SICKNOTE

BY THE SAME AUTHOR

HERETIC
ANTICHRIST

SICKNOTE

a novel

ERNEST JORDAN

PAPER RECORDS

PAPER RECORDS

Published in Great Britain 2025 by Paper Records
paperrecords.co.uk

British Library Cataloguing-in-Publication Data
A catalogue record for this book is available on request from the British Library

First Edition

ISBN 978 1 9192 7680 9
Typeset in Dante MT Std 10.8/13
Printed and bound in Great Britain by Clays Ltd, Elcograf S.p.A.

FSC www.fsc.org MIX Paper | Supporting responsible forestry FSC® C018072 for Nirvana and Ché

I

Ever opened your eyes to a foreign ceiling, unsure if you were dead or alive, mouth sticky, the stench of dope on you and in you and all about you? Ever wondered if there were many versions of you, slipping between countless realities with countless names and countless faces?

I'd gone again to Disco 2000, the last haven for junkies, dealers and prostitutes. Jezebel slipped a pill on my tongue before disappearing with her new boyfriend. Jacob, my best pal, had limped out on his crutches. And in my maddened and paranoid state I reckoned three junkheads were waiting for a punchup at the bottom of the stairs.

Seagulls squawked about the streets.

The morning sun narrowed my eyes.

I balled my fists. Exhausted.

But instead of fighting, I slid into a cab with one of those characters.

Staring up at his ceiling, memories flooded back. My gut churned. Climbing on to my elbows I looked blankly at a wall. In the corner of my eye I see the junkie puffing a cigarette, wearing my jumper, hanging loose over his skinny body. I wondered how he came to wear it. Then the sound of loud music, cranking between my ears, sent my head to slam back against the mattress.

My eyes rolled back, my spine tensed up. The music thumped on while a single blue light danced about the room. Then in a flash, I'm back where I started, calm, staring up at that ceiling.

Gasping for air I wiped spit from my lips and coughed. Minutes ticked by as I tried remembering when I'd blacked out and the bastard had fucked me—assuming that I was also queer.

Although that was the least of my worries. Loaded up on pills and booze and all else, I had followed this guy back to smoke some hash to take the edge off, but after a weeks run of comedowns with little sleep, I was already half out of my mind.

I tried again to sit up. Another convulsion racked my body. My chin jutted forward and my head slammed back to the bed. From here, I drifted in and out of consciousness, the music still blaring and the blue lights swirling. And through it all, I caught glimpses of his scrawny, junkie body writhing on top of me, his black greasy hair whipping across his face.

Wiping away more spit, I realised I was having flashbacks, along with some kind of seizure. What I didn't grasp however was how this moment, fueled by a weekly cocktail of pills, speed and booze, was dredging up everything I had undergone since my childhood life. Call it psychosis, a mental crash, a radical awakening of the soul. In any case, I believed I had died—as strong as the belief that once convinced me I was alive—that I had overdosed on too many pills, and now I was in Hell, surrounded by demons.

This epiphany of mine was no holier-than-thou baptism. I didn't receive *the Good Word* from some Latter-day Saint. I was a speed freak, an amphetamine case, a smalltown kid chasing his own tail on the bleak coast of England. I knew Hell like the back of my hand. But it ain't the Hell from the Bible. It's that human kind, the kind that reeks of piss in the hallway, fagbutts clogging the toilet, people leaping from building tops. I pitied the do-gooders and all them preachers spouting their stuff. Perhaps I was too stubborn to swallow their lines, or too reckless to give a damn. But one thing's certain, from the time I was a young kid I've hated God with a nocuous fever. It wasn't a consideration or some chewed-up idea, it was raw, primal hatred. And as I got older and encountered more of the world, that hatred grew into a rage, a rage against Him. And as I did not suffer envy I had plenty time to observe the stupidity of man. Maybe I was too lazy to follow the path laid out ahead, too simple. Yet something old had taken root inside me, some old and ancient dispute feeding through the skin, the nerves, tossing and turning behind the eyes.

Straightening up my trousers I stumbled to my feet. Too tired to buckle my belt, I gripped the strap in my fist. It was an odd thing to wrap my head around, that I somehow believed so deeply in some malevolent crawler—that all these people about me had been demonic all along, sucking up the same air, living in the same sick world.

I summoned the urge to beat the blood out the queer, but as I moved closer, readying my fists, a wave of terror swept over me, flashes of memories flooding my skull, all the things I'd done to end up here, choices I'd made, like water rushing into my lungs. The madness of a monk, beneath it all I was mad with holy fucking suffering.

Stumbling across the room gripping my belt buckle, I stopped ahead of him, the air thick with smoke. He handed me my jumper as a lover would. I snatched it from his hand, my eyes intense, big. He recoiled in fear. With the jumper now over my head, barely able to catch the belt strap, I staggered away.

The staircase was narrow, the carpet worn to shreds. I moved toward the front door, thinking quietly:

'Just keep moving, the demons are on your trail!'

At the bottom of the stairs I pushed the front door, blinded by sunlight. My eyes half-closed I inhaled, holding the air and releasing it slow from the gut.

Walking through a gate I turned into a desolate street with small checks over my shoulder. Crouched behind a parked van, I watched some gypsy kids play in the road, thoughts racing wild and murderous. As I turned to tie my lace I spot a young boy across the way, stood there unafraid, holding a ball beneath one arm, his other arm limp by his side. The look in his eye told me he knew something that I didn't. And yet, there was a strange familiarity to him, like the kid was me in some parallel fucking universe, looking forward at himself through time.

Once the kid scooted away I stood back up and buckled my belt. Catching a glimpse of my reflection in the window of the van, I saw myself with no clothes on. Frozen stiff, I was convinced something had taken over my body and had tricked me into walking out of that house naked. Carefully looking down, I saw shoes, jeans, a jumper. I moved my foot to be sure it was me. It was me. I was moving my foot. But as I faced again the reflection, there I was, stark naked.

I stood there like a lost cause, my head churning like a meat grinder. It was like waking up knowing you had died and had arrived in Hell. And that the world hadn't changed, but beneath it all everything was now twisted. And no matter how hard you try, you can't shake the feeling you're stuck in a sadistic game. You try to convince yourself it's all in your head, that maybe you need sleep, food, television.

Snapping out of the nightmare I slipped down a back alley toward Central Park. Along the way I passed the town's football stadium, where I once strode through the gates, thousands of fans cheering my name.

Continuing toward Jacob's place, I kept up appearances, just like every other fraud. When he answered the door I followed him up to his attic and sat at his window, examining the world below.

'What is it, Judas?' Jacob asked, stood behind me.

I turned to him. Seeing worry in his eyes, I wanted to tell him what I knew and what the situation is: God is no good. Everyone is a fucking demon! But Jacob was tricking me to say it out loud, I was sure, make me sound like a nut.

'I don't know what's going on, Judas,' he pleaded.

Pointing between his eyes, I said, 'Who the *fuck* are you?'

'What d'you mean, Judas? *It's me!*'

Needing to keep moving I pushed by my friend and slipped out the door, hurrying through his backyard before jumping the wall and disappearing into daylight.

2

I heard tales of Africa. One in particular of rebel gunmen coming to execute my old man. He was an Englishman working overseas as an engineer, and his chalk-white skin made him a target for retribution. Fearing for his life, he hid in the wardrobe while my mother stood in the door with two rifles pointed between her eyes.

It's an image that stuck around, told and retold by my mother, how she stood there ready to give birth to me while those men and their guns loomed over us. She said she wasn't scared, the lunatics didn't frighten her—in fact, she took a step closer to the guns.

My father, on the other hand, weighed up his options before hiding in the wardrobe. He was a Londoner, and this was downtown Africa. So on his instruction, his pregnant woman answered the door to talk it through with her fellow people. My old man wasn't heroic, he was resourceful, and wanted to live. And he did. We all did.

This was all before the Liberian coup d'état, before thousands were murdered, raped, and the hearts of babies cut out and eaten for spiritual gain. As the story goes, my mother scolded the rebels at the door, and they both lowered their guns. Meanwhile, her brother and chief of police was patrolling the area, and chased the crooks away with his pistol.

When my mother finished telling the tale, she refused to accept her brother having saved us. She didn't like him. It was chance he happened to be patrolling the area, she'd say. 'God saved us.'

The day of the fighting was blistering hot, and my sisters—Esther, Rudy and Tabi—played in the backyard. My father had just received an urgent telegram that morning, sitting down to slice open the letter with his paper knife:

> Dear Mr Judas Nobody stop Half-caste babies are reportedly being stolen from JFK Hospital in Monrovia stop The disappearance of these children has been attributed to a speculative case of local voodoo stop The mothers have been institutionalised at the E.S. Grant Mental Hospital, having supposedly lost their minds with grief stop Doctors at the hospital continue to claim no record of those babies ever existing or of those women ever being pregnant stop

Once my father finished reading the telegram, he slid it into his pocket, lighting a smoke and pondering the news the whole morning before escaping to the wardrobe at the sound of flying bullets.

Once the rebels had fled and with my mother close to giving birth, my father crawled out of his hiding, insisting that I be born in a hospital. He had money, and wasn't about to let anyone cut out his son's heart for some corrupt war. 'Dammit!'

But his wife, well-versed in the town's superstitions, particularly those surrounding half-black, half-white kids, had other ideas.

Instead of following her husband's plan, my mother waited until her English newlywed was deep in conversation with his Western pals, pouring themselves gin on the patio while yammering over the looming mutiny. Creeping into the bedroom alone, she encouraged me out of the birthing hole in silence.

'Tay-tay w'ter,' she whispered to me as I arrived, roughly translating as 'titty water,' or the more custom 'drink mammas milk.'

And so that was that. I was born at home and kept alive. And my mother, eight pounds lighter, kept her sanity. Eeh-menh. 'Amen.'

So we fled the war by plane to Plymouth, England. The old man, who had brought us here in search of refuge, suffered slowly from lung cancer. As we walked the streets—a motley-coloured family of white, black, and brown—people would spit on us through windows, skinheads jeered from passing cars. From inside our home we watched as our door was kicked by drunken yobs late into the night, making threats, urinating through our letterbox. We had escaped one war only to have found another.

Some years went by. And I'd watch the fall of rain from the window, washing away the dogshit on the pavement, and people scraping gum from beneath their shoes, tramps digging through bins trying to catch a meal. Married women drifted the streets with black eyes and swollen lips, and the pubs were always crammed with celebrations, waving British flags, ending with the occasional fistfight.

My mother soon had my father thrown from the house. He was too old to protect us, sick, too poor, and now a racist toward his own wife and kids, she'd claim, seducing a young trawlerman to grab him by the collar and break his nose, tossing my father to the kerb like a gutted fish. And yet he'd turn up to our doorstep every day, coughing and pleading, grieved by a simpleminded woman. He'd lost it all, and finally turned away a sad, defeated old fool, made to live alone by the sea and quietly await his end.

3

Yanking the chain and freeing the plug, the murky water slithered down the drain with a gulp. I was meticulous with cleaning, scouring the sink, polishing the basin and tap until it sparkled like sunlight. When I was done, I'd take a deep breath and inhale the soap mingling along my skin.

My father and I would get into his bed and go to sleep. But when I woke the next morning he'd be lying on the sofa, while I watched the ceiling, fixing back up my pajama bottoms. I was a kid, maybe seven years old. His eyes would be big and sorry and strange, guilt running along his face. He told me I kicked in my sleep, that he bruised too easily. But when I saw him in the corner of my eye I didn't feel good. I didn't know him and it frightened me.

'You kick too hard, Judas, as I live and breathe, dear boy, too hard!'

Placing down his sketchbook and his pencil, resting his glasses on the table, he'd turn to me. 'Okay, Master Nobody, let's inspect you.'

Stopping at the foot of his wooden stool where he sat, he turned my palms up. 'Hmm, good me boy,' he would remark. 'That's a good half moon. Now let's see your neck?' I'd lean my neck to one side.

'Yes, good cleanliness.'

Bending my earlobe, I opened my mouth wide at the same time.

'It has only now occured to me you've got your mother's teeth,' he said curiously. 'Nice and strong, yes. Of course you'll have to keep them clean also.'

My father peered down at my knees while making noises through his nose, raising one brow. Peering down with him, we both wonder what to do about the dry mud from wrestling Jacob in the field.

He gave no smile. I don't ever recall him smiling, or talking that much. What I know is that he was a keen swimmer when he was young. Joined the RAF Academy aged fourteen with false papers. Became a Master Engineer during World War II. Smoked a hundred Woodbine a day. Caught his first wife having an affair. Abandoned a kid daughter in Yorkshire. Divorced a pretty Cypriot prostitute before taking up work in Liberia. Got poisoned by an African sex worker. Married my mother. Had more kids. Dodged a bullet during the Liberian uprising of Samuel Doe. Got old. Got lung cancer at age sixty-five. Got broke. And died. None of this he said to me. It was told to me when he died. And yet I still didn't know who he was. Vaguely I recall his voice, the way he repeated things. But he was a recluse, a hermit. And when he died, the silence he left chewed me up, like being watched by something that isn't there, something that knows things that I don't.

Handing him his handkerchief, he'd say, 'Thank you, Judas.' To stop his hand from shaking, he often placed it firm on my chest and declared, 'I'm an old man now, Judas . . . a very sick old man.'

He coughed again, beginning to wheeze. I go grab an empty glass. 'Papa,' I'd say. He liked that we called him *Papa*.

'Thank you kindly, Judas.'

He'd cough up clumps of red phlegm into the glass, and I enjoy watching the cancer slither until it reaches the bottom, the bristles along his chin brushing the glass like sandpaper, his tall nose breathing heavy inside, his neatly combed silver hair as he'd turn away with pride to spit more.

'Okay, let's move to the desk. A letter we must write.'

'Yes, Papa.'

'But first, dear boy, let's fold the bedsheets and polish our shoes.'

His home was small, filled with cages of chirping parakeets hung lowly from the window above a round writing table. The table is crammed with sharpened HB pencils, sketchbooks, and sealed letters. The morning light filters through the window, casting a glow over the room. The floorboards would creak beneath our feet as I help him settle into his chair. And I watch as he positions a writing pad, selecting a fountain pen and shaking it, listening for ink. Then he would slide a blue diary across the table, running his wrinkly finger along the alphabet.

'Now, a letter to my old sister, your Aunt Irene Beaver,' he says. 'She would very much appreciate it, yes she would.'

I'd stare at the side of his head, where a skin graft had been, crawling with blue veins. And then, like a sudden rainstorm, the flair of his penmanship would come alive, a steady stream of cracks and long, elaborate scrapes as he whipped the point of the pen with the art of wartime calligraphy, crafting letters to loved ones. Outside, a few pigeons land on the balcony, cooing over a puzzle of grey tower blocks. The windowlight illuminated the red liquid in the thermometer. Giant maps of ancient worlds are nailed to the wall. And a pile of old books stacked on his chest: dictionaries, several atlas, one vegetarian cookbook.

My old man was born in 1920. 'Just a few years before a little old Irish firecracker named Violet fired a bullet at Mussolini, clipping the fellas nose!' he'd say with rare emotion, a woman he seemed fond of.

My father adjusts his Air Force beret. I help him into his coat, grab his walking stick, zip up his camera bag and fold my fishing rod under my arm, ready to march.

The rain came down. People running into doorways. But my father always walked on strongly like it was the sunniest day. 'Chin up, Master Nobody!' he'd command. 'And shoulders back, me boy!'

We came across a homeless drunk pushing a shopping trolley filled with junk. The rain stopped. As soon as the tramp saw my father he stashed a bottle of drink, clipping his heels together with a salute. They talked in a hush, like they were planning a robbery.

'Okay, let's be on our way, me boy,' my father said to me.

We made our way to Mayflower Steps, the pier of the Pilgrims. Here he'd take photos of me fishing, pull out his sketchpad and draw, while I cast my line, willing my first mackerel.

'Judas,' my father said, 'I'm going to die soon. Do you understand?'

I nodded.

'What I wish to know, dear boy, is do you accept it?'

I thought about it.

'Do you accept that I will die?'

I stopped thinking. 'Yes, Papa.'

'You understand that I will soon die and you accept it fully?'

'Yes.'

'You accept it fully?'

'I accept it fully.'

'Okay... good... good, me boy. Right, now, to the library.'

The library was a fortress, a large gray structure that had been the same before the war. We always sat at the same table to read. It was short and wooden, with thick legs. We'd dump our coats and bags and stroll between the shelves.

When my father returned he stacked his picks on the table. And the people sitting nearby didn't speak, reading as if no one was there. I liked how people were in the library. They were calm. They read. And this was how we spent most Sundays.

Later on sat patiently in his livingroom while Astaire tap-danced on the telly, my father gazed out the window with one leg across the other. And I would sit and wonder about his bruised leg and the way he often looked back at me from the sofa after escaping the bed, leaving me to think why he looked so afraid—how different and distant he became, afraid. You never saw him afraid. So I watched the bad feelings inside until they just went away. Sometimes I'd eagerly anticipate this part of the day, where I'd sit on my stool and wait for the bad feelings to go. Perhaps he was doing the same?

During these moments a fly would always find its way into the room. I'd watch the fly stop on the wall, remaining very still for a long time. With nothing else to do while the old man stared out the window, I'd decide to stay as still as the fly, to outdo it. Not even blink, I promised myself. Eventually the fly would find its way back to the window, and I'd let off a long sigh, glad to see it free.

'I need to go now, Papa,' I said. He called me over, and we shared our usual nose rub before handing me a letter.

'For when you get home,' he said, and I tucked it safely into my pocket, ready to sit and read once I reached my mother's house.

4

On my way home I made a pit stop at the fishing port to cast my line, squeezing out a maggot onto a shiny hook. And wait. All you could do was wait. An hour passed. The streets were empty, everyone indoors eating Sunday Roast. I packed up my gear and kicked a stone back to Moon Street.

The stinking tramp asleep on the stairway didn't wake as I climbed over him, running up four flights of steps to my block. Before pulling off my backpack to see my first caught fish, I paused at the door, staring at the doormat, imagining dead faces from the scuff marks. I then opened my bag and looked at the mackerel, its black eyes staring up at me from the bottom, pleading for life.

First thing I hear when walking in was screaming, loud, high pitched, murderous calls. I tiptoed to the livingroom door, wide enough to peer in and sneak a look. There, in the centre of the room, lay Esther, my eldest sister, with our mother on top of her again, tearing off Esther's clothes.

Esther yelled to me, 'Help, Judas!'

Swinging me a glare, our mother dragged Esther to the next room by her legs.

'Get help, Judas! She's crazy! CRAZY!'

Our mother had a grip on Esther's mouth. Esther held on for dear life, her fingertips digging into the doorframe, white splinters scattering to the carpet.

But our mother was relentless, her thick arms like a cartoon villain, unpicking Esther's fingers one by one.

'Please, Mum! I'm sorry!' Esther cried.

'You mast learn, oh. I will beat you an'til you learn.'

The door slammed shut. And Esther got a cruel beating.

The next morning, as the kettle whistled, my mother stormed from our flat down the landing and out to the courtyard. Her target: Fleur, the neighbourhood troublemaker, who had pulled our clothes from the communal line and thrown them in the bin, sniggering like a maniac. My mother charged down four flights of stairs and fought Fleur. The two of them went at it like wildcats, until Fleur was half nude, both white tits bouncing up from her bra like double-whipped ice-cream. All that was left were her slippers and stockings, as my mother gave her a thrashing.

A dogfight wasn't only for the men in our courtyard. Women were just as likely to have a scrap, tearing at each other's hair and ripping each other's bras off. It wasn't as violent as the men, but it was more entertaining and lasted longer. We would wait for a flash of boob, or if lucky, a rare glimpse of a fanny. Whenever a fight broke out the whole of Moon Street would rush to their doors and windows, twisting their necks to get a look.

Esther became known as what was called a *hardnut*, and the beatings she endured only made her tougher. After being ambushed by school bullies, my mother threatened her, warning if she ever came home again with spit in her hair she'd be beaten even worse.

'I will beat you more than them!'

My mother hailed from a smalltown village, illiterate and only knowing one way to fight. And she could fight. So Esther no longer ran away from the bullies. And it was only a matter of time before she left a grown woman unconscious on the pavement, the broken heel of Esther's shoe laying beside her in a pool of blood. From that day on, my sister was respected. No one messed with her, no one except our mother.

The evening mood settled the house. The hob was boiling stew. And the dog had been out all day walking the streets. The dog always took himself for a walk. There were no favourites, he, like us, had to muck in, fend for himself.

Twelve hours of caring for the elderly, tidying beds, wiping asses, washing willies—that was my mother's work. And as soon as she left for another night shift, leaving us kids alone, our home became a whorehouse.

I watched as Tabi, the youngest of my three sisters, rubbed pink lipstick over her mouth, pressing her eye to the spyhole. The boys came tumbling in like wild dogs, swinging plastic bags and rattling glass bottles. I sneaked behind my bedroom door and watched as drinks were poured, glasses topped up, beer cans popped open, the start of sex-making.

A tall blonde named Tasha stormed in like a whirlwind, her giant boobs barely contained in the bra. Her red lips stood outside my door, chugging back cheap wine. One guy held her ass, another her neck, before dragging her to a room. I prayed they'd keep the door open. 'Please,' I said, 'I want to see the boobies.'

Tasha's screams filled the air, sending a strange chill down my spine. I waited patiently for a guy with slick hair to stagger drunk down the hall before seizing my chance. Creeping near the action I feel my heartbeat in my face and arms. It was everywhere, the heartbeat. Soon enough, I had my eye between the gap of the door, rooted to the spot. Tasha groaned as her giant boobs bounced. She grabbed hold of her giant boobs to keep them from bouncing. I noticed her nipples were larger than mine, pink and perfectly round, with a thick teat, like a cow. Suddenly a hand reached up from beneath her, belonging to a boy. The boy pushed Tasha's hand away from one boob, causing it to droop. And he slapped the boob, and Tasha yelped, 'Ow! Jesus, that hurt!' My head flinched back, I blinked, before peering between the door once again.

'Ahh, shut your cakehole,' said the boy.

'Too hard! *Too hard!*'

'Shut ya hole, ya bitch, YOU LOVE IT!'

She soon let go of the other boob, both boobs again jumping up and down. And sometimes making circles, big swinging circles.

And he slapped the other one, this time harder.

'Ow!' she yelped. 'Too hard, Joey!'

Joey laughed. 'You love it you whore! That'll make your tits blue!'

And then the other boy came into eyeshot from behind the bed, I'd forgotten he was in the room. Shuffling his socks along the floor with his trousers about his ankles his willy stood very strong in front of him. Then from behind me came a voice:

'Judas, you little perv!'

I got out quick, leaping back to my room and behind my bedroom door, pressing my ear against the keyhole. 'Ow! Too hard! Too hard!'

Much later on, Esther walked in with some guy and his little freckled-faced niece. Her name's Breena. Breena is five.

'Go play with Judas,' the guy said to his little niece.

I stepped aside and motioned Breena into my room, holding my finger over my lips for her to keep quiet. While we were alone, I got to work unbuttoning her little denim skirt and pushed my hand down her pants. I knew exactly what to do, and where to touch. I was in charge, like *she* was now the child and I was the grownup.

Something felt moist. I put my finger there. Breena looked down too. It made me excited. And just as suddenly it made me snatch my hand back. Quickly buttoning her up I forced her to leave. I was mad at her, and went and stood in the corner of my room with my arms crossed, looking at the door while smelling my finger, afraid of who might walk in next, who'd Breena gone and told.

5

My eyes opened wide to the ceiling the next morning, the air thick with burnt toast, and the kettle whistling like a lunatic as usual. The dog was thrown from the house for shitting outside Tabi's door again. She stood in it with her bare foot. Poor boy, I thought, watching the mutt lower his eyes pass my bedroom door.

My mother was cooking and singing to Jesus in the kitchen. And the potato guy had dropped off a full sack. I picked up my spud gun and walked to the kitchen. My mother was stirring a large bowl of porridge, adding drops of water.

'No money for milk an'til to-morrow,' she wanted me to know, continuing to sing, *'Jeeesoos loves me! Jeeesoos loves me! Jeeesoos loves meeeeeee! for the Bible tells me soooo . . .'*

I dragged in a chair and stood up by the sink to watch insects float to the surface of the water, above the potatoes and cabbage. My mother wore a new tropical gown that she had made on her little sewing machine, wrapped around her fat body, her finest piece, orange and green and yellow. Grease dripped from the wall behind the cooker, the doors peeled, the floor had a thin layer of smut with metal rings from spaghetti cans lying here and there. And yellow use-by-date stickers that came with the bread had been at the foot of the fridge for days, everybody saw them. And the bin stinking of rotten food, gathering more and more flies. And giant rats busying beneath the cupboard chewing on all the crumbs swept out of sight before the spud man arrived.

I picked out a floating bug and brought it close to my eye.

'Can I use a potato?' I asked, watching the bug's legs come alive.

My mother handed me a potato. 'Help your sistah to set de table.'

I stepped down from the stool and passed placemats to Rudy, the middle of my three sisters, who was awake waiting by the door when our mother pushed her key at 6 AM. Rudy had recently changed schools. She didn't walk with me anymore. Instead, a special bus with special kids picked her up outside our Moon Street estate. Some of those kids drooled on the bus window, boss-eyed with mouths permanently open like strange deep-sea creatures. Others waved at everyone all of the time, just waving and drooling and banging their heads against the window.

Each morning I'd watch Rudy climb onto that bus looking back at me, clutching her little pink lunchbox. And I watched her sit by the window and, over time, wave like those other kids. My mother said it was the white man's food putting disease in her brain. Rudy complained about some of those kids hitting her in the canteen. She told me everything. Just saying whatever came to her head, mostly laughing and repeating it over ten times, even if it was bad news somehow it seemed funny in her new world.

'Gravy,' Rudy said, turning the placemat. 'Gravy, Judas, gravy.'

'I'll clean it,' I answered, taking it back to the kitchen.

'It's got gravy on it, Judas,' she repeated behind me.

'Yes, I know. I said I'll clean it.'

As we sit for breakfast, I keep my arm over my porridge, not wanting who my family were and what they believed to find its way into *my* brain.

We were the first to have Cable TV on the estate. After breakfast my mother invited some neighbours and all their kids to come and fiddle with the cable dial. *Click Click*, went the dial. It made me nervous, strangers in the house.

'Mum, can Katie stay?' I asked.

'Who's Katie?'

'You know!'

'I don't know any *Katie*,' she replied annoyed, shuffling her fat buttocks in her chair.

'She was here with your friend. She said your friend was her mother. We were playing right next to you. You know!'

'Oh-kay, oh-kay, she can stay,' she agreed, just so I'd shut up.

Esther whispered close by, 'Judas, psst, Judas—Katie died *years* ago.' Esther smirked. I got angry and walked to the window and breathed onto the glass. And all the handprints I made weeks ago with Rudy appeared again.

'*Please*,' my mother begged, pointing to Rudy, 'trow your hair down de toilet when you finish makin ah mess!' Rudy looked up and nodded, gathering together the hair from her little doll brush. Leaning forward from her chair my mother's eyes smiled like a crazy person. 'If dey get your hair dey make voodoo, voodoo, *VOODOO*.'

Rudy kept nodding while pulling the hair from her little doll brush, excited with fear.

'Oh-kay, I will now prepare da food for when we meet him,' announced my mother, climbing to her feet.

Tabi had been writing to a prisoner. She'd never met him. He came to visit. She had been unusually quiet the whole morning, trying on different skirts. He had gotten out of prison that day. I don't know why he was in prison, but I think I liked him. And I think I was afraid of him. When he arrived and sat down, I saw that his skin was the same colour as mine. I thought he was very handsome. He was muscular and tough-looking. And he appeared calm, very calm. But he didn't *feel* calm. He had a tattoo on his hand of a bird. I kept trying to look at the bird. He told me it was a Kingfisher, and that the Kingfishers are shy birds, but the greatest hunters. My mother cooked rice and chicken for everyone when he came to visit. And we all ate in silence.

And then he left.

Later that night I poured a glass of flat lemonade and took it to my room, stuck a pretend chocolate fag between my lips and hit balls on my miniature pool table. The balls disappeared down the little holes. My light bulb was dying, but I didn't care. I liked the darkness. And then Henry walked in, a new friend of Esther. He was a full-grown man with pale blue eyes and yellow hair, always thinking and looking about. He walked into my room and whispered beneath the flickering light. I offered him a chocolate smoke. He turned it down. So I fetched my other cue for him to put down some balls. He slipped a wad of cash into a plastic bag, signaling for me to keep it hush-hush, before stashing the money above my wardrobe.

I nodded with the cue held out.

'Later, Judas. We'll play later . . .'

As he turned to leave, he hit his head against my light. And I watched, mesmerised, the flickering, dying bulb swinging back and forth like a dancing moth on fire.

I pointed my chewed-up cigarette at the light. 'It's a moth on fire,' I said to myself.

6

It was almost midnight. My mother was at work. Tabi and I stayed up watching a French black and white film on cable. Two kids dug a hole in the soil, unbuttoned their jeans, and were slamming the earth, their tiny bums shining like silver coins. And their trousers twisted about their ankles in the dirt. They would stop and speak in French, seeming very serious. And this would go on: burying their peckers into the earth, to then enjoy a long speak about their efforts. Me and Tabi couldn't take our eyes off the telly.

By sunrise the milkman had been and gone, and the big-booted rat guy had changed all the poison in the kitchen. My mother, as usual, made sure to sweep before he came, make it look decent.

I was in the front room spinning beneath the light with a cape tied around my neck, pretending to fly up to the sun like Superman. Realising it was just a stupid costume I wandered into my sister's room. The room stunk of plastic dolls and cherry bubblegum, and the damp sweaty soles of girls' shoes, making my nose scrunch up.

Immediately I'm made to sit on a stool and lick plastic ice-cream, while Rudy yapped on about this thing called *romance*. Then the swine slipped our mother's heels onto my feet, and tricked me to sip pretend tea from her little plastic teacups.

Her mouth blabbered on about a dream house. I swear she was talking with someone else 'cause I weren't listening to the maniac. Then I'm told to dance, which I reluctantly do in high heels like a sore-footed pigeon, before bolting out the door and grabbing my trainers and running as fast as I could down the steps, chased by my dog barking as we both race as far away from girls as we could.

Stepping out onto Moon Street, I strolled along the sea beside the fish market on the Barbican. The market bustled with big-eared handsome fishermen wearing bright yellow overalls with thick beards, yelling over the crowd while unloading baskets of fish and crab and squid and eels. The smell was great and the sky full with yakky seagulls. I got a closer look at all the fish with their lifeless eyes, crabs pincing and fighting, clawing above a heap of red mayhem. And the cobbled streets a mess with sea cartilage, hauled in from the ocean, and locals bidding for the best-looking cod, loaded onto green trolleys lined with newspapers.

As the bidding carried on, I stole a stray prawn before taking a seat. It squirmed in my hand, its spindly legs thin and many. Its tentacles twitched and they reached. The shell was hard and the eyes as black as anything. I peered deeper into its eyes, its small, dark holes, and then tossed the critter back to the ground. I watched it struggle, writhing meaningless on the cobbled stone. Falling into some sort of daydream, I started to feel like the prawn, like I couldn't move too. I liked the feeling, but mostly I didn't like it. So I kicked my foot to stop feeling that way, called on my dog and headed to the chip shop for leftover scraps.

As night fell I snuck into my mother's closet while she went out to the pub with her new boyfriend—some fisherman with a leaky boat. Huddled between a heap of bamboo sticks, studying the stains of Esther's blood on the tips, my sisters burst into the room making a racket.

I held my breath as they tiptoed about, looking under the bed and whispering my name, threatening to tickle me until I wet my pants. The room reeked of nail polish and tacky perfume, making me sick. They pawed through our mother's trinkets, rifling under a red chest overflowing with cheap baubles. I watched from my hiding spot, catching glimpses of their greedy fingers as they fondled the stash, jewellery our mother had gotten from door-to-door thieves posing as salesmen.

On the count of three I sprung from the closet. The girls shrieked and I roared, catching the swindlers. Bamboo sticks clattered to the floor. Esther snatched one up and snapped it twice against her knee.

'Good riddens!' she yelled. 'She can't smack me now!'

I pointed at her. 'Mum's gonna chin you,' I said.

'*You* snapped it!' the lunatic fibbed.

'Liar!' I shouted back.

'Judas snapped it! We will pray for Judas!'

I shook my head furiously, begging, 'Don't pray! Don't pray!'

Esther and Tabi ran out the room, yelling, '*Judas is going to Hell! Judas is going to Hell!*'

I rolled up my fist and chased after them.

An hour later I found my mother in the livingroom, her crusty feet propped up on a stool, sipping Napoleon brandy with a distant look in her eye. She had begun to drink. Gone were the days of her bright village dresses. Now, she wore strange wigs and dull-looking blazers with oversized shoulder pads, and straightened her hair with chemicals. All the girls straightened their hair, the smell of burning scalps taking over the whole house, driving me and the dog crazy.

Esther had slipped out before our mother returned, leaving behind chewed up nails and a worried mood. Our mother had been waiting for Esther in her bedroom, brandishing a rolling pin, ready to bash Esther for staying out late smoking with the prostitutes.

But now, sat in her chair, our mother was retelling the same old story, the one about the rebel gunmen in Africa.

'And that was that,' she said, pouring a little extra Napoleon into her glass. She wiped away a tear before taking a drink, and looked aimlessly as if she didn't know where she was, a lost child forming behind the eyes. The temperature outside dropped, blowing a cold chill into the room. And it was then, as I recall it, that I had this crazy idea, coming to me like a flash . . .

I want to be a priest, I thought. Not like the ones at her church, not like them, but a real one, a *real* priest.

7

Sometime in the spring Tabi and I brought home two parakeets from Papa. He was making a little extra dough on the side taking in unloved birds, promising the owners a good home before flogging them in the local CLASSIFIEDS. I was glum. Our birds had to live in the same stupid cage and get along. I hated the way her bird glared at mine, constantly pecking his wings, while my bird just wanted to be left alone. And I hated that he didn't fight back, that he was *weak*.

A gang of kids returned the dog after finding him in the park, eating out of bins and chasing squirrels. He came and sat beside me and we watched her bird, we sat and we observed. We watched. Then my dog licked my hand. There was something about my hand that tasted good to him. I let him lick the other side too. He then started chewing fleas off his back. I sniffed my hand before wiping his slobber on my shorts, and we both resumed looking up at the cage. Her bird was a bully and we knew it. I wanted the beady-eyed, yellow-beaked flying rat dead.

The next day I couldn't wait to get home from school, eager to check on my parakeet. I walked straight to the cage to discover my bird laid out on the floor, looking like the boogeyman had snatched him up in his sleep. Her bird squawked, climbing about the steel bars as I came closer.

'You murdered him,' I said quietly. 'You murdered my bird.'

Grudgingly, I pried open the cage and reached inside, grabbing the murderer in my hand and squeezing the killer while it chewed my knuckle.

'Die, you feathered devil,' I whispered. Its beak shot open, its tongue poked out like a hot lizard. I stared the demon in the eye and squeezed tighter, one last time, one more *squeeze*, before letting go.

Why couldn't I finish her off?

I picked up my bird, which was cold and stiff. It felt hollow. I didn't know where he had gone. And it scared me. I slammed the cage shut and walked out the door with the dog close behind.

Heading down the stairway I passed a couple kids on the second floor smoking cigarettes. Kicking a syringe down two more flights, I watched it smash into pieces before jumping over the tramp passed out on the bottom step, avoiding the pool of dark piss pushing out from his trousers and stepping into the sunshine.

Gail and Charlie, the two fat sisters on the ground floor, were hanging out the window, teasing passersby with their lollipops, offering to suck their willies. The adults who gave them a telling off they told to go fuck their filthy mothers, calling out to me as I crossed the street, 'Judas! C'mere! Play with us!'

Remembering what Esther'd said, I avoided the double-yellow lines, not wanting to be cursed by sleeping witches. My dog stayed put as I sprung across the main road, dodging traffic, holding tight my dead bird. Finding a lane with fresh soil I crouched down and dug a hole the size of a pencil case. Once covered, I said a prayer, made one up in my head, touching my fingertips together just a little so no one would notice how stupid it was that I was praying on the street. It was stupid. It was an act. I knew I was acting, like all those hymn-singing morons. Snapping a twig in two I twisted it together making a cross and sticking it on top of the grave. Then went to meet Papa for Friday fish and chips.

A strange sight watching old aged pensioners eat. They were always in the chippy, all at the same time, making a right mess of mushy peas. I sat chewing my fish, trying not to look at them.

Once we were stuffed I helped Papa to his feet, handing him

his walking stick while he fixed his Air Force pin, straightened his tie. He talked on about how important and strong and caring I am, like he always does, before heading off alone to the watchsmith, shouting over his shoulder, 'Keep your feet straight, Master Nobody! And chin up!'

Turning away, I faced the ivory heights of Moon Street estate, a huge oblong asylum, a madhouse, an ungoverned bedlam harbouring hundreds of inpatients born to eat, shit, and vote.

My dog found me again, his docile white and brown mongrel face looking delighted, chewing something he shouldn't. We both then turn the corner up toward our block.

'Look, Judas! They're fighting! They're fighting!'

The two fat sisters rushed toward me, snatching me by the hand.

'What is it?' I asked.

'He's beating him up!' they both screamed.

The girls led me to where Thane was, his eyes crazy and his nostrils flaring. He wasn't very big, but he was strong and off his nut. Thane never smiled. Men often told him to cheer up, telling him things like, 'Go get some fanny, Thane, that's what you need.' And he'd say, 'Go fuck y'self.' Or they'd say, 'Have a wank first thing in the morning, clears the head.' And he'd say, 'Go fuck y'self.' And the girls would sing, 'I'll suck you off, Thane, I'll suck your cock dry behind the bins, that'll put a smile back on your cherry.' And he'd say, 'And give me a disease? Slag, GO FUCK Y'SELF!'

I got close to the action. Thane's shirt was torn, his broad chest panting. Red claw marks ran along his neck to his stomach. He picked up the other guy by his hair, dragging him toward an abandoned car. A trail of blood followed them along, with more on the kerb from where the other kid's head bashed against the stone. I saw big purple lips busted open and eyes blue and swollen closed, his shoe slipping away as Thane pulled him along the ground. One girl picked up the shoe and put it safely inside the doorway. Thane opened the car door and rested the head perfectly down to the steel frame and slammed the door, breaking his cheek, his nose, blood oozed from the ears and from the eyes. He pulled the guy's head back up from where it had fallen and placed it carefully back and restarted over.

Slam! Slam! Slam!

Thane didn't stop, pulling the head back up again and again, yelling for him to keep still so he could bash it without it moving.

'Stop moving!' his mouth frothed as he yelled. 'Keep it still!'

I understood then that people kill. And that I could be killed.

An adult rushed out from a nearby doorway hearing the commotion, and wrestled Thane away, barking for everyone to get going.

'Get goin ya liddle bastards!' he cried with a closed fist.

Me and the dog legged it as fast as our legs could take us.

8

Jacob lived outside of my estate, over on the better side. It wasn't great, just better. Jacob and I knew each other since I arrived on this island as a foreigner. He also had curly hair. Some kids called him *cauliflower head*. He didn't seem to mind. His grandma was a lovechild between an English factory worker and a black Yankee soldier during the war. And he could run fast like me, and scale trees pretty quick too, and skim stones along the sea with at least ten hits. He wasn't afraid to dive off cliffs or pick up crabs, and he rode his bike alongside without ever breaking a sweat. And he always bit his fingernails, chewed the suckers till they bled. I don't know when he started doing this, but he did it often, especially if a gang of skinheads booted by chanting '*Rule Britannia!*' or if a girl came along popping gum, wanting to kiss. He didn't like that. He thought girls ruined our fun, tried to take over and all that. I liked to kiss the girl, and he would get worked up and kick a stone. And I'd tell him I got a stiffy in my pants, that she made my ding-a-ling go hard. He didn't like girls. He just wanted to get back to finding slow-worms and centipedes and other stuff. And he didn't mind taking a piss in public too—he could even chew his nails while pissing. Me and Jacob were best pals.

The scaffolders had finished turning Moon Street estate into a towering climbing frame, set to be painted cream, we were told. The same cream but a newer cream. It would look the same, but new. Jacob shrugged. 'I think they should paint it black,' he said.

Telling Jacob to guard our patch, I went and fetched my prized rubberstamp collection, pulling out the orangutan. A few more kids joined: Carlisle, Mick, and Freddy. I stamped everyone's hand with the ape and gave them each instructions on how to be a chimp.

Moments later I'm leading the clan through the block, descending four flights of stairs without touching a step or the homeless guy and his stink. Tiny, a cool kid from landing 3, was sitting outside his flat, wiping endless bubbles of snot from his nose. I asked if he wanted to join climbing the scaffold. He shook his head with his eyes fixed on his lap. The back window still had stains of blood from his stepdad busting his old lady's nose on their way back from the pub. His mother then rushed out with a black and purple eye, laying a few more marks across Tiny's little legs with a wooden spoon. Tiny stretched out his arms, trying to shield himself, his gasps plunged deep inside his throat like he was drowning. Yet his mother, boiling with rage, just hit his fingers away and kept going at his legs, his screams heard down the block as we legged it.

We shot out into a hissing sun with monkey whoops. Jacob joined when he saw us coming. During all the chaos I pulled out the stamp and stuck one on Jacob. We circled the scaffold, sizing up the roof of the block with our heads sideward. A young blonde hurled past, her little sister close behind, crying hysterically.

'Don't go down the slide!' she screamed. 'G-L-A-S-S!'

We watched them run by and vanish into the estate.

'She's always crying,' said Mick.

'She lives next to us, cries all fuckin day,' Freddy joined.

'Her leg looked pretty messed up,' Jacob said, chewing his nail.

'Cryin's worse,' repeated Freddy.

'I bet it was Lonny who stuck the glass in the slide, the gaylord.'

'He once put glass in Nancy's shoe and it cut her foot.'

'Yeah, it definitely was Lonny. He's such a tosser.'

'Don't reckon we should use the slide, lads.'

'Slice your balls in half!' laughed Freddy.

Mick joked, 'Your balls are too small, Fred, like peanuts.'

'My balls are massive,' boasted Freddy. 'I'll fuckin show ya.'

Mick laughed. 'Go on then, show us your balls!'

'There're too many people about, someone'll tell my dad.'

'Her leg looked pretty messed up,' Jacob said again.

Mick elbowed Freddy. 'Peanut balls.'

Freddy's face shot red. 'I'll smack you in the nose, Mick!'

'Pea! *Nuts!* Get it?' Mick was in hysterics. I laughed too. So did Jacob. It was funny.

Freddy made a fist. 'I'll clobber you right in the gob, ya scab!'

'You don't have the BALLS! *Ha Ha Ha.*'

Freddy paused before yelling, 'Your mum's a slag!'

Mick stopped suddenly. 'Did you just call my mum a slag?'

'She *is* a slag! Yer not laffin now, twatface!'

'C'mon,' I said, 'let's just climb the scaffold.'

Mick got Freddy in a headlock. '*Your* mum's a slag. Say it!'

'Leggo of me! Leggo, Mick! You're hurtin!'

'SAY IT!'

'My mum's a slag! She's a slag! I'm sorry!'

Mick pushed Freddy to the floor. 'Peanut.'

Freddy jumped up. 'Your mum's a fat slag with a FAT FANNY!'

Mick balled up his fist. 'I'll get you, Freddy!'

'Let'm run. Let's just climb the scaffold.'

'I'll get the gaylord later,' said Mick.

Jacob had a new thought. 'Why don't we play Tracker?'

'We're climbing the scaffold!' I said again.

'Or Burn, yeah, let's play *Burn* . . . Hands up for Burn.'

'Scaffold.'

'Scaffold.'

'Three against one. Fuck Burn.'

Suddenly, Blake Chambers, a tough older kid came walking. He picked me out and whispered a dirty joke in my ear. I laughed. He then told me to hold his hand. So I did. He raised our hands to our mouths, and told me to suck my thumb so we looked gay. And I did. And he sucked his thumb too, while making sex noises.

'Gay!' shouted Mick. 'Gaylords kissing!' I quickly pulled away. Blake stuck up his middle finger to Mick before walking off down the street laughing. Then an old guy, having heard us, stuck his bald head out a 2nd floor window with a chin full of white foam, sucking a bottle of beer and making monkey whoops. The whole clan went berserk. All but me and Jacob, straightening up and taking a step back. We'd seen white men making monkey noises and it didn't feel good. Esther beat a girl about the block for making them. The old man then yelled down the safety rules for climbing the scaffold, before slamming shut his window.

'Just don't fall boys,' he told us. 'It'll be a helluva mess to clean!'

Just as we got hold of the lower bar, my mother appeared from the top floor, shouting to throw up the house key.

'A Neanderthal!' I yelled, setting off a hoot from the posse, a deep throaty chatter that highered in pitch until we were all screeching up at the blue sky like nutty apes.

'Judas! I'm tired! I just got home from work!'

The monkey chatter faded. The gold key shone as I took it from my pocket and held it above my head, like I was damning the wicked, to then spin like a disc thrower, tossing it skyward. My mother clapped her hands but the key sailed by, landing on the roof of the estate.

'Get it at once!' she yelled, before vanishing.

Eyes fixed where my mother once was, patting my pockets, I whipped out the stamp, planting new orangutans on everyone's cheek. We had the orange ape on our hands, arms, and now our faces.

I pointed to the roof and said, 'Monkeys, climb!'

We swept up fast. I kept a fraction ahead, keeping the pace. The bald man waved his beer as we skirted by his window. Close to the top, Mick got spooked. It was too high, we were too high.

'C'mon,' I said, hanging with him until we were back on the up.

'Thanks, Judas.'

'You don't need to go so high if you don't wanna, Mick.'

'I can do it.'

'Just make sure you grip tight.'

'I can do it, I can do it.'

'And stay on the inside, close to the wall.'

'I can do it, Judas!'

The top of the estate jutted out, coated in waxy tar, fairly sticky from the heat. It took a foolish effort to hook our legs over the top of the scaffold. The scaffold shook top to bottom. Mick and Carlisle hung back, something in the air said not today. And there I was, stood next to Jacob, looking over our bleak city from the very top. We jumped on all fours and whooped like monkeys, howling across the jungle.

Collecting the key I leaned over the edge and put it in the hand of my mother. She didn't seem to mind that I was fifty feet above ground, above the cranky scaffold. She had climbed similar heights in her youth—only it was up coconut trees escaping her brothers wanting to stick leeches down her pants.

As the posse made their way down the scaffold, fear crept upon me. I stared down at the tiny people below. The height made my head spin, encouraging strange thoughts of falling off the edge, arriving as firm suggestions, as though nothing else existed but to fall. I was almost excited by it, overwhelmed by some strange manic pleasure, like there was no more fear, nothing to be afraid of. I felt alive, full of aliveness, beginning to make the thoughts up myself, causing my cheeks to tense as I imagined breaking my face on the pavement in every which way again and again, bones cracking, snapped spine, eyes busting open of reds and yellow pus. I had to step back, back against some force drawing me closer to the edge.

Kneeling, I placed my hand to the floor.

'What is it?' Jacob asked.

'I'm just dizzy, that's all.'

Jacob was already on the move. 'I'm scared, Nobody, I'm going.'

My mother poked her head out the window again, telling me off for climbing to the roof and waking our elderly neighbour from her afternoon snooze.

'Get to your room!' she yelled, knowing full well she'd ordered me to throw up the key and then to go get it after missing the catch.

Reaching ground, I handed Jacob the orangutan stamp in case she'd try to take it from me.

'Hold onto it,' I told him.

Jacob snatched it and ran home.

9

My mother married the beer drinker with the fishing boat. His name was Arnold Arnolds. His friends called him AA as they cheered with their cans of beer, laughing, they always laughed and sucked their beer whenever they called him by his initials. It seemed to be some inside joke that only grownups knew. I laughed along anyway, it sounded funny.

Papa took pictures of us on his Maxxum 7000 at the wedding without anyone knowing, hiding behind a tree. And the fridge now had more beer than milk. And there were always cigarette butts floating in the toilet, calling for me to take shots with my pee pee. And Esther, she started getting into cars alone on the streets past midnight, returning with a purse full of cash. She had more money than anyone on the estate, even after she gave her friend Henry some once he dropped her safely to the door.

After the wedding, I swiped two cans of Heineken and escaped to my room, sweeping up the dog's bowl.

'Good boy,' I said. 'You're a good boy.' I took many swigs of beer and burped. I was still speaking to the dog while burping. It was fun.

We chugged the first two cans, so I stole another, popped it open, and poured half into his bowl. Soon I left him there and stumbled ahead to the livingroom where the wedding party were watching Dallas. I felt good, like I could outwrestle a bear. The pooch staggered in behind and collapsed to the floor, while I pretend to have the bear in a headlock. The mutt then tried to lick his balls but soon gave up, slumping to the carpet with his tongue lolling out. I could smell his beer breath, stinking of accusation. Unable to stand much more I took him by the collar and slogged us both to the kitchen.

'Be careful, Judas,' my mother whined as I growled on my hands and knees, displaying my canines to the mutt.

My mother then said, 'We're not having chips again to-day, we're having *vegetables*.'

I stopped growling. 'Chips *are* vegetables,' I said.

'They're not vegetables, Judas.'

'Yes they are.'

'Stop it, Judas, they're *chips*.'

'But Muh, chips *are* vegetables, they're potatoes.'

'Leave me alone!'

Retreating before she lost it, my pup followed me out the front door and we sat on the landing facing the peak of the old burnt down church, bombed during the war. And I wonder if anyone was in there when it got bombed. Esther said it was haunted, said the ghosts of the monks lived there, she'd seen them.

My dog sat beside me, panting and drooling, his breath humming of vomit and bone and Heineken. He licked my face while I connected words like those old phone operators connected calls. I couldn't help it. I did it through fear and of the need to feel good again. I knew what my mother meant about chips not being vegetables, but she could snap in a second. Her eyes became black and she eclipsed any source of light from the bulb or that of the sun. And the only book she ever read was the Bible, word for literal word, which made her some sort of medieval person. It's been a week since my ears started to twitch. I liked to think it was a call from the aliens, that I was really from another planet pretending to be human. As I pondered this my dog's breath wafted up my nostrils. He stopped licking my face and began licking his pink willy instead. I watched his willy grow like lipstick, unsure if he was cleaning it or was just as surprised as I was that it suddenly got stiff.

Should I touch his willy? Would he act funny if I did? I reached out and touched it anyway. It was slimy. And jerked when I touched it. Then he farted. I don't think he knew farts as we did. He never looked embarrassed about it. He just checked my eyes before going back to licking his gonads. I liked smelling his farts, they were disgusting and worse than ten of mine put together.

Deciding to go throw stones by the pier, I told the mutt to stay put and to not shit in the house before running out the door.

When I returned, my mother was playing a Doris Day LP. I disliked Doris Day very much. Her music forced me to smile and she always smiled, even when she wasn't smiling. Her eyes smiled, her nose smiled, her stupid ears even smiled. So I had to smile back at my mother smiling and singing along to Doris Day songs. It wasn't fair. It was cruel. Child cruelty, I was sure of it. I felt trapped in pretending to please my mother so she could be happy and not angry. I don't know what was worse, pretending to be happy, or being in the way of the anger. I didn't like either outcome, they both felt uncomfortable and very confusing. And it only forced conversations in my head to argue, like she lived inside my head always with something new to say, and I had to make sense of it all.

So reluctantly I smiled, watching my mother sing all the wrong words like she did at church with all the people. Slowly and gradually she played her old village cassettes less, all those old tapes were put away in a brown shoebox stacked behind the latest Hollywood blockbusters and magazines of the Royals, alongside glossy LPs of Doris Day.

'Once fried,' I said, 'chips are not *really* vegetables . . . not really.'

'Leave me alone!'

IO

It was Sunday when I woke to my father holding his shin, telling me I kicked him through the night again. I'd watch him in the corner of my eye, pulling back up my pajama bottoms while pretending to be more interested in the ceiling. He'd lie back on the sofa, going on about it. We were strangers again. Why'd I kick him? I don't remember any of it, but I felt bad anyway.

Dressed smartly by the window with the light against his face, I'd wait for the old man to come alive, usually when Harry James and his orchestra played out with *It's Been a Long, Long Time*. Then off we'd go, train ride across the coast. 'An adventure, terrific, that's what we need, Master Nobody, adventure dear boy.'

As usual, the carriage was crazy. Kids with crumb-infested seats and empty wrappers thrown over the floor. I'd sneak a glance at the countryside pass by, trees and cows and sheep, counting electric pylons while falcons soared high above fields. A couple of fat boys started playfighting, slamming against me, spilling their drinks and mine. They cackled, talking all kinds of gibberish with spit falling from their chubby fat faces. I watched them choke, watched them foam at the nose. And I'd think to myself, unwilling to understand how they continued waddling about with crisp smothered over their chins, bumping into everyone and everything. What could I do? There was nothing to do, other than watch a couple blubbers play human Pinball. It was amusing from a distance, yet sudden intrusions by either dipstick grabbed me by the guts, forcing me to sit still and endure, even while I was afraid. And I was afraid of everything, a nervous wreck of a kid. I wanted to leap up and grab both fatheads and leave them on the tracks for spilling my drink. But I couldn't. I couldn't even tell them to wrap it in. *You coward, Judas!* I was a mixed-up rubble of leftovers, that's what, just a rubble of mixed-up wires. I hated it. I hated feeling weak. And I hated the thought of bumping into anyone. That's why I dodged humans. And I was good at it. But what kind of priest would that make?

I glanced at my father as we rode along the coastline. He was in his own world, looking out the window. He then pulled out his notebook as though he had puzzled the meaning of everything, like a jigsaw piece somewhere in the middle, revealing the big picture. And off he went in one of his fits, writing and sketching. But I couldn't complain, watching him figure things out with his pen helped buy me time from the fatties, a small break as I quietly sipped the rest of my Coke.

By late afternoon I left my father and headed home. Some kids from the estate were lugging tables and chairs to the bonfire pit we'd been building for a month, the estate buzzing with excitement.

The pit was as tall as the pubhouse. Trucks and vans would roll up and dump scraps—old couches, beds, and nail-cladded wood. Aerosol cans were hidden inside the pit, ready to explode in the fire. Despite some dads fishing out canisters, there were always explosions, like miniature stars, spitting out space debris.

That year, a group of older kids got itchy, paced about all nervy as I stood mesmerised by those tall, magnificent flames. And they were right to be nervous. The eruption of a foam fire extinguisher combusting at the centre of our bonfire was enough to change the once ineffable gathering beneath the inky black sky into a night of total shit. Shards of metal lodged in everything in its line of fire, slicing through the air like a hot knife.

The pub was a right mess, the streets heaving with locals falling on the cobblestone. Some squabbled with bandages wrapped about their faces, throwing drunken fists. I somehow managed to walk away from the explosion unharmed—not even a scratch.

Last orders had yet to make its rounds, it was 'drink till you can't stand', a common rule to a group of men picking up an old-timer who'd smacked his head cruelly against a wall on his way down, trophying up his pint as he hit the deck. Everyone cheered as the old coot was hoisted to his feet, a drunken Hercules. I watched in awe as he wiped a spill of cider from his chin, straightened out his woolly hat and fixed his sea-boots. And with a crazy glint in his eye, he saluted the mass like a madman. *Hoorah!*

I bolted past just as the old-timer hit the deck, seeing my way through like Moses. Peeking back from the grim doorway of my block I caught a whiff of human shit in the murky unlit corners of the passage, mixing with the thick aroma of Old Spice. I gazed at the curious stout of alcohol, gathering up the wounded, celebrating the suffering of fallen angels. I was afraid of fallen angels. They had no sense. No way out.

Fleur of Block-H on the other end of the estate, called to me, clutching hold her massive tits. Her makeup smudged about the eyes and her hair was big and red, with a black bow tied around her chubby thigh. She had more tattoos than any man, on her fingers and arms, with a big sea anchor on her leg. She called to me, pulling down her top while sucking her fag. My chest grew warm, then everywhere again the heartbeat, my feet glued to the floor. I prayed to see them—I said to the Lord, 'Show me the boobs, dear Lord. C'mon, Lord, show me the boobies.'

Fleur winked. 'I'll teach ya, Judas. Teach ya howda hold 'em.'

'Leave the kid alone!' laughed Hercules. 'Get on inside, me boy,' he told me. 'She's too big for you lad, she'll gobble you up.'

The homeless guy at the bottom of the stairs stirred as I quietly toed past, grunting words to himself. I paused as he slid his swollen boots along the murky hall, tugging at his trousers and crouching in the corner. I don't think he knew that I was watching, it was only me and him in the passageway. He didn't seem to have feelings, his eyes hung low and his greasy hair fell over his dirty face. He didn't make much noise, just pushed the shit out in silence. You could hear the squeeze if you listened closely, then a spit and pop, making its way to the concrete.

But his shit wouldn't last long sat there. As Eileen, the old grump on the ground floor would toss a bucket of hot bleachy water to be rid of it—until he'd squat again in the same corner, pushing out another hot, steamy load, sending all the flies.

I leapt from the railing and landed on my doormat, and slipped inside our flat. Our door was wide open, which was just how it was on Moon Street.

A tall stranger came rushing toward me, zipping his trousers in a hurry. He didn't live in my house, or on the estate. I sidestepped and pretended to be invisible as he ran out the door with his face the other way.

When I found Rudy she was sitting alone mumbling to herself with her clothes all spoiled. She tried fixing her skirt with nothing in the eyes, like they didn't want to see.

As she buttoned up and wiped her tears, I grabbed hold the telly remote and flicked through the channels.

Sitting back to watch Danger Mouse, in staggered Arnold Arnolds, fixing his Teddy Boy hairstyle with a pocketcomb, leaned against the cabinet. Me and Rudy jumped to the couch. Arnold tried lighting a cigarette but the drunk couldn't keep it steady, crushing the fag on the table. Now on his knees, he tried straightening his socks, bashing his head against the door. Me and Rudy watched on. Our mother's new loveboy crawled his fingers up the wall, accidentally hitting the light switch. The room turned pitch black, only the shine of Penfold holding a bomb on the telly. Arnold then found his feet and tripped, falling headfirst into the glass coffeetable, pieces of fine glass puncturing his arms and his neck.

'Arrggh,' moaned the drunk, 'arrgggh.'

We watched blood run down his cheek, with lots of small red cuts all over his face and hands, dripping to the carpet.

Arnold stopped trying to get up and soon passed out in the glass.

'Is he dead, Judas?' whispered Rudy.

'No.'

'Blood, look Judas, there's *blood*.'

'Yes.'

'Is he alive?'

'He's alive.'

'Mum's going to be upset.'

'More than upset.'

'Shall we help him, Judas?'

'No. Let's go bed.'

I switched off the telly and we crept over him. I then bolted the front door shut. 'It's locked,' I told Rudy. 'No one can get in now.'

Rudy checked the locks while fixing her skirt again.

'Let's go sleep,' I told her.

'Okay,' she said. 'Nighty night, Judas.'

'G'night, Rudy.'

II

The potato guy changed. This one didn't wipe his feet at the door. My mother didn't ask him. Maybe he didn't think it mattered? She never needed to tell the other guy. I tried not to let it bother me. But it did. It did bother me.

My mother pushed me out the door in the hands of two local women who often came knocking for me. They'd take me by the hand and walk me about the neighbourhood, kissing my cheek and touching my hair. Other women on the street would stop and also kiss my cheek and feel my hair. They liked to kiss me and say how curious I looked, from the other kids, and how they wanted to kidnap me and take me to their home and kiss me all day long.

When we finally returned to my house, my mother would smile at the women, waiting for them to hand me back. And when they went away she would become normal again and spit on her dress and wipe all the lipstick from my cheek. Each week for as long as a summer, different women would turn up, each with new lipstick and new smells.

The day was bright. Beside the park, kids from all over the block jumped about a single bush. It was a large, green bush, with big purple flowers, shooting out like broomsticks, where a hundred new butterflies beat the air.

I rushed to the kitchen and made holes in the lid of a jar with my pocketknife. Then I'm out the door.

'Where you going with that there jar?' Mildred asked, sweeping her doormat with a cigarette stuck between her lips.

'To catch a butterfly!' I yelled.

'Mind how you hold 'em! They're delicate little fings! And don't you keep 'em for too long!'

'Where you goin with that, me buhy?' asked Frank the ferryman.

I ran on. 'Butterflies!'

Frank laughed. 'Get on, ya scallywag!'

Jacob was on his way up with his bike. Seeing me race toward him he ditched his bike and we both run along the passage and out the estate into the high sun. The sun spread across the sky. We hurdled over the rubber on the playground, zipping past the new steel slide that had replaced the old plastic one, preventing kids from making boobytraps with broken glass bottles.

A few more strides and we slowed the pace, one hundred wings punching the air like spastic flies. The picture was different from my window, more idyllic. I looked down at my jar, counted the holes. SEVEN. I counted again, slower. NINE. We crept to the bush, avoiding a load of blondies legging in and out the swarm, screaming at everything. As we reached the bush I plucked two twigs and several leaves and stuffed them in my jar.

'Are you putting a butterfly in that?' asked a little girl, picking dried snot from her cheek.

I kept plucking leaves. 'Yes. Shush. Your scare 'em.'

'I want a jar, I want it.'

'Shuddup, your scare 'em,' I said again, now adding too many leaves, having to take some out.

'It's not fair!' she cried, folding her arms.

'Will you just shuddup. Go ask your mum.'

She pointed at my jar. 'I want *that* one, with the *leaves*.'

'Jesus Christ. You're doing my head in.'

'Yeah, you're doing our heads in,' Jacob said.

She managed to pick her snot. She made a face.

'Owwer,' she whined.

'Shhhh! Christ, be quiet! We have to be quiet!'

'It hurt!'

'I don't care!'

'Yeah, we don't care,' added Jacob.

'You're both not nice.'

'Look!' I said, 'just get away, you're too loud.'

'I'm going to get my dad on you,' she huffed, finding her feet.

Jacob looked at me as she ran. 'Will her dad come get us?'

'He might,' I said. 'We'll have to outrun him if he does.'

Leaning back, we waited patiently.

The same girl came back and whispered, 'Get that one.'

'It's too far,' I told her. 'I won't get it in time.'

'Yes you will, yes you will.'

'Bloody heck, just go away,' Jacob told her.

'Right, I'm really going to get my dad now.' She skipped away. A small group of butterflies settled nearby. Jacob looked at me, then at the butterflies. I lunged and threw one in the jar.

'KILLER WASP!' yelled Freddy.

We ran as fast as we could away from the bush, me and Jacob pushing our way through all the girls.

'That was close,' I said, shutting the door to the block.

'Yeah,' Jacob said back. 'That bee almost killed us.'

We climbed the staircase, seeing Tiny being dragged indoors by his mother with that wooden stick again. 'You're not allowed to hurt me!' he yelled at her, this time without showing any tears. Me and Jacob nod at each other, agreeing without saying so.

The lady at No. 46 stood in our way. 'What you got there, boys?'

'A butterfly,' I said.

'Oh yeah? What'll happen if you keep it in that there jar, eh love?'

I peered down at the jar for a second, noticing my laces undone beneath the jar before looking back up. 'It won't get out,' I said.

Jacob shrugged. 'Yeah, it won't get out.'

She gave us a curious look. 'It won't get out, eh?' she asked suspiciously. 'Is that what you want, huh?'

Jacob tried glancing at me, but his head was frozen stiff. His eyeballs darted back and forth between me and the neighbour, who reeked of burnt sticks—the same sticks my sister Tabi set on fire and waved about her room speaking gibberish while pretending to be Japanese. This neighbour had a big nose. And she was bony, with dirt in her hair, her arms covered in small papercuts. We couldn't pass, couldn't even dare try, stood there as she was looking us over with her stupid finger on her lips and that filthy dustpan in her hand, repeating over what we'd already told her. 'It won't get out, eh?'

Eventually giving in, she sighed and continued sweeping her door.

Me and Jacob bolted up the steps.

'Wait!' she popped, jumping back to her feet.

We spun around and faced her again, her brush raised high like a machete. 'What'll happen if the butterfly can't fly, hmm?'

Again I looked down at the jar and at my laces. Having thought it over, I stooped down and tied my shoes, stood back up and lifted my eyes. 'Then it won't get away,' I said.

'Yeah,' shrugged Jacob. 'It won't get away.'

We finally got away and back to my room, setting the jar next to my window with plenty of light.

'Does white stuff come out your willy when you stroke it?'

'Yeah,' said Jacob. 'And then I rub it on my face.'

'You rub it on your face?'

'Yeah . . . you're suppose to rub it on your face.'

'Who said?'

'My dad.'

'I didn't know.'

'Yeah, and my dad said someday I can rub it on a *girl's* face—yuck.'

'That's weird. Does he rub it on your mum's face?'

'I think so, yeah. And my auntie's face, too.'

'Are you making this up?'

'No. I swear it.'

'It's called spunk, I think. Yeah, spunk.'

'Does it make babies, Judas?'

'I think so, yeah. Inside the spunk is sperm.'

'Ohhh,' he said.

'Yeah, sperm. Inside the spunk.'

We both sat still continuing to watch the butterfly do nothing. Bored, we sprang out the door and hopped on our bikes. We pedalled by the skinheads sucking beer on the wall, riding faster to avoid them. Before reaching the main road Jacob slammed his brakes, while I collided with the front of a passing car.

The car swallowed my bike beneath its tyres as I ricocheted off the bonnet and flew over the roof. The old banger coughed my bike out its rear-end as I landed on the concrete, rolling beside my mangled pedals. The brakes of ten cars shrieked along the road as passersby gasped and pointed. A bearded Janner with a flabby gut bouncing beneath his shirt tumbled out his car and grunted toward me, repeating if I was okay.

'I'm okay,' I croaked, rescuing the frame of my bike.

Jacob had already turned back for help. The whole world was just pain and people staring and pointing and closing in. And the skinheads cheering and clapping.

'Are you sure?' glugged the driver, looking less concerned.

'*Yeah*,' I croaked again, 'tickety-boo, mate.'

He started shouting, 'You came out of nowhere!'

I didn't answer. I tried to breathe. I tried not to look hurt.

'You could've been killed! You almost got yourself killed!'

It felt like an elephant had its foot on the spine of my ass.

'And the other cars behind! You could've hurt someone!'

Like being underwater in a swimming pool, observing all the people above, everything became a blur of colour and noise, dreamlike apparitions occupying another dimension, able to watch them without being seen. A spy beneath the water. A figure. A blob.

Picking myself up, I hobbled back to the estate, passing the cheering skinheads while trawling my broken bike. Thudding the door closed with my foot I slid down and hid from the crowd, allowing the pain to be what it is.

Holding my leg in the dark, Dolly the cupcake lady stepped from her door carrying a fresh bake, hearing the disturbance. 'Oh! You kids making trouble! You kids! Get back to your own block!'

I found my feet again. Dolly never offered cake to any of us except her grandkids whenever they visited. I wanted to eat them all, wondering if when she had a heart attack I would have the guts to climb through her window and stuff my face before the ambulance came. The sight of my whole thigh blue was a definite sign that what was happening was real, not a dream.

'Judas! Keep away from old Albert's door. Away child! Shoo!'

Pushed on again, this time by old pissy pants Margeret hanging out her yellow knickers, telling me to steer clear of Albert the pedo's door. He seemed fine to me. You never saw him outside. Only peeping through the window. 'Off you go my love!' she fretted. 'Shoo child!'

The next morning my mother walked in from work with a boy my age and his parents. On her way home she noticed them sleeping in a car, huddled together in the backseat. They had driven all the way from Berlin with little money for petrol and sandwiches. My mother went straight to the stove and got to work stirring a pan of porridge with the last bit of milk. They moved in. All of them. That very morning. Our front room became their Jesus-loving pray-pit until they sorted something with the council. I hated the kid from the moment we met. We hated each other. Not sure why. Some things do not need understanding. Hate is hate. It is what it is. We fought all the time, me and the German kid. He had a constant swollen lip from some lip disease, and his mouth remained permanently open like a mongoloid. He busted my basketball and said it wasn't him. I even saw him put the dart right through it. I chased him in and out every room, and grappled him to the floor, squeezing the truth out of him.

'Tell the truth! I saw you!'

'I vill not!' he fired back.

'You busted my ball! Say it!'

'I vill not!'

'You busted my ball with my dart! Say it you liar!'

'You vont make me!'

'You're a liar!'

'You are a lie! You, Judas No One!'

I snarled, applying the Randy Savage chokehold.

'You are hoorting me, Judas! I can-not bwreev!'

I squeezed tighter.

'Get auff me! Get auff me!'

I leaned into his ear and hissed, 'The madness is runnin wild.'

Everyone was out, including the Germans, which meant the TV remote was mine. Then in stumbled Arnold Arnolds, stinking of beer and stale farts. Today his eyes were different. The room shrunk. I stared at the door he just slammed shut. I tried ignoring him, but he came straight for me. Without room to leg it past he grabbed my arm and pinned me against the wall by his hand, wrapped around my neck. Spit rolled from the corners of his mouth, his silver tooth shining. My face warmed each time he tightened his grip, his cold rings pressed against my throat.

'D'you get what I mean, eh kid?' he grunted, gripping tighter. 'When I say no runnin in the house—is what I mean . . . '

My breath narrowed and whistled, my tongue pushed out by itself until I could no longer catch air.

'Is what I mean . . . what I mean, ya little nigger.'

My cheeks swelled up. I tried loosening his fingers. Faintly, I detect a key turn in the front door. Moments later my big sister Esther walked in, leaping toward Arnold and grabbing him by the throat. I crashed to the floor. Our mother's new husband got Esther by her throat too, one throat possessed by the other, her eyes tigerish, wild, his a rolling alcoholic mess. She flung her head toward him, thudding his nose. Losing footing, Arnold stumbled back and fell to the floor.

'Run Judas!' she yelled, standing over him as he moaned holding his face. But I didn't run. Sometimes you just don't run, or can't. Sometimes you're frozen stiff, caught by the fear, so much fear that there's just nowhere to run.

For the many days and nights I had to duck past Arnold, often staying out late with my dog until he collapsed drunk, and at times barricading myself in my room with my back against the door.

Following many more weeks of dodging his shadow, finally, too fed up of blaming me for causing problems, my mother told the beer-swigging lunatic to pack up his stuff.

12

Kicking my ball against the wall in the yard, I kept one eye on the butterfly inside his jar. The whole night he didn't budge.

I kicked the ball without hitting the jar, which I placed on the ground. Though I wanted to, wanted to crack it open and wake him up. Setting the butterfly free was soft, like he knew he was trapped in a jar. But he didn't know he was in a jar. He didn't know anything. And he didn't even care.

The jar spun on the gravel but the butterfly didn't give much. So I kicked the ball harder, and many pigeons flocked close with their swollen feet and their heads bobbing. Does he know he's in a jar? Like goldfish stinking up tanks and chickens shitting in cages—does he know he's trapped?

Glancing about my estate, the new cream paint didn't make much difference. The walls still looked dull. Then from nowhere Loner Leon appeared, dragging a dead bird with cotton looped about its neck, cleaning his pocketknife of blood. Hey Judas, he said. Leon, I said, watching the weirdo turn a corner.

Lonny was spying down on me from his bedroom window, having been grounded for sticking glass in the slide. He didn't think I noticed but I saw the dip ages ago. And then there was old man Gregg, tossing out a broken chair by the bins, telling his wife to quit her bloody yap as he clobbered the concrete with the chair, sending splinters flying. 'You'll take an eye out, you silly fool!' she piped, throwing up her hands. I could've sworn I saw Albert the pedo's curtain twitch as old man Gregg beat the chair. Along the top of the courtyard hurried brothers Reggie and Rory, the two door-to-door salesmen moving fast with an armload of designer shirts. Behind them walked Duke, the thickset gypsy who loaned everyone money, doing his weekend rounds.

'Judas!' yelled Tiny as I picked up the jar. Tiny was much smaller than all the other kids his age, that's why we called him that. His hair was greased back with half a tub of Brylcreem, looking like a hedgehog. He was a cool kid. Slick. Collar up. Tiny spent a long time playing with action figures. After school I'd often watch him play, watch him make those noises with his mouth all alone. He didn't mind that I sat on the slide close by and watched him move his toys about the air and make those noises. But I decided that it was strange. It was strange that he did that.

Tiny stood on top of the concrete slide with his football boots slung over his denim jacket.

'Yeah?' I said back.

'Wanna come to Saint Budeaux fields for football trials?'

I nodded, though I didn't know what he meant.

'Okay, let's go!'

I opened up the lid and shook the butterfly until it crawled itself out and sat on top of the jar. It was okay to let him go this way, I told myself, pretending he did all the work.

'Wanna come with us?' shouted Tiny to Carlisle.

Carlisle lived in the pub. He was a pub kid. The pub was called The Blackhorse. He hung out the rear balcony of The Blackhorse which faced the courtyard, holding the estate together like a buckle to a belt. Carlisle was a skinny ten-year-old skinhead, a good skinhead who sucked his cheeks and popped his bright blue eyes whenever he felt trouble. And there was always trouble in The Blackhorse.

'I got the shits!' Carlisle yelled down.

So me and Tiny made our way to the fields, the farthest either of us had been outside of the estate alone.

'What is it?' I asked Tiny.

'It's a trial day to play for a *real* team. None of this courtyard shit.'

'A *real* team?'

'Yeah.'

'What they called?'

'Saint Budeaux.'

'Of course,' I said. 'What do we do?'

'I don't know. My stepdad told me to get out the house.'

'Your stepdad was drunk yesterday.'

'He's always drunk yesterday.'

'I saw your mum's boobs when she was fighting Connor's mum.'

'I saw Connor's mum's boobs too.'

'Were they big?'

'Medium size. Why is Connor albino but his mum normal?'

'Maybe his old man's albino. What colour were the nips?'

'What?'

'Connor's mum's nips?'

'Bright pink, like you could hardly see 'em.'

'Knew it,' I said.

Approaching a park, we had to leg it past a gang of older kids smoking and drinking. They shouted at us but we kept running until we reached Saint Budeaux fields.

About fifty boys stood about the grass with nearly as many parents, clutching their bottles of Gatorade.

Tiny plonked down and laced up his football boots. I thought my pink bermuda shorts and plimsolls were alright. And then a big shine of sun split open the clouds, spilling over the field.

I set off. 'We should get there quick!' I called back.

'Wait for me!' Tiny yelled, running behind.

The coach gathered everyone together, and as me and Tiny gave our name to a guy with a clipboard, a lady with enormous knockers and a permanent smile handed us each a slice of orange.

'Welcome to the Under-10 Saint Budeaux football trial!' said the coach. 'Now, we've a long day, so please listen very carefully. Put your hand up if you've not given your name and address to Tod?'

Tod waved. His hand was bandaged.

The coach went on: 'Good. Now, we're gonna split you kids into four teams. Tod'll give you all a coloured bib to wear.'

Tod was now waving beside two black sacks.

'Now, we'll play ten minute games and change teams so that everyone gets a chance to play at least twenty minutes.'

Coach looked at his watch. Tod looked at his watch. They nodded at each other. Tiny was slurping his orange and I didn't know what to do with my peel so I dug a hole and buried it.

'Peels! Peels!' called the lady with the big boobs, shaking a white bucket. Tiny dropped his peel into the bucket and began sucking his fingers like he hadn't been fed in weeks. The lady stared at me with that same never-ending smile. She then lowered her whole body, blocking out the sun, and tilted her nose to a peel that wasn't mine. It belonged to a ginger kid. Unable to take her boobs an inch from my face I quickly picked up the peel and dropped it in the bucket.

When she moved on I tapped the little ginger kid on the shoulder. He shook his body and yelled something to the sky.

I tapped again. 'Where's your orange peel, mate?' I asked the kid.

The dummy searched all around with orange skin smothered over his freckled face. 'Where's my peel?' he said. 'Who took my peel?!'

I pointed to the lady with the fat boobs. 'In the bucket,' I told him.

'BUCKET!' he screamed out. 'IT'S IN THE BUCKET!'

Tiny paused with his finger in his gob, his eyes switching between me and the kid. Ginger was a maniac.

'Blues versus Reds!' announced the coach.

The coach assigned us each a field position, which no one seemed to understand. Then the whistle blew, and everyone chased the ball.

I watched them all run, charging with their heads down. It was a disaster. The sun blazed. I only ever kicked a ball alone against a wall. But now here were fifty lunatics, all trying to kick one ball at the same time.

'Get involved, lad!' the coach barked at me.

'Go'n, sonny!' roared an old lady in support.

This is it, I think, setting off toward the mob. Tiny was already in the centre of the riot. A few players had understood the coach, standing in their positions about the field. One mean-faced chub got all the action, flinging other kids to the ground. Pushing my way inside I nicked the ball away from Chubs, and was almost free when a bunch of kids tripped over at my feet.

I took a step back.

'Get involved, lad!'

'Go'n, sonny!'

An excited boy spoke over my shoulder, 'We need to pass the ball,' he said. I spun around, the kid was kitted out like his future was made, and spoke of tactics and strategy. I liked his talk.

'We need to spread out first,' I said.

The kid agreed. 'Yeah, open up the game,' he said.

'That's right, yeah. Take our time, set up chances.'

'Yeah, use the whole field. The ball moves quicker than us.'

I really liked him now. 'Exactly,' I said.

We both stared at the riot continuing to chop about the field like a crazy tornado.

'I think I'd play a free role, make things happen,' I added.

'Nice,' the kid said. 'I prefer the wing, me, working the line.'

'Sounds good. But first we need to spread out.'

'My name's Bow,' he mentioned, picking his nose and chewing it.

'Bow?'

'Yeah, like bow and arrow.'

'I'm Judas.'

'Like the Bible Judas?'

'Yeah, that Judas. Right. I'll go get the ball and try to pass it to you, and then you pass it to that kid over there.'

'Aye aye, cap'ain!' Bow said.

So I took off again with a plan. Pushing my way through the mob, I snatched the ball from Ginger, sprinting in the opposite direction with a load of kids on my trail. As planned I passed the ball to Bow. He took it clean and turned sharp, waking up the other kid who was waving for the ball. Bow made the second pass. Suddenly a stampede of twenty kids came barreling toward the ball, including Chubs, which got the other kid nervous. Me and Bow yelled after him. 'Pass again!' we called out. 'Pass again!'

But he was crushed by the mob, crawling himself out and hobbling back to his position.

Then the whistle blew.

13

I received a letter in the post, addressed to Mr Judas Nobody. I glanced at the telephone so I could look at the letter again new.

Welcome to Saint Budeaux Football Club!

So I got proper boots and shoe polish. Shining my boots before each game. I joined the worst team in town. We lost. We always lost. The other teams scored all the goals. We lost count the number of goals they scored. But when the ball somehow found its way to the back of their net, our coach had to run onto the pitch and calm us down. And this went on, ten, fifteen goals by them, and our coach breaking us up when we scored our only one. And the parents laughing. We were terrible.

Soon I received an invitation to join the best team in town.

Welcome to Elm United Football Club!

And I played against my old team, and I watched them celebrate when they scored their only goal, the coach running onto the field to break the little crooks up. I saw Ginger trip over his laces and curse the sky. Chubs causing havoc. Tiny more concerned for his hairdo. And Bow high-fiving my new teammates, clapping when we scored. You couldn't get a crazier bunch.

I soon realised I was the only street kid among my new teammates, the only kid playing with fear. And so I got serious, like one of those religious crusades. And I became pretty good. Really good, actually.

14

My father died of lung cancer, age 72. I had turned 12.

The last time I saw him alive I was ushered from his room at the care home where my mother nursed his final days. They hadn't spoken in years, I have no memory of them ever being present in the same room, yet there she was, washing down his legs and feet, spooning the old man porridge.

Catching his eye on my way out his room, he held that same expression when I kicked in my sleep and he'd escape to the sofa and I'd lie alone, fixing back up my pajama bottoms again while staring at the ceiling, wondering what happened, like we were strangers. Though I felt closer to him as a stranger than I did his son. There was something straightforward to it, something you couldn't ignore.

No one spoke much the morning of the funeral. Sitting with my mother and sisters I fell into a daydream, imagining if he could feel the warmth of his casket descend into the theatrical black-clothed stage of fire that the Undertakers cheaply put together. I felt no loss, no sorrow. No one he knew saw him off, no child from his previous divorce, no old chums, not even his good pal the watchsmith—no one except his nephew, who gave no clue to who my father was.

Commiserations were awkward, long, pitying condolences. So I made an effort to avoid them, sidestepping my way out of situations. I just didn't mind that he had died. It didn't upset me.

Hovering about the sandwiches my mother mingled with her church people as though she'd been adopted by overrich slave sympathisers, circulating supposed Aryan sovereignty, correcting her wig, inching her narrow heels across the carpet that made her walk like an overused, foreign whore. The sight of it made me cringe. The ceremony was small and insignificant. Above the exit, at the far reach of the hall, a large stained-glass window shone all kinds of colour, ambers and yellows, reds, some gateway to something beyond, something near perhaps.

What is now proved was once only imagined, wrote this fella Blake, what I read the morning before in the library. I turned my father's camera to my eye and took a snap of the window, noticing the colour, thinking nothing.

From here on I collected my mother from the care home where she worked, having to sit among the forgotten folk and the stink of decaying breath clinging to false teeth. I was never used to the stench, just recognised it more.

'Worry is a disease, me boy,' this one old fella Harold repeated to me. I wandered room to room, stopping and spying on Harold being checked over by a pretty nurse, his large saggy bum slung over his bed with big hanging turkey-testicles in her soapy hand. This time he noticed me spying. Harold had a sweet tooth, all the oldsters did. Me and Edna got on with sherbet. Edna never said more than two words, just grounded her dentures in circles like a goat.

'Frank died this morning,' said my mother as I walked her home.

I thought of the space left now old Frank had gone.

'I'll put you in a home when you're old,' I told her.

'You cheeky boy!'

'You should be nice to me then.'

'You're too cheeky! I give birth to you!'

'I didn't ask to be born.'

'You'll leave me in there to rot with all those sick people?'

'I'll let you choose what home you want to rot in.'

'You can't leave your mother! Your poor mother!'

'Yes I can.'

She tried changing the subject.

'We found Harold in Betty's room with no pants on!'

'Harold's a rascal.'

'Yes, he is a rascal.'

'I'm still putting you in a home.'

'You cheeky boy!'

Old folks' homes were the last bus for oldsters, passing tea through plastic tubes. Many had to make an effort to remember me, reintroducing myself again and again with a nurse repeating my name louder and louder until they pretended they knew, sat back and reached for their bag of sweets. They scattered the room like nail clippings. Perhaps leaving them in a forest with chickens and blankets, a radio and some easy board games would do the trick, a small patch of nature where the dead just die, see themselves out.

One Sunday, a nurse switched on the gramophone, Glen Miller and his band, causing a few to rise from their chairs, have an afternoon waltz. The livingroom had more of a stench. The news broadcasted a severe downpour for the afternoon, sunshine soon after. I read a picture frame on the table during the waltz: Da-vinci, Old Men: *'While I thought that I was learning how to live, I have been learning how to die'*. Edna caught my attention, smiled and chomped down on a soggy shortbread before turning her eye back to the tea dance happening on the rug. I always got offered a cuppa tea. I never took it. The cups smelled like the seat of the chair once they all got up.

It was everywhere.

I was cautious not to take it home with me.

That stink.

It's been a week since my father died. The dog's been gone for days, no one saw him. The new potato man still walked in without wiping his feet. And Rudy came home with a Silver Star for her attempt at reading Matilda.

Waking up, I saw a figure in the corner of my room. Rubbing my eyes I saw that he was very tall with long thick hair. His face hid behind the shadows, seeming to bend the light pushing in from the streetlamp outside. I held my breath beneath my quilt as the figure came closer. Drawing a sleeping bag from his back, he then rolled it next to my bed and lay on the floor.

I bolted out of there and made it to Tabi's room. 'There's a man in my room', is all I needed to whisper at three in the morning, it woke people up and kept their mouths shut. Tabi quietly unpicked three locks and raced down the stairs and out the estate half-naked and barefoot with me and Rudy close behind.

My mother got the call and made her way home from work. There was no doubt the man was real, stood there shivering in my underpants.

'You okay young man?' the police asked me.

'He's in my room. I saw him.'

'Well, we've checked. There's no one there. And no one's gonna jump the top floor without us knowing about it.'

We all looked up at my window. I didn't like what the cop said or his stupid grin. My mother reached home just as the police left.

'It's the ghost of your fahda,' she said. I didn't believe her. I told her to settle down, it wasn't Papa.

A few months later Tabi called social services to stop the beatings at home, she wanted out. It failed. The welfare treated her to a breakfast in the caff around the corner but returned her straight to the place she was desperate to escape. So she tried killing herself again, this time swallowing the whole tub of paracetamol. That failed too. It's been too long since I last saw the dog. I started to really miss him.

15

I dialled the number. My mother was on her way home from her night shift. We were late for school again. It was nine o'clock in the morning. Tiny and Carlisle and Jacob huddled in close to hear her voice. Tiny held the back of the CLASSIFIEDS open with the number circled in red felt and his finger pressed against it.

'Hello,' came a voice. 'What's your name, lover?'

I hit the loudspeaker. 'Judas, Judas Nobody,' I said.

'Hello, Judas Nobody, my name's *An*gela.'

I nodded at the phone. 'Hello Angela.'

'So, Judas, what d'you like, honeybunch?'

'I like my radio,' I answered, and meant it.

She laughed. 'I like the radio too. What else d'you like, Judas?'

'Football, I like football.'

'Is that all?'

'You're sexy.'

Carlisle threw his hand to his mouth and coughed.

'Thank you, Judas. You like to get straight to it, eh soldier?'

'Yeah, I do. Straight to it.'

'Have you got an erection, Judas, a big fat hardon, eh babe?'

I looked around at everyone. 'My friends are here,' I said.

'Oh, so you like orgies, eh Judas Nobody? You like group sex?'

'No. I don't know.'

'I think you do.'

'No.'

'Maybe you do.'

'Maybe.'

'You wanna touch my pussy, Judas?'

'Yes. I want to touch your pussy.'

'*An*gela.'

'*An*gela.'

Jacob had a big smile. Carlisle was still coughing.

'Mmm, come touch *An*gela's puss puss, loverboy.'

'Okay.'

'It's here, Judas. Can you see it? Can you see ma puss puss?'

'Yes. I can.'

'It's wet and waitin for you to come lick it.'

'Yes. I can.'

'*Oh Judas,* be quick honey—slip your cock in your hand and come with *An*gela baby boy.'

With that request I panicked and hung up.

'Ahh shit, you hung up again, Judas!'

I shook my head at the floor.

'That was just gettin good!'

'*An*gela . . . bet she was an old biddy, wasn't she, Judas?'

Tiny shook his fist. 'I'll stick my cock up her fanny.'

'Yeah, yeah . . . what cock, *Tiny*?' laughed Carlisle.

Tiny turned on Carlisle. 'Shut ya face, knobnuts!'

Jacob looked at his watch and panicked:

'We gotta get to school! We're late again!'

With that we all run from my house, passing my mother.

'Have a good day at school, boys!'

16

The weekend came. Turning out my drawers for my wetsuit, Jacob and Tiny and Carlisle loitered outside. I stuffed a lingerie catalogue I pinched from my mother beneath my bed and took off downstairs.

One year later and we'd escaped Moon Street estate amd moved into an actual house. The neighbourhood was a mishmash of hard-working families thrown in with your regular druggies, dealers and stealers.

'Where you going?' my mother asked.

'Seafront. Wanna come?'

'I've been working, Judas,' she stressed.

I hung about the kitchen to lift the mood before getting off, hearing her sing gospels as I slammed the door.

Stepping outside, my crew erupted in an overblown cheer, decked out in rubber suits and their best trainers. I already decided the mood of the day late in the night, scribbling two more pages of my latest story.

We dived off every rock, step and pier, as long as the water was deep enough, we took the plunge. We dove into hidden lakes, off cliffs, and into hotel pools. We hit the upperdeck of Mayflower Steps, charging past a group of canoeists.

'High tide lads!' yelled the skipper.

We raced by the boathouses, counting them as we ran. The cobbled path long and uneven, rusted chains clanking against the pier.

'Let's go!' yelled Jacob and Tiny running ahead. 'C'mon!'

We jumped the pier like a pack of rock-hopper birds. Swimming around the fort we came to Corinthian, a 40-foot drop into an undisturbed cove of blue and green ocean. To get there, you had to skim over a rocky slope, followed by a short hike along a dry trail, finally making it up the concrete mound known as Corinthian, extending from the promenade like a broken sword.

Reaching the peak, we rest to soak up the sun, when Jacob hollers, 'High tide, fellas!'

Before Jacob could fill his lungs I legged it past, gliding up over into the blue. Jacob punched the air soon after, all that sky and wind, the sea rushing toward us.

I gasped as I returned to the surface. Jacob bobbed up soon after, shooting snot from his nose with a big happy grin.

We dodged jellyfish and hoisted ourselves to land, unzipping our rubber suits on a dry patch of grass. Tiny then jumped. He didn't make much a splash, cutting through the water like a pencil. Carlisle paced along the edge, trying to get out his head and leap.

'We could be fishermen,' Jacob said while we watched Carlisle.

'Yeah, fishermen, a good life.'

'Simple life.'

'Hard work.'

'Good work.'

'Maybe.'

Jacob turned to me. 'Do you believe in baptism, Judas?'

I picked up a crab from beneath a rock. 'I believe in drowning.'

'I mean *baptism*. Not drowning.'

'I know what you mean,' I said, looking the crab in the eye.

'Baptism ain't drowning, Judas.'

'Maybe it was back in them Bible days.'

'Drown people?' he asked, plonking down with a fistful of pebbles.

'Yeah, pull 'em out the water when they blackout.'

'Oh yeah? But what if you die?'

'Just get yourself alive,' I said, placing the crab back on the rock.

'But what if you DIE?'

'You're supposed to die,' I said. 'That's the whole point.'

'To die?'

'Yeah. Then get yourself alive again. That's the *real* baptism.'

Jacob skimmed a pebble along the ocean. 'I like living,' he said.

'Yeah? Well maybe we should baptise *you*?'

'You mean *drown* me?' he asked, tossing another stone.

'Yeah. *Then* you'll know what living is.'

'Alright then,' he said. 'But you first.'

I jumped up. 'I'll do it. I'll get myself back,' I said.

Jacob continued lobbing stones. 'Yeah, yeah, Judas. Nice try.'

I crouched to him and said, 'Imagine coming back after dying.'

Jacob studied the ground for more stones, flashes of excitement in his eyes. 'No one can see the Kingdom of God unless they are born again. John three three,' he said.

I leaned over and helped Tiny out the water. 'I don't know it,' I answered, grabbing Tiny's arm. 'Something like that, I guess.'

The sun soon got lost behind a sheet of cloud. The sky was all cloud. Carlisle jumped from the rock. We all cheered.

It was past midnight when I left the boys. I walked home, keeping back thoughts of ghosts lurking in the dark. The wings of a thousand crickets rang in my ears. Looking up at the night sky, I searched for Orion's belt, a habit I picked up from old man Gregg. Once spotted, I just stood there, contemplating the cosmos.

As I walked, I peered over my shoulder, catching sight an old blue Honda rolling behind, keeping its lights low. I don't know why it kept behind. The street was empty. I kept walking and it kept rolling. Too afraid to run, I didn't want to think I was in trouble. But I was, I was in trouble. The car lights switched off and the engine quietly hissed. Get going, Judas, I said to myself.

Then a voice in my head said, Run Judas . . . RUN JUDAS!

I legged it that fast my feet couldn't hit the ground quick enough.

Twisting my neck as I ran I saw the engine fire up. The car accelerated, meeting me at the foot of the road. I shot past the bonnet too afraid to glimpse who was behind the wheel. When I reached my house I shoved my key in the door, expecting to be lynched any moment.

Shutting my door, I toed lightly up the stairs to my bedroom, kneeled along some carpet and peered between the curtain. The car's headlights suddenly switched to full beam, lighting up the whole street. I watched it roll past like an alligator along a black river. And I tell myself:

'That was a good decision, Judas, a good decision. And exciting! Exciting?

I slinked down beside my bed and gobbed twice on my wall: one for God, the other the Devil. I don't know when I first started this, it just seemed to find its place, determining the outcome to a shoddy situation. The two lines of spit slithered down the wall side by side. And I waited, waited for the outcome.

'God it is,' I muttered to myself.

Kicking off my shoes and lying back in bed, I wondered what I should feel. Nothing came. So I imagined the headlines along the canvas of my ceiling:

Boy Found Tortured and Almost Dead
Man Killed with Bat
BOY KILLS MAN!
Abducted Kids Chained to Walls
Beaten and Molested by a Cult of Pedophiles
BOY SAVES KIDS!

The scenes kept coming, having to escape time and time again, bludgeoned and hacked, molested. But I could never *actually* die, could never *think* myself to death.

I buried my head in my pillow. 'You wimp, Judas,' I said, rolling and facing my mirror, my eyes looking back awake and dark, as though some cunning angel smiled at me, and kept on smiling as I slept.

17

Reading my father's final letter before he turned up his toes was the cause of the tear. I made myself do it. I was good at making myself tear up when needed, thinking, You should cry, you should be upset that he died. So I read the letter for the sake of crying. But in a strange way I watched myself cry, and thought, You need it, poor kid.

Finishing up the remaining sicknotes that I had written for kids at school on behalf of their unsuspecting parents, I had forged the final signature, ready to hand them out before the bell. A pound a letter seemed a fair price.

I inherited my old man's gift of penmanship and was putting it to use. It took several tries to differentiate one note from another, rewriting each one until the use of words were like characters to a play. Unable to sleep until it was just right, I'd be up for hours scribbling the thing down.

Writing sicknotes gave me something, witnessing the faces of kids light up, being thanked, admired. I cared less about the money, and not much for the lies: flus, migraines, *domestics*, diarrhoea, suicide attempts. It was important before handing out the notes that each kid knew their lie back to front.

Pretty soon demand skyrocketed, so I had to recruit a classmate to take orders and keep track of names and sick days. Our policy was simple: no deposit, no note. Donny, a street smart handsome wily kid with a lazy left foot, that gave him the scuffle of a crazy schizoid, had a knack for numbers, was sharp, reliable, and didn't waste time with small chitchat, cutting straight to the deal.

Some days I'd watch the morning sun fill my room, having been up the whole night possessed by all kinds of twisted tales. I split half the dosh with Don. Soon enough I had to shoplift a variety of pens and writing paper to throw off the teachers. It no longer kept me awake with excitement, but with a tense fever.

Once business was booming my pal and associate Don and I added a second service: designing front covers of school exercise books. Fifty pence a cover. My workload doubled. Sitting on the floor of my bedroom I stared at a tall deck of textbooks alongside a fictional stack of half-written sicknotes.

Almost two in the morning and needless to say I had to get the lot done by 8 AM. Wedging a towel beneath my door and pushing a window, I burned some hash I got from Don, see if it helped as he assured it would.

7:40 AM: My vintage nudie magazine stuck out from beneath my bed. C'mon, Judas, she teased, remember my sweet pink pussy lips?

I was too tired, had already beaten off four times to the same muff since midnight, penned seven sicknotes, and sketched all sorts of madeup patterns on a pile of covers, followed by tired navel attention. I hunched down and managed forty pressups. Climbed up. The mirror reflected back something I imagined made the girls want me, made them all want me, flexing my bicep with a spliff protruding from my lips. I then peered down at the arc beneath my foot, the little arc that should be tall like all the white kids, like they were a perfectly evolving species. I pulled out my knob and gave it a good inspection. Those Christians or Moses or whatever madman who had the idea to snip the foreskin must've been off their bloody rocker. Maybe Moses was a sadist? Whatever the case, that foreskin was mine, not theirs. Those selfish bastards.

To be whole like my fingers were born whole, and my leg and toes functioning as they were meant, how *their* God meant. And I wasn't sure if I had a small knob or a medium knob or a something in-between. It wasn't massive like in some dirty mags, or teeny like how some kids would get labelled 'maggot dick'. I didn't have a maggot dick. But I couldn't shake the feeling of something shy and full of quiet panic. Perhaps my dick just wasn't as confident as my arms, I thought, raising my bicep in the mirror.

Zipping my todger away, I gathered the books and the sicknotes into my rucksack, packed my football boots, straightened my tie and splashed on some Old Spice, ready for school.

On the turn of eight a small posse of local neighbourhood schoolkids had gathered outside my window. I signaled one more minute, taking one last hit of the joint while stretching open my eyes in the mirror. I hadn't slept a wink.

Stashing the dope at the far reach of my bed beside a stack of subscription magazines, I fingered out the latest edition of *True Crime*, rolled it up and squeezed it into my rucksack.

8:05: Brushed my teeth, brewed my mother a cuppa before listening to tales of the hospital nightshift, how she was bullied by this and that nurse. I gave my best team talk, and made it downstairs and out the door.

Just the previous day the police had blocked our street leading to the old farmhouse at the end of the road where a kid had killed himself with a shotgun, blowing a cartridge through his own skull.

'That kid who killed himself fucked a chicken,' said Duke, a blonde dude rolling along on his skateboard, handing me a silver coin.

'Let's walk,' I told the boys, passing out textbooks and sicknotes. 'I can't have my mum seeing.'

'How'd you fuck a chicken anyhow?'

'Reckon you'd have to knock it unconscious.'

'Jesus, it's like fuckin a baby.'

'C'mon, man, too far.'

'Well it is . . .'

'Yeah? So how'd you know?'

'It just is, thicko, it's called *physics*. Maybe it was a good thing he banged a chicken.'

'Instead of a baby?'

'Yes, genius. Instead of a fucking baby.'

I handed Cal his sicknote and said, 'How in the hell did you two go from chicken molestation to kiddie-fiddlin?'

'He must've had a maggot dick!'

'The chicken was actually frozen. He buggered a frozen chicken.'

'I hear some minges are frozen.'

'There he goes again with his facts. So how's that, Casanova, eh?'

'I got frostbite from your mum!'

'Twat.'

'*Ha Ha Ha.*'

'Poor guy. Feel sorry for him. No *won*der he shot himself.'

'Feel sorry for him? Killing yourself takes *guts!*'

'You don't know what went on inside his house. None of us do.'

'The chicken was actually alive, it wasn't frozen. He grabbed its neck and squeezed hiz pecker between its feathery butthole.'

'Yeah, and hiz folks caught him so he blew hiz head off.'

'Stop making shit up.'

'True story.'

'Jesus Christ, enough.'

'Here Ed, your sicknote, your Nan died in her sleep.'

'Thanks, Judas, but she ain't dead.'

'I know. But you never see her. You got the week off.'

Ed hands me a shiny pound coin. 'Cooool,' he said.

'Judas, you knew the boy who killed himself?'

'Not much, saw him about the shops a few times.'

'How'd you get your pecker in a chicken anyway?'

'Frozen chicken.'

'How'd you get your pecker in a *frozen* chicken?'

'Boys, enough with the chicken conspiracy, fucksakes.'

'It's one-fifty a note now lads. WHSmith upped prices on paper.'

'You steal the paper!'

'Exactly,' I said. 'The risk is more expensive.'

'Can't take any more days off anyway, Judas. Me old man's fishy.'

'Mine too.'

'Yeah, I've had three this week. I'm meant to have chickenpox!'

'Best cool it for a bit then. But it's one-fifty next time.'

'What makes you wanna kill yourself anyway?'

'Happens all the time. Just watch the news.'

'The news ain't real.'

'The chicken was! *Ha Ha Ha.*'

'Will you PLEASE give it a break with the CHICKEN!'

'Dunno what you boys are on, but he shot himself cus a London drug gang. He owed them money. Thousands, I was told. He was storing crack or somefin at the farm. That's what my brother said.'

10 AM: Kitted out in school gym gear, I ran laps around the track while the other half of our class swung Lacrosse sticks.

Our PE teacher, Grenshaw, was a serious fella. His eyebrows punched down and his little black whistle remained permanently lodged in his mouth. He wore very tight shorts that always presented a dick-bulge, with his socks sprung high over his knees.

'Oi! *Pakee!*'

With no sleep the morning was already rough. And now I gotta deal with this stinking kid, swinging his stick and chewing gum. I didn't know his face too well, other than his older sister being a supposed hardnut in fifth grade.

'Yeah you!' he snotted again, laughing with his little sidekick.

'Is he talking to me?' I asked some kid running alongside.

'I guess so,' he shrugged. We both knew I was the only brown kid slogging it round the track. I was in fact one of just two brown kids in my year, and one of maybe four in the entire school, all seeming to have warning in the eyes to stay the hell away from each other, don't draw attention to us, the eyes said, *spread out!*

Grenshaw was busy chasing students with his whistle when I scaled the fence. I would've preferred reasoning with the kid, but his eyes were funny, and his front two teeth were much bigger than the rest, already a natural sign of my victory. In any case, the plonker harped it again. He could be yelling nigger or chinky. To him I was anyone who just wasn't white. I didn't even know what I was? Just some kid casted between the feud of two old enemies: a mongrel. Yeah, *mongrel.* I was a crossbreed, the go-between, an experiment that slithered out the cunt waving a neutral flag.

And so he ran, this kid, picked up his feet and pegged it. He took aim and flung his stick over his shoulder. His mouthy companion shouted for me to leave his mate alone. There were no wild screams or erratic bouts of rage, that didn't seem to fit my temperament. I didn't want to catch the bastard but I could run. So I shoved him to the ground. Gasping, the toad sprung to his feet. 'HOH SHIT!'

Grenshaw came in fast to break us up, his arms and legs striding with textbook precision. Wiping my hands on the grass, not wanting to have the kid's stink on me, I heard Grenshaw's whistle. Meanwhile the kid ran away. And I watched him scarper, thinking I may have developed a problem with his older sister.

'No need to explain, Mister Nobody,' said Grenshaw, catching his breath. 'Just get back with the running team. Off you go, lad.'

11:30 AM: Passing through the schoolyard peering over both shoulders, I expected a hillbilly lynch-mob waving pitchforks, preparing to haul me off to the woods with rope and a flag. But instead I noticed books that all looked the same. All my drawings. And Donny collecting our cash with his little notepad and busy pencil way out in public, like we were The Untouchables. And all my classmates kitted out in black leather gloves like it was mandatory schoolwear, all thanks to my shortlived shoplifting spree with a gang of five I assembled, before being outsmarted and chauffeured home by the police. It was getting out of hand. Me and Donny needed an emergency meeting.

'Don, it's over. Stop taking orders.'

'No way!' Donny cried out, counting the last of our takings. 'I'm good at this, Judas.'

I realised we were speaking too loud, lowering my voice, I pulled Donny aside. 'I'm shutting it down, Don. We're too known.'

My business associate dropped a bunch of coins into his pocket. 'What about me, Judas, huh? Don't I have a say?'

'Sure,' I said, moving us to another spot, lowering my voice some more. 'Keep it going if you want. But I'm out.'

'Wait!' he said. 'Okay, no more gloves, or book covers. But we keep the sicknotes.'

I shook my head, took another glance about the yard.

'How's two a day?' he begged. 'Enough for chocolate and fags.'

I said nothing.

'*C'mon, Judas*. We're making twenty quid a week!'

I shot Donny an eye. 'I don't care about the money. The teachers, Don, they'll be up our ass in a flash. It's getting out of control.' I placed my hand on his shoulder.

Donny let off a long sigh, nodding to himself. He then slipped away his notepad with a reluctant shrug. I gave the mopey crook a larger cut of what we had left before heading along to English.

'Mister School Trophy Winner,' hooted our English teacher, Mr Farringdon. 'Please, enlighten us!'

I gave Farringdon a cocky smirk. 'Si señor, I mean . . . yessir!'

'Amusing, Mister Nobody. So tell me, have we finished our story?'

Farringdon came down the aisle of the classroom like a man

who lived by his values. His pale blue shirt scruffy and well-worn beneath a purple sweater, his rusty yellow hair combed to one side like the SS, his bulging, ever-present blue eyes glaring and frightening, as though we were preparing for something so paramount that he would not hesitate extending the class.

'May someone offer at *least* a line?' His dirty-brown loafers had all the swagger of a crazy professor, with cream-coloured cords rolled raggedly at the ankle. 'Right you lot, you've got two very patient minutes. Otherwise we take this to afterschool detention!'

His voice is a mixed bag of savoir faire and common country bumpkin. One kid tried catching Donny's attention, tapping a fiver on his shoulder. Donny shot me a problem look, ignoring the kid and instead raising his hand, willing to read.

I had a story. But the idea of reading out loud scared the jizz out of me. I couldn't do it. I hadn't written my story for the class. Fuck them. Fuck them all right to hell.

As everyone began talking over each other, getting amped up by Farringdon, the room was slowly being brought to a hush by red fingernails tapping the door.

'Tap tap, hola, muchachos.' Farringdon's lady, Ms Garcia.

Garcia was a beaut: lilac tights, yellow miniskirt, pink waistcoat, little blue shoes, with an intense, in your face bang. Her tall legs catted between the aisle and popped a print of rouge on Farringdon's cheek, uttering something in foreign before striding back along the aisle, back to teach the Spanish class next door. 'Adios, muchachos!'

Farringdon wiped his cheek. 'Alright, alright, calm down you lot. Judas, for chrissakes, tell us the name of your story.'

I unwillingly opened my book. 'Sour Milk,' I said.

Farringdon chalked SOUR MILK on the blackboard, then walked to my desk. 'May I?' he asked, taking the book from my hand.

Adjusting his spectacles, he began reading my story out loud.

'The boy and his dog crept along the hall, freedom in their sights.

The floorboards creaked as they slowly made their escape. A tall man with a wooden face and cold, beer-soaked eyes stumbled from a room and faced the boy. The tall man glared in the direction of the boy but he couldn't *see* the boy. Then a woman, very fat, with thick arms and a sore spine, appeared from the same room. Her eyes were seasick, and her knees swollen blue. The woman dropped to her swollen knees and raised up her arms, praising the coming of the Lord. She then started to weep, but her eyes were not wet. She wanted to cry, to show tears, but her eyes remained perfectly dry, like the ending applause of a good show. Then, suddenly, her shirt began to wet, two small circles where the nipples were . . .'

Farringdon stopped the class from giggling.

'Okay, Mister Nobody. Giving the reader something to think about, hm? *Sour Milk*. It's simple, yes, but there's something. Though perhaps you could be bold enough to write what that thing is exactly, hm? Tackle it straight on!'

Farringdon stopped thumbing through my book and placed it on my desk. He then called for the next story. As he waited for a show of hands he leaned back to my desk and whispered, 'And please try to keep your handwriting consistent, Mister Nobody, it changes on each page. If I didn't know any better, I'd say you've had too much practice penning all these *sicknotes*.'

'Si señor.'

He stood up. 'Congratulations, one more lunchtime detention, very good.' He then pointed at Donny. 'Mister Parker, you're up next!'

12:30: The field was yellow with summer grass at the rear of the school, overrun by hundreds of kids during lunch hour.

Farringdon rubbed away the chalk from the board in small and slow anti-clockwise circles, revealing sweat staines under his armpits. He then scooped up a good chalk and began scribbling before dusting his hands and walking to my table.

Tapping my textbook, my English teacher left me with this: 'Making words say something, Mister Nobody, may just be your luck.'

The ugly kid with a huge hairy mole, who stank of something fowl inside the gut, tried striking up conversation with me. Some kids nicknamed him Pig-Poor—on account of being too fat to breathe through his nose and for kicking a plastic Coke bottle in the yard with his only friend, Scabies, a kid covered head to toe in blisters. They put me at ease, Pig-Poor and Scabies. I preferred exchanging words with these than the popular kids. I even joined a game of 'bottle-ball' in the schoolyard now and then. So did Don. We liked them. We liked feeling unpopular—not that it was a popular school.

1:30: The Battle of Little Bighorn in 1876, led by Colonel Custer, a US Army officer and Cavalry Commander. We were being inducted by an historian who scratched his balls in plain sight. I pulled a late seat at the back of the class and dropped an ear on two girls discussing a lesbian who'd just come out. The girls seemed turned on by the fact that she openly declared her liking for vagina. I just about caught a lecture on tribal handprints in the caves of southern and eastern Australia, just about kept awake to hear how aboriginal folk spat a mixture of ochre, water, and animal fats across their hands, sinking into rock like ink to paper, marking an initiation, a vision of the soul, while earwigging the girls speak about masturbation. I was shocked girls did it too. I didn't know. I grew a little beneath the table just listening, careful to rub my finger along my zipper as they chitchatted.

Leaving the girls to whisper I turned to Denver Becker, a hefty kid with a yellow flat-top. I wanted to know what the lunatic was reading.

'Mein Kampf: Hitler and the Nazi political agenda,' he said. Denver was a quick-witted kid with large ears. The book stood out beneath his pale hand. The cover was neat, distinguished, unlike any

I'd seen. I liked it. I asked him, 'You allowed to read that in school?'

'You allowed to talk about wanking with girls?'

You see, *large ears*. Becker was surrounded by a mysterious kind of madness, the loner type who held a grudge always. He didn't have any mates. But the nut didn't need any, he needed troops, followers, people who voted. Those kind of folk. Adjusting in his chair, he kept his big nose straight with a strong jaw. I kept my gob shut. I was actually impressed. That Hitler book took good care of him, kept him moving along the trenches of the school corridors while all the kids pinged elastic bands his way.

2:30: ART CLASS. Ms Jankowski drove a Beetle. It was yellow. With blue flowers. She was something from the hippy days. Petite, with a pitchy voice, bouncing about the classroom. Jankowski wore colourful tutu dresses with thick ballerina stockings, a true art nut. I thought about Jankowski often, imagining her muff wild and sticky, like the 1950s *Bains de Champagne* addition tucked beneath my bed.

Trying to conceal another boner, my finger brushed an old wad of bubblegum stuck under the desk. I sniffed my finger. Strawberry. I couldn't think straight until I washed it off, couldn't hear a thing Jankowski said. And rubbing the stink on my trouser leg only made my hardon grow stiffer.

Another fine situation, I thought, looking about to see if anyone noticed. Maybe big ears Becker did, looking to the air just ahead of me. I kept an eye on him. We both know he's acting weird, his gaze darting between me and the front of the class. You don't pick a spot across the classroom mid-lecture unless you're looking at someone. The sneak rolled up his eyes to the ceiling while fiddling with his pen, pretending to muse over some hanging volcanic sculpture before dropping his fat nose to face Jankowski again.

3 PM: DRAMA. 'Now, let's all move slowly to the floor, feeling yourself as a withering flower. *That's it!* Keep moving. Super-duper! Okay, as you reach the imaginary soil, I want you all to roll toward the person nearest to you. Now, once you reach your partner, I want you all to take hold a part of their body and lie as still as you can.'

The sole of Boris's mangy foot ponged something rotten.

'Chrissakes, Boris, stop wiggling your bloody foot.'

'I cannot help, Judas,' Boris bleated. 'I don't like touch.'

I yawned, thinking again of being stalked by that car. Maybe there were two child snatchers? One driver, one killer? I considered the possibility while holding Boris's pinky toe, recalling scenes of the Moors murders, rereading it several nights back in *True Crime*.

18

The next day I woke up and reached for my book, a short paperback of some 170 pages on decoding the Bible, something I swiped from the library. But it wasn't there. Did I leave it there? Instead I grabbed a book of essays by Carl Jung and fanned open a random page, trying, again, to get my head around this 'unconscious projection' thing—this idea, that, someone, who claimed so little of themselves, would have *you* believe that *their* delusions are *yours*.

Sliding out of bed, I went and knocked on my mother's door.

'Come in!'

I stuck my face in. 'That's not your book.'

'It's not good, Judas. The pastor say so.'

'Where is it? Where's my book?'

'I gave it to Pastor Tom.'

'That's not very Christian, Mum, you pinched my property.'

'It's not a holy book. He say so.'

'I think I might become a Muslim, like Malcom X.'

'Not under my roof!'

'Stay out of my room,' I said, closing her door.

Charlotte Griffin had no friends and carried a peculiar odour. She never smiled or spoke much. And I liked that, I liked how she walked about school alone, having gotten rid of kids somehow. But most of all I liked her big tits. Just one eclipsed both Jankowski's. I tossed off to them when laid in bed. I stopped using Ms Jankowski's small but wonderful ones and instead imagined Charlotte's, bouncing beneath her school shirt.

It was a hot day. All the kids walked home in a sweat. Charlotte held her bag as the girls laughed. I warned the bullies to leave her be. 'Listen, lesbians,' I said, 'go tongue an asshole.'

'Oh, Judas,' the chavvy dykes sighed together, walking away hand-in-hand. 'We bet *you'd* like our tongues up *your* asshole!'

They weren't wrong. Charlotte wiped dust from her knees and struggled her weight back to her feet. She then carried herself through the fields, allowing me to stroll alongside.

The sun glistening between the trees drew attention to dark hair above her lip. I don't recall what we said, or if it mattered, but what we said didn't try to make us laugh or smile or like one another.

She stopped and gazed at things, and I watched in astonishment how long this girl could go without tying her shoelaces, laces that dragged along the muck.

Charlotte wasn't a looker, and she couldn't care less neither.

I said, 'Hey Charlotte, you have the biggest tits I've ever seen.' It was a compliment. I was being complimentary. Her face remained the same, not even a flinch, kicking leaves as we walked.

I told her she lived near me.

'I might just walk you home,' I said.

'Fine,' she says. 'No one's home,' she also wanted me to know.

Charlotte invited me into her house for Dr Pepper. Her mother had been gone with her new boyfriend for days. The television was on, bowls piled up in the sink with crusted cornflakes and small flies jumping.

I picked up a family portrait and put it back exactly between the dust and asked Charlotte when I could see them. It sprung out my mouth without any trouble. No one cared for her and I knew it. I knew no one cared.

'Go on,' I pushed again, 'show me your tits.'

Charlotte motioned to the back room, her chubby finger pointed, the brown matted hair floating along like fluff off a broomstick, her pleated skirt, hung stiff like paper, above thick legs with a patchwork of blue veins. And her busted shoes still undone and two sizes too big, with dirty frilly socks adding no favour to her appeal. My God, I liked her.

We sat on her bed beside yellowed-stained pillows. Charlotte unpeeled her shirt, tugging her large bosoms. She presented them to me from her white bra and I observed how they both drooped over her fat stomach—stretched out, the biggest kind, with large round purply nipples. And veins, lots of them, crawling up the skin. Though they looked different to how I imagined, swung low, with her bra remaining up high, where I had always pictured the tits would be.

Charlotte became more relaxed. 'Wanna kiss 'em?' she asked me, taking one giant boob in the cup of her hand for us both to admire. She suddenly seemed better at this than I expected, more optimistic. Her window was generous with light, shining directly upon her chest. I rested my lips on the left nipple, performing tiny kisses.

She yanked up her skirt. 'Wanna feel my fanny flaps?' she asked.

I stopped kissing the nipple and took a look. It was a thick bush. More moisture climbed the air, with a fishy odour. The kitchen flies had tracked our whereabouts, stink flies continually landing and flying and landing.

I felt a fear. 'I have to go,' I said.

'But why?' she asked, tugging up her knickers with a little embarrassment. 'You don't wanna feel my flaps?'

'I've got a football match,' I said, frozen stiff.

She nodded, and didn't put away her tits, they just hung there, with great power over me.

Shooing flies, I got up and left. And thought about stuff as I walked the streets. And we said hello along the school corridors the next day. And I remind myself, those quiet girls can't be fooled.

19

My wallpaper made it easy to lock eyes on one spot, pausing the horrors of life. Uncapping the glue stick and taking another long sniff, I turned my attention to my mirror.

'What the hell is going on?' I asked myself.

My skull warmed, vision thinned. Soothing my temple with my fingertips, I allowed my head to drop to my navel.

I wasn't good with pity. It was an illness, a disease. What I needed was wise direction:

'You're doing alright, kid, keep it going, just keep it moving.'

As my head hung low a drip of mucus spilt from the roof of my nose, pooling liquid inside my nostril. It itched. And I let it itch, soon becoming unbearable, putting myself through the misery. All I needed to do was wipe it away and that would be that, no more torment. But I refused, stubborn as shit, choosing instead to endure the itch—endure the suffering!

Finishing a yawn I finally gave in and mopped up my nose and reached again for the glue stick, noticing blood on my hand. Fixing my eyes to the ceiling with my head tilted, pinching the bridge of my bleeding nose, my mother begins to call.

'Your coach is on the phone!'

I made it downstairs.

'Your nose! It's bleeding again!'

I ignored the woman and took the phone.

'No problem, I won't be late. And thanks again, Mr Stanford. See you at the ground on Tuesday, seven sharp.'

I put down the phone.

'What is it?' my mother asked.

'Football trials for the England under-sixteen squad.'

I couldn't get excited. Perhaps the glue was still working.

'That's brilliant, son, well done.'

I picked her up. No one ever picked this 15-stone woman up.

'Blood! Blood! Put me down! Put me down!' I plonked her down and walked back upstairs and kicked my door closed and slid out my little dope tin from beneath my bed and rolled a celebratory spliff.

Later that day I took a wander round the block with thoughts of last night's game. Maybe the England scout was lurking? I had emptied half a can of deep-heat over my legs to keep them from turning blue before hitting the field, leading our team through a rowdy gauntlet of supporters. I recalled gazing down, hating the cold and rain. We pounded our chests like a bedlam of pygmies. I stretched out my calves before sauntering over to the forward and giving him the brief.

'Let's get this done,' I said.

Coach waved me over, reminded me again of the danger players. The pitch was where I could let it all go, live by my own rules. I beat my studs and took several leaps into the air like the Maasai.

Then the whistle blew.

Sucking up the stench of defeat, hunched over my knees, there below me, in the muck, squirmed a crushed worm defying death, cut in two and still fighting. The worm shook me out of my stupor, fixing my captain's armband and hollering at the squad:

'Keep formation!'

We were still in the game. I picked up the ball, barking commands like a drugs raid, swinging the thing out to the wing for quick one-twos. One hard-looking kid charged straight for me with his studs airside, propelling along the dew. I nicked the ball over his head.

'Keep formation!' I yelled again as we surged on.

Collecting the ball from the back of number 6, I juked it between his legs, lobbing it over one square-footed player and sending our winger on a hundred-metre dash down the line.

'Formation, formation, formation!' I called again and again, that being paramount to victory. One rat-headed nit tugged my shirt, playing dirty. 'Ref!' I yelled, but the ref was too far.

I promised the pissbag a beating.

'Touch me again, dicko,' I said, 'and I'll break your face.' Although a sharp elbow to his rib proved enough to spin on my boot, leaving the crook splayed out in the mud.

I was unmarked, coming in wide from outside the box with my hand raised high, just as our winger swung the ball after a good dash, giving it plenty spin. Some antenna jogged me back ten paces, volleying the ball with accuracy, striking the top right-hand corner of the net.

Goal!

One-nil.

'Keep formation!' I yelled immediately, saving a wink for the shirt-puller picking himself up.

We held our turf for the final few minutes, leaving the pitch as though wild pigs had smashed the earth.

Game over.

'Well done, lad!' praised a short gent with receding hair and long rubber boots, his green wax jacket slung over his shoulder. Lowering my eyes and rolling down my socks, I said, 'Cheers mate,' removing one clammy shin-pad and inhaling the victory.

Knelt down looking out at the dads huddle their kids, I took another sniff of my pad before the coach arrived.

'That's what happens when you put the work in, son! Great game! *Great game!*' Coach gave me a pat on the back. Nothing more. I wasn't sure if he wanted to. I stood close to his side anyway, not knowing when to go alone, opting instead to listen to him exchange strategies with a bystander. The space between us grew. I wasn't sure whether to close it. I chewed dry skin from my lip and looked up at the rainclouds. I laughed when they laughed. I felt impertinent, a tactless idiot waiting to be excused, taking a quiet step to one side and heading back to the locker room.

Hours later I'm back home cleaning out a muddy bathtub with my mother stood outside the door with a basket of laundry reminding me what the gypsy recently said: 'Keep the boy away from motorbikes. He'll end up in a wheelchair!' vowed the cider-quaffing mystic.

It seemed irrational, but the premonition ached both my legs the whole week, dreaming or wide awake. Sometimes I'd let their crazy prophecy just break them, allowing imaginary limbs in some fantasy world to be taken beneath a steam train just to relieve the tension.

Crack. Crunch. Hoot Hoot.

'Mum, not now please.'

'My dead sister told the gypsy. She watches over you in the spirit world!'

'Mum, I'm not going to be in no wheelchair. Enough.'

'Promise me you won't ride a moto bike?'

'I'm not promising you anything.'

'Your auntie warned the gypsy, Judas. Please, it upsets me.'

'I'll ride whatever I like at whatever speed I please.'

'Judas!'

'Enough with the crystal ball, Muh. Give it a rest.'

'You're not riding a moto bike while you live in *this* house!'

I stepped from the bathroom. 'I'm tired. I'm going to bed.'

'Stop it, Judas. I said no!'

'I can't even ride a motorbike. I'm fourteen, for chrissakes.'

'Stop upsetting me!'

'You're upsetting yourself.'

'I'm not upsetting myself. It's *you* that's making *me* upset.'

I walked to my room. 'Not now, Mum.'

She followed me. 'The gypsy said don't let my son ride a bike!'

'Goodnight.'

'I'm not going to bed.'

'I'm going to bed.'

'Then go to bed!'

I slowly shut my door. 'No more tea, Mum. It's late.'

She stormed off and screamed, 'Leave me alone!'

The woman slammed pots and pans in the kitchen, yammering nonsense to her God. It was about a quarter to nine. It didn't take long for my mother's latest manfriend to march up the stairs, swinging open my door like a pissant hero. The five-foot pest in tartan sweater came straight for me, demanding order and respect. I never liked the guy, he was under-height and grouchy, like a tumbleweed, and buckled his trousers too high. His mouth clapped, sending flecks of spit below my eyes. With each brave step forward her protector became more furious, his finger angling nearer. Putting an end to his performance the idiot finally buried that appendage in the centre of my chest.

Switching off my light, the street became illuminated from my window, the sky a sheet of black with razorblades of blues and purples. Outside, my mother begged her fella to stop yelling ahead of the house as her fancy man nursed his bleeding head and vanished up the street. 'That swine!' he roared. 'No respect!'

My mother's feet soon thumped up the stairs, mumbling 'Jesus' and 'that boy will not speak that way to me in my own home' before slamming her bedroom door. With that bone-crushing prophecy of hers still ringing in my ears, I locked my hands in some fisted sort of prayer, pausing my thoughts and slowly unsticking my eyes. The coil in the streetlamp flickered to life. I spit twice against my wall, today a win for the Devil, and cleaned up the broken glass from where I'd slammed his face against my mirror.

Her manfriend never returned.

But the Devil, as always, stuck around.

20

Being false, fictitious, make-believe, the word read. Fanning pages of a dictionary it felt right to settle on *spurious* and dogear the page. I could likely chip away to find something a little more exact for Benny's sicknote, but this'll do, I thought, this will do.

My mother had the volume on Doris Day on the VCR all morning, trying to get me out of bed with that awful yippy sound. Unfortunately for her, it had the reverse effect, causing me to dig out a few untested magazines, finding a similar sweet-faced gal.

Spreading pages across the ledge of my duvet I started greasing, holding back until the very last moment. Fingering out another nudie mag from below my bed—FIFTY PLUS XXX—I discovered the small and delicate buds surrounding the nipple. I hadn't noticed that part before, all those tiny buds getting me excited. I shot my load immediately. My last thought that of sweet Doris.

Then a bang outside shook my wardrobe. Followed by more.

Bang! Bang! Bang!

Tilting my head out the window I cranked down, 'Tabi? It's eight o'clock in the bloody morning!'

Bang! Bang! Bang!

Without pause I yanked on my bottoms and threw on a shirt. Doris shuts up, followed by my mother hexing to the door. I jumped from my room, shouldering my old dear back and slipping outside.

Tabi hot-footed away with a filthy pram and an open rucksack, glancing back with swollen red eyes.

'Chrissakes,' my mother hissed. 'That sister of yours!'

Running across the yard, I waved her back. 'Tabi!' I called. 'Tabi!'

Watching her trip and fall, missing a parked car by a nose, she managed to keep the pram upright. Instinctively I rushed to help but she warned me away. 'LEAVE ME ALONE!' she cried out, dusting her knee. 'LEAVE ME ALONE!'

Like a wounded animal she hobbled over the hill, leaving behind in her panic several nappies.

I scooped them up and headed back, tossing the nappies on the kitchen counter. 'You two need to talk,' I said.

'She's crazy! Crazy!'

'She's not crazy, Mum. She's upset. The past is eating her up. Just make an apology and be done with it.'

'I've done nothing wrong! NOTHING!'

'No one's blaming you.'

'Jesus took away my sins! I'm born again! The pastor say so!'

'Okay, alright,' I said.

It was always the same, one sore-eyed sibling of mine would come and go like an angry windstorm, usually pregnant or rocking a pram. After their showdown, I'd make my mother a commiserating Tetley's and leave her sitting by the back door talking to nobodies.

'What about me!' she'd weep, cleaning her teary face. Turning for me, for anyone to notice her pain, she'd then cry out, 'I came to this country with nothing! And your father left me alone! HE LEFT ME ALONE!'

'Drink your tea,' I'd tell her, before walking upstairs and scribbling myself a sicknote, something or other of the neighbours arguing through the night again: police, ambulance, mayhem, he hasn't slept, was too tired, no school today.

21

Hestia walked beside me, her long Malaysian hair swinging in the breeze. She had migrated to Plymouth with her old man from Brooklyn, New York. She was all I could think of the moment I stole her picture from the drama club noticeboard. She was a year older, fifteen, half Malay, half Yankee Doodle, with full pink lips, big brown eyes, light cocoa skin and skinny all over.

She pointed to a cloud and noted, 'That's a raincloud.' I made an inquisitive thrump through my nose, picked up a stone and chucked it into the woods. She looked on without seeming impressed. So I scooped another and threw it harder, which hit a tree and almost returned to our feet. Hestia laughed.

I handed her a stone. 'You throw one,' I said. And she did, tossing it farther than both of mine, clapping dust from her hands and turning back to that cloud. I picked up another and flung it with every male fibre I had, sending the rock high over the trees. We both hear the rustle of a bush somewhere out there. And then we walked on.

My home was one of a few grey houses on the street, the few not painted. There were nicer looking homes with trim little gardens and brass door numbers, making me wonder what'll be like to lead Hestia through a painted gate with a little picture of a spaniel or some other smug pooch, greeted by a slim and personable white lady waving from our kitchen window, with mittens, tattered old cookbooks and interested questions.

'Almost there,' I said, passing one of those gates.

'Sure,' she returned with excitement.

The two stinking crackheads at 58, Baz and Charleen, were

bickering on their doorstep, screaming at the top of their lungs with their little inbred bull terrier, Wedgie, barking at pigeons.

Jack, the snobbish kid from number 70, who claimed his old man drove him to some fancy private school each morning, burst from his door, a bright, shining house boasting a British flag flapping from the rooftop. His ginger mop bounced as he skipped across his trim lawn in his blue slippers, taking cover behind a hedge.

Me and Jack swapped Dreamscape cassettes and got stoned in the back alley. His folks never seemed to be without a newspaper. And they didn't send Jack to Happy Shopper for emergency toilet roll, Tampax, and a pint of bloody milk, recounting a fistful of dirty copper. I never liked Jack, the ginger dickhead was too sure of himself, always eager to hand out advice.

'Pssst, Judas! Can you score any weed?'

I swung my arm around Hestia and ignored the dipshit.

All the lights were on in my home, smoke pouring from the kitchen window. My arm felt strange around Hestia's neck, like a prized possession that didn't belong to me. But I couldn't let go, my arm didn't seem to be mine either.

Little Wedgie the ugly-nosed terrier had a twig between his teeth trotting happily, those dopey eyes stretched back inside his skull with his minuscule pink nuts swinging. The dog stopped a foot from our toes and began biting his scrotum, really going after all his fleas. 'Fackin stupid mutt,' moaned Charleen as she belted by, kicking the dog to move. 'Hey Judas,' she said in passing.

I watched her rotted scheming smile as she and fleabag sped toward the telephone box.

The end of the street was still plastered in yellow police tape along the gated entrance to the farm. The one about the kid who sprayed his wall with his brains didn't seem appropriate. I kept shtum.

'I live here,' I said, like a boy without Christmas.

Tabi was back in town, a busy shadow in the kitchen with Rudy.

As we turned to the house, I saw all the muck I would usually pass without care: cigarette butts, sewage excreting from inside the walls out of a dirty white plastic pipe and down the crease of the house as though some homeless alkie had hiked his way to the roof and let himself go in the gutter. And Rudy, I had hope for Rudy more than any of these women, she was easy work. But I doubted her role in my climb to a better life, the girl would give too much away, ruin me at the peak, I was certain, rabble over my golden lines with absurdity.

My arm was still latched to Hestia as we strolled the path. The door swung open. Making use of Rudy's sudden appearence, I took back my arm, with Hestia folding loose strands of hair behind her ear, as though she'd suffered too.

'Mum's gone work, Judas, she had to go work,' rattled my sister, nodding her delighted head.

Tabi, the other one, appeared from behind. 'Mum asked me to cook for you and your girlfriend,' she said.

I glanced at Hestia. We'd just met a week ago. It was our first walk. I didn't ask anyone to fucking cook anything.

'This is Hestia,' I reluctantly inform the two of them.

My special needs sister jumped first: 'Hello Hestia. Nice name that! Hesti-a! Hello, Heeesti*a*. BEANS ON TOAST! It's beans on toast today, look Judas! We're making beans on toast for you and your lovely girlfriend, Heee*stia*.'

'And sausage,' bleated Tabi from the stove, rocking her second kid in the pram. Rudy giggled. 'Sausage for your girlfriend, Judas!'

'Her name's Hestia, Rudy. *Hestia*.'

'Whoopsie! Alright Hestia? How are you today? Do you want to come inside? Judas hid his lady magazines before you came.'

Hestia looked at me. I shrugged, defeated.

On entrance I noticed the broom infested with weeks of shit, with slow-reaching grime on the door and on the walls. This is not hygienic! Chrissakes. This ain't good hygiene. Hestia belonged in a palace with sphynx cats and fresh watermelon. She was my declaration, like Jack's fucking house, informing my family how better I am and to clean themselves up, aim higher, for chrissakes. I am not like you. I am not grime. You are grime. I am not. You are.

'Just call when it's ready,' I said to Tabi.

'Okay,' she said, continuing to rock that filthy pram.

I lead Hestia up the stairs, her scent unfolding throughout the hallway like spring dancing through the sewers.

Fiddling shut my new flimsy door lock, Hestia hovered about curiously. 'So this is your room, mister. You can tell a person by their room, dontcha think?'

'I guess so,' I replied, half-distracted.

She quickly followed her finger. '*True Crime*? Is that all yours?'

I nodded while jamming the lock. 'Correct.'

She picked up this month's copy and started fanning pages. 'Don it make ya feah?' she asked, her Brooklynness coming heavy.

'Well,' I said, 'I like to know the worst of us, the dark stuff, and then, I guess, I feel better for knowing.'

'But don it make you feah?'

I gave up on the lock, stood up and faced her. 'Fear what?'

'Feah people, out there, ya know... who muhder?'

'It ain't so bad.'

'Ya know whadamean. It's creepy, gives me the heebie-jeebies.'

'We been killing each other forever, no doubt about that.'

'Yeah, but dontcha think we can change?'

'Change what?'

'The muhdering!!!'

'No.'

'You don think people can stop killin n' stuff?'

'No.'

'You think they'll always be muhders?'

'You learn quick.'

'You're a pessimist, Judas. I knew all along.'

'Maybe I am. *Or maybe I'm a realist.*'

Hestia paused. 'You don go round killin peoples' pets, do ya?'

I thought about that for a moment, humans who slaughter their animals. It horrified me.

'Well,' she continued before I could defend myself, 'I'm an optimist I think, or maybe pacifist. Haven't decided.'

I started straightening my bed. 'Could you kill someone?' I asked.

'Me? Noooo, I could never. Liddle ol me?'

'Yeah, little old you.'

She placed my magazine back precisely where she'd found it. 'No, no,' she said again, making a sweet face. 'Pacifist's don kill.'

'I don't mean it like a bad thing, given the circumstance.'

'I don have it in me, Judas. Ama scaredy-cat.'

'Maybe you haven't thought about it.'

'No, no, nuh-uh,' she said again, continuing to glance curiously about my room. 'I get not all muhders are intended, but your magazines are *different*, Judas. These people *choose* muhder.'

I started to giggle.

She jumped in my face. 'What?' she demanded. 'What's so funny?'

'The way you say *murder*, your accent, it's sweet.'

She smiled self-consciously.

'I think it's the scariest thing, to take another life,' I said.

'Maybe somethin spooked you as a kiddo.'

'Maybe.'

'Alright, can we *please* quit talkin muhder now? It's creepy.'

'I like your beads,' I said.

'Oh thanks. My mom made them. I like 'em too.'

'You're really pretty.'

Hestia sat down beside me on the bed. 'Ama dork, Judas.'

'And a fine-lookin dork you are.'

'Gawd, no, stop. I'm no good with compliments.'

'Okay then—you're an ugly dork.'

'YOU BRAT!'

Sat on my bed, our eyes meet in the reflection of my broken mirror. The sweet stench of her skin filled the air between our lips as I went in for the kiss. Her lips were very soft, like cotton. I inhaled her breath. She had nice-smelling breath. My hand gently cupped one small, perfectly round breast while folding her back to my bed, picking my buckle. Her boots slip easily to the floor with a delicate clunk, her tiny feet vanish beneath her baggy jeans and reappear on the other side. I felt harder than ever. We both strip away her blue knickers, leaving them wrapped about my finger. Dropping them over her boots I rolled off my jeans while she took apart her shirt. She unclipped her tiny bra. Her pretty brown eyes looked into mine and I felt alive and happy. She pushed her bra along the bed until it slipped to the floor. Her nipples were small and dark, like pennies. Her chest heaved as I kissed the pennies. Her thick jet-black hair spilled over the pillow.

She whispered into my mouth. 'Judas, it's my first time.'

'Mine too,' I whispered back.

With her lying naked, I looked down at my hardon, then at her tuff of pubic hair, knowing I had to put my hardon *inside* the hair. And so I made my move and pushed myself inside. It took a few attempts to find the hole. With help from Hestia, placing it just right, I was in.

The new feeling felt moist and narrow, more narrow than moist. Her legs hugged my waist with a tremble. I pushed inside and out again. Hestia made a face and pressed my shoulders.

'It's okay?' I asked.

She spoke quickly, 'It's okay, it's okay.'

Her pubic hair burned my dick, but I didn't mind. We were making it.

'Slower,' she pressed.

Slowing down, I shifted my gaze to her slender shoulders, noticing her nipples perk up, her chin cradled to mine. And I lost all knowing of what the hell to do other than push in and out, overcome by her beauty.

Hestia moved beneath me. *'Judas,'* she pined, this time with a stiff smile.

We fixed our eyes together. And that's when it all went to shit.

'FOOD'S READY!'

My new flimsy lock flew across the room, followed by Tabi's grotty foot punting the door open while balancing two plates of beans on toast. With one look she calmly set one plate down with her eyes semi-closed, snatching the door handle and shutting it closed. 'Oh my god,' she said.

Hestia and I looked everywhere except each other, searching the floor for clothes. She touched my hand and said sweetly, 'It's fine, it's okay.'

I was embarrassed. Her smell was new and wonderful. She made me feel good. She made it all feel good.

Cowering away so she didn't catch sight of my shrinking pecker, I threw on shorts and headed for the door. 'I'll get our food,' I said.

'Okay,' she said with a cheery smile. 'Am starved.'

Tabi was waiting in the kitchen as I charged in.

I snatched the food. 'Jesus, Tabi.'

'Hands full. Couldn't knock. *Sorreee.*'

I stretched my neck and whisper-growled. 'Don't ever walk into my room without my bloody permission.' I then spun out of there before the trollop could snigger, glancing at Rudy sat at the kitchen table who had paused her fork an inch from her gob, thinking she'd done wrong.

I stopped and waved at her. 'Not you, Rudy,' I said.

With a minute spare I returned Hestia safely to her door. She lived on a nice street, good part of town. Hearing her voice, her old man dropped his head out the top window. He had long yellow hair, like a woman, with chalk-white teeth. 'Hey kiddos,' he waved.

'Hey Pops,' she waved back.

'I'm off to bed now, Hestia. Got an early start. Feel free to come inside and have a drink before you leave, Judas.' He gave Hestia a wink before vanishing, leaving us kids gazing up at the stars.

Several moments later her jeans and knickers are on her bedroom floor with two glasses of cranberry juice on the bedside table. The insides of her legs were soaked in my drool, her big eyes instructing things I had to follow. Her thick pubes crawled over my lip. I wasn't sure what the hell to do other than wiggle my tongue, listening to what she liked and to keep doing that. Just as my tongue was getting numb, she reached and held my shoulder and clenched her eyes, letting go a light squeak before collapsing back to the pillow.

22

I'd done it with Hestia.

Taking a shortcut along Mount Gould Park, I jumped the gate over Dartmoor View, ripping through brambles and popping out the other side like an escaped felon, finally reaching Old Laira Road to Stevie's house, sniffing my fingers with sweet thoughts of Hestia.

Stevie's old dear swung open the door cradling a tall glass of wine with crusts of red in the corners of her mouth.

'Hello Judas, my love.'

'Hey Jan.'

Stevie ordered his tipsy mother inside, lurking behind with two tins of Heineken, a full flaxen moustache at age fourteen, and one hairy leg in plaster up to the knee—having busted his ankle jumping a fifteen-foot wall being chased by a steadfast copper.

I picked out a dark strand of pubic hair from my teeth and held it up. I held it up and felt bad that I had done that, that I had somehow cheapened Hestia.

'Geddon, ya seadog!' cried Stevie.

We cracked open the beers. Stevie tried getting the scoop but I kept it between me and my girl. Beers finished, we went inside.

Since his old man took off, Stevie took charge of the house. His mum held a flash job in an office out of town and drank wine like water, and could never seem to gain the respect of her son.

Stevie didn't know his old man but insisted his *grand*father was black. His mother would sip her wine and roll her eyes. 'Oh yeah, Steven? So is that why you blast that horrible jibby-jab music, huh?'

As we entered his bedroom, there was Darcy, this older kid who knew everything about weed, perched on the floor crosslegged alongside Mookie and Lenny, all watching *Executions* on VHS, a tape Stevie always played of public killings from all over the world.

Mookie was so short he was almost midget, but the kid had bite. Though now, as I plonked beside him, his eyes fixed on the carpet, he said, 'Eddie punched me,' in this sad, pathetic tone.

Things immediately escalated. Stevie limped across the room on his plastered foot and unlocked The Tool Box.

I jumped up too, snatching a cosh from the box, a short dumb-bell fitting snug in my hand. Lenny, a scrawny kid with boils on his neck, got hold the knuckleduster. Mookie wiped his tear, sprung up and snatched out a bike chain, gritting his teeth. 'Let's go have this bastard,' he snarled.

Finally, Stevie slipped a blade down his shorts and we all race out the door, leaving Darcy with his latest pot-smoking invention.

Several hours later searching the streets, we all surround Eddie. The bastard didn't look much, but he had a reputation for knocking grown men to the floor with seamless combinations. But he also messed with younger kids, clapping them on the nose whenever he was ratted. Eddie left school years ago. Had a spikey hairdo. A calm, mean-faced stare—with a tattoo of a naked woman on his arm.

Stevie slipped out his knife, a crazy glint in the eye. Lenny hunched over, tapping the palm of his hand with that knuckleduster, while Mookie gently swung the bike chain.

Seeing he didn't have a weapon I threw my cosh to the grass and stepped up. If we were going to scrap, I wanted it even-stevens.

'You like hittin kids, huh?' I said. 'Well I'm a kid, Eddie. Try me.'

Eddie studied me with that calm look on his face, finishing his can of beer. The streetlamp lit up our patch. I wondered if the bully didn't fancy his odds. Stevie signalled a nod with his little knife ready.

But I knew Stevie wouldn't use it. He was crazy and smoked and drank with his own mum and cut his arms when he had problems, but he wasn't a maniac.

Eddie finally threw down the empty can and burped and balled his fists, ready to roll. We circled each other like killer cockerels, a brawl to the finish. I was half scared shitless of his legend but more afraid of backing down.

'Guard up, Judas! Keep that guard steady!' put in Lenny.

'You got this champ! Duck 'n weave! *Duck 'n weave!*' said Stevie.

'Just belt the twat!' Mookie yelled.

'Amma fuck you up,' I snarled, staring Eddie in the eye as we jigged. I don't know why I said that like some Harlem gangster, but I did. And repeated it. With a murder face. I quit speaking like a Janner kid from a rusty fisher town on the bleak country coast of England and instead chose to call upon the spirit of a negro killer pimp from the ghetto. I don't know what everybody thought. But I kept at it, knuckles tight.

'Amma make you ma lady, *bitchtits!*' I said. 'Put your dukes up!'

Eddie kept his fists raised but with a confused look on his face. And before we could roll, Mookie yelled out 'PIGS!'

Sure enough a siren shot up Blandford Road. We all scrambled away, scattering into the night. Stevie caught me up on his crutches, crying out in pain as we took off running.

'Ho Ho, fuckers!' cheered Lenny. I was on my sixth beer. My hands had stopped trembling. Mookie was back to his old self. Today, it seemed, we had become men.

'Say hello to King Henry the Eighth, fellas,' said Darcy. It took two to carry his makeshift bong once filled three quarters with water—double silver-rimmed gauzes topped with an eighth of dope, with two rubber tubes of which Darcy and Mookie shoved into their gobs.

Stevie scooped up the top half of a plastic bottle, with the bottom half resealed with a plastic bag and marched me to the bathroom.

'You need to catch up,' he said.

'What the fuck is that?' I asked. He had this crazy grin, like brain freeze. He even did it when he wasn't drunk, flaring his nostrils and popping his eyeballs with his lips all crooked.

'Darcy calls it *the head-fuck*,' he tells me, proceeding to inflate his cheeks from puffs of a joint, blowing the smoke into the bottle and filling the plastic bag until the the thing swelled like a balloon.

I leaned back in the empty bathtub, feeling pretty good about life. We stood up to Eddie. And I put it inside Hestia and licked her muff. I was drunk. It felt easy when I was drunk. Being drunk and screwing just made it all easier. Why wasn't I told this sooner?

The plastic bag had filled with smoke. Stevie, red-faced and light-headed, cupped his hand over the nozzle and passed me the bottle, instructing to do the same. I swigged some beer and set my can between my legs and took the bottle.

'Just suck it up and hold it in for as long as you can.'

'All of it?'

'All of it.'

Stevie's crooked grin paused as I began sucking up the smoke.

'Good lad,' he said. 'Suck it all up.'

The dope shotgunned straight to my skull. The bottle slipped from my hand as I stared at jars of bathsalts, watching my thoughts run away from me. I looked up to the ceiling and blew out a cloud of thick smoke.

'Yup,' said Stevie.

'I'm gonna be sick,' I said.

'Caam down,' he said, slumping beside the tub. 'Just be sick in the bath if you need to, mate. That's why we do the head-fuck there.'

I was close to vomit, water rolling along my cheeks. Attempting to straighten my eyes I said, 'I'm too high. I'm too fucking high.'

'Yer fine. Just stay *caam*, that's all. You're juss havin a whitey. That's what Darcy calls it. You'll be right as rain in a sec, you'll see.'

'False. I've lost control. I'm gonna be sick and shit my pants.'

Stevie rolled back in a fit of laughter. As he did my brain told me I was laughing too, but I wasn't, I wasn't laughing.

'Blooming hilarious!' he cried out, climbing to his knees and dabbing his eyes. My instincts told me to focus on a wall tile, then my hands, beer can, now shoes, shuffling between objects with no reason while Stevie belted out a tune, some old sea shanty.

'How much dope was in that?' I asked.

He stopped singing. 'The whole joint! It's a proper *head-fuck*, eh?'

I hunched down for my can and gulped.

'Better?' he asked.

'Christ,' I said, still trying to see straight.

He snatched my arm and hauled me to my feet. In doing so I produced several phantom pukes, gagging toward the plughole, wanting to be sick and not wanting to be sick.

'You okay?'

'Next question.'

He slumped against the tub. 'I had one before you got here,' he says.

'I had your mum before you got here.'

'And yer welcome to again! Might cheer the old hag up!'

'I'll put a cheer on her face,' I said. 'And you'll thank me alright.'

My friend sat up against the tub with a cheap grin, turned and looked me in the eye. 'I just needed the music to bloody end when I did my head-fuck,' he says. 'I thought my ticker would stop. I went to the other place and thought, Stevie boy, we may never get home.'

'Cheers for the warning,' I said.

'Ya welcome! So, was it good?'

I broke a string of spit from my gob. 'It hasn't ended, numbnuts.'

'Nooo, I mean that girl, *Helia*. The Yank. Did you fuck her?'

'Hestia, her name is fucking Hestia.'

He kept staring at me.

'Yeah,' I said.

Stevie smiled to himself. 'Think it's time for me to have my end away too. I'm wanking four times daily.'

My cheeks exploded with puke. I tried getting up.

'Stay in the tub!' Stevie yelled. He tried catching me. I stumbled back and kicked over my can. And it helped, watching all that beer spill down the drain somehow helped.

By eleven, Stevie's cutting his arm with his pocketknife. Lenny and I watched in a dope-haze. The lunatic folded his eyebrows, as if looking for something beneath his skin. He then raised his bloodied arm like some trophy, wearing that same crazy grin before turning the blade on his thigh. That's when Lizzie and Libbie barged in, two frisky schoolgirls looking for a good time.

They both begged for their bottles of 20/20 to be opened. I wobbled to the next room, seeking refuge from the volume. The room shook. Unwilling to shut my eyes, I swallowed vomit and prayed. The door creaked. A sliver of light touched the wall before plunging back to darkness.

Libbie's long hair hovered above my eye, the occasional sparkle of her jewels flashing in the dark. She tried for ages but couldn't unzip my fly. She went gentler, fiddling my zip to and fro. Zilch. She then huffed in annoyance and left.

By the time I kept down more puke, Lizzie was in the room. She smelled fresh, like washing powder. One of her hands traced my arm, while the other caressed my bulge. I couldn't get it hard. I wanted to, christ, but I was too spaced out. She whispered in my ear, promising me great head. I thought of Hestia, my sweet Hestia. Stevie's mum suddenly called for everyone to get going. 'I need sleep, Steven!' she yelled from downstairs. 'I work!'

'I don't give a monkey's ballsack!' I heard him shout back.

'This isn't fair!' she yelled again. 'I'm the adult! I make the rules!'

My ears detect Stevie's plaster hobble along his bedroom floor, swinging open his door. 'Leave me alone, woman!'

'Well at least turn that bloody horrible video cassette off of people being killed! All I can hear is death screams! It's driving me mad!'

'I'll turn it off when I'm good and ready, wench!'

I forced myself to my feet and staggered out. Lizzie had already bolted down the stairs and out the door with Libbie and the boys.

'Your mum's going spare,' I told Stevie.

'Don't you listen to her,' he said. 'She knows her place.'

'Well, I'm off anyway. Goodnight and sahlou, old boy.'

I made it down the stairs to the front door. Jan was all elbows in the kitchen, twisting the cork off a late bottle of red.

'Bye Jan,' I said.

She turned and waved. 'Oh bye Judas, me lovey!'

I found my house, my room. Collapsing beside my bed I slipped out a black .45 replica from my shoebox that I traded for a sicknote and turned the barrel to my skull with thoughts of that farmyard kid, the cold steel pressed against his eye.

'Bang,' I whispered, clicking the trigger.

Stashing the gun back in my box, I reached for my can of lighter fluid, gripping it between my teeth and inhaling several hits of gas. My eyes rolled back, an iciness enveloped my chest and skull. Like a snake full on a good meal, I slithered into bed with all my clothes on.

'G'night, boy,' I said.

23

I woke to the sun blazing through my curtains, the sound of my mother singing her joy to Jesus. A warm haze filled my mouth. I tried speaking, but no sound emerged. I was asleep with my eyes fully open, completely numb head to toe.

Perhaps the logical thing to do here is to remain mortal, to strongly consider life. But I welcomed death with open arms, some sort of celebrated end.

My muscles tensed, delivering spasms up and down my spine. I had the idea to think my body awake, think myself to move. With some luck my right arm received the memo as I tumbled out of bed, landing flat on my elbows.

Crawling on all fours, I paused at the foot of my wardrobe. My eyes fixated there, two small kids materialised before me. The girl wore a white frock, the boy a drab waistcoat. They both glided right through my bed and the walls as if I was someplace else, someplace near to where they were. Twirling in circles the pair enchanted me with their dance, vanishing as quickly as they appeared.

Climbing to my feet I made it along the hall, swinging open my mother's door. 'I just woke up and couldn't feel a thing,' I said.

She stopped hymn-singing. 'Maybe you need a laxative?' she said.

'No, Mum, no laxatives.'

'You need to flush the Devil out!'

'Okay, okay, that's enough now,' I told her.

I said nothing of the ghosts or whatever they were, lessening any unwanted prophecies and went back to my room.

'I'll fix us a cuppa tea,' she said, rolling out of bed.

Stopping outside my door, she looked at me nervously.

'Your headteacher rang,' she told me. 'He said you've been writing sicknotes for students.'

I kicked my magazines beneath my bed. 'Their parents don't care. It's no big deal,' I said.

'Judas, this isn't good.'

'It's fine.'

'Why did you do it?' she begged to know, her fear placed only on speaking with my headmaster. You see, people who were anointed the authority by the civil public, who counted the votes, purported the rules, scared the life out of her.

'They just needed days off school,' I said. 'And I gave them.'

'I don't want to speak with your headmaster, Judas.'

'It's fine, drink some tea, me and the chief had a chat.'

'Please, no more,' she begged. 'You're a good pupil. He said so.'

'Listen, he won't expel me. His name is mentioned each time I'm in the newspaper holding up another trophy. It's a two-way deal.'

'He said you wrote sicknotes for all your class!'

I laughed. 'My class? More like half the school!' I put my arm around her and planted a kiss on her forehead before confessing, 'I even wrote my own sicknotes, signing them *Ms Nobody*.'

'Ohh, Judas.'

24

Leonard sold dope from his home and from school. He was good at selling dope for a fifteen-year-old kid, both shrewd and likeable. He kept track of profits to the penny, with a knack for puzzling schemes that often arrived while caught in some idle chitchat, as though his mind was always a degree someplace else.

Like most kids in the great unwashed, Leonard felt the loom of inheriting his share of family grief—mostly matters that a little extra cash would unburden. And so on a night's supply of Nik Naks, the kid would clamp on his headphones and press play. And by nightfall, he'd chopped and bagged a couple ounces into perfect seven-fifties, eighths, and quarters, ready for trade.

Leonard lived in Stonehouse with his mother, while his old man was serving ten years for paying a hitman to kill a cop. His old lady was pretty, from the Seychelles, with a pair of Indian ocean eyes, wrists full of gold bangles. Inside their little flat she kept ouija boards nailed to the wall. Rita, his mother, handcrafted and sold them. I'd heard rumors about the ouija, mostly bad stuff, but I was curious to try.

Leonard palmed me a bag of dope at his door, took my cash and asked if I'd fancy a séance on his mother's latest toy. Moments later I'm sat on a rickety chair in the livingroom, staring at Rita across the room while she waited for her date.

Leonard let out a long whistle as his mother ratted her nails impatiently against her knee-high boots, watching us with suspicion.

'What you kids up to tonight, then?' she asked.

Leonard made another whistle, a warning to watch out.

Checking her watch again, she said, 'Where the hell is that man?'

Being some sort of speaker to the dead, she'd cleverly left her previous question sniffing about the room like a crack hound. Leonard whistled again. This time adding a few cryptic loops, catching me off guard. I hadn't a clue what the fuck this one meant. I glanced at Grendel, a blonde-haired kid who'd also come for dope and agreed to the séance, clasping his little bag of hashish next to me.

'So?' his mother asked, now stroking upward thick black mascara while gazing into a pocket mirror.

Then Leonard said, 'Don't be so paranoid, Muh.'

Grendel agreed, nodding while chewing his already ravaged nails. And his knee gyrating up and down against the chair, eyes full of relief as though that was the end of that, no more questions. And then he sniggered, a wry, rattling snigger cutting like a knife. He even sniggered to himself, laughing at his own thoughts, his head bursting with things he found privately amusing, that strange, busting black thrill—the recall of an old headline where an elderly man had tried tirelessly to squeeze himself inside a child but kept losing his erection, that utterly misplaced cry of dark laughter, no meaning or purpose, just simple depravity that fell into the mind of such a kid.

There came a knock at the door. 'He's here! How do I look, boys?'

'You look fine, Muh,' huffed Leonard.

'A sight for sore eyes,' I said, inhaling the last of her.

She jumped to her feet. 'No ouija board,' she said.

'Why not?' Leonard dared ask.

'Not without me, Leonard. You're not ready. It's not a game.'

Rita took one last suck of her cigarette, clawed her wild hair back with her long fingernails and shook down a hundred bangles to her wrists before clapping her little pocket mirror back inside her purse, eyes pointed at Grendel. 'You tell me if he goes on that board, got that?'

Grendel cracked. He was no good being singled out.

'I'm just going to the pub for one, Leonard,' she finally said before running out the flat. 'I'll be back soon!'

The door slammed.

We waited in the silence, only the sound of Grendel's knee chuffing against the chair.

Several moments later we're stampeding up the stairs, shooting past a collection of homemade ouija boards nailed along the wall. With symbolism etched. Numbers and letters. And three words:

YES NO GOODBYE

We gathered in a room. Grendel claimed the first chair at the table. Leonard followed behind, hugging a white pine, slab of wood.

I took my seat as Grendel fired up a joint. Leonard walked us through each step without being distracted by Grendel's relentless snickering. He reminded us of the spirit world and how every question, in our heads or said out loud, would be heard and answered. Everything is heard and everything is answered.

Speech over with, he propped up a shot glass on the ouija board, flipping it upside-down.

As instructed we all placed one finger on top of the glass.

Leonard then said, 'If there's anyone there, please speak. We are here and we are ready.'

Some time passed. The doorbell rang. Leonard wasn't expecting anyone. And his mother had a key. He said it with surprise, putting a wary dart right through our already black imaginations. We heard men arguing outside, all while our fingers stuck to the glass. The shoes of whoever knocked soon faded down the street like shovels in grit.

'Wensit suppose to start?' asked Grendel.

'Patience,' answered Leonard.

'Just clear your head,' I put in, taking the joint from Grendel.

'I don't think that's possible!' he sniggered.

And then the glass moved.

I spun to Leonard as the glass nudged across the board, sudden bursts forward, some sliding inches here and there.

'Are you moving it?' I asked him.

Leonard shook his head and kept quiet.

I spun to Grendel and sneered. 'Gotcha!'

Grendel removed his finger from the glass to prove it wasn't him.

'Keep your finger on the glass!' Leonard cried out. 'The spirit can't get out! You mustn't break the circle!'

Grendel hurried his finger back with another misplaced smirk. The glass oscillated between letters, not making any sense. It spelled a name: Alice. How old? The glass stopped on the number 9.

'She's nine,' explained Grendel.

'No shit, Einstein,' I said, passing the joint to Leonard.

'I know who she is,' declared Leonard reluctantly. 'She was a stillborn. It's Alice, my baby sister. She's our ghost.'

I leaned to Leonard's ear. 'Are you fucking with us?' I asked.

He lifted his finger half an inch above the glass. 'I'll prove it!' he reacted. 'Ask her a question. Go on!'

I looked at Grendel. I had nothing. Grendel shrugged. And then the glass moved without Leonard touching it. It made its way to the word NO and stopped.

'What was the question?' Leonard asked us, switching his eyes between me and Grendel. We shook our heads. Leonard lowered back his finger. 'Told you,' he sneered at me. 'I'm not moving it, Judas. It's Alice, Alice is doing it.'

The glass moved again, this time sharply to YES

'Who asked another question?' demanded Leonard.

Grendel shook his head again.

'Not me,' I said with a shrug.

'What do you want?' Leonard asked his dead baby sister.

This time the spelling came quick: K I L L Y OU

Grendel jumped from his chair, keeping his finger pressed on the glass. 'Rat shit!' he said.

'That ain't Alice,' Leonard said nervously. 'She don't spell so quick.'

I'd never felt something so strongly and with so much hatred spike inside of me, begging to die so I could go hunt this dead fuck wherever it hid. I was ripping inside with total loathing, making myself go nuts, my cheeks tensing as I exchanged imaginary fists in some imaginary other world.

'You okay?' asked Leonard, seeing me flinch.

'Fine,' I said. 'I'm fine.'

The glass then spelt N I G G E R. They both looked at me. Christ, I didn't know what the hell was going on.

The glass moved again.

Leonard shot out his chair and pressed down harder. 'Keep it on the board! It can't get out! The spirit has to stay in the glass!'

We were all now on our feet with our thumbs pressed down on the glass. A long time passed. 10 minutes. 20. No one made a peep.

'Who the fuck are you?' Leonard finally asked. The glass moved to the letter D and kept crisscrossing the board until it was done. D E V I L

I glared at Leonard. 'This ain't funny anymore.'

'I'm not doing it! I'm not doing it!'

The glass busied itself again.

Leonard looked at us. 'Who asked a question?'

'I did,' I said. 'I asked how.'

'How fucking what?'

'How's he gonna kill us, dickhead.'

And then came the letters E S over and over.

'E S? I don't get it?'

'It's the 13th today,' snickered Grendel. 'Friday the 13th.'

I grabbed Leonard by the shirt. 'Why didn't you say before?'

He pushed my hand away. 'It's make-believe bullshit. It doesn't fucking matter.'

'It clearly fucking matters, Leonard!'

The glass made a run for the edge of the board.

'Please leave us,' Leonard commanded. 'We ask for you to leave. Goodbye. Goodbye.'

'Please leave,' repeated Grendel with a wonky grin.

A key worked itself in the front door downstairs.

'Mum!' Leonard cried out. 'Get up here!'

Me and Grendel started shouting too. 'We're upstairs! Help!'

'I've just walked in, boys!' Rita yelled back. 'Keep your wigs on!'

'Get up here now!' Leonard yelled.

'Alright! Alright!'

We hear her make apologies to her date at the door, followed by footsteps and moaning and finally the woman appearing with her wild hair and noisy bangles. We all look at her in horror.

'Save the shit for later, Mum,' pleaded Leonard in a sweat. 'It said it's the Devil.'

'Chrissakes, Leonard,' she hissed. Wasting no time she unpicked her crucifix from her neck while repeating a prayer: *Hail Mary Full of Grace, The Lord is with thee. Hail Mary, Hail Mary, Full of Grace.*

We all watched as she gently lowered the cross in the palm of her hand. 'Not my new board, Leonard,' she whined between prayer. 'It's not been *cleansed.*'

'Just get rid of it!' Leonard barked.

'Okay, now everyone listen very carefully. I want you all to tilt the glass just enough so I can slide the crucifix underneath.'

We cocked the glass. Rita slid our Lord and Saviour beneath, upfacing. We dropped the glass immediately over the cross as she told us to. The cross sprung to life, hiting the top of the glass with a sharp ting, the Second Coming landing face down.

I don't know what I saw. It happened and didn't happen.

Rita tapped hurriedly at her pockets while muttering nervously to herself. Finally pulling out her cigarette lighter she calmly told us to tilt the glass once again. We tilt. She cranked the lighter, holding the flame beneath the glass. We all stare into the flame, watching the Devil burn.

'Okay, now put it down. It's done,' she said.

We each pull our fingers away from the board.

'Are you boys okay?' she asked us.

Me and Grendel bombed down the stairs and out the front door. As soon as we reached outside I watched the white soles of his shoes vanish under the dark. The air drew faces. Trees swung axes. I took off running along Greenbank, passing Mount Gould Church and up Pike Road until I was back in my room. Kicking off my shoes I lay stiff on my bed, locking eyes on a single spot on the ceiling while repeating, 'Hail Mary Full of Grace . . . the Lord is with thee . . . '

25

Perhaps an hour had passed as I stared at the same spot. This is all there is, I told myself, *me and sweet Mary of Nazareth.*

'Pssst! *Judas!*'

I opened my window. 'What you doing?' I whispered down.

Almost midnight. Dion's face hung over the window of a beaten-up red Escort, thrown across the pavement.

Hestia had recently migrated to another city with her father. He got offered steady work as a guitar player for some band called The Wets. We strolled the parks and said our goodbyes. I wrote her a soppy love letter. She handed me a kiss. I then watched her walk away for good.

'Come for a ride!' Dion yelled.

Dion, the guy hollering up at my window past midnight, is Jezebel's older brother. I saw Jezebel on a bus travelling to Notre Dame—an all-girls Catholic school—along with fifty other girls fixing their bras and puckering their lips. But Jezebel, she stood out like a mole on the face: spongy black hair, coffee-with-milk skin, and an untameable gob with lips as pink and plump as a peach. Jezebel's half brother, Dion, was a low-rent drug peddler, running an artless operation from their mother's kitchen. I met him only once when I walked Jezebel home. This being the second . . .

The engine grilled and coughed on the kerb as he tried to start the thing back up.

'Whose car is that?' I asked him, leaning out my window.

The engine started back up. 'I stole it!' he yelled.

'Bollocks,' I said, running out the door.

We shot past the farmhouse, still with that yellow police tape muzzled to the gate, speeding down Military Lane. I attacked the lever for headlights. 'No lights?' I asked, swinging a sideways glance.

'Smashed'em,' Dion mumbled, hands slipping from the wheel.

The car was freezing cold. I wondered who'd he nick it from. Johnston played on the stereo, *Honey I Sure Miss You*. I'd heard it once before. It was a good one. Grabbing hold the wheel before he'd murder us I steered back to the road whenever we skimmed a wall or missed a parked car. I couldn't believe he'd made it this far being so wasted. His long blonde hair whipped about his face, a drugged-up maverick racing across the hot desert. Removing one hand from the wheel, he slid strands of hair from his glassy blue eyes, his sickly colourless skin, sick from all the junk, a brilliant white in the darkness.

We bounced off a kerb, missed a tree by an inch, and demolished a whole street of garden walls, flying sixty miles an hour. Swinging the wheel from the passenger side, I sailed us back to the road. All we had was the moonlight and my sober eyes as we wound down an unlit lane, coughing us into an empty motorway.

The car stalled in the middle lane, Dion's face now slumped to his chest, burning the engine with his unconscious foot. The bonnet smoked and popped and hissed, with Johnston continuing to rattle uneasily out the open window.

I slapped his cheek. 'C'mon, Dion,' I said, 'we need to go!'

Flinging off my jumper I got to work polishing the steering wheel and levers, door handles and locks, before leaping from the car. Dion fell through the door and found himself moaning on the concrete, tangled up in his seatbelt. I untwisted his leg and got hold the lunatic, dragging him up a mound under the old gypsy camp.

Within minutes a light display of blue sirens surrounded the wreck as we spied between a small hedge.

'Bleedin heck that was close,' I said.

'I can't see,' Dion moaned, rubbing his eyes.

'What'd you take?' I asked him, watching the cops search the car.

'Dunno man, E's, a bit of acid, some other shit. I dunno.'

'C'mon,' I said, picking him up. 'I'll take you home.'

We reached his place around two in the morning. I heaved the ninny up the stairs and sat him still at his door, waiting for Evel Knievel to produce a key. I wondered if Jezebel was asleep, dreaming naked beneath her sheets. Their overfed Persian pawed past, her chubby body collapsing against my leg. I couldn't resist giving the furbag a rub before she threw herself at the cat flap.

I turned back to Dion. 'Found 'em yet?'

'Found what?' he said, twisting his pockets with his eyes closed.

Abandoning him wasn't a bad idea. So what if he woke up some other twit? But instead I found myself walking round the back of the house, checking if any windows were open.

When I returned the pillock had dozed off. Shit! I was exhausted. Christ, Dion! Without much enthusiasm I patted down his greasy jeans, searching for his door key, only to find a soggy pack of Lamberts and a broken lighter. The guy reeked of weed and dead farts. The only other option was to vanish round back again and sweep up a grit of stones and start throwing at Jezebel's window. Which I did.

On the third try her big sleepy eyes looked down. I waved stupidly. Jezebel unlocked the door slowly at first before swinging it open, sending her brother collapsing inward.

'What the hell is this?' she said.

Dion tried hauling himself up with all his fingers stretched, looking like a helpless infant. I managed the fifteen stone water-monkey off the floor, one half of his foot refusing to turn on its sole, dragging along like a brick on a rope. Jezebel hopped out from behind the door, wearing just an oversized shirt over a pair of naked legs.

'I think he's taken too many pills,' I said.

'Fucking wanker,' she barked. 'Wait till I tell Mum. He can't even bloody stand up! Sorry Judas.'

With Dion slung over my shoulder I hauled the carjacker inside. 'I'll leave him on your couch,' I said.

'Fucking jerk,' she sneered over him. She didn't mind to be stood there half-naked in front of me, crossing her arms in protest, her eyes black and indignant. Dion seemed to weigh more than he looked as I folded the lump to the couch, kicking over his bong beside a neat assortment of blue pills. Jezebel tiptoed across the room and tore a chunk of weed from his tobacco tin and held it over his unconscious eyes. 'Now I fucking need this to sleep,' she snarled at him. 'I've got fucking school in the morning, Dion!'

She looked at me. 'Sorry again, Judas. He's a cunt.'

'It's fine. I'll get going.'

She saw me to the door. Turning to say goodnight, we kissed. Simple. No fuss. No trying to impress.

'You can stay if you want?' she said. 'It's late.'

'Nah, I need to get back. Been a strange night. I'll run home.'

'Get home quick!' she called as I raced off. 'All the weirdos are out!'

'See you later, Jezebel!'

'Bye, Judas!'

26

Another hot summer, the year '95. I was fifteen and had returned from Lilleshall, England football trials. I didn't think I played well. The standard was high. Those premiership players were hungry. I started to think I was an imposter, that I didn't want it as much as those kids. Stepping from the bus I headed for Jezebel's.

The sun crackled like a sparkler. I wiped the sweat from my head and turned down Channel Park. There she was, stroking her cat at the window. She unchained the door and kicked Dion's nunchucks.

'Fucking move these nunchucks, Dion!'

'They're there for a reason, Jezebel!' he shouted back.

'I don't care! They're in the fucking way of MY LIFE! *Please,* can I live in a normal house for one day.'

'Hey Jezebel,' I said as she opened the door. Folding her arms with a madeup smile, she replied, 'Hey Judas love, come on in.'

Frida, her mother, was cooking rice and peas in the kitchen. She was a good cook, stirring a pot slow and easy over a hot stove.

'Hi Judas dear,' Frida said over her shoulder, taking a large swig off a bottle of vodka. Frida looked like an aged flower-child of the sixties, with seen-it-all eyes and a magnificent bust. She refused to wear a bra. Her nipples were very thick, pushing through her blouse like a pair of metal screws.

'Dion, can you roll me a joint, please?' Frida asked her son.

'Make it yourself!' he popped back, sat in the lounge with some guy from the neighbourhood, dope-giggling at *Up in Smoke* for the fifth time this week.

'Hey Dion,' I said.

'Judas, hey man, how was footy?'

'Yeah, it is what it is.'

'Okay,' he replied, raising his spliff. 'But you'll have to stop smoking this shit. You gotta think of your career now, bud.' He took a puff and stretched it to Alfie, the other stoner who hardly said a word, just a delayed stutter as he woke from his bong-smoking abyss to receive the passing of the joint, the livingroom ritual.

'Oh, Judas,' Dion said, snatching up the newspaper and dusting off tobacco. 'You're in *The Herald* again!'

I stood back as they gave a riley cheer. Pleased the cat wandered by, I stooped down and gave her all fingers and thumbs. 'Right,' I said.

Jezebel winked and vanished upstairs. 'C'mon, Judas!' she called. 'Don't hang around those stoneheads. Let's go to my bedroom!'

But I stalled, taking the moment to whisper to Dion, 'I can't sell these anymore,' I told him, discreetly handing him a bag of valium.

Dion took them. 'No worries, man . . . was a stupid idea.'

'C'mon, Judas! Don't get trapped with those losers!'

'Oi!' shouted Dion. 'Watch your mouth, Jezebel!'

'Judas!' Jezebel cried again from upstairs.

I leaned to Dion. 'Those fake fivers, too, I can't get rid of 'em.'

'Keep 'em!' he said. 'Just watch your fingerprints.'

'I'm all alone!' Jezebel yelled. 'Waiting for you, Judas!'

I made it upstairs to her bedroom.

'Shhhhh . . .'

'What?' I said.

She looked excited. 'Close the door,' she said.

I wedged it shut. 'What is it?' I asked again.

She slipped out a small bag of weed from her tiny bra and squealed with joy. 'I nicked it from Dion. He's too stoned to even know!'

We both sit on her bed while I rolled us one.

'Why'd you speak to him like that?' I asked her.

'Like what?'

'You know what.'

'You don't have to live with him, Judas. All he does is fart, watch kung fu movies and gets completely wasted on that couch with his stoner pals. He never sleeps in his room! And he's always in debt because he shoves it up his scabby nose or gives it away. And the house *stinks of weed*. Can you smell it, huh? IT'S EVERYWHERE! And my poor cat is obese because she's got the munchies all the time. Stop laughing, Judas, it ain't funny.'

'Calm down, Jezebel.'

'If you'd just come upstairs I wouldn't have yelled.'

'Don't blame me.'

'You're just as bad. I'm sick of this shit!'

I stopped laughing. 'I said calm down.'

'Don't tell me to calm! You fucking calm! You didn't follow me up the stairs and instead stayed down there with those losers! So don't tell me to calm!' She shoved me. We got into a tangle over her bed. She caught me with a sharp claw to the neck, screaming her face off. I grabbed her by the mouth. 'For Pete's sake, Jezebel, calm down.' She mumbled something behind my hand before biting my finger and looking at me with pure rage. I threw her to the other side of the bed where she hissed like some terrified jungle child.

I pointed my sore finger with gritted teeth. 'If you don't calm down,' I told her.

'What?' she snarled. 'You'll do *what?*'

'Christ, stop pushing, Jezebel. Enough.'

'Or else you'll *hit* me? Is that it?'

I picked out the squished joint from beneath her foot and straightened it out. 'Someday I just might,' I said.

'You're better than those lot,' she said, relaxing back to the bed.

'Just calm down. And stop swearing so much, it don't sound ladylike when you swear all the time.'

She wasn't listening, busy investigating a cigarette stub in her pink seashell on the windowsill, retrieving the tobacco. She was sensible that way, liked to hoard things. When for me it was all or nothing.

Jumping to her feet, she pushed her trousers to her ankles, with her buttocks perked out ready. 'Hurry!' she said.

A cold breeze blew across my behind as I swung in and out of her gooch, Tarzan and his ululating call to the wild, swinging tree to tree. I glanced at her Troll Doll collection along her dresser while my thighs slapped against her cheeks.

'Be quiet, my mum might hear.'

I slowed it down, peering sideways at the new tattoo on her hip, some grim-faced gremlin. I then stretched beneath, cupping one tiny developing tit in each hand.

'Not too tight,' she whined.

I kept slamming.

'Go faster,' she said again.

I sped up, pounding the fladge twice as fast.

'Finish quickly,' she pleaded. 'My mum'll hear us.'

After I came we smoked the joint out the window, listening to a mixtape of Liquid and Ratpack, and then I left.

'Psst, Judas,' whispered Alfie as I came downstairs. 'Wanna bong?'

Dion was snoozing against the couch. I was on a nice high, the sweet spot, thinking only a packet of Chewits and a SunnyD.

'It's Grade A stuff, man, blow your socks off,' he said.

In most cases you ignore the sofa stonehead and proceed on your merry way to the candy shop. Yet I, with a considerable lack for moderation, tiptoed across the rug and took the bong and sat myself on the arm of the couch and inhaled a big hit, watching the thick, yellow smoke float above my eyes. Christ, I'd tipped over the edge again. There was no way back. 'Shit,' I said. 'I'm too high.'

'Didn't I tell ya?' the crook smirked.

My head nodded by itself, busied with all the usual small horrors, not able to move, stuck between the abyss of the couch and somewhere in the galaxy. Glancing across at Alfie, his dazed, dopey face bothered me. I was no longer high, I was stoned, deprived of common sense. My face felt unsure of being a face. And now begins the tremendous overthinking of how the fuck I was going to stand up and collect my bag, and which shoulder I should rest it upon. Should I tighten the strap so it doesn't pat my hip as I walk the street? That'll be pure hell, I thought. Should I say goodbye or just get up and aim for the door, ten steps of ignorance to save myself sounding like a dunce goat. Do I lock the door behind me? I considered that one a great deal, seeing the mechanics of the lock spin in my head. What if I bump into Frida, what I'd say, would I blake any fense? Can I make it home without pissing before I leave? I think so, yes. Do I need to piss? Yes. Absolutely need to piss. My ears rang. My legs go numb. Panic sets in. Footsteps clank down the side of my skull—*clank! clank! clank!*

'For fucksake, I told you not to hang around those losers!'

My glassy eyes observed my girlfriend's rage migrate to the kitchen, returning with a glass of orange juice with rattling ice. She walked right by me. 'Do what you like, I don't care,' she moaned, thumping back up the stairs and slamming her bedroom door, cracking a hole in the universe.

The door startled Dion, sitting him upright, immediately setting fire to the joint that hadn't left his fingers. I wanted to pass the bong back to Alfie, felt it the right thing to do. I see myself do it a hundred times, a hundred thousand times, finally dropping the bong to the floor like a tired toddler of his toy and walking out the door.

Along the streets, I asked God for His mercy, knowing the brute was there behind all those twisted eyes, bestowing His trickery along the tricky street. I shoved my hands in my pockets. Jezebel was right again. She was mostly wrong about stuff, but with this, with getting too high and useless, she was always right.

Some dirty-faced kid with a ball waited for me to pass before continuing a lonesome game of kerby. The sky lowered above my head. I duck a little, shrinking my upper body, a frightened, barely formed fetus kicking its legs along the road.

When I arrived home I dropped my bag and headed straight for the loo, pissing sat down. I spit twice on the wall, the Devil winning by a nose, flushed and walked to my bedroom.

Staring into the mirror, I watched my mouth twitch, wondering if there was some dark entity inside me, pushing its black soul to the surface. I prayed to be normal again, made a promise to myself not to ever smoke pot. The last time, I vowed, seeing the madness through for the next few hours until

I'm

myself

again.

27

The latest issue of *True Crime* arrived in the post. I flicked the pages and read a small article on the Susan Smith killings.

My mother shouted goodbye. The door shut. I watched her walk to the bus stop from my window. She looked tired. I squinted up at the sky. A few seabirds flocked over. It was cloudy.

I picked up a book and tried starting it over. Something Shakespeare. It was full of old-speech and overly dramatic. So I read the last sentence of the final page and put it away, yawned, threw on some extra clothes and took a cigarette for a walk.

Robert was my mother's new love interest, a six-foot-five uneasy kinda guy, all limbs and feet, with large, twitchy eyes.

It was Sunday morning when her new friend wheeled up in his blue Honda bought by my mother and licensed in his name. Walking to him, I informed the weirdo that he'd just missed her and to go catch her up. His big hand nervously tapped the steering wheel, the other fiddling with the car stereo, and the eyes, uneasy. He stopped on Radio Devon before sweeping his gaze in a full, half-tragic spin, meeting my eyes as a stranger would. Without saying a word he revved the engine and shot over the hill. Nutcase.

A few days later I turned my key in the front door, back from a football trip to France. My hands were frozen stiff. I picked the key back up from off the floor and tried it again.

Stepping inside I hear fatal screams. Rushing to the crime scene there was Robert over my mother on the floor, eclipsing her body with his mass of pink flesh, wrenching something from her fist.

'Help, Judas! *Ahhh*, Jeesos God! Somebody help me!'

I dragged the psychopath to the livingroom, blood oozing above his eye from the glass that I picked up off the table and slammed in his face. More blood freckled the walls as he shook his head sober. I got him by the collar, his polished shoes slipping along the carpet. His arm managed to hook a finger to my jumper, climbing from the ground up. He was tough, you could feel it in his agony. Reaching out he ripped a handful of my hair, yanking all he could from the roots like it was velcro.

My mother kept screaming, nursing her limp wrist on her knees. Overcome by survival I merely heard the rip before seeing a small thatch of black wool fall from his hand. I delivered an elbow to the bastards neck and slipped his bloodied head between my arm. I threw the guy over a chair, his nerves bounced back from the spring of the chair into my fists, his chest, his ribs. I kept at the ribs with a succession of one-twos, his eyebrow now a fleshy gush of blood, splattering over my shirt.

'It's my car!' the maniac pleaded, spitting blood through his teeth. I needed to make sure he couldn't move, couldn't hurt her. So I gave his ribcage several more solid hooks, each blow a knowing the man could jump to his feet by some compelling bug-force of nature.

I turned to my mother. 'Give me the key!' I demanded, leaving the schizo in the chair hugging his waist. He found his feet and stumbled after her as though I didn't exist, wiping blood from his eyes and murmuring, 'Hand me the car key, woman.'

I snatched the key from her and led the nut to the street. 'Stay in the house!' I warned her, swinging the key while backing out the door.

And I could see it all, a spy behind my own eyes, dangling this key like it was the thing that lit him up, a real-life lunatic on my trail. His hands stretched pitifully. I'd met another madman, turning up his fire for a Honda Civic. Madman? This was no madman, but a dead man, living for his newspaper and his politics, and this goddamn car. Christ, this was no madman, but a sick man!

I looked at him, his arms begging farther and more sad, following me endlessly up the street. I looked at him from my own desperation, my own rage, my own fear. And the people stepped from their houses hearing his pain. Some calling for help, others watching on, waiting for the next thing. He pushed more blood from his eyes as a queue of cars brake either side of us.

'You want this?' I teased him, swinging the key. 'You want *this?*'

His head bounced. He clasped his ribs with a gutful whine.

'Ugghh . . . aaahh . . . mmmph.'

'Stay back!' I warned him. 'Stay where you are!'

But my words were useless, as he squeezed his ribs and stumbled toward me with his arm outstretched. 'Give me the key, boy!'

I stepped over a drain. 'Stay back!' I yelled again. 'It ain't worth it!' But the lunatic kept coming, leaving me no choice but to drop the key down the gutter.

He came to a sudden halt, both arms around his waist. You could see it fully and share with him all his suffering right there, his face a gory mess, the dim whites of his eyes looking helplessly at the gutter, as police sirens wailed up the hill.

An hour later I was sat in a cell at the police lockup, listening to junkies plead for clean air, hardmen threatening to make serious trouble with everyone in the station once they broke free, and some strange fellow in the next cell laughing whenever the hardmen threatened, or the junkies whined, simmering his delight with faint titters and crazy talk in the small passings of silence. I sat upright on the hard bed and stared at the floor, listening to all these familiar sounds till nightfall.

'Okay, Mr Nobody, we're taking you home, son. Robert Jones decided not to press charges,' said an officer, unlocking my cell.

'Two of his ribs!' he joked.

I stood up from the bed. 'Is my mother okay?'

'She's a little shaken, but she's fine. Let's get you home, champ.'

I stepped out from my cell. 'Where is she?' I asked.

'Back home. She was with Mr Jones at the hospital yesterday.'

'Did she come here?'

The cop hesitated before shaking his head. 'No son.'

28

'He wanted the car to go see his ex-wife in Cornwall,' she later told me. 'I paid for it! It's my car! It's my car!'

'It's over,' I said, stepping inside. 'Just no more of him, agreed?'

'Okay. No more.'

The cops drove off. I looked at my bruised knuckles. She flew off to the kitchen, her slippers running along the floor.

'Let me put a bandage on your hand!' she said.

'It's fine. I'm fine, Mum.'

She turned and faced me. 'You got a football game tomorrow?'

There was no remorse. Her so-called apology was being a nurse, a guilted one, absolving herself of any wrong. As a fifteen-year-old kid I'd learned that her issues would become my burden if I didn't hurry up and see her for who she was against who I wanted her to be. This woman was my mother. There were things about her that I didn't like, things that mattered, and I was having a hard time accepting that. But for the most part, the day to day stuff, we got by.

'Let's get some sleep,' I said.

Turning out the light, I stood at my window. The streetlamps glowed. I counted stars, watched dogs sniff the grass and take a dump. I saw the last #9 bus come and go, a woman tapping cigarette ash on her doorstep. Some alkies huddled together across the street, swigging cider and sucking fags, their cigarettes dancing like fireflies. Over on the green a fox hustled between houses, looking for a meal, cats unafraid, adapted. I watched all these things from my window, yawned, thought nothing more.

Slept.

29

Walking to Channel Park alongside Tommy and Champ, two of Dion's mates, Tommy asked me, 'So how was footy today?'

'Lost.'

'Listen,' he said, putting his hand on my shoulder, 'you know this ain't gonna help.'

'What ain't?' I said.

'Drugs, man. Don't waste your chance, Nobody. Not like I did.'

My edgy nature told him he'd gotten too close. He took back his hand. I didn't take advice well. I thought Jesus looted a good one: 'Do your thing and be prepared to die for that thing.' And this fella Blake, he had something decent: 'Excess leads to wisdom—we never know what is enough until we know what is *more* than enough.'

Frida was stood in the door watching the pink sky with a large glass of homemade punch. The wind moved her long, reddish hair as her lips sipped from the glass. She wore a white shirt over a pair of tight denims, barefoot.

'Hi gents,' she said, taking a puff of her joint.

'Hey Frida.'

'Hey Frida.'

'Hey Frida.'

'Shoes off. And tidy up after yourselves.'

'Will do.'

'Will do.'

'Will do.'

'And no ash on the floor. Use a tray. There's plenty. And tell Dion to open up the bloody window. It stinks.'

'I'll tell him,' volunteered Tommy, smitten by Frida, as we all were.

The cat was rolling about the garden. She climbed to her feet as I got close, arched her back. Frida turned to me. 'She likes you, Judas,' she said, tapping ash to the wind.

'She likes anyone who gives her attention,' I answered.

Frida smiled thoughtfully, took another sip of her drink, then said, 'You must be really fit with all that running about the field.'

Something told me to kneel down and fiddle with my laces, untie the knot and fix it tighter. 'Yeah, I guess so,' I said.

She stepped nearer while admiring the sky, the cold wind lapping against her chest. 'All Dion does is get stoned,' she wanted me to know. 'I keep telling him to get a job, or at least a bloody girlfriend. I worry about him, Judas. And those nunchucks. I should toss 'em in the goddamn bin.'

She took her eyes from the sky and pointed them at me.

'He's not bad, though. He thinks things,' I said. I think about relacing another shoe but instead stood up and faced this woman.

'I love these boys, Judas, but they're just wasting their lives away with too many drugs. If it wasn't in my home it'll be someplace else, you know? At least I'd keep an eye on them.'

Her big earrings reflected the lowering light. Nervous, I ran a finger down the wall of the house. 'Maybe needs a lick of paint?' was what my fifteen-year-old brain responded.

She smiled cruely while sipping her drink. 'Well *maybe* you can paint it for me, eh darling?'

I shrugged.

She sighed and faced the hills of Mt Edgcumbe, looking out at that horizon. 'Thank God for this view,' she said.

I was nodding from behind, wanting to be there and not be there. She was a fully grown woman, way out of my league. She rubbed her breasts beneath her shirt like I wasn't there. My dick did a turn.

Jezebel threw her head out the door. 'What you doing, Judas?'

I pointed at Frida. 'I'm with your mum.'

'I've been waiting for you all afternoon,' she said.

'Calm, Jezebel, he's been running about a field all day. Give the boy a break.'

Jezebel had saved us a seat. Dion was performing a seminar on the credibility of these acids he was peddling. Tommy and Champ almost have a real bust-up. Champ handed his beer to Alfie and told him to hold it for just a sec. Tommy apologised. Dion slipped me an acid, delicately placing the tab on my fingertip.

'At the same time?' suggested Jezebel, holding her acid too.

I swallowed mine. Jezebel swallowed hers. Tommy and Champ and Alfie followed suit. Lastly Dion tossed his down before diving into the pile of drugs scattered on a newspaper at his feet, meticulously filling his little wooden box with bits of cigarettes and rolling paper, counting valium into small resealable bags like some pharmacist.

'Anyone wanna buy before I put 'em away?' he asked.

I gave Jezebel a nudge.

'I'm not fucking buying drugs,' she said. She then leaned close to my ear and squealed, 'I stole a stash upstairs in my knicker drawer!'

Over on the couch, Tommy amused himself with impressions of Chinamen, while Dion continued bagging pills, muttering calculations and names and dates. Tommy then snorted a line of white powder off an encyclopedia, before jumping up and squatting on the rug. Champ got handsy with Alfie, giving him a nipple-twist.

'Faggots,' shot Tommy, shaking his head while squatting.

'Alfie's just playing hard to get,' joked Champ, his thick arms hugging Alfie to a purple pulp.

'Heeello, there's a girl in the room for fuck sake. I don't wanna hear any of that *faggot* shit please.'

Tommy apologised.

'Thank you.'

Dion chimed in, 'They're juss messin, Jezebel, don't take it so serious.' Dion started swinging his nunchucks in slow, rhythmic patterns around his back, a routine he'd seen a thousand times on Game of Death.

'Why don't *you* try taking yourself seriously, Dion! And stop thinking you're a fucking Chinese monk!' barked Jezebel.

I gave her an elbow. 'Stop swearing,' I told her.

'You're suppose to stick up for me, Judas! He's being *sexist!*'

'It's not sexist, Jezebel,' laughed Dion, swinging his sticks wildly.

'Yes it is! And you need to grow up and stop swinging those fucking sticks everywhere, it'll take someone's eye out!'

Jezebel and I both squint at the fret of one chuck flying loose across the room. Jezebel gave a nervous giggle-screech. 'Ahhh!'

I covered my face. 'Yeah, leave it out, Dion,' I said.

'I know what I'm doing,' he insisted, placing the chucks between his feet like some honourable sage before rambling on about Eastern philosophy.

Jezebel got mad. 'Dion, stop talking shit. You don't know shit. You're not fucking Chinese. You've had those nunchucks for five fucking minutes and you think you're some zen fucking monk. *You're stoned, Dion. Stoned*. Last week you were a Samurai with that fucking sword before Mum got rid of it, and the week before you were teaching everyone Wing fucking Chun. You don't fucking know Wing Chun, Dion!'

'You don't know jack shit,' Dion snapped back before addressing the room. 'Martial Arts started long before any of us knew what it was. It's the movement of the wind, the trees, life. We once knew what it was, we've just forgotten. It's coded in our biology, in our genes. We just have to remember. We don't need to take classes an' all that crap, we simply connect to the spirit. It's all right here, like electricity. I'm remembering, not learning, remembering.'

Dion looked at me with sermonlike eyes. And in these moments, these dust-star of the skull holy lecturous moments, the whitewashing high of getting stoned, you got seduced to Dion's galvanising headcloud without end. No end. Only retreat. You had to retreat from the sermon, the certainty, the mad oration of the wise word speaketh what is virtuous, maddening the already insane.

'You got a point,' I told him.

He snapped his fingers. 'Thank you, Judas!'

Jezebel spun her eyes to me. 'You serious, Caesar?'

'*Ha Ha Ha* . . . it's Brutus, Jezebel, not *Caesar!* Et tu BRUTUS.'

Jezebel faced her brother. 'I know what I mean, Dion!'

Dion smirked. 'You just ain't ready to master the secrets.'

Jezebel looked about the room at the rest of us. 'Am I the only one here who thinks he's talking complete and utter rubbish?'

Everyone shrugged. She turned back to her brother.

'Okay, *Dion*, what did you just say, just now, about electricity?'

'It don't matter, Jezebel. That's gone. Old news. It has to flow. When nothing is done, nothing is left undone. You just ain't in the flow.'

'BULLSHIT! You don't know what you're talking about, Dion! I don't wanna be in any flow. DO NOT include me in your flow.'

'Well don't include me in *your* flow.'

She gritted her teeth. 'What'd you mean, *my flow?* I ain't got a flow, Dion! And I don't want one thank you very much.'

Dion perked up. 'Everyone has a flow, Jezebel. It's your thoughts and feelings spilling out all over the place, like cosmic diarrhea, creating all this here *stuff,*' he says, rubbing his thumb and fingertip together. 'But what you really wanna master,' he went on, rotating his eyes about the room, 'is a natural flow with nature, without resistance, just coming and going and letting go. Most important to let go, and accept what is, just what is . . .'

On that note he leaned back and fired up a spliff with a smug grin.

'You can shove your flow up your ass, Dion! I've had enough.

I'm gettin serious psychological issues listening to your shit.'

'Just calm down, Jezebel, you might learn something. It'll be a bloody miracle if you do, but you just might.'

'What is it, Dion? Am I *learning*? Or am I *remembering*? Make up your bloody mind! I've had enough!'

Dion shot forward. 'You see, you're listening!'

'No, *Dion*. I'm trying to remain sane in this madhouse. And you're twisting things cus you're stoned! That's what happens when you sit on your ass watching kung fu films and smoking dope all day, you speak rubbish, and I have to take it, and it's not fucking fair!'

'Enough swearing, Jezebel!' yelled Frida from the kitchen.

Dion smirked. 'You see, that's your flow, Jezebel. You're like a black hole, sucking life out of everyone.'

Jezebel raised her hand. 'Talk to the hand, cus the eyes ain't listening.'

'*Ha Ha* . . . the *ears* ain't listening! Not the *eyes! Ha Ha* . . . you see!'

Jezebel threw down her hand. 'What, Dion? See what?'

Dion sighed before saying, 'Jezebel, when you stress, you make everyone else stressed. You only wanna get what *you* want. You don't listen. It's called havin an ego, Jezebel. You got a big ego. That's your flow. And that ain't a wise flow to be in. It only attracts problems you can't handle alone. You'll need people to tell you what to do, how to think, where to go. You'll be a slave to the mind, a puppet.'

Tommy got down for twenty pressups while Champ sat quietly in the corner rolling tobacco. Alfie, in a sudden burst, decided to chase after the cat.

'Mum!' Jezebel yelled. 'Tell Dion to stop speaking rubbish!'

Alfie came running behind the cat, tripping and landing on his face. Jezebel cupped her forehead. 'Why do I even fucking bother.'

Then came a loud bang on the door.

Dion immediately scooped up his nunchucks and shifted across the room, returning with a bat, peering out the corner of the curtain.

Bobby Bundy, a tall, olive-skinned tough guy, sprung from below the window in the front garden and yelled, 'Arrrghh!'

'Jesus, Bob,' huffed Dion, lowering his bat.

Bobby was a known hardman about town, a twenty-something kid who collected owed money. He was lofty and charming and handsome, with something dark behind the eyes, something offended. He never spoke of the scar along his cheek, cutting to the corner of his mouth. I heard stories. Jezebel said he could be my older brother. There wasn't much of our kind about town. In any case, I was glad he just dropped by to collect his pills.

When Bobby vanished, Dion began pacing about the room, picking up things and putting those things down someplace else. Placing some papers there and bringing the ashtray here. His obsessions were always the same, fissuring sentences between three or four subjects at once with a fresh joint in one hand while working his fingers over his swollen pockets, forgetting where he left his lighter.

Frida was still at the stove, chain-smoking and leaning her way down a litre of booze. And then the acid kicked in.

Hovering my hand ahead of my face, I watched vapour trails of reds and golds. Dion drew the curtain, while Frida shouldered the door with a cigarette and a glass of vodka. A surge of joy lifted the black soot of the mundane, casting light over the lowly neighbourhood. Jezebel's face was incredible. She beamed a yellowish glow, circling her hand about the air the same as mine.

'I'm coming up,' she said. 'These acids are trippy.'

Tommy opted for the floor, caressing the fine tassels of the rug with his fingertips. The cat lay on Alfie, massaging her claws into his lap as he worked both hands beneath her fur, while Dion nodded with self-amusement, blowing smoke rings.

Jezebel then clung to her Troll Doll close to my side. I didn't like that she still played with dolls. It was strange. I told her that it was strange, not even toddlers should play with dolls. 'It's weird,' I said.

'Don't be upset,' she pleaded.

Moments later the acid really hit us. Everyone in a fit of laughter. Jezebel pressed my side and held my arm like she just found me. 'I've been looking for you for hours,' she said, close to a tear.

It grew dark outside. I walked us to the sofa. And saw all kinds of things, otherworldly goings-on—aliens passing through, strange creatures with big heads walking from here to another here. I spoke back without speaking. And they knew. They knew everything.

In a moment of happiness, I turned to Jezebel. 'I think you're wonderful,' I told her, starting something I wished I hadn't. She looked to me with big, dewy eyes and told me the same.

'I love you,' she gushed, clasping my arm, 'I promise not to swear. Please don't leave me. I'll stop playing with dolls, I mean it.'

Before she could ruin our trip I scooped up the cat. When I turned around, Jezebel was gone. I dropped the cat and searched the house, finding her on the stairway picking the woodchip wallpaper.

A chill ran down my arms. I tried to keep a grip, but eventually plopped down. Jezebel placed her hand on my shoulder. A large purple snake twisted about my leg. I thought about fighting it off but somehow knew to let the thing swallow me whole.

'Judas,' Jezebel whispered, 'you're scaring me.'

I tried opening my eyes to tell her I'm okay, that a giant snake is eating me whole. But my eyes wouldn't lift.

'Judas,' she said again. 'Let's take our clothes off and go to bed.'

I found my feet again, my fingers finding her lips, her cheeks, as though I was old and blind, wanting one last stroke of a pretty girl.

Several moments later we crawled up the stairs and dropped our clothes on the bedroom floor, sinking into an act of bizarre cosmic love-making continually until daylight.

30

Frida was heading down to the '95 *Run to the Sun* summer festival in Cornwall with her sweetheart. Me and Jezebel decided to tag along. Noah, her sweetheart, a burly, hippie-faced, wide-chinned carpenter bloke, pulled up outside in a rundown VW camper, slamming the horn. We bailed on Dion watching reruns of Drunken Master and tossed our bags into the van.

I sat upfront with Noah. Jezebel couldn't stand the cool breeze against her face in the backseat. She also didn't like the idea of roughing it up in a tent in the middle of a field on the Cornish coastline, surrounded by mud and horseflies and thousands of campervans.

'Here she blows . . .'

'Shut up, Judas. I don't have to like sleepin in a fuckin tent.'

'Language, Jezebel,' cautioned Frida.

'A few good bevvies and you'll sleep just fine,' assured Noah.

'If I can't sleep then I'm not staying.'

'Jesus, Jezebel,' I said. 'Cheer up, we're not there yet.'

'Don't care! Not sleeping with fucking insects crawling over me.'

'Jezebel! That mouth!'

'Shake your sleepin bags off before you go to bed,' Noah advised. 'And sleep with your mouth shut so spiders don't crawl in.'

'Fucksake, Judas!'

'Jezebel! THAT MOUTH!'

Two hours later. The sun smashed over the hills. We wheeled behind an unending queue of classic German engineering, with every tenth festival-goer asking at the window if I'd any pills to flog.

'Must be somethin about you, Judas,' Frida joked.

Jezebel smirked. 'It's because he's black.'

'Please try to be subtle, Jezebel dear,' Frida told her.

'I'm not black,' I said.

'This van's a bit dodgy, could be the van,' humoured Noah.

'But I'm not black.'

'I am smoking a joint, that could be why,' Frida added.

'Where's the dope?' Noah asked.

'Tits,' replied Frida, sunning her face out the window.

'You are black,' whispered Jezebel over my shoulder.

'We'll break some dope off for you kids, so make it last.'

'You got all that dope between your tits?' Noah asked.

'Yes, Noah, *tits*. It's the safest place till we get settled.'

We were stuck behind a sea of campers. Some guy lifted his head to my window. 'Hey man,' he said to me, 'you got any magic beans?'

'No, no beans.'

Slowly, he eyed all occupants of the van before vanishing.

Jezebel sniggered. 'Black.'

'My dad's white. My mum's black. I'm an experiment.'

'You're a black experiment.'

'Shut up, Jezebel.'

'Where'd you put my flask of vodka, Noah?' asked Frida.

'Glove compartment.'

'I'm actually brown,' I said.

Jezebel laughed. 'Well I'm black.'

'You're a dumb dumb, that's what you are.'

She giggled to herself and fell back to her seat. 'I'm holding onto our dope, Judas,' she said.

'If it makes you happy.'

'I am happy.'

Frida fussed. 'I can't find it, Noah. I need my vodka.'

'Yes, you're happy, Jezebel, full of joy,' I said.

'Noah!! Vodka!!'

'It's in there!!'

'I know I'm happy,' Jezebel answered.

'And who cares . . . ' I said.

'Sorry Noah, found it. Why'd you hide it way back there?'

'So it didn't bounce about and smash to pieces.'

'Almost gave me a heart attack. Did you pack the whiskey?'

'You saw me do it.'

Jezebel had been quietly thinking. 'You care if I'm happy,' she said.

'I really don't,' I said.

More quiet, and then, 'I'll keep our dope in my zip purse, Judas.'

'Jam it up your butthole for all I care.'

'Judas! That ain't nice!'

'Is the tonic in there too, Noah? Did you pack the tonic?'

'Six bottles,' Noah said, swinging left into the festival carpark.

'Does anyone want some of this joint before we get to the gate?'

Jezebel reached out. 'I'll have some,' she said.

Another guy appeared at my window. 'Scoosmie mate,' he said.

I faced him. 'What is it?'

The guy cupped his hand over his mouth. 'You got any candy?'

By mid-sun Jezebel and I had pitched our tent. She wasn't much of an outdoorsy human, mostly commenting on the crowd and what we should do later.

'We should eat *hotdogs*,' she said.

I peered up, squinting away rays of sunlight. 'Pass me a peg.'

'Peg?'

'For the tent, in that bag, next to your foot.'

Her skin was already a few shades darker under the sun. She wore her hair bundled up beneath a little white hat, with tight jean-shorts and a blue vest, looking worryingly at all the noise about camp.

Frida bit off a chunk of dope and passed it to Jezebel, telling us to make it last before going for a dip with Noah in the sea.

Every fifth or so van passing our tent stopped to ask if I'd any extra supply. Jezebel was in fits. I laughed too.

'I could've made a boatload of money.'

'Don't you dare!' she said, taking a hungry bite of her hotdog.

By nightfall we decided to party.

Jezebel later found her mum and Noah in some gong massage tent.

'They'll meet us there,' she said out of breath and smiling when she returned. 'Just you and me, Judas.'

Within an hour we're dancing beneath a giant dome full of hundreds of ravers. Jezebel was in her own world, twisting her arms about the air like some snake woman. Gazing up at the roof of the dome the euphoric reverie beat the backs of our necks, sweat dripping from our faces. We danced and danced.

With Jezebel close behind, we made our way nearer to the stage, to that deejay I liked. As we nudged through, one pudgy guy with a CREW badge swinging from his neck, pointed to me then to the stage. I got a mouth of Jezebel's cheek-sweat as I kissed her.

'Wait here!' I yelled over the music, weaving through the crowd.

Jezebel bounced up and down waving, trying to catch the attention of the guy, but he'd moved on.

A pretty brunette in a zipped down peppermint jumpsuit also got hoisted up on stage. I noticed the brunette, gave her a wink, before trying to spot Jezebel. Glancing across the darker lanes to my left, I catch her there toying with some tough-looking security guy, an inch from his pressed white shirt. Her gaze roamed up and down his tie. He pulled her near as she stepped away. Her head dropped semi-displeased, as though he had done nothing too wrong, a small lovers quarrel. She fixed her vest strap back over her shoulder the second time, her eyes searching for me then back to the floor, a side-glance at the security guy, back to me again. I turned and acknowledged the girl in the peppermint suit a second time.

Several moments later my girlfriend zigzagged between the crowd and stopped below me. 'I've lost the dope!' she shouted up.

I jumped down from the stage.

'I think I dropped it on the dancefloor,' she added.

Hundreds of revellers all about us were jumping to the music. On top of that, that prick of a security clod had followed her, stood like a retarded action figure a few feet away. He surveyed the crowd while fiddling with his earpiece, catching her in the corner of his eye, checking her out, checking me out.

I looked Jezebel in the eye. 'Why were you flirting with him?'

'I wasn't!'

I snatched her by the arm. She snatched back her arm.

'You left me alone to go dance on stage. You left me alone!'

We stared at each other for a second, both of us at a deadend.

I huffed. 'How'd the dope get out the purse?'

'Must've fallen when I opened it,' she shrugged.

'Where'd you open it?'

She pointed across the crowds. 'I think over there,' she said.

Seconds later I'm on my hands and knees, sweeping the dance floor like a toothless tramp madly grinding his receding gums, searching for his misplaced junk. I was relentless, in a panic, couldn't leave it alone. Jezebel walked alongside, shoving people out the way while yelling, 'Watch your backs!'

I jumped to my feet. 'I found the dope!'

Jezebel threw her arms around me.

31

I sat facing Dion and Florence, one of Jezebel's schoolmates.

Jezebel didn't know I was dropping by.

'She's upstairs,' Florence informed me.

'With Bruno,' Dion whispered with caution.

The chair I was sat in had lost its spring, knees up against my chest, eyes in line with Dion's armpit.

Dion looked nervous. 'He's been here all night,' he said.

Florence gave it to me straight, 'Jezebel had sex with Bruno.'

A friend of Jezebel once said Bruno's cock was substantially larger than most guys, and how much it hurt her, in a good way. It hurt her in a good way. She liked that it hurt. Both Jezebel and I were intrigued.

My eyes stood down at my lap, then back at their faces all tense and worried. 'Just thought I'd drop by, surprise her,' I confessed.

Squinting up at the pin of sunlight piercing through the window, I sucked in a lungful of air, thinking of the argument we had a few days earlier. It was a big one. I said I had had enough. I was done.

'Judas, listen, best you just *go home* and talk with her tomorrow.'

Dion fiddled with his zippo. I noticed it had an engraving of a wild stallion up on its hinds, a free and fearless-looking creature.

'He's upstairs?' I asked them.

They both nod together. 'Yeah, upstairs . . . with Jezebel.'

'*And* Bobby,' added Dion, naming the two toughest guys in town.

Great, I think, fucking perfect, Jezebel.

Footsteps came down the staircase. In stumbled Jezebel with bunched-up hair and guilty eyes. The bitch kept her eyes low and away from mine, dragging her stupid piglet slippers to the kitchen. Florence pushed herself up slowly from the chair and followed her.

'Alright,' I said to myself. My brain couldn't comprehend how she'd gotten this far without knowing she was on her way out. We were just a pair of sixteen-year-olds, with stuff changing and creeping up on us new, like the volume strength of alcohol, and the serial impact of a lie. It was all a bit foggy and my sixteen years of life couldn't work this through. So as Dion cranked the stallion, I stood up and went for the door.

As I walked up the stairs I was afraid. But when I reached the top I had pushed through the worst. Hearing the usual banter between older guys, the noise came from Dion's room. I stepped in. The noise grew. Bobby Bundy was laying fists into a punchbag which hung from a metal wire, with Bruno on the other end counting blows. *One-two! One-two!*

My head was empty, like a dream. I walked like a dream toward Bruno with my spine up, ready for something. His neck was much thicker than I recalled, like his face was a continuation of neck. He grew up in a boxing family, his nose flat and rearranged, chin tough as stone. Dion's face had only just recovered from being pounded by Bruno in the alleyway beside The Bluebird over a disagreement on pool rules, which somehow escalated to glasses being smashed and Bruno's fists continually finding Dion's face. Only Bobby Bundy, the debt collector, was brave enough to step in, telling Bruno enough was enough. Dion, the poor bastard, couldn't see for two whole days, with a face swelled a quarter size.

'Whoa now, Judas,' said Bruno. Bobby stopped punching the bag. Bruno stretched his palms out wide, pleading like a cheap saint. I had no plan other than to face him. Whatever it took.

Bruno held out a joint as an offering.

I shook my head.

Why couldn't I throw the first punch?

And another part of me said: it's like hitting a child, that's why. There was no glory to it, no decency. I needed something, something worthwhile. Fighting over a girl seemed crazy.

Bruno stretched the joint farther. 'It's cocaine,' he tells me.

So what if I took a puff. So I did. This is cocaine? Talcum powder. Not worth shit. I passed it back.

'Smoke more,' gestured Bruno, with a big dumb grin.

Within minutes I'm laughing in the corner of the room, my head a supernova of racing red hot tales with a disregard for any girl, only I mattered and I loved it. I was fucking spectacular!

Bruno handed me another coke-spliff. I took more drags.

'Fancy a few pops on the punchbag?' asked Bobby.

'Sure!' I said, jumping to my feet and giving the bag a few light jabs—*bam! bam!*—throwing naturally from the hip. Bobby looked at me with intrigue. And it was easy to leave, I just turned around and walked out the door and down the stairs without a word.

'All okay?' asked Dion.

'Great,' I told him, grabbing my kit bag. 'Just great!'

I raced out the door, passing the girls whispering in the kitchen. My adrenaline wanted to leap all the way home, my heartbeat thumping through my chest as I sprinted along, lit up like a Christmas tree.

When I finally reached my front door I pulled out my key. My hand trembled. I closed the door behind and walked slowly up the stairs. A grey mood filled the house. I faced the back of the door, sat on the toilet, feeling faint and low and stupid.

Why couldn't I punch him?

A catch of wind whistled through the window like a thousand demons. I spat on the wall and cheered the Devil. Pulled up my trousers and noticed a peculiar change: my dick had shrunk. And my balls had shriveled up too . . . *Cocaine?*

In the livingroom I put on a song that reminded me of Jezebel, and forced myself to dance and make my eyes sore. It was ridiculous.

I thought that to myself, I thought, Judas, this is ridiculous. But I couldn't stop. Then Frida phoned and said she'd heard the news and that she was sorry. I told her it's the best news I'd had since forever before hanging up and going to my room to sleep off the mood.

But my teeth kept grinding and my eyes watched the ceiling the whole night through, unable to stop thinking, thinking, thinking . . .

32

Just one month until twenty-four footballers from thousands across the West Country are chosen for a scholarship with Plymouth F.C.

'Meet you upstairs!' yelled my teammate, Pauly.

Strolling through his livingroom, I passed his old man, a Social Club deejay, sorting through 70s vinyls. Pauly darted into the bathroom as I hit the top step. His mother was a chubby woman with looky eyes. She wasn't a stunner, but she was woman.

I paused outside the bathroom door. We spot each other in the squared mirror above the sink. I kept my gaze steady. My heart raced. We didn't have much time. Pauly left the door open just enough for his mother to be admired. And I admired her as she stood starkers below the mirror, drying her mop of hair with eyes looking at me and not looking at me.

Just as things were heating up Pauly's kid sister came running. I made a move to Pauly's room. The little spoiler followed me in and planted herself on her brother's bed near to where I began packing my football kit.

'Are you captain today, Judas?' she asked.

'What's with all the questions?' I said, my chest still thumping.

The door swung open. Pauly appeared in a panic. 'We gotta get a move on!' he yelped, spitting flecks of toothpaste. 'Hey Kal,' he then said, 'show Judas your boobs like you showed me.'

Kal turned away from her brother and looked straight at me, pulling up her vest without a hint of shyness.

Pauly chimed in again, 'Show him properly, Kal,' he said.

She yanked her little vest up higher, revealing two little infant tits, all the while remaining plain-faced. I scratched my leg, feeling a sudden itch creeping over me. Both Pauly and his sister stared my way. I didn't know what they wanted. I wished I had a sister like that. I thought Pauly was very lucky.

After a moment of silence I blurted out, 'Your nipples are puffy.' And they were. There was more nipple than tit. I'd never seen puffy ones before. Kal shrugged in agreement like it was nothing. Pauly looked closer. His mother then passed between the hallway from the shower, her half-naked body sweeping by the gap of the door. I was warm, getting warmer, burning up!

Kal twisted her vest down while Pauly got on combing his hair like it was just another Thursday.

I formed words from the babbling inside of me. 'They're almost perfectly round,' I said. Pauly agreed. Then something miraculous happened, Kal pulled her vest back up to take a look. And I thought, she pulled her vest back up because I said something *nice?*

'I don't know what it means?' she asked, studying her chest.

I bounced my shoulders and added, 'They're like little plums.'

Pauly came and stood beside me. 'You mean, her tits, Judas?'

'That's right,' I said, staring at them. 'A couple of lovely plums.'

We all bunched eyebrows together, inspecting each tit for some time. I couldn't believe my luck. Kal soon had enough and fixed her vest and wandered over to Pauly's desk, snatching up his microphone.

'Can I borrow this?' she asked him.

'Yes. But I need it back tomorrow, Kal.'

'Fanks!' And off she ran.

33

The team coach raced across the country of Wales, entering the small town of Aberystwyth. The town was cold and wet and far from anything.

One hundred players stood cheering team Brazil as they collected their winner's trophy. I didn't know how the hell I won Player of the Tournament with those Brazilians being there. But I did. With the announcement I untied my laces and followed meekly behind.

Once the ceremony had ended, Pauly and me made our way to the pier. Team Ireland had instructed a player to shadow me during our match. The worst players often got the shirty task of keeping the good ones out of the game. Pull the sleeve, they're told, get in their heads, commit fouls without being seen by the referee. Whatever it takes! So during our game, me and this Irish kid struck up a conversation.

'Pull my shirt again, cupcakes, and I'll chin ya.'

'Guwan den fella,' the idiot laughed.

'Get chor fucking hands off of me you stinky inbred.'

He kept laughing.

'Prick.'

He laughed harder.

'Glad I'm amusing you you Irish cunt.'

That did it.

'The feck you call me, fella?'

'The little leprechaun speaks!'

'Ye black bastard.'

'I'm not black.'

'Ye black coont.'

'Ale give your sweet ma-ma a black *coont.*'

He started laughing again. 'Ahh, good'en! I ligh tha!'

'Keep it.'

'I juss migh . . .'

He tugged me again while the ref wasn't looking.

'Leggo my shirt!' I yelled.

'Go feck yourself.'

'Chrissakes, you cheating twat.'

'Juss doin me jawb.'

'Shit fucking job.'

'Is wha'dye do.'

'You should have a serious rethink, little elf boy.'

He laughed again, tugging me from behind.

I missed the ball and spun around. 'Leggo my shirt!'

The referee caught sight. 'Number seven! Watch your mouth please young man!' Irish let go of my shirt before the ref turned on his boot.

I let the ref have it. 'How about *you* do *your* job and *watch him!*'

'I'm doing my job just fine, young man! You got yourself a warning, number seven! Cool it down!'

I faced Irish. 'You're an annoying little gingercock, know that?'

He smirked. 'Juss doin me jawb.'

'Fuck your job, Tintin. Meet me by the pier tonight.'

And that was that.

Most of the boys back at camp tried talking me out of it. 'It's not worth the hassle, Judas,' big Bob said. I patted his big docile head and walked off alone. Pauly caught me up.

We couldn't be farther into Welsh land, with slow-moving tractors and rundown farmhouses, bundles of hay stacked along tops of green fields full of roaming sheep. Yet by six-thirty I'm haggling dope from the only dealer in this part of town who so happened to be loitering beside a bus stop in a shiny red tracksuit. With the hash stashed in my pocket, Pauly refused to speak to me until we reached the pier.

The pier was grey and the sky pale blue. Tens of seabirds napped along the promenade, comforted by the crashing whitewash of the ocean tide. Irish kept his word, stood there waiting with a lucky charm, half-shivering with their hands in their pockets.

Pauly whispered, 'The hell do I do if you guys start swinging?'

I stopped and looked at Pauly. 'You don't need to be here.'

'Don't be daft,' he said annoyed. 'There's two of 'em, Judas.'

'You still don't need to be here,' I assured him.

Pauly looked out to sea, taking a moment. He hated violence.

'Listen,' I said. 'I don't wanna fight him. But I have to be here.'

My teammate cracked. 'No! You don't! What if the police come? Did you think about that? You've got drugs!!' He also hated drugs.

Ignoring his dramatics, I turned to Irish. In doing so I noticed a bearded guy swing a metal detector along the beach. Both Pauly and I stare at this guy for a moment, watching him scour the sand with his oversized headphones, listening close for some sort of change of frequency detected by his little machine. We stared a short while more before continuing along the promenade.

'Just let me do the talking,' I said.

Irish and I look plainly at each other. His head was round and hard, eyes unblinking. I gestured to his friend. He looked nervous, eyes darting about like a spooked animal. Pauly took a step back trying to get my attention. I gave the idiot a crazy lookdown, fearing he'll make us seem soft.

The bearded fella advanced his metal detector along the beach with his belly in front of him, searching for that change of frequency. We all, for some reason, turned and looked at this guy, his eyes rooted to the shoreline, running that thing along every grain of sand.

Me and Irish had it out on the field. It was done. I knew that. I was just some kid who felt uneasy being touched. I hated it. I hated being touched. The slightest brush from a human made me skittish, like a wary street cat. I didn't hate people, but I wanted to get away, predisposed to either war or solitude. What would Mishima do? Maybe he'd make a pot of tea, watch the good sailor choke on his knees.

I had gotten to appreciate my bunker, a welcomed break from the caricatures of daily life, people with a cloudy, domestic fuzz behind the eye—defending countries, towns, tradition, uncaring whether they lived or if they died. I figured the deceptions of this world didn't come from those politicians or some mouthpiece news reporter. It was hiding in plain sight, right there beneath your nose, wrapped up in those closest to you. I was dark inside, it was always there, a tight-lipped observer to the things that made most people shrink. And my inklings looked after me, told me the shit, such as prizewinning authors showcasing their literary snot upon bookshelves, or the voting queues of lamblike degenerates readying to better their lives with a red tick in a box. My inklings didn't try to make stuff up, twist a tale to have me feel good. It simply aimed toward clean air whenever things got murky, dragging me along with it, cutting through the same old jinglebells and hallelujas and seeing things for what they truly were. My inklings were easy, befriending souls, not shells. But the masses will nail you to the block if you don't vote or love Jesus, celebrate your fellow human.

'Name's Connor,' muttered Irish.

Nods passed between us. We shook hands. Pauly smiled. Connor said nothing more, he just stood waiting. They all did. Waiting for me. I pulled out the dope from my pocket that I'd just bought.

'You got any papers?'

Connor mumbled something to his Irish pal before facing me.

'Whey feckin not,' he said with a grin.

Several moments later we're all sat by the pier on a bench painted in birdshit, throwing chips to Welsh seagulls.

Afterwards we said our goodbyes and good lucks. I had smoked too much again. Everyone watched me, the eyes in the cars watched, the people up in their houses. We made it back to the hill and I stopped to roll another joint. The rationale was to keep smoking, picking a fight with the world of bonds and chains and tyranny.

'Just get rid of it!' Pauly howled.

Afraid of playing the accomplice, my teammate steamed up ahead. Seeing him run made me more sketchy. I ditched the dope and caught him up. Yet in his upset the crook continued to hurry away. 'You're trouble, Judas!' he said. 'You're bad news!'

Out of breath, I stopped chasing the bastard and yelled at his back, 'No one asked you to come! No one bloody asked you!'

34

'Say goodbye to all if not most of your friends. From here on, other than eating and sleeping, the academy is your only priority. If you try to do more, you will fail. If you do less, you will fail. If you have a lady friend, please inform her she won't be seeing much of you—those of you who are single, try to remain so. Be prepared to work harder than you have ever worked before. I expect nothing less. Be prepared to give your absolute best. I expect nothing more. If you persistently turn up late, you're out of the academy, no question. If you turn up too early, it counts for zip, other than more work. You will be the first to arrive: seven o'clock sharp. And the last to leave—that time depends on the proper completion of tasks. Each of you will be allocated two professional players to shadow each year. You will be responsible for washing their kit, towels, boots, and whatever else is needed. Be warned, we have plenty superstitious players. You will be training every day with the occasional rest on Sunday. Each of you will be allocated cleaning areas, which I'll run through now: *showers, bathtubs, corridors, changing rooms, utility room, kit, kit room, laundry room, boots room, balls, ball room, carparks, vans, the training pitch, park entrance and exit*. I will be spot checking all areas once complete. Again, do not expect to leave until everything is cleaned to specification, you work as a team. You will be paid sixty pounds weekly, congratulations. If you wish to be paid, please see admin with your bank details at the end of the day. Now, get your running shoes on and meet me by the front gate, we're going for a twenty-mile run.'

The air was thin, warm, summertime, end of school and the start of my football career. Just one week following the completion of perhaps more than a decade of mostly inapplicable and vague curricula studies, I had heard that Carlisle was kicking down doors of smalltime dope dealers, taking their cash and whatever belongings he could flog, and doing pretty well too. And Donny, he was off to juvenile for his role in a sizeable cocaine plot. Tiny, he'd decided to go in search for his real dad someplace up in the Netherlands, armed with a photograph, a hundred Dutch coins, and the family name of the mistress his old man took off with. Jezebel got a job cage dancing in a popular nightclub. My best pal Jacob got on with odds and ends with his old man, drifting along. And here I was, gassing out the first mile of nineteen more to come.

Me and all the other rookies ran along the edge of the moors, along the flat coast of the next town between narrow country lanes and over banks and muddy mounds, passing cottages and cattle and tractors. We ran by old pensioners, coughed our guts through empty villages. Once we reached the closing five-mile mark we legged it up a yellow field and fell on the other end, exhausted, climbing back to our feet and continuing to run until we reached the stadium.

'Good, very good,' said the coach, breathing as though he could run another twenty. 'Now you lot, get a decent stretch then meet me by the pitch for an hour of circuits.'

By nine o'clock that evening my mother shook me awake where I'd passed out on the sofa, my kit bag strapped to my back, telling me to take myself to bed.

35

The final year of the academy. I woke up with a migraine. Tiptoeing downstairs, I didn't possess the importance to convince the coach I couldn't play because of a useless headache. Unless something was broken or seriously injured, it was business as usual. My mother fixed me a bowl of porridge, said it'll do the trick.

By eleven o'clock we're smashing the field, playing a touring team from Luxembourg. The pain in my temple twitched my right eye, cracking my skull in two. Then suddenly, my stomach curdled.

'Coach!' I recall shouting. 'I need to shit!' I couldn't wait. Deserting the pitch I sprinted the four hundred fucking yards straight for the outdoor loo, shoving my pants down with milliseconds to launch.

My mother confessed. As a villager, she unequivocally believed in flushing out toxins as the cure to all health anomalies. And so, to counter my *migraine*, she chose to pour laxative in my porridge.

'You don't go round slipping laxative into someone's food, Muh!'

'I wanted to flush it out!'

'I had to run off the field in the middle of the game!'

'I know! You told me! You told me!'

I put my face in my hands. 'Jesus, woman.'

'I only put a little bit! Not so much!'

'Enough,' I said, walking away. 'Just don't do it again.'

'Okay son. No more laxative. I promise!'

Now the pressure was really on, having to play through strained hamstrings, one torn tendon and numerous ankle injuries. There was little hope. I kissed my old lady on the head and suspiciously sipped the tea she'd just brewed before running to the academy.

The coach leaned against the wall of the corridor seeming to have a serious chinwag with his assistant. He was a lanky fella, a thin sheet of flesh on bone with a hooked nose that could sniff out trouble from a mile. Marathon fit, a tough-talking northern bloke with something tender behind the eyes. Only I didn't see much of anything tender. He swung toward me, threw his clipboard to his side. 'And what yer gonna tell me now lad, eh? You got the mumps!'

I cleaned up my nose. 'It's just a cold,' I said.

'*Good lad,*' he said, tapping my shoulder with his clipboard before marching off. 'Discipline!' he belted, vanishing down the hall.

'You need to want this more, come on, Nobody,' I told myself while mopping the showers. I mopped until the floor glared, striking off *shower room* on the little white list before getting started on washing kit.

Waiting for an available machine, some senior players caught my attention, frolicking naked in wet flip-flops with towels flung over their shoulders. Some held themselves proudly in their fists, twiddling their balls, with apprentices collecting their sweaty shorts and muddy boots strewn about their feet. A few respectable seniors left a neat pile of used wear on the bench with their shirt number shown plainly for the apprentice to notice with ease. But these, this fine fucking lot, they always left a tip for us academy kids like spoilt little sweethearts, calling it *initiation*. What kind of initiation was this?

'This is the second time this week, Nobody!' The coach scribbled on his clipboard. I slept through my alarm clock twice in a week. 'Twice!' he said. So I set a couple clocks beside my bed: one digital, and my usual windup and steel bell, a minute apart. Along with this, I started to peg it the five miles to the academy so I didn't have to rely on the bus running on schedule. The arguments with the coach in my head were endless. Did I want this? Was it for me? Do I give a damn?

Bob and some other kids joked about. The coach joined, gave

them each a victory wink and a few champion words. I was winning games, completing tasks on time, playing through injuries, and punctual—*mostly*. Yet he would always remark: 'Give it more, lad! You got more! Give me more!' sliding his finger along the filthy wall as he passed me by, his prizewinning commentary fading off with the tyrant as I scrubbed the bath on my hands and knees.

Later, while firing up the hose, I got to thinking some more. 'Is this it? Is this all I got?' It was a good use of time, cleaning, a bit of space when everything was all right.

'You gotta want it, lad! You don't want it enough!' bleated the stumpy, tongue-in-ass assistant at the start of another day. The coach interjected: 'You're training with the seniors this morning, Nobody. Off you go, son.'

My teammates didn't seem surprised to see me jog to the pros pitch, lugging with me the newest balls and nets and cones.

'That's the spirit, laddy—good session!' The senior coach punched me a wink and shook my hand as though I had signed up to kill an Arab. 'I've got my eye on you, Nobody. You've got potential! Oh yes. You won't be a junior for too long, sonny.'

On my way to Dion the town was electric. Friday night. Police vans parked on all corners of the street, spying on the yobs and their drunken mayhem. Dion swung open the door with his nunchucks. 'Christ,' he huffed, easing off. 'You almost got murdered.'

I shook my head and followed him in, glad Jezebel wasn't around.

'I'm juss watchin a documentary on the cosmos,' he tells me, collapsing back to the couch with a fresh joint dangling from his lips. I sat in a chair and hoped he'd fire the thing up. Several minutes went by, the orbiting rings of Saturn were forming on the telly. Noticing my exhaustion, Dion jumped back to his feet, motioning to follow him to the kitchen.

Swinging open the fridge door he carried out a snowball the

size of a child's fist. *'It's speed,'* he whispered.

Breaking off a couple pieces, he set the remainder of the powder back in the fridge and led us to the kitchen table. With a couple rolling papers, he carefully parcelled those pieces, passing one to me.

And away it went, no question. We both swallowed the speed clean with a gulp of tap water, sitting back down to learn the composite of gasses that made up Jupiter.

My eyes soon burned awake fully alert, my mind a cosmic fireball in the brain. This is it, I think, *this is the answer!*

Dion got to know a bit about the coach. In between all that, he told me of his dope-selling dreams, The Psychedelic Cartel. With this speed, we could form new civilisations with just our minds, right here on the sofa! I glanced at the clock, summed the minutes till I needed to wake up and run to the academy, plotting all the great and wonderful things I was to achieve the next day. Life was good. Life was real good. I'd found the answer. I found SPEED.

It took just a minute for Dion to start moving things about on his little newspaper, changing bags, taking things out of his little wooden box and putting them back. He counted pills and weighed dope. He then lay back and said nothing more. I needed more, I needed to remain high and optimistic.

'I know what you're thinking,' Dion muttered behind the cushion. 'Don't worry about me, Judas, I'll figure it out. I've been meditating night and day, channeling my energy, like Laozi. Dow*wizm*. Ancient stuff. Anyway, hope it works out with coach Gustav.'

I jumped to my feet. 'Thanks, Dion. Okay, I'm off.'

'Hey Judas! Chip off another piece before you go.'

And that was that.

The once black sky soon became morning blue from my bedroom window. Eyeing the drawer where I stashed the speed, the wait for the first alarm was hell. Finally I was out the house with no sleep, just a thousand hundred solutions to be the epitome of success.

A few strides along my new conquest my lungs croaked. Speed didn't make you run faster I had discovered. Catching a breather, I took a break by a bus stop. The bus rolled in with pairs of morning eyes looking bleary, like they too needed a hit of this stuff. With my hands on my knees I waved the bus on. The old git shook his head and took off down the road.

Before reaching the academy I swallowed the last of the powder instead of waiting till midday as agreed with myself at around three o'clock this morning while staring into the abyss of my ceiling. I chewed a Mars bar, sunk a can of Cherry Cola in five victory gulps, and belched big from the gut. The champ was ready.

Pirate FM assaulted the airwaves from a stereo in the changing room. Glancing into a mirror, someone curiously looked back. Was I the impostor?

The next hour the coach summoned me to his office as I was coming up on another amphetamine rush, my jaw torqued to one side, wiping endless spit from my mouth. He told me something needed to change. I had been late too often. There was a hotel close to the academy where boys from outside of town resided. A club bus collected those boys each morning and returned them to the hotel each evening on schedule. There was a room available. Unable to form a coherent reply, lockjawed, eyes transmitting information like television sets, I simply submit to the offer with a puzzling nod.

The Club hotel was simple—dull, chintzy furnishing with musty carpet room to room. It was run by a hairy-chinned, seventy-ish-old lady named Maureen, with an untidy white mane of hair screaming from her scalp. She roamed the hotel corridors stinking of burnt toast and detergent, upheld the rules and made sure I understood them perfectly. She was a generous, hermitlike creature, who spoke only necessary things. I liked her instantly.

Three flights of stairs behind Maureen's enormous buttocks and I was mesmerised. The size and weight of those things mounting each step was remarkable. Her breath grew heavier with each floor conquered until we reached the only single room in the B&B with a bay window.

On the way up, I had time to wonder when Maureen might have had a stiff cock inside of her—if a woman of such ugliness had even considered she owned such a fortune between her thighs. There seemed to be no limits to my delectation, all fannies were just fascinating to me—but especially the undesired ones belonging to the outcasts, the hideous, the disabled, they fostered the most beauty, the most wisdom it seemed, the most sincerity. I would have woken at dawn each day to go plunge my pecker inside Maureen on her musty mattress, twist and squeeze her hairy nipples as she sucked me stale. *'Oh Judas,'* she'd groan as I'd grope her mouldy vaginal meat. A mighty delicious feast of a woman she was! I'd unclog that fat hole and smother her wild hermit pubes in morning cumshine, all before the boys yawned from their little rooms. And I wouldn't need an alarm clock for that.

'Breakfast starts at 5:30—finishes at 6:30. The academy van comes to collect you boys at 6:45 sharp.'

'Understood.'

'And no girls in the house, Mister Nobody!' she flatly stated while hyperventilating back down the staircase.

A few lads whispered loudly on the ground floor. 'He don't give a damn,' said one. 'It's a joke! He's from this town and he's living here at the hotel—pisstake!' joined another.

I seemed to always attract the immigrants, being one myself in a peculiar way. Yet this foreign mob spoke too privileged for my liking.

We made it through a cold winter. I kept myself locked in my room. Uninterested in who came top of the league or what star player had been transferred to which team, or when game seasons stopped and started, or the score in the World Cup Final back in the sixties—irrelevant horseshit. These boys could talk a load of championship drivel yet still be average on the pitch. What was I? I was a pretender, that's what, trying to figure what was really going on here. Some sort of cowardly spy watching it all pass, humans rushing about the streets calling out todays news like it was all coming to an end, putting everybody into a spin.

Later that day, following another toe-crushing marathon, the whole team was summoned to the media room for a random drug test.

Acting quick, I coughed up my last wrap of speed into my rectum, a handy takeaway from issue 24 of *True Crime, Smugglers Paradise.*

The coach appeared looking flat and annoyed, calmly informing the team we were each about to receive a standardised drug test and to meet him on the field straight after for an hour of ball work. But before he left, he stated that anyone who failed the test will be dismissed from the grounds immediately and out of the academy for good.

Sat at the rear of the boardroom my chair received the full weight of my problem, arms folded. A few cheerleaders sniggered, seeming to already know my future.

'Nice knowing you, *Judas,*' joked a puny kid called Elmore. All I could produce was a scrappy grin, butt clenched, thoughts on how this humiliating saga was about to pan out. I'd walk pass Elmore and his employee-of-the-month mug to collect my kit and drag my feet out the gate, plotting revenge. Although secretly, I admired their passion. This was it for them—this was it.

'Okay, first three rows, please come with me,' instructed a bald-headed chap from the doping body, clasping a white clipboard. Within minutes my peers are back in the room, laughing between themselves, confident, smug. The next row stood up and returned in the same manner. Then the next. Next. Next row. Next. Leaving me and one other backrow suspect, ready for the boot. Then the coach returned after being absent the whole time, announces the regulator did not bring enough test packets.

'He'll return later in the day to complete the final tests,' he said.

I stood up, held my bumcheeks together and shuffled along quietly to the toilet. And the little bald man and his clipboard never returned.

36

Saturday night. I dragged some of the boys away from the hotel to a nightclub on Union Street for a tipple. We were warned by the academy to watch out for lipstick-ladies on the lookout for fresh-faced athletes. They even made us watch some VHS tape on how such girls work a room. The problem was . . . all the actresses in the educational presentation were dressed up like porn stars, huge tits squeezed inside PVC outfits. I was seventeen scribbling notes.

Heading straight for the bar, I quickly bought a round of Jim Beam. Big Bob from Penzance, who could grow stubble in the time it took to finish a pint, waved over a pretty girl and her tipsy friend from the other end of the bar.

By eleven we're sidestepping puddles of beer. A few songs more and we're spitting against each other's cheek above the music, trying to express how much we hated each song. Stumbling back to the bar alone, I took two more shots, pouring both into my beer and knocking the mix back.

The barman kept an eye. 'One more?' he asked.

I climbed on a stool and held my glass aloft. 'Make it two,' I said.

Elmore appeared by my side. Some people you just won't get on with, ever. 'Be prepared for Monday. And don't be late, Judas.'

'You're a funny boy, Elmore,' I said, knocking back the shot.

'I'm not joking,' the slaphead answered.

I swiveled on my stool and faced him. 'Well then, you're a natural comedian. A very funny boy,' I said, patting the kid on the head before swivelling again, signalling to the barman.

Elmore snarled over my shoulder. 'Touch me again and I'll . . . '

I put a cigarette in my mouth. 'You'll do what, Tinkerbell?'

He straightened up. 'Fuck you, Judas. You don't deserve a place on the squad. You don't wannit as much as us boys. It's wasted on you. You fink you're sommink special.'

I thanked the barman. 'I've zero interest in being special.'

'Special is earned, you think you were *born* special.'

'Not now, Elmore. Get yourself home. There's a good chap.'

'I was going home.'

I lit the cigarette and took the shot. 'Good. Go. Sleep.'

'You sleep!' he snapped back before turning for the exit.

I spun on the stool again, twirling round with my Sambuca held high. 'I'll be sure to call you before bedtime, sugarplum!'

Bob could drink. He was good company. A happy drunk. Elmore and the gang had left. The two girls hung around. They liked me and Bob. I chatted to one called Juliet, whose family originated from old Cyprus. She had big, flowy brown hair and large brown eyes with a round sweet face, a young *Monlaur*, and said things straighter than I'd heard any girl talk. It was new to me. I found it very attractive. Bob got close to her pal Daisy, keeping his tongue busy down her throat.

Then the music cut out and the lights stung our eyes.

'Time to leave!' barked the doormen. 'Shows over, folks!'

Bob hoisted Daisy over his shoulder. They both laughed. Bob laughed like an inpatient. His whole body chugged, his ears, his big docile chin. Daisy clutched hold her dress and kicked her feet as Bob carried her away. Her underwear was pink, like the dress. One doorman asked Bob to put her down. But King Kong continued walking and laughing with his girl slung over his shoulder while Juliet and I strolled out behind, tipsy and in fine spirits.

'Taxi!' yelled the big fella, placing his prize down to the kerb before wandering drunkenly into 2 AM traffic. Daisy's teeth rattled, holding tight her little pink bag while keeping up that smile for her man.

Meanwhile, my chick slipped off her shoes. 'I'm not going to have sex with you tonight,' she wanted me to know.

'Okay,' I said.

'I don't do it on the first night.'

'Fine by me.'

She paused. 'You don't care?'

'Not really.'

She picked up her shoes. 'Boys normally care.'

'Girls do too.'

She paused again with a curious look. 'Where do you live?'

I pointed east.

'Me too! Fancy a stroll, Judas? What kinda name is Judas, anyhow?'

'A well-suited one.'

I had a word with Bob. Juliet chatted to Daisy. When we rejoined she was blowing cold air up to the stars, pointing out astrological animals.

We walked, sharing a wrap of piping hot chips. 'What do you want from life, Judas?' she asked me.

Like a flash I recalled something I had read: 'If you come out the other end with your humour still intact, give the Devil his dues.'

'You're weird,' she said.

'Well maybe you should lighten up your questions.'

'I want to be a muse. I think that's what I want from life.'

We continued walking. 'How do you become a muse?' I asked.

'I don't know. I think Camille Claudel lived with passion! She was a sculptor. I think sculpting is the most beautiful artform, don't you?'

I put a hot chip in my gob. 'Right, you're a romantic.'

She spun on her heel. 'And she was! But her life was also pretty tragic. But I think that's just part of art, of being an artist.'

'Maybe.'

'You don't think so?'

I pinched another chip. 'We each have our own tragedies.'

Juliet fell silent. And then said, 'Maybe what is tragic is a gift.'

I scoffed three chips at once. 'A gift from who?'

'Camille spent half her life in an asylum when she wasn't ill.'

I reached for the ketchup. 'I understand she was dealt a shoddy hand. Though living in a nuthouse may have its upside.'

Juliet snatched the chips away, eyes fully on mine. 'You don't think being declared a crazy person when you're an artist is tragic?'

I shrugged while chewing.

'What's *wrong* with you?' she said wryly, stuffing two chips in her gob before clasping back my arm and continuing to walk.

'I think Crazy is a slippery word,' I said, 'like Love and Happy. She's told she's crazy. Okay. So what? There're worse things that could be suggested, words you could pin down, like Devious and Cheap.'

'Oh, so you think being an artist and being crazy are the same?'

I swiped a dollop of red sauce. 'I think you try too hard to be a muse,' I said.

'I'm also thinking of opening a flower shop.'

'Sounds good. I live down this street.'

My walking companion gushed. 'So do I!' she said.

Her house was chalk white with a Mediterranean-blue door. 'Home from home,' she told me. I kissed her cheek and staggered back up the street to the hotel and masturbated before sleep.

The next day we sat on the church green. 'What do you think the pastor does when no one's in there?' she asked.

'Gives his crucifix a polish?'

Not sharing the funny, she led us to the church to peer inside. The pastor was collecting Bibles. 'This is stupid,' I whispered.

'What?' she whispered back.

'He's just some guy in uniform, doing his job.'

We walked back to the green and sat down. Juliette removed my hand from her breast.

The following Sunday she led me down our street, stopping short of her house. 'Don't worry,' she assured me. 'It'll be fine.' Her old lady stared at me. I stared back. She was very short and quiet and spoke mainly in Greek. Her home was full of colour and life and fresh fruit. She made a pot of chamomile tea and sat with us and spoke with me through Juliet. It was sweet and it was simple.

Later on that evening, I escaped the guys sat watching football and instead chose to run the mile and a half to Dion's across town to score some speed, returning to the academy hotel before curfew.

Pulling my ear away from the door, I stashed the toot and turned off the bedside lamp, lay down, looked up at the evening sky, and allowed my eyes to close by themselves.

Then a stone rattled me. Followed by another. Peering down onto the pavement, I see Juliet there alone glowing beneath the streetlamp like an angel, looking as pretty as ever.

Wasting no time, I reached beneath the bed for my stash and dropped several crumbs on my tongue, forcing the stuff down with dry spit. Following which I plumped my pillows and straightened my bed, and doused the air with Old Spice.

The staircase creaked as I made my way to the ground floor. Reaching outside, I shushed my girl from her burst of excitement before pulling her inside. We both closed the door together as though we had spent our entire lives mastering the cogs of its mechanics, waiting until spring. Ignoring then the wide grins pointing at us from the boys, we quietly made our way up to the penthouse.

Juliet sat on my bed, keeping her eyes fixed on the moon.

'Beautiful view,' said she. I heard her fine yet my attention was mustering the usefulness of speed beneath the sheets, an all-night fuck monster was the motive, to give this girl what all girls wanted.

As we slid off our clothes, a sour, putrid odour fell over the air.

'Wait Judas,' she whispered before completely undressing. 'Turn off the lamp.'

With that I rolled and switched the thing off, leaving a dim glow from the streetlamp outside to hang over us. Secretly I worked my hand along my shaft, resuscitating the shrinkage caused by the amphetamine. A minor obstacle, I assured myself, soon forcing an erection as she fed me her tongue. She then stopped my hand from wandering, drawing her tongue away in some sort of reconsideration.

'I have something to show you,' her voice said in the dark.

I nodded while trying to unbuckle her bra. She helped the bra off and carried my hand to her chest and we both held a beautiful, full breast together. We rubbed and explored the beautiful breast, her nipple perky and cold to a tremble—a circular ring of raised trembling bumps that I petted between her fingertips. And the odour of something nauseating, something malodorous and foul always there growing stronger. She then took our hands again, sloping away from the beautiful breast and over wrinkly loose skin. A patch of her body where the second breast should be. 'It never came to be,' the voice spoke gently in the dark. She then pulled away a gel mould formed inside the left cup of her bra and placed it in my hand.

I was both turned on and repulsed, beginning to lick the loose, nippleless skin with a burn of filth and pleasure. And the blood rushed, and I grew rock hard, turned on by what was not desirable. I was animal and tender and heated with curiosity. And her head pressed the pillow and her eyes watched the ceiling, my hands caressing the one good tit and nipple and skin, my lips running along her ample pale hips, petting her plump buttocks. And the smell intensifying, making me more and more repulsed. And I found and faced the source of the odour, yet my hunger to do as I pleased took over any disgust as I licked her putrid pussy with depraved hungry enjoyment of the flesh, groping her one beautiful breast and rubbing the loose monstrous skin until she moaned and squeezed my hands to a stop.

'Put it in,' she gasped in the dark. 'Please, Judas, *put it in . . .*'

37

The final week of the academy. I was glad I'd made it this far. Two tough fucking years. Monday. Boiling hot. The mood strange about camp—strangers among ourselves upon our final week where only a handful are chosen from twenty-four boys to join the big league.

Following the last minute of pressups I headed to the showers. The room thick with steam. Thirty or so players, from juniors to seniors, looked remotely about a tired and bleak wetroom.

Handing myself a few more inches with several cock-strokes, enough to appear average, a soft-mannered, tiny-footed kid from Japan, passing through the southwest trying his talent, flip-flopped his way between two changing rooms to the shower with a towel flung freely over his little Japanese shoulder, unabashed by the head of his teeny brown penis nestled deep inside a moth of perfectly straight, black pubic hair. He pinned his towel to the wall, gave a crooked smile to the guy to his left, and fired up the hose.

Behind him came Patrick, an even shorter but more muscular black guy from Trinidad. We all wondered how Patrick's wife managed with that thing. He always wore a permanent grin, and didn't mind the fellas making fun as his Caribbean meat swung and crashed against each thigh. Today I was pleased the Japanese kid showered close to me.

'You've all done well. You should be very proud of yourselves,' upped the coach strolling through. 'If you get everything cleaned by five you can all go, I'll see you in the morning, seven sharp!'

One junior cranked up the radio, while Elmore got to work on his future with the seniors like he'd already made it.

'Did you hear about Umberto?' I got asked in the lockers.

I hadn't a clue who that was. 'Umberto?'

Elmore piped in, catching what I'd said. 'Jesus, Nobody!'

I watched on as their mouths spilled forth the same talk, as though they were one organism with three exact tentacles.

Folding my towel into my duffle bag I escaped into the afternoon sun, strolling across the gravelled carpark feeling pretty good that the end of the academy was near. I moved down the lane alongside the stadium and over the fields to collect some training cones, stopping to say hi to Sully, a kid who didn't make the senior squad last year, so instead convinced the groundsman to take him on as an apprentice because he just loved the shit out of anything related to the game. He spun the wheel of his lawnmower, breaking a foot away with a cowboy grin and green fire in his eyes. We both admire the job he'd done, the field looked good. I congratulated him and walked on.

As I continued, a bunch of kids yelled from behind a fence waving paper and pens with desperate little pink faces. They called me over, asking all sorts of questions, little doting fans of the sport rather than playing their way out of a hopeless situation. I scribbled on their little white pads, mentioned *Umberto*, and watched their tiny mechanical eyes light up before continuing on.

Once at the top of the field I admired the view, took a whiff of the shrubs. As I looked up, a flock of starlings whizzed overhead, with one flying loose behind, trying to keep busy. I willed the little fella on as the flock twisted and turned, flew up then down, the single bird exhausting its little wings, trying to determine which way the flock would fly next. After many failed attempts, the bird eventually swung a lucky left and hit the centre of a seperate flock nearby, fluttering away with his new pals.

I took my time picking up cones, thinking small things, threw a net over my shoulder and headed back down the field.

38

The final day of the academy arrived. The changing room was spotless. Glancing about at all the faces looking at each other, I stay stood with my duffle bag over my shoulder.

'Seven-thirty!' shouted the assistant. 'You'll eached be called to his office one atta time! *One atta time!*'

This is it, I think. Placing my bag in the corner I climbed the wooden staircase to his office, meeting the coach's name in the small metal slider fixed to the door. 'Bobby 'Magic' Tompson'.

'Come in!'

Twisting the brass doorknob, my head slid in first.

'Hey coach.'

'Judas! You're keen, son. We start at seven-thirty.'

'I know. Could I have a quick word?'

'Of course!' he booted, shuffling paper to his drawer. 'Take a pew.'

I sat down and kept my nerve, good eye contact.

'I had a feeling,' he said, tutting to himself. His shelves toppled with championship medals and winner's trophies, with framed pictures of his young son holding a ball donning *the kit*.

'Well, I appreciate you telling me now, lad.' His blue eyes studied mine with suspicion, waiting for the doubt, the change.

'Thanks for everything, coach, I appreciate it.'

'Okay,' he sighed, falling back in his chair. 'If it's what you want.'

Feeling both relieved and shit scared, I stood up and made my way back down the staircase. Most of the lads looked on speechless. I kept it short, and wished them all good luck.

The extent of my decision fell from me like a heavy weight as I ambled between the carpark and through the stadium gate for the last time. The path before me seemed far, endless.

Closing the door I stepped into my house to break the news to my mother. Though the coach had made a call and was on his way.

'It's fine, Muh. I know what I'm doing.'

'Are you sure, son?'

'Yes. Yes I am.'

Bobby Tompson's car heckled outside. He knocked. Took a seat.

'Now look 'ere, lad, you can buy yow poor mother a house, get out of this damn neighbourhood! Do you understand?'

I kept my eyes low.

'You've gotta fortunate career ahead of you if you wan'tit. You juss gotta wan'tit! This club is only the start fah yow, lad.'

I lifted my eyes. 'Thanks again, coach, but it ain't for me.'

'*Now you listen 'ere, sonny*, this is yow life we're talkin—I've seen many a lad waste his talent . . . too many! This club is juss the beginning fah yow. Last chance, me boy, ah won't beg.'

I was empty, a good empty, a fine feeling. 'Thanks, but I'll pass.'

He jumped out his seat and shook my hand. 'Well, it's sad, but alright then, *all right*. Good luck, son.'

My mother and I watched as he climbed into his Jaguar.

'So what now, Judas?' she asked.

'I'll figure it out,' I said. 'I'll figure it out . . .'

It was a day of getting things in order. The afternoon mood was small, easy. I packed my things and got out the academy hotel before the apprentices returned, thanking Maureen for the room.

'No problem, Judas. And good luck with everything.'

'Yeah, you too, Maureen.'

Swinging a left out the guest house, the plastic wheels of my cheap suitcase jumped over the cracked pavement. A car roared close behind. The driver punched the brakes. I glanced over at a shiny SUV. Out jumped a senior player, Joey Dion, leaving the engine rumbling in the middle of the street and the door flung open with loud hiphop music tumbling out like a small rebel army. Joey was a popular player on and off the field, a boisterous display of championship material, a Londoner, with a short afro, one gold tooth, and bags of cockney charm—recently out on bail for a kidnapping while in possession of a Colt Combat replica and a ten-inch cleaver. As he approached, a slim, sheltered looking fella froze nearby with undecided fear in his eyes, hurrying on when he realised the incoming spectacle was for me. A taxi slammed his horn behind Joey's Range Rover. Joey stepped to the cabbie, offering a few choice words before calmly making his way back to me.

'You're wasting your time, Joe,' I said.

'See my motor?' he riled up. 'You can have one next week with your new salary. Full leathers an' all. It's alright, this club, you'll get used to it. You juss gotta play the game, nah whot I mean? Don't mess this up, fella. We're from the same neck of the woods, you an' me. C'mon, hop in, I'll drive you back to the stadium.' He walked. I stayed put. He cursed and threw up his arms. He looked at me then at my cheap suitcase. The taxi slammed his horn again. More cars stopped along the street, lining up like raffle tickets.

'Alright, Judas,' Joey finally said. 'Be lucky!' With that, he climbed back into his sixty-thousand-pound motor and sped off.

Walking along some more street I meet Juliet talking with a guy at her doorstep. I knew he was the one who was with her before me. You could tell by the distance he kept. He told me he loved her, he'd always loved her. He was mad but gentle, mad at himself. I saw the heartsick stooge was trying to make things good again and that she still admired the poor sap. I wished them both well and went on my way.

39

It had been raining nonstop. The sky was grey. And the cars locked together along the road gave the impression of a mechanical serpent, corroding the surface of the earth. I fed the handle of my broom down my boot and gave the top of my foot a scratch.

It was a muggy Saturday morning. The air stunk of grit. I dug into my pocket and pulled out a rollie, put aside the broom and pitched myself under a tree.

Pinching the rollie between my lips I traced my pockets for a light. As I glanced up, I caught sight the supervisor wagging his head and flapping his hands, opening and closing his mouth like a fish out of luck. I shot my hand up and stuck the rollie back in my pocket, glancing up at that sky.

I'd been up since the crack of dawn, made my old lady a Tetley's when she got in from work, walked the twenty minutes to the petrol station, and said 'alright mate' to the supervisor, before slipping on a yellow Mac and rubber boots. My new boss unlocked the utility shed and grabbed a hard brush, sending me to work scouring spilt petrol from filling stations. There were queues, as far as the eye could spot. I kept a lookout for spillages, watching folk and other things too. Life, passing along, doing its thing. The rain eased up and the clouds soon moved away. The roof of the station was black with smut. I wondered if anyone would recognise me beneath this oversized, banana-yellow Mac with a loping yellow hood. I rehearsed what I'd say—I'd have a minute to twist some bullshit before some customer got cheesed off waiting, punching their horns to get a move on. Life was good.

The supervisor came and had a word, told me to go slower.

'You've got the job, Judas,' he said. 'Now please, *take it easy.*'

I lifted the broom and wiped my brow. 'Alright mate,' I said.

The sun began to dry everything up, the leaves, the road, the air. When I arrived back home I tossed my bag aside, crumbled up several leftover roaches from my ashtray into a single paper, and stashed the secondhand smoke for later. My mother was thumping about the house like a banshee, getting on my back as she was lately. Hesitating to eat for the first time, I made my way to the kitchen to put together a sandwich. Things had changed.

'I'm going church tomorrow,' she starts up. 'You should come.'

'No.'

'Pastor Tom said he would like to speak with you.'

'Why?'

'I don't know, Judas! He just said so . . . '

'What have you said?'

'I haven't said anything!'

'Not now, Mum.'

'You're still under my roof!' she yelled. With that reminder, she stomped her feet up the stairs, nagging all the way to her room.

The food I was about to consume suddenly held consequences, so I placed the bread and butter, ham and that juicy ripe tomato back in the fridge, counted some copper, and took myself to the shop, purchasing cheap porridge and a carton of milk, enough till payday.

'We have porridge! There's lots of porridge!'

I dug a spoon into the slop. 'I prefer this one.'

'You're doing this on purpose, I know! I KNOW!'

I forced down another spoonful. 'You're imagining it.'

'We have porridge! The one you like!'

I stopped eating. 'Listen, I'm not getting much right now, but I can put a hundred toward bills each month till I find something decent.'

She calmed down. 'I didn't say I wanted your money.'

I pushed the slop to one side. 'It's simpler this way,' I said.

The postman managed a few letters through the letterbox. I tailed after him, asked if they were hiring. 'We're always hiring!'

A few weeks went by. I came home from scrubbing oil to another church meeting, a weekly run of hallelujah's at our house.

The pastor jumped up. 'Hello, Judas me boy!'

I said hi to everyone from the livingroom door. My mother looked at them as they all faced me. All I see are big corny smiles, like walls of a dental clinic. 'How's church life?' I asked the pastor. Pastor Tom was a pint-sized, pigeon-toed fellow, with beady eyes and elfin ears. His hair was a receding grey mop, his voice an eclipsing, high pitched, almost comediclike cackle—Paul Daniels on the pulpit.

'Oh, Jesus is GLORIOUS!' he howled with a punching fist.

'Right,' I said. 'Well, that's good news. Everyone okay for tea?'

They all picked up my mother's finest knockoff China and sipped.

'Muh? Another Tetley in your lovely cup?'

'No,' she answered, raising an eyebrow to the pastor.

'Oh! Hey! Judas! I don't ever see you at church, young man. I think your mother here would like that very much,' he said. Taking his cup and saucer from the coffeetable, he took the teaspoon and squidged the teabag, tapping the cup three times like some Saturday-night magician. He then wondered where to place the spoon while everyone watched, slipping it back on the saucer with theatrical glee. '*There we go*,' he sighed.

'Church, yeah, *well* . . . maybe next week,' I lied.

'Ohhh, Glory be to God! A-men to that.'

'AMEN!' chorused his congregation.

My mother looked sheepish. She tried joining them, but couldn't. Not in my presence. Her lips moved a little but nothing occurred. I raised an eyebrow at her. Made a comical face. The traitor kept it straight.

Pastor Tom continued muttering to himself while wiping his brow with his handkerchief. 'The Mighty Lord is good, *oh yes.*'

A young lady with beautiful emerald eyes and a Mormon bust looked nervous, keeping her tea close to her chest, her spine upright.

'Okay,' I said, 'I'll leave you all with the Big Guy.'

Slipping open the fridge I took my last slice of bread, dipped my knife into her butter, stole a spread of jam and retreated to my room.

Fingering out some new porn, I flipped the pages and went to work, catching a moment of feel-good.

Stuffing a towel along the foot of the door and firing up the smoke I'd made earlier, I tuned the radio to the shipping forecast.

'Same time tomorrow! *Glory! Glory!*' roared the pastor outside.

'Glory be to God!' followed the congregation.

I peered onto the troupe from my window as they made it to their cars, performing worthless nods and plastic laughter. Keeping an eye on the young girl with heaven's breasts made me want to jerk off again. I wanted to caress those devotional cups more than any in my magazines.

They all waved when they caught me watching.

'Bye, Judas! God be with you!'

'Goodbye, Judas! God bless!'

The pretty one then called out, 'See you at church!'

'So you're coming to church?' my mother asked.

I sat down with another slop of porridge. 'Nope.'

'Judas, please . . .'

'I'm gonna stay with Esther for a while.'

The next day I packed a bag and went to stay with my crazy eldest sister, Esther.

40

Esther swung open the door. She lived in a large house in Saint Judes with her partner, Big Henry, and their kid, little Henry Jnr. She told me to hurry in, glancing up and down the street like a crackhead before pushing the door shut.

'You never know who's watching,' she said. 'Cops are everywhere!'

'And so they should be,' I said. 'Riding unicycles along tightropes.'

She paused, gave me an odd look. 'You don't mind the couch?'

'I could sleep in a doorway.'

'Mum driving you insane?'

I put my bag down. 'It's Jesus I'm worried for.'

Esther's skin was dark as a midnight train, her eyes white as salt. She could've been a champion runner, a finely groomed prize-fighter, an athletic dynamite of a girl, somewhere to pour all that aggression. But instead she chose to stop cars as a fille de joie at age fourteen, a beautiful black prostitute swinging her adolescent curves along Hooker Lane. She was sharp-witted, a wily street cat, and all the men all over town wanted a piece of the exotic. But Henry muscled in first, raised her from the kerb elevating my sister to a fully bloomed Madam, building by hand for his lady a modest house and a bustling busy brothel.

'I heard things didn't go to plan in Egypt,' I said.

'Don't get me started! We've given away the three monkeys. Bad omen—*evil*.' She then whispered as if the spirits were listening, 'That old toothless hag tried putting a curse on me!'

Soon after she yammered to a parrot in his cage, who squawked back, tapping his little claws.

'He keeps plucking his feathers, poor boy,' she tells me as we walk to the kitchen. 'They don't like to be left alone. They get depressed.'

'He sleeps in the front room?'

'You don't mind?'

'Not at all.'

'So,' she said, continuing to explain her time in Egypt, 'they thought I was the reincarnation of Nefertiti! If it wasn't for Henry and the men looking after us with rifles, I don't know what they would've done.'

Three Egyptian desert crooks took off on camels with Esther along the dunes of Cairo beneath a blazing hot sun, yelling, '*Allahu Akbar!*' She screamed and screamed and kicked the camel. Once caught, the dusthill mob confessed immediately, swearing she was who they believed. 'Nefertiti has returned!'

Esther brewed us a cuppa while informing me how the house operated. 'Henry's up at five every morning. And expects us all up.'

Out the back window a giant tortoise was chewing lettuce.

'You've got a giant tortoise in your garden,' I said.

'That's Tommy the Tortoise, for little Henry. He did a runner last week, made it all the way down the back lane. Gone the whole bloody day. Poor Henry was so upset. We found him hiding under a bin. Imagine putting out your rubbish and seeing a giant tortoise?'

'Old Noah would lose his damn mind.'

She paused again. 'Judas, you speak funny.'

The door swung open and little Henry came crashing through, leaping toward me. I scooped him up. 'Uncle Judas!' he cried.

'Go play in the other room, sweetheart, grownups are speaking. Uncle Judas'll play later.'

I dropped the kid and the little sprog vanished. I then sat on a stool and listened to whatever leapt from Esther's head.

Henry Snr soon walked in. As always, since I recall, he'd been as big as a door, with a square chin and shifty blue eyes, hands two swinging clubs with a cunning mind.

'Judas!' he cheered, tossing me a beer.

Henry sucked joints from sunrise till sunset, and they were wet, sodden with anxious spit, always stuck to his lip, like a toothpick.

He immediately lists jobs to do, things to get on with each day, earn my keep. He talked me through the list as we footed to a building site stacked with bags of cement.

He took the joint from his lip. 'We gotta plaster all this 'ere,' he said, sweeping his hand across two large sections of brick. 'And then I'll get you to tile all these 'ere walls.'

I shrugged. 'No problem.'

He clapped my shoulder with his big spade of a hand. 'Don't look so worried, me boy! I'll teach ya. While you get on with that, I'll be building extra rooms at the back of the house for the girls. Bleedin crazy the punters turning up for a bit of rump. Lawyers, politicians, doctors, *coppers*, you name it, they all flock here. Corrupt bastards.'

'Coppers?'

'Ask your sister!' he said. 'We got the constable of police 'ere once. We made sure to get the toerag on VHS with two of the girls spanking his little rosy bumcheeks. That'll come in handy if ever we need it. Anyway mate, welcome aboard, we start work tomorrow at six.'

41

The next morning I faintly hear Henry treading about the kitchen, getting on with tasks. His lighter cranked every minute. The kettle whistled. Then in stepped little Henry. *'Uncle Judas?'* he said quietly, padding his tiny slippers and balancing a chewed-up dinosaur on my pillow.

I jumped up. 'ROAR!' I yelled. The little munchkin dashed out the room. I slipped back beneath the duvet. The door creaked, little feet padding, the undecided giggles.

'ROAR!' I booted again, sending the kid off like a firecracker.

Esther came down the stairs, shushing Jnr's laughter.

'Uncle Judas is sleeping,' she told the kid.

Hearing this I got straight up and slipped on my jeans, buttoned a shirt, clawed crust from my eyes and pushed a window, balled up the duvet and re-shaped the sofa with a few one-twos.

'Morning,' I said, stepping into the kitchen.

'You're up early!' said Esther.

I winked at Jnr. 'Been up for a while.'

'Lemme grab you a towel,' she says as I dangle the kid upside-down. She handed me a towel. I dropped the kid and walked up the stairs. Before reaching the bathroom I paused at a door, listened for voices below, before pushing it open. And there it was: leather straps pinned to the wall, with carnivallike masks and every possible length and colour dildo stacked on a table beside a big white adult-sized cot with man-sized nappies and bottles of baby oil.

I shut the door quietly and took a shower.

'Just one scrape along the wall like this,' motioned Henry. 'Keep it neat as you can.'

'Got it.'

'Good. Now fancy a bevvy while you work?' he asked, already spading his pockets for loose change.

'They sell beer this early?'

'Get whatever you want once they're open—'ere you go, boy, get us a couple cheap cans for breakfast.'

The local shop was a two-minute walk.

'Judas Nobody!' screamed the shopkeeper, my old dinner lady from Mount Street, Ms Chomsky. 'Look at you! You've grown!'

I picked her up. Her hair was still overgrown and wiry, with rows of lofty yellow teeth, a large nose and a stubbly chin.

'Still married?' I asked her, placing her back down.

'Hah! Nuthin's changed, eh? You been asking me that since you were in Year Two!' She fixed her hair. 'I hear you're a big football star.'

'Not anymore. Got out in the nick of time.'

'Well that's a right shame,' she smiled dimly. 'Wait till I tell my Graham I saw you.'

'Say hello from me, will you?'

'Oh, I will, I will. So, what you doin round 'ere, mister?'

'Staying with my sister for a while.'

'Well, that's nice, that's nice, well ain't that nice . . .'

We smiled at each other. It was just after 9 AM. I noticed again her wedding ring just as I did as a kid, when I would drop my last twenty pence in the tuckbox and recieve an extra Wham Bar or Curly Wurly, thinking how kind she was.

The shop doorbell chimed.

'Morning, Mr Fletcher!' An old gent with a dapper brass cane poled the door open and gave Ms Chomsky a salut.

'Morning love,' the old timer grunted, examining my presence from the edge of his spectacles.

'Gimme a sec, Judas.'

Chomsky got on gathering bits, carrying them back to the counter, pricing and stacking the items neatly into a brown paper bag.

'Thanks, love,' said old Fletcher. His polished shoes and finely creased trousers were immaculate, with a shiny chain-watch dangling from his blazer pocket, and a pair of gold links fastening the cuffs of a perfectly pressed white shirt, just like my old man.

'See you tomorrow at nine!' he commanded, using his cane to yank open the door.

'He's a smart-looking chap,' I said.

'Mr Fletcher? Oh yeah,' she said. 'Only ever leaves his house to come 'ere or walk to the post box. Always dresses the same,' she went on, nodding her head as Fletcher marched past the window. 'Six eggs, rye, a pack of plain digestives, bunch of ripe bananas and a pint of skimmed milk. Never changes—unless he's out of teabags or sugar, or if he fancies himself a bit of jam pudding.' She stopped daydreaming and turned to me. 'Anyway, Judas my precious, what can I do you for?'

I opened up a fistful of coins like a cheap magician.

'Two cans of beer?'

'Oh, nice 'n early then, eh?'

'Just helping out with some building work.'

'Don't you dare explain yourself. How much you got, lovey?'

I made a quick count. 'Two pounds and ten pence.'

She turned to the booze. 'Right then, Red Stripe?'

I shrugged. 'That'll do.'

42

By midday I'd tiled two walls and finished four beers. I was a tiler. I liked tiling, working the hands, just me and the thing, the thing becoming some other thing.

The sun had come out. With the two Henry's stalking the tortoise in the garden, Esther said to me, 'Let's give you a tour of Paradise.'

We jumped in her car and drove ten minutes to the East End. Esther tightened her lips and raised her chin, drained her eyes of pity and humour, stretched out the spine, shoulders back, the Mistress, the Madam. She swung open the door to Paradise. Sat there looking bored on a cream couch in what seemed to be the reception were three pretty girls: one Filipino, I was told, the other two local. They all wore long gowns that brushed over the thick white carpet. I didn't know what to make of it. I was excited and terrified.

'Girls, this is my little brother, Judas.'

Two sprung up together, calling me to sit.

'Just put it at the back for now,' pointed Esther. I dropped the box in a side cupboard.

Esther then asked me, 'Judas, you don't mind if I leave you here till about two-thirty? I've got a quick errand, that okay?'

'Sure,' I told her, making eye contact with the brown-skinned girl. She was slender, childlike small, and wore excessive red lipstick, springing wonderful images to mind. She put on a smile and held it to please Esther, I could tell, I recognised performance.

'Look after him you lot. Turn that bloody radio down. And give me a call if you need anything.' She then turned to me. 'Judas, if any punters turn up, just make sure you're out of sight.'

'No problem.'

'It's by appointment only so no one should just knock out the blue. But don't answer if someone does. Might be old bill.'

'Got it.'

'He'll be fine,' said the blonde.

Esther stuck her manicured nail under the blonde's nose. 'I know he'll be fine, cheeky. Now back to work!'

As soon as Esther started up her car and drove away I sat down and wondered if this was a setup—if Esther and Henry were watching me on camera. It was something they'd do, it's how they invested their time: watching people.

With my sister gone the Filipino, Jaslene, footed over to me and lowered her buttocks and put her small hand on my leg as I looked about the parlour for hidden cameras. The blonde, who called herself Ellie, walked to the kettle and switched it on. 'Tea?'

'Thanks, please.'

The third 'masseuse' remained on the couch opposite me with legs together and a book on lap. Her name is Daria.

'You like?' asked Jaslene, a dozen pearls brimming between her lips.

'Yes. I do.'

'Tea!' Ellie placed my cup on a side table. 'It's hot,' she tells me, before jumping on the tip of her pink toenails, her bleached yellow hair lapping over one shoulder and her plump lips grinning with confidence. She spun around, performed a little pirouette, and teased her gown apart, her bumcheeks suspending like a drunken heart. It was magnificent. The first pornographic ass I'd seen up close and for real. Her red thong was wedged up real high. By now I was certain it was a setup, scanning the room once more for cameras.

Jaslene continued rubbing my leg. *'You like, huh? You like?'*

'Yes,' I said. 'Yes I do.'

'You can touch if you want?' Ellie offered. I couldn't tell her age, mid-twenties maybe.

'Alright,' I said. Her buttocks were smooth and tender. Grabbing hold of one cheek, then the other, I lifted them apart. As I did more of the thong came away, releasing white sprinkle-dust into the air.

Jaslene patted the cheeks like bongos. The tiny Asian girl then slid her hand a little farther inside my leg, an inch from my cock. She was about fortyish, give or take, you could see it in the eyes, the only part of her that couldn't cheat. I was told she had kids back in the Philippines and was trying to smuggle them over, start a new life—that she was in a bad state when she arrived to Paradise, escaping a Chinese gang who brutalised their hookers and kept them always high and docile.

Then the phone rang.

Ellie quickly fixed her gown and took the call. Her voice changed. I think she's in charge. Jaslene snatched her hand from my crotch and faced Ellie with a pensive look.

'Okay, let me just check our diary,' spoke Ellie, flicking through a leafy notepad.

Daria was a chubby girl, much larger than the other two. Her skin was blotchy and pale, her lips English thin, almost non-existent, and she wasn't wearing any makeup that I could tell. She lifted her green eyes from the book she was reading and dogeared the page. I started to feel nauseous with all the stink of talcum powder and perfume and cheap air freshener. Peering down at Jaslene's feet, her little webbed monkey-toes wiggled like fingers.

Ellie put the phone down and foots it back.

'So, Mr S wants Jaslene at five for one hour,' she said. 'It'll be the usual. But be sure to bruise him this time. He wants it *rough*. You got that, Jas. RUFF!' Jaslene agreed. Ellie continued: 'Mr P our twelve-thirty will be here soon. We should get ready.'

Jaslene licked her teeth and they both left the room. Ellie's head reappeared around the door. 'Judas,' she said, 'you can hide under the reception table when he buzzes. Just make sure you're not seen, babe. The slightest whiff of another man makes them run a mile. And don't worry, we lead the punters straight to the room.'

'Under the table. Got it.'

Ellie smiled and rejoined Jaslene in the back.

'How old are you?' Daria asked me.

'Eighteen.'

'Will you be driving us to jobs?'

'I don't have a license.'

'That's a shame,' she said.

'It is?'

She nodded without explaining.

'How old are you?' I asked her back.

'Twenty-three tomorrow,' she said without any pleasure.

'Right,' I said, glancing up at the ceiling before performing a covert look at her tits and back to her pretty green eyes in one clean move. Daria turned her attention to the telephone while reopening her book.

'You study?' I asked her.

'Circus school, yeah. That's why I'm here, to pay the fee.'

I was surprised. 'Circus school?'

'Clowning, that's right. They were once the philosophers, did you know? Life being an act, one mood to the next.' She became more excited. 'If it wasn't for clowning, I'd be labelled just another fruitcake unable to hold a nine to five.' She sat back. 'Anyway, this job pays the fee.'

'Right,' I said, not expecting a prostitute to be this smart.

She spoke on, 'It's easy money. What my girlfriend makes in a week I pretty much earn in one afternoon.'

'Girlfriend?'

'Yeah . . . well, we broke up a week ago. Third time this month.'

'Right,' I said, reaching for my tea.

'You know those cups are the ones we serve punters?'

I set the mug back down. 'Thanks,' I said.

Ellie strutted back in wearing a tight leather dress and black fishnets, with high heels like screwdrivers, emptying a can of freshener.

'He'll be here soon, Judas. He's always on time. He's a lawyer.'

'Right,' I said, getting up and crawling behind the reception table. The skirting board behind the table had two plug-in pine smellers. My stomach did a flip from all the morning beer.

I whispered to Daria. 'Have I got time to use the toilet?'

'Is it a number one or a number two?'

'.......'

'Well?'

'One, it's a one.'

'Once he's in the room I'll let you know, then you can go pee.'

A minute later the doorbell buzzed.

Daria whispered again, 'Okay, that's him.' She ran to the door.

'*Hello my dear*,' came the sound of Mr P as he entered the parlour.

'Hello, Mr P,' replied Daria. 'Let me take your jacket.'

'Why thank you. Thank you ever so much, my sweety. You look *wonnn*derful as always.'

The door closed. 'Thank you,' Daria said.

'Do you mind if I just make an extremely brief phonecall, dear?'

'Of course not—Shoes?'

'Oh yes,' he sniggered. 'How very rude of me!'

I hear shoes slip off and heavy feet trudge across some carpet, pausing by the couch opposite the reception table where I lay hidden.

'Smells fresh!' he cracked.

'Tea?' asked Daria.

'Oh no, thank you, dear. It'll just take a mo-mo.'

'Sure thing,' she noted.

There was some silence. And then, 'Hello? Katie? Hi, could you please get in touch with *Mr Edwards* right away, he's at the airport and desperately needs to see something in writing before he boards. Can you please do that now—thank you. Yes. Right now. And copy me in. And pleeease be sure to have it *pro*ofed before you send. No mistakes now. See you later. Bye bye.'

Mr P coughed as he stood up. 'I'M READY!'

'Follow me,' said Daria.

I watched a small spider run along the wall until Daria returned.

'Just a few more minutes,' she whispered to me.

'Okay.'

'I won't be here for long,' she continued to whisper.

'What time you leaving?'

'*Nooo* . . . I mean here, *at Paradise*, doing this.'

'Sure, well, that's good, I guess.'

'I've already paid for my clown studies.'

'Well done you.'

'Promise you won't tell your sister.'

'Cross my bones.'

'Thanks. I'm just saving extra cash for my clown outfit.'

Mr P started to cry. I could hear Ellie shouting.

'You can come out now,' said Daria.

I climbed to my feet and stretched my legs.

'You need to take your shoes off. Put them in the cupboard.'

I slipped my shoes in the cupboard and followed Daria to a small makeshift toilet that Henry had built. I bolted the door and pushed my trousers to my ankles and pooped. The smell consumed the room. Clenching my rectum, I hadn't noticed the room had no window, just a small extractor box stuck in the corner that wasn't turning. I spun around and found an air freshener and tssst quietly. The smell worsened: lavender poo. I flushed the toilet. Waited. Flushed it again. Waited a little more and cranked the fucking thing again. In a panic I wiped myself and yanked up my trousers, twisted out the toilet brush from its little fucking holder and beat the bloody toilet bowl like a lunatic. I then got hold some bleach and squeezed half the bottle in there. Christ, it stunk like hell.

Daria looked up from her book as I came back.

'You okay?' she asked me. 'You look nervous.'

'Fine. Everything's fine. What you reading?'

She lifted her hardback for me to read: *The Art of Clowning*.

'Your sister's pretty fair,' she says, resting the book back to her lap. 'I've heard horror stories about other parlours from Jaslene.'

I sat down, hoping the stench hadn't followed me.

'I wouldn't know,' I said.

Mr P stopped crying and instead started whimpering. The little Filipino took over from Ellie, screaming at Mr P to shut his mouth.

'Shut you mouth!' she yelled. 'You have smelly mouth!'

'I'm sorry, Miss! I'm sorry!' the man cried.

Daria went on reading. I picked up a Vogue magazine on a sidetable and flicked the pages. The clock on the wall soon struck ten past one.

'I'd better go hide,' I said.

Daria looked up. 'Yeah,' she said. 'He's about done.'

'I FUCKING KILL YOU PIECE OF SHIT!'

'I'M SORRY, MISS! I'M SORRY!'

'I HATE YOU UGLY FACE! YOU HAVE UGLY FACE!'

43

'A little more gas,' motioned Henry. I gave it more, skimming shopping trolleys and a delivery truck.

'Woah, Judas, me boy!'

Henry grabbed hold the wheel and sailed us toward the exit.

'We're leaving the carpark?' I asked.

'You'll be fine,' he said, taking a swig of his breakfast beer. 'Just keep it steady. Not many cars about this time of morning.'

Exiting the lot, a scrawny kid with big headphones in supermarket uniform crossed the road with his eyes to the floor. I jammed my foot on the brake and stalled the car.

Henry barked out the window, 'Oi! Knobtits! Wake up!'

The kid turned and jerked his fist. With that reckless act, Henry unravelled his seatbelt and rolled himself out the car. 'Stay 'ere, Judas,' he said. Once the kid saw all of Henry he ran away.

The man-mountain fitted himself back in. 'Now, where were we?'

Flipping the ignition I rolled us to the foot of the motorway, and away we go.

'Easy work, eh?' the big man cheered. 'You'll be driving the girls round in no time, make some extra bob.'

We spent each morning at five-thirty wheeling about town in Henry's cigar-brown S-class for an hour. They had two cars. I was keen to drive their Classic 507. That was Esther's. Only she drove that car. Not even Henry was allowed to drive it. He sat in it once, it looked like a toy.

'We need to get some gravel,' he told Esther. 'Back in an hour.'

'Gravel, huh?' she replied with suspicion. 'You come straight back.'

Falcons circled the country fields. The sun was white-hot, everything else blues and greens and long greys of endless road. I heard Henry rummaging through the bins at four in the morning, cursing to himself. He'd scrounged several joint butts and rolled a crusty cigarette, sighing nostalgically. But the dope hit wasn't enough. He was on edge. His face thickened. His breathing heavied, bulllike, his knuckles gripped to the wheel.

'What kind of gravel we getting?' I asked.

'It's all the same,' he said back.

He turned off the radio. Switched it back on. Continually changing the channel for as long it took the traffic to take off. Then out of nowhere an old grey estate cut us off with the driver keeping his fist on the horn, speeding ahead—just a loud, condemning horn and rushing black wheels and blue skies.

Henry threw the car to third. Then forth. He switched to sports mode and took us to fifth, his face a metallic red, eyes two hot coals, fixed on that estate.

The driver glanced at Henry as we sped up alongside pushing eighty miles an hour. Henry glared, calmly mouthing at the fellow, 'HELLO AGAIN, YOU CUNT.'

The driver, a guy in his forties maybe in a cheap navy suit, seemed to be an accountant, a business exec, corporate tax manager, solicitor, inventor of white goods, technology officer, data resource executive, financial advisor, auditing clerk, or very possibly a furniture sales rep, with his tie loose and hair greased to one side. He tossed his eyes between Henry's big stone face and the long hopeless road. Henry signalled the guy to take the next exit by simply pointing to the exit then at the guy. The suited man shook his head like a small child and instead willed to ignore Henry, devoted to that horizon and his escape. Henry signalled again. Yet the clerk refused to acknowledge the big angry man's existence, speeding on.

'That little minx,' Henry muttered.

We struck a hundred miles an hour, smoking past the driver. Henry swung up front and slowed to seventy, wound down his window and clawed into the sack of gravel we'd just bought on the backseat and began delivering stones to this guy's windshield. The driver swerved a swarm of flying pellets. Henry towed it to sixty while fingering another handful, catapulting hard and accurate. I turned to witness the victim angling sharp onto the hard shoulder before coming to a violent stop.

Zigzagging in and out of lanes, Henry slammed the brakes just ahead of the guy. With his seatbelt already popped he pounced from the car without a word, screaming like a crazy Viking.

In a desperate act of self-preservation, the resourceful vacuum seller threw it into reverse, raising a fume of dust all the way back up the hard shoulder, attempting to make enough space between Hulk Hogan on meth and his bumper. With a move deserving a standing ovation the terrified taxman jacked his '92 Volvo Estate to 1st and 2nd then 3rd in three racing gear shifts, speeding back onto the motorway, swerving a five-ton oil truck as he flew toward that glorious horizon. I caught his eye as he raced by, a terrified born-again, life-winner.

Looking up at the rearview I watched the over-big hothead saunter back, pausing to catch his breath, grip his waistband, talk to the sky. Slowly, he squeezed back into the car and buckled up.

'Fucking Volvo drivers,' he said.

By three that afternoon, while I was learning how to skim walls, Esther dove into the backroom where Henry and I were plastering, whispering in a low voice, 'Three guys—with guns.'

Jesus, I thought, they're a couple of maniacs!

Henry slithered along the kitchen floor with a spatula of cement like it was a military radio. 'Close all the curtains,' he commanded.

Esther disappeared, gliding over floor tiles on her hands and knees, while I made a run upstairs to go grab the kid.

BOOM! The door went, followed by shouting, Henry shouting inside the house, then outside the house, while Jnr rubbed his tired eyes in my arms.

The front door slammed shut. Henry was now outside, arguing between the front of the house and the garden, lasting as long as it took the kid to stop crying.

'It's okay!' Esther yelled up. 'You can come down, Judas!'

The six-and-a-half-foot lump had a calm, unfeeling face. He walked to the kitchen and we all trailed behind.

'Goddamn drug gangs,' he said, rolling himself a joint.

'What'd they want?' asked Esther.

'To supply the girls, otherwise they'll make trouble.'

'So you said yes?'

'No, but they'll keep trying. Once the girls are hooked, it's over. They're no use to us. They can do whatever the fuck they like outside of here, but when they're at the parlour or visiting clients, NO DRUGS. We can't be involved. It's too messy. The judge won't allow it. A little midnight hanky-panky he'll let slip, but dealing drugs, forget it.'

The kid stretched his arms to his mamma. I handed the child over.

'Judas, run to the shop and get us a couple beers, would ya?'

'No.'

'He's not going out there, Henry,' said Esther.

The big-faced prat kept on at me. 'It's fine, bud. They're gone.'

'Get your own beer,' I said.

'HENRY!' Esther yelled.

'Fuckit,' the oaf huffed. 'I'll juss have a cuppa tea then, eh?'

Esther covered the kid's ears. 'No swearing in front of Jnr!'

The maniac petted his child's little head like a lapdog. 'Did Daddy swear, bubba, eh? Awww, naughty dad-dad.'

'Christ,' I said. 'You two are nutjobs.'

'It's him!' screamed Esther.

Henry grinned at me like a man out of luck. 'Wait till you get more involved,' he said. 'We'll have the best-looking girls working all over town. Now, be a man and go get us our beers.'

Slipping my hands in my pockets so no one noticed them rattle, I stepped to the madman and snarled, 'Get your own *fucking* beer.'

Esther switched on the kettle like it was just another Monday, singing *Wheels on the Bus* to the kid while dropping three teabags into three cups. Henry, wagging his head at me, casually picked up a flat-headed screwdriver and jerked out a panel beneath the kitchen worktop. He wedged it open and freed five or six thick bundles of pink banknotes.

'Well,' he chuffed to himself, 'best move this lot for now.'

44

'It'll all be fine,' I told Daria, watching her puff her cigarette in the passenger seat as we crept away from Paradise. 'It's not for you. You'll never get out. You'll never be a clown!'

'Shit, Judas, your sister's calling.'

'Don't answer.'

'You got your driver licence?'

'Not yet.'

'Then whose car is this?'

'It's Henry's.'

'Shit shit shit.'

'*Remain calm*. It was me. I forced you to leave.'

We made it to her flat over at Prince Rock. We got out the car and sauntered along the quiet road to her door. Daria lived on the ground floor of a Victorian build, with flowerpots along the windowsill.

Straining the last of her cigarette, she flung it to the street.

'C'mon, Casanova,' she said. 'You may as well come inside.'

The hallway was tall with a large brass-framed mirror, and one of those Chinese lucky cat's sat on a shelf, its yellow paw rocking back and forth over a wrap of Golden Virginia.

We walked inside her flat. 'Tea?'

'Thanks, much.'

She advanced with an urgency, kicking her shoes off into the air before fixing the rug on her knees. I stayed stood by the door as she hopped her cardigan off on the spot, her monstrous tits bouncing up and down.

'Milk?' she asked.

'Plenty,' I replied.

With that she kicked the fridge door and threw water into the kettle, hit the switch, dropped a couple tea bags, then shamelessly swept up several thongs, scolding herself to the laundry basket.

I wandered across the room to a bookshelf while she continued cleaning up the place.

She had curriculum books, books on psychology, a Marxist social philosophy number, a few new-age hippy hardbacks, *The Magical Folly of the Jester. Clowns and Priests.* And music books: The Who and Peter Gabriel. Poetry. A treatise on Greek mythology, another French cinema. Rimbaud? 'Take it,' she said, 'you'll like him.' I read some lines and put it back. Too soft. Dated. Had its time.

'What books do you read?' she asked

I continued along the shelf. 'Crime magazines mostly. And Jung. Sometimes Sun Tzu.'

'Sun who?'

'Tzu . . . Sun *Zoo*.'

She paused and looked at me. 'Why Jung?'

I thought about that for a moment. Had never considered it.

'He doesn't seem to rest,' I said. 'The man just keeps going, opening himself up, right down to the thing.' I picked out another book.

She continued sweeping. 'What novels you read?' she asked.

'Haven't,' I answered, flipping through some Odyssey.

'You haven't read a novel?' she mocked, close to laughter.

'Correctamundo,' I said, sliding the over-written showpiece back on the shelf. I looked around. Her walls were a dull white, still with the remains of a Victorian ceiling, of which I could now appreciate the craftwork after lending my hand knocking up dominatrix suites.

Daria footed to the curtain and dimmed the room. Catching her by the hand I brought us to the bed. Her skin was cold and shaking with small pimples. Her heavy frame sunk us deeper into the mattress, her skirt gathering up her chunky thighs. She climbed on top of me, pinching the hair away from her pretty eyes.

'Judas?' she said.

I stopped kissing her neck. 'What is it?'

'Your sister. I'm worried.'

It took only for me to rub my dick against her crotch for the girl to twist her tongue inside my mouth. Yanking her skirt, I grabbed hold her thick behind in both hands and tugged the girl over me. With her cleavage in my face I couldn't resist letting go of the haunches and digging out her tits—a great bursting need. Yet as I fought with the bra, inexperienced with the art of the double-clip, she grappled my hands and slammed them down either side of my head, arched up her back, and began rubbing her clit back and forth with small sighs of relief. Managing one hand free I reached down and investigated her panties, pulled them aside, and slid in a couple fingers. She hurled her head back down, once again busying her tongue inside my mouth, my fingers now three, four.

The phone rang.

Daria stopped instantly. 'I'm scared,' she said.

'I'll deal with it,' I assured her. 'Don't you worry. You need to get out of that place and go join a circus.'

Then came a loud knock at the window. We both look up at a small shadow jumping about the street.

'Daria!' the shadow yelled.

'Shit. It's Jesse.'

'Who's Jesse?'

'That's Jesse,' she said, pointing to a picture. 'My girlfriend.'

'Ex-girlfriend.'

'It's complicated, Judas.'

As she sprung up I couldn't help sniff my fingers. Rolling from the bed to my feet, thinking of a convincing lie, I straightened my shirt and said, 'Just say I drove you home and we were having a cuppa, that's all, an afternoon tea before making love.'

'Daria! I know you're in there! Answer the door!'

Daria didn't take the funny side, pacing the room in a panic. Not able to hear me, she seemed afraid of Jesse.

'I know you're there! Esther told me you took off with her bruva!'

Daria was reluctant to open the curtain. Why were they closed? Why were we sat in the dark drinking tea at three in the afternoon?

'Listen, it's fine. I'll leave you two to sort things out. At least you're out of Paradise,' I said. 'Good luck with the clown thing.'

"Thanks, Judas—Oh hey! Take that book with you!'

'Rimbaud? Nah, can't ingest that stuff. Seeya, Daria.'

'Bye, Judas. And thanks again.'

I walked down the hallway, giving that wrap of Golden Virginia a little shake before opening the door and pocketing the baccy.

Jesse was a skinny grunge kid, an upset lesbian-boy with a crew cut. 'Where the fucks my Daria?' she said.

I zipped up my trousers. 'Your tea's gettin cold,' I told her.

She barged straight by me, maffling where I could stick the tea before slamming the door to her girlfriend's flat. The force of the door shook the little Chinese cat, but it didn't fall, remaining on that shelf, its lucky paw beckoning me toward the exit.

45

Finally arriving back to Esther's street, the petrol gauge remained red. It was red as soon as I started the car. I don't know how I made it back, but I did. As usual, I'd jumped in headfirst without considering the consequence. But what the hell, the game—as Esther always called this line of work—had liabilities. And I was one of them. Whose bright idea was it to leave me in a room full of hookers anyway?

I thought of what I'd say driving along the roads, concluding that I just liked her and she liked me, etcetera, etcetera, and to just take all the shit that came my way. It was better than getting into a scrap with Henry. Although that bothered me too, that I had to lie my way out. Lying always makes it worse, makes you *weak*, I told myself, clenching my hands over the steering wheel.

Stepping into the house, I walked slowly along the hallway, pushed the kitchen door and saw them both huddled around a small television. It was cream and oblong with a black and white screen, like one of those 1970s Orbital TV sets. 'Shhh,' Esther hissed, waving me in.

Stepping closer and peering over their shoulders, I see a young girl smacking an old feeble-looking gent on his buttcheeks, with a second girl stood sadly in the corner. The old guy wore a giant nappy and nothing else, his breasts and waist drooping with neglect.

'Henry put CCTV in the new rooms,' Esther said.

The old fella moved as though he had shit himself in his nappy, stopping short now and then to tense his knees together. I knew instantly the dominant one was that blonde, Ellie. She circled the old guy in long, black shiny boots that crawled up her thighs, clasping a large wooden paddle, sneering. She sneered and walked in circles, clapping the paddle with the other hand. The old boy looked lost, desperate.

'He's a county judge,' Esther said. 'We're recording everything.'

The old guy's nappy fell to his toes. He tried catching it, but soon threw his hand out in defence as the paddle swooped down over his saggy bruised backside. The poor bastard landed on his knees, trying to soothe the pain while desperately arranging the nappy back on, looking a sad, trembly old mess. Ellie's fingernail stabbed at his cheek, her mouth gossiped, the veins along her neck visible as she flung her head back with sardonic laughter. The old man's bare ass was flattened out, hard and gritty, as though it could withstand any amount of punishment.

The timid coy girl stood in the corner began pleading poorly to Ellie. She was short and fat and wore an old raggedy dress, the arms of the dress loose and unkept. She leapt forward in protest, pinning the nappy back on the guy, encouraging the old man to his feet. His knees were shaky. She nursed his back and hugged him. She hugged and rubbed and held him tight, his shiny bald head nestled between her tits. He shook his shiny head between her tits, pleading to the genteel servant or cook or whatever the fuck she was pretending to be to put an end to it. But Ellie high-heeled back over with that disgusted grin and spun the old man around, catching him flush across the cheek. He clasped his cheek in both hands and turned and buried his bald head once again in the fat girl's chest, whimpering like a small child.

'Mummy's boy,' muttered Henry, taking a composed drag of his smoke. Esther nodded in agreement. 'Each to their own,' she added with a shrug, both glued to the screen.

'Where's my car?' Henry asked me.

'Parked outside,' I said.

Esther interjected. 'She wasn't popular, Henry. She was only doing two punters a week. Probably best she moved on.'

'We can't have that,' Henry said coldly, taking another puff of his smoke. 'We can't have you runnin off with the girls, Judas.'

I shrugged behind him, crossed my arms.

The thick-necked pimp then spaded out a few gold coins from his trouser pocket. 'Go get us a couple beers, loverboy,' he sniggered.

I took the money and walked out the kitchen and along the hall, passing the kid playing with his new trainset.

Outside on the streets, I felt a sudden spike of brutality, needing to prove something. With my jaw clenched I eyeballed some guy swinging his weight down the road, strutting alongside his muscle-headed mutt. I went looking for action. I was sore and needed some dumb idiot to take the bait so I could punch and be punched.

Stepping from the shop with three cold cans of Red Stripe, I popped one open, sunk it down, and belched deep from the gut. A blanched old lady with a little green shopping trolley crossed over the road, she crossed over without daring to look my way, as I raised my chin, cigarette in mouth, switching my eyeballs at anyone who passed.

46

'Look!' blasted Henry. 'Look at this, Judas!'

The squareheaded lout had the local newspaper pressed up against the air with his big thumb tapping an advert in the CLASSIFIEDS under MASSAGE. He whispered from behind the paper: 'Those cheeky sonofabitches, they haven't a clue what they're doing! AMATEURS!'

Sunday morning, not yet eleven, and I was half drunk. I had pieced the final floor tile for a new bondage room, swept and admired my work. Henry sat perched on a stool, looking like that statue 'The Thinker', sucking a wet joint while exploring every corner of his lecherous intellect. It was the Sunday morning phonecalls.

'Try this one and just get 'em to confess. I'll record the call.'

It was the same each Sunday. We'd call the competition, other massage outfits, and Henry would record the call, attempting to cajole the crooks into admitting to running a whorehouse and have them shut down, stealing their girls and clientele. Yet they always said the same thing: 'I'm afraid we do not offer sexual services, Mr X. But I'm sure one of our young ladies could accommodate, we *never* disappoint.' The receptionist had the backstreet tone of a bored seductress, likely squatted beneath some desk painting her toenails.

I hung up and shook my head. Henry hit the voicemail machine, listening to more punters while Esther fed the kid spaghetti hoops.

I got a kick out of listening to society's most regarded half-beg a return call with false names as though it was a formal business matter. Henry was good at fishing out the scammers and time-wasters, and those curious enough to dial the number, too afraid to cheat on their wives or risk tarnishing their reputation. It was mostly old white affluent men with a degrading desire and a bit of pocket change, getting their kicks once or twice a week.

'What about that guy?' Esther suggested as one commoner left his details, sounding like your typical Janner ruffian.

'Too much hassle,' Henry told her. 'You know how it is, babe, that kind are normally coked-up and crazy. That's why those rotters always call Sunday morning after a boozy night out.' Henry turned to me. 'I let some in a few times. It's not nice for the girls or for business. And it ain't easy gettin the bleeders out the door, either.'

Then a woman's voice came through the machine.

'We got another female!' Esther said delighted.

Henry lowered his paper and grinned—all that guesswork of women and their dirty little secrets showing up like a rare toad in an Amazonian swamp.

'Someone has to do the business,' declared Esther.

Henry said nothing, sitting back enjoying this rare moment, cranking gas and blowing smoke. It normally came down to a cash incentive for one of the working girls. Mr and Mrs Pimp would pop open a cheap bottle of plonk to loosen her up, have fun, cast predictions before the female punter arrived.

Henry had a theory: 'She'll spread her thighs and beg for Alexa to beat it—release all that pent-up stress of fighting her point against suited pricks all day at the office.'

Alexa, a pill-popping new hooker on the books, a blue-eyed bisexual who had happily taken the job, just smiled and sipped the wine.

Henry snapped his fingers. 'Pussy punishment!' he declared.

Esther was quick to give him a sharp smack. 'Oi!' she laughed. 'Not while my little brother's in the room!'

'He's not a kid!' Henry shot back. 'He knows all this! He knows!'

Meanwhile I poured me and Alexa more wine.

47

The house had been a battlefield for a week. That lipstick mark, which left a perfect print when Esther carefully held Henry's dick in her mouth before he was allowed to go out for a rare drink with his old pal Davy, had returned home a different shade. Henry assumed it stopped there with Esther, just a bit of lippy on his knob to make sure there was no funny business. Of course he knew there were different shades of red, many shades, but he did not suppose the depths of Esther's paranoia in their line of work.

So on inspection, usually the next morning, all she did was give the returned lipstick around his dangling member an eye exam, likely squinting at the thing, keeping a serious face while Henry quietly sniggered. However on this particular cold Sunday morning, nearing Christmas, she ordered the accused to stay right where he was, abandoning her inquest with his pants round his ankles before running up the stairs past me and the kid, returning in a flash waving the original lipstick.

'Oh, c'mon!' I heard the defendant yell as the door slammed shut.

'You stay right there!' she yelled back.

To his credit, the man stayed put. 'Great! She's final gone loopy!'

Chewing jam toast with the kid next door, discussing species of dinosaur and the various sizes of their poop, I heard the curtain drawn and the light switch leaned to max voltage.

'LOOK!' she said. 'The colour! It's not the same! *It's not the same!*'

'Jesus, Esther, stop being so goddamn paranoid.'

'*This*, Henry Cooper, is *Ruby Woo*.' She must've held that stick right against his nose. 'That, on your willy, *is not* Ruby fucking WOO!'

I was later told she took his thumb and made a copy with the unknown red he'd brought home and stuck a fresh print with Ruby Woo right next to it, and raised his thumb up beneath the bulb, right up to his good eye. Her suspicions had won. No matter if Ruby Woo had faded to a *Dior Rouge* in the man's pants while he and Davy shot pool down The Old Ship, he'd had it.

They fought all over the house the whole week. She punched him out the door every night. He tried holding her back, nothing left in the poor sap, pleading to me that she'd finally lost it and to call the mental hospital. She was in a rage, a firestorm.

'Go back to your whore!' she yelled, kicking the front door shut with the bottom of her foot.

Each time she threatened to call the cops he'd jump back in his car and speed away. She changed the locks and argued from the upstairs window. He pleaded and begged, told her to just pack in her nonsense, expressing his innocence on the street, line for line, appealing with fair manner for her to cool the fuck down and to please unlock the bloody door, that he loved her, and the kid, too.

'Go back to your whore!' Esther shouted down at him.

'I built all this!' he hit back. 'You're nuthin without me!'

Esther secured the home, window to back door to loft with a flashlight before throwing her head back out the window. 'It's all in my name!' she laughed wildly. 'I own it all! *Ha Ha Ha!*'

Another cold afternoon. I drifted through the front door and into the kitchen with a sore hangover, and found Esther, stood there staring at the back window facing the garden with her arms crossed and a face without feeling, shrugging her shoulders and muttering insanities, looking as though she hadn't slept for days. I stepped a little closer. Her eyes remained glued to the window.

'Esther?' I said.

'He's bluffing,' she said.

I turned, and there was Henry, stood at the back of the garden with a red petrol canister, slowly pouring the contents over the top of his big shiny head with the same sullen expression as Esther, gazing at one another. He then threw the canister to one side and produced a large box of matchsticks.

'Do it,' Esther quietly hummed.

'I'll do it!' Henry yelled.

'I'm waiting!' she hit back.

He struck a match and stretched it out ahead of him.

'Esther?' I said again.

'He's bluffing,' she said.

He held the match. The flame died. He picked at the box, struck another. 'I'll fucking do it!'

'Well get on with it!' she yelled out.

Her arms remained folded, eyes bloodshot and empty. She wanted it, wanted to see it all go up in flames and away into the night sky. For him to burn like a smoking lantern, twinkling in some far off universe. You could see the twinkle in her eye, a beaten child lying naked on some cum-soaked mattress, making wishes to outer space.

A twenty was folded in my pocket that I'd pinched from their money tin when she was dumping clothes out the window a few days earlier. I wished I took more.

I noticed a bundle of fifties next to the dishwasher, ten thousand perhaps, with a pile of credit cards and several new chequebooks. Esther was going after the money.

Henry struck another match.

'Do it,' Esther quietly hummed again.

I had recently read of the monks of Tibet setting fire to themselves on the streets of Amdo, the sacrificial act of immolation. There seemed to me nothing more brave, nothing more courageous, nothing more desperately alive, than to be in the flame, burning.

Henry took his shirt off, his large, golden chest looking meek and tired, his burly fingers delicately clasping the little match, his other arm hung loose to his side. His face was red and exhausted, wishing to die, his swollen eyes awake for too many days.

'Do it,' said Esther again and again.

The sky was blue. The garden a lush green. The tortoise slowly crawled behind Henry's feet. The flame lasted a long while.

'Esther, I stole twenty quid from your tin.'

'I can't do this anymore, Judas,' she said, ignoring me. 'I'm losing my mind. I'm going crazy.'

Henry fingered the box again and produced another match.

'He's right,' she went on. 'I should be in a nuthouse by now. All these twisted perverts and their goddamn issues is taking its toll. All of 'em. All of it. But none more than *him*.'

Henry lit the match.

'I've seen it all, Judas. It's sad, really sad, but it bloody helps, you know? We do our bit for society. God knows what would happen otherwise. Rape would be fucking legal, that's what.'

We continued to watch Henry go through all of the matches. Tossing the empty box to the grass, he walked slowly toward the window, drenched in oil, repeating something over and over.

Esther tried reading his lips. 'Eats bau-ber?' she said. 'What? What's he saying, Judas? Eats ball-der? I don't understand?'

Henry kept walking and repeating himself. We couldn't hear a thing. He then stopped at the window and pressed his wet nose against the glass. 'IT'S WATER!' the idiot yelled, laughing.

'Cunt,' said Esther.

48

I hadn't seen or heard from Jacob since I escaped the academy. I don't recall how we found each other again, but we did.

Jacob and I walked back to his house head to toe in mud. We'd been kicking a ball about the field, sliding about like dogs.

'Let's pick up some bevvies and get clobbered!' I said.

He fretted. 'Mum ain't gonna let us in the house with all this mud.'

I laughed. 'I've got mud up me jacksie!'

He twists his key in the door. 'I'm glad we're back together, Judas.'

When the door swung open his mother was coming down the stairs completely starkers, drying her hair with a towel.

'Jacob!' she yelped, darting back up in a flash.

Jacob turned to me and shrugged.

'It's okay, Joan!' I called up. 'I didn't see anything!'

Yes, yes I did. I saw everything.

Joan was slender and attractive and forty-five, with olive skin and almond-shaped eyes. Her hair was boyish short, legs narrow all the way up to her buttocks, like two pencils. Her nipples were dark and big and perfectly round, like taking a brown crayon to a piece of paper and drawing circles on circles on circles continually without lifting the chalk. I saw her from the front and then from behind as she ran away, all beneath a skylight beaming with marvellous sun.

'C'mon, mate,' Jacob said, tapping my chest, 'let's go inside.'

As we stepped in Joan yelled from somewhere above. 'Take your boots off and go straight to the backyard! No mud in the house!'

Following orders, we hopped over the paving in the backyard that his old man had built. His old man, Fred, and his grandad,

Fred Snr, both worked together as handymen. They were always knocking down and rebuilding the house, always in white overalls with paint spattered to the hair.

We slipped our muddy socks off and piled them to one side. Joan hurried to the yard wearing a simple white tee-shirt and a pair of tight denims she'd thrown on.

'Okay you two,' she said. 'STRIP!'

On that instruction, she footed over to the yellow hose in the corner of the yard and lugged it over to the outside tap. Jacob was already down to his skivvies. Me, I held my shorts for dear life. It was cold. I was cold down there.

'And our pants, Muh?' asked my pal.

Some magpies sat yattering on the rooftop while Joan was going at that tap, leaning into the thing with her lovely shoulder.

'Do what you like, Jakes,' she muttered to herself, grappling the hose.

I swung an eye at him, kicked off my shorts and kept my pants firm. Luckily naturist boy kept his too.

Joan finally fired up the hose, snaking the thing around the concrete bed like a meteor storm taking hits at planets, steadying toward us, ripping up moss and weeds and small stones—worms, lice and snails flung in all direction.

'It's cold, boys,' she warned us.

She went to work on Jacob first, hosing him down proper. He fought the water with the palms of his hands, hopping on both feet.

'Jesus!' he shouted. 'It's freezing!'

'Now turn around,' she told him.

It took only a few minutes until he was done.

'Okay, now in you go, Jakes.' With that he grabbed his clothes and disappeared back into the house.

Once he'd gone, Joan let the hose rip again: worms, snails, planets. I noticed her wet hand grip the nozzle, the long, slim fingers, the sparkly wedding ring, her bare feet advancing.

'Okay, now it's your turn, Judas.'

Her face was without mercy. Were we thinking the same?

'How's that?' she asked.

'It's . . . c-c-cold,' I quivered. 'But I can take it,' were the following words that shook from my jaw.

Fixing my underpants, I had to move my bulge, sought to get that extra show. I was cornered. She crawled the water up my legs, getting me comfortable with the temperature. But it was cold, my teeth trying always to hack my tongue. Her face was untelling, but I didn't care. I just packed away the image of her beautiful tits and ass and that wild feral fanny-bush tightly inside my masturbation memory box. I owned it. It happened. *She was mine!*

The water beat my chest. I tilted my head and just allowed Joan to do her thing. Have her way. Water bashed over my eyes like a newborn. With one hand still gripped tight to my pants, I limped my head to one side and noticed a slug being waterlogged. I watched the slug. I watched him rolled to his back, his slimy, slug-white underbelly facing all that blue sky. I shook my hand over my scalp, loosening up the mud. Closed my eyes. Opened them. Felt my balls shrivel. And Joan, keeping the water steady above my waist, gradually shooting lower.

Gaining confidence to edge my hands away from the front of my pants, I saw that she was now concentrating so well on pointing that hose that I could get a real look at her. It seemed easier to look at a woman when she was preoccupied. She lowered the hose some more, the rush of water forcing my pants back and my bulge forward. I abandoned the bulge, hovering my hands above with unease and infancy. With my hands out of the way she immediately took aim at my dick while I noticed again her slim fingers, the eyes in quiet, tender revenge. I straightened up, encouraged my shoulders back, being sure—be sure of yourself! The blackbirds took off suddenly, cackling away into the same sky, causing my hands to nervously judder back over my pants, shoulders hunched once more, teeth hacking my tongue.

I soon gave up on the belief of me and Jacob's mum, there was too much riding against us, too big a risk. So I cowered. And instead took all that sun against my rattling spine.

'Okay, Judas,' she said looking satisfied. 'You can turn around.'

The back of the yard was a tip, with open bags of cement and recycled wood plotted about.

She seemed out of breath. 'Okay my love, we're done, that'll do, that'll do just fine. Get yourself in and dried up.'

I turned back around, stood in a puddle. We caught eyes briefly, neither of us looking for too long. She then graced soundlessly over the concrete toward the tap, a naked nymphet springing across the water. I made my way back inside, fixing my pants, pausing by her wet feet as she struggled off the hose.

'Need help with that?' I asked.

49

Jacob had already dressed and was running his finger through his King James. Freeing fresh clothes from my bag, I towelled up in the corner, listening to his mind rummage between verse.

His room was a mess, stuff all over the place. Slipping my pants on, I folded the towel over a chair.

'Your room's a shittin tip,' I told him, kneeling under his bed.

'I like it this way,' the blight answered, his head stuck in that book.

'And you still got pints of piss beneath your matress.'

'Alright, alright, I'll take 'em down later.'

'How long they been under here?'

'Dunno, a week—maybe two. *Who cares?*'

I moaned at him, before standing back up and buckling my belt. Jacob lowered his book and grinned. 'Dare me to drink some?'

I took a seat and put on my socks. 'I dare you to piss in the toilet.'

He put his Bible aside and fingered below his bed for one jar of dark amber urine. He raised the jar to his lips and took a nip.

I paused buttoning my shirt. 'What's it taste like?' I asked.

'Hmm, warm, pondlike. Tastes like piss.'

We both take a closer look at the jar.

'It's got bits, look?' he said, pointing to the bottom. He circled the jar mid-air between the sunlight shooting through the window.

'You gonna drink all that?' I asked him. But the idiot had already started gulping, stopping suddenly at the third mouthful.

'Swallow it,' I said.

He shook his head.

'Swallow!'

He shook his head again and spat it back in the jar.

'Chickenshit.'

'It's not that bad, Judas. It's just piss,' he tells me, wiping his chin.

'Those floaty bits are probably rotten skin and insects and other shit living right under your mattress, plopping dead into those jars.'

'Probably.'

'Years and years of rotten assfluff.'

'I guess so,' he shrugged.

I pointed my finger around the mess. 'Clean your bloody room!'

Flipping over his beloved Bible, I checked out the cover. I had a thing for old-looking books. The covers were modest, ordinary, one or two tones, uninterested in competing for your attention.

'Did your mum say it's cool for me to stay awhile?' I asked.

And he said, 'My home is your home, Judas.'

'You didn't ask her, did you?'

He set down the jar of piss. 'She's fine. Don't you worry.'

'I'll speak with her. I'd better ask if it's okay.'

'Have you spoken to Jezebel?'

'Not since she fucked Bruno.'

'I don't like her.'

'She's alright.'

'All you do is argue. She's a bitch.'

'Swearing doesn't suit you.'

'No, I know.'

He closed the book in my hand. 'Open it at any page,' he said.

I shook the book at him. 'I'm warning you, stop with this come-to-Jesus shit.'

'Just do it, Judas! Trust me!'

The pages were dull and battered and musty. His grandmothers: 'read a verse a day to keep the Devil at bay', as they did for generations. I took a moment, let off a long sigh, and flipped a random page:

ST MARK Chapter One. Jesus is baptised by John—He preaches the gospel, calls disciples, casts out devils, heals the sick, and cleanses a leper.

Jacob gawped at me, nervously chewing his nails.

'What?' I asked.

'Dunno,' he shrugged. 'It's supposed to be an *ana*logy, like a *meta*phor or somefin. My gran does it. She closes her eyes and opens a random page every morning.'

I tossed him back the book. 'I'm a Buddhist now, like those monks catching fire. I'm one of them now.'

'I'm not a Christian, Judas!'

'Good.'

'Why don't you ever trust me?'

'I'll trust you when you learn to wee wee in the toilet and tidy your bloody room.'

'I'm serious,' he said, clasping his precious book.

'Yeah, *too* serious.'

'I mean it, Judas—why don't you ever trust me?'

I moved my eyes along Jacob's eyes before snatching back his book. 'Trust is a rare commodity, my friend,' I said, absentmindedly flipping pages. 'We have to pass through Hell together.'

His eyes lit up. 'I know Hell,' he said.

I closed his book and held it under his nose.

'You know the Bible,' I said.

50

Jezebel circled back and called out my name. She was excited to see me. She told me all about her new flat opposite the graveyard, her face bright and cheery. Finally she moved out of her old lady's place and into her own little flat. There was no mention of Bruno. I didn't ask. I could tell she was single. She had a strange piercing on her lip. I didn't like it—but I said it looked nice. She spoke of her friend who'd just got her breasts enlarged with this new thing called *sili*cone. Jezebel laughed about her small tits, making hints while cupping her little ones in both hands. She moved her hands farther away, showing me what they'd be like triple sized.

'Did you sleep with him?' I asked her outright.

She dropped her hands and looked to the floor. 'Yes,' she said, before straightening up. 'But only after you broke up with me!'

'We had an argument, Jezebel!'

The rush of anger ran to rage then betrayal until it was all right. I got it. We were young, she was young, noticing her power as a woman, and of a whore. The whore in the woman. And the whore needed protection, I was convinced of it, a dumb brute with muscle. Someone who didn't bother you with meaningful questions. That was Bruno. She needed to feel safe from the world to express herself as a whore. I got it. She hated that I never fought for her. She said I was too soft. I guess I was afraid of being a brute, of hurting someone without good cause. It wasn't me. I was too in my head, musing stuff over, seeing outcomes and choosing wisely, or cowardly perhaps. Maybe I was a coward? I oftentimes wanted to be a brute, fuck whores and manhandle the enemy. Perhaps I could? I thought about it. I always thought about that. Maybe Jezebel *was* good for me? I agreed to meet the next day.

Jacob shook his head as I ran out of his place and reached the graveyard and walked all afternoon with Jezebel, reading all the stones.

'Ralph Henderson, died aged 9. So young!' she said. She almost cried, almost. She could almost cry easily. It didn't take much—but it didn't last long either: the almost crying. She would pretend to wipe a tear and move on like it never happened. I watched her wipe her hand on her dress. She hardly wore a dress. She preferred jeans. But today she wore a pretty yellow dress.

We both look at a tombstone. 'I hate my feet,' she told me.

And I say, 'You've got nice feet.' And she does, she knows she does.

'You're just sayin that, Judas. I know my feet are ugly.'

'They're not ugly!'

'I've got troll feet.'

'Well, I like troll feet.'

'Hah!'

'Shut up, Jezebel.'

I stooped down and read a stone:

Alma and Robert Tucker. They lived always in each other's hearts. And now forever in dust.

'Alma, that's a nice name,' she said.

I agree but I didn't care, I didn't care for Alma or Robert. They lived. And who knows what comes of death—an endless replay of the Black War, a hundred virgins on their knees, a hellish wormhole swallowing you up. Who knows! What really caught my interest was how they both died just two days apart, after fifty years of wedlock.

We walked some more. The sky was patchy but it was warm. Jezebel studied an old lady in a white hat dropping a bunch of flowers near a grave. I don't know why she pretended to care. She asked me to wait a minute. I couldn't see her nipples anymore, they'd gotten flat in the heat. Tying her hair up she chewed her cheek and took her eyes from the old lady.

'Stop chewing your cheek,' I told her. She complained of blisters. She caught me up. We waited for a squirrel to pass by us.

Jezebel hopped on her toes. 'If it comes near, I'll scream!' she said.

'He's fine. He just gets fed by humans so he thinks we might serve him lunch. He's lost his nature, his gut inklings, just as we have.'

She shrieked, 'I'll kick him in the bleddy head!'

I snatched her by the hand and we curved down an old pebbled path with a well-trimmed line of grass and antique picture frames of more dead faces. Jezebel treaded over the graves while I picked a flower, a yellow daisy—yellow like her dress. I handed it to her and watched as she twisted the stem between her fingertips. She wasn't sentimental. She said thanks and held it. That daisy soon became a sore between us. She needn't carry it for so long, I thought, picking another and ripping off each petal, one by one. Jezebel did the same. We both then ditched our petalless flowers and kept walking.

'Fucksake,' she said, folding down to unclip her buckle again. 'I've got another stone in my shoe!'

An old pair strolled by. They said good morning. I said good morning. Jezebel peered up and smiled perfectly and said hello. We could all see Jezebel's knickers. They were white.

'How's your old dear?' I asked as she stood up.

'She's getting more pissed each day, Judas. Cleans off a bottle of vodka before lunchtime. She doesn't stop! It's Dion and my dad, they stress her out. Noah bought her a diamond necklace. He spoils her rotten. She deserves it. She deserves to be spoiled.'

'Right,' I said, pulling apart the word spoiled in my head.

'There's my flat!' She wiggled her finger across the graveyard. 'I live on the top floor, the one with the blue door. Number 33!'

'You finally got your own place,' I said.

'Took ages to find. Thank christ I'm not waking up to Dion's stupid nunchucks. Anyway Judas, come see my flat.'

We past more gravestones, more people handing down flowers. It was a strange place, the people here were deeply reflective among the dead. Maybe we ought to have open graves paving the streets, a reminder of the inevitable, a keepsake.

'My ass sticks out in this silly dress,' she said, 'like a baboon!' I got a little hard, as often the case. I always got a little hard. I was used to it, growing a little. I hadn't seen Jezebel naked for some time.

As we watched a hundred swallows dip and dive, I couldn't help pity all these folk dragging around their tired shoes, busying between old stones. It was endless. It wasn't real. Nobody gave a flying muck what lay beneath these rocks. They only cared of their regrets, of getting old and losing the will to live each day, handing down their troubles to the kids. They didn't take heed of life. They clung to loss, and the consoling tales of others who had suffered too.

While Jezebel dropped down to fiddle another stone from her sandal, a sweet voice came over my shoulder. 'Are you Judas?' it said.

I spun and faced a pretty blonde. 'That's me.'

'I'm Corby's sister. I used to watch you play football.'

'Yes, I remember you,' I lied. 'How's Corby?'

'He's a policeman, can you believe! Anyway, *so sorry*, gotta get on. Just thought I'd say hi. I'll tell Corby I bumped into you!'

She hurried away with a bunch of flowers.

I waved behind her. 'Nice seeing you again!'

Lowering my hand, I watched the blonde leave, fixed on her beautifully-shaped legs, racking my brain at who this Corby kid was.

51

Jezebel twisted her gold key in the lock. 'Moses just moved in downstairs. Small world,' she whispered, kicking open the door.

The hallway was narrow, with a single flight of stairs straight ahead. Jezebel swelled with pride.

'He lives there,' she whispered again as we passed by his door. We then climbed a set of steps to a blue door—33A.

She swung open the door and there stood a small cat.

'This is Lily! Ain't she adooorable, Judas!' She scooped up Lily the cat and kissed her little brown nose ten times, the tenth being the loudest. 'She's been shittin nonstop all weekend, the poor thing. Could be the cheap food. I might have to buy the posh stuff!'

Lily was another Persian, like her old cat. But this furbag was a ginger, with big green eyes and a dopey tongue that stuck out.

We stepped in. I closed the door behind me.

'Tah-da!' She skipped to the lounge, dropping the cat like old news before fussing through her vinyls. 'We need music,' she said, choosing Do Nothing by The Specials.

She started dancing about the room. 'Dance with me, Judas!'

'No.'

She kept dancing. 'C'mon! Dance with me!'

The cat rubbed up against my leg, readying to piddle on my shoe. I kicked her away and looked back at Jezebel. 'That's my record,' I said. She turned it up and swung her hips. 'No it's not! It's mine!'

I kicked the cat again and yelled over the music, 'IT'S MY RECORD!' She stopped bouncing and turned the music down and grabbed me by the hand. 'Kitchen first!'

The kitchen was a squeeze, room for one. There was a large bowl of oranges and bananas and purple grapes. 'Mum bought the fruit. I don't know why. She knows I don't eat fruit. Looks good though!'

I stood in the door. 'Yeah, looks nice.'

'Shoes off please, mister!'

I kicked off my shoes next to her sandals. She put a beer in my hand and led us back to the lounge. Lily jumped from the sofa and plodded aimlessly in one direction. Much light poured in from the bay window, overlooking that graveyard.

'It's a good size,' I told her. And she told me what it'll look like in a few weeks: plants, pictures, rugs, little dainty flowerpots, a forty-inch TV, a red vintage telephone she spotted in a charity shop, cat house for young Lily, a bright yellow Smeg fridge, a dildo drawer *and*, a lava lamp in every corner of the room.

She took us to the bathroom.

'It ain't much. But it's got a bath. Just needs a scrub. Bah.'

I took a swig of my beer. 'It's a good start,' I said.

'I know it's shit. But I'll make it look nice.'

'Make it look whatever you want. It's your liberty.'

She shook with excitement as she walked us to the bedroom. 'Tah-da!' Her room was all bed, with a matching dresser and wardrobe wedged together. The bed was draped in red silk with all her baby toys sitting upright along the pillow.

I tipped my can. 'Still playing with those toys, huh?'

She big-eyed me and started chewing her cheek, pointing to the other stuffed puppets above the wardrobe. 'I know it's sad. But I can't let 'em go just yet, not yet. Do you like my bedroom?'

'Yes,' I said, racking up the lies.

She plonked on the bed and gave it a beckoning pat. I sat my beer on the dresser and plonked down beside her. It smelled like nail varnish and wigs. I told her about Esther and Henry and we laughed together. She reminded me of the time my sister tried cajoling her into joining the parlour, learn the ropes, become a Mistress. And how she always noticed Henry's persuasion over me, to do what he had done, take good care of Jezebel. Put her to work.

'We're all a little screwed, Judas. I know you know that.'

I didn't answer. I didn't want to get into it. Not now. Leaning over I gave her a kiss. Her eyes turned. I pushed her back to the silk.

She suddenly jumped to life. 'Wait!' she yelped. Acting fast she clipped off her earrings and tossed them on the dresser, unzipped the back of her yellow dress in a hurry and guided it neatly over her curly hair to the floor. Unstrapping the bra, she kicked away her white knickers, sprayed something lemony in the air before shuffling her naked body to the centre of the bed.

'Okay now,' she said, spreading her thighs . . .

52

Dion jumped back from the bar, steering clear of Bruno sinking pints, throwing air jabs. We were in The Newmarket Tavern on Market Way. Legend has it, there was something missing from Bruno's brain, some sort of *brain defect*. The crooked-nosed nit didn't say anything clever. He was just some lout who roughed around whoever he could.

Gulping my beer I watched on as he danced on his hooves. I was on edge. Dion told me again of his dreams to get out of this town. I tried listening. I see his lips moving but I was too preoccupied scanning the same old mob about us.

And there they all were, the typical hardmen with their steely eyes glaring from tops of beer glasses, cheap medallions glistening in smokey light. Every one of them had tattoos scribbled across their forearms: birth dates, jail dates, swallow birds, bleeding hearts and sailing ships, all poorly inked with a common man's pride. I took another swig of my beer, tuning in again to Dion's rambling.

'Just watch, I'll have a small army touting for me. I'll be invisible, like that Machi-avelli fella. You know Machi-avelli? No one'll know who I am. I'll pull in twenty grand a week, juss for starters.'

I flipped a beermat with my thumb. 'Who's Machi-avelli?'

He gave me that all-knowing look. '*Exactly*,' he said.

I shook my head. 'What'll you need all that money for, anyway?'

'Coke's in high demand. No one touches speed these days. Two years of solid work, then I'll leave this shitheap and go start a new life in south of Spain, or maybe *Jahpan!*'

'Better weather in Spain.'

'But that little Japanese pussy, imagine!'

I flipped the beermat again. 'I'd miss a good Cornish pasty.'

'They'll be pasties.'

'Not like 'ere there won't.'

He took a swig of his beer, belched. 'Sometimes you gotta make sacrifices to ride the road of destiny,' he said, the ring of another Master Lee film.

The barmaid handed me a look while pulling a perfect Guinness. I fell in love. It happened instantly and abandoned us just as quick. Then Bruno, in an upheaving fit, dropping left hooks, failed to hold his pint, smashing to the floor and spilling across the pub. Annoyed or embarrassed, the hard-headed ape immediately got hold the guy to his left and stuck his finger between the poor bastard's eyes.

Bobby tried to compose the brute, sliding a wad of cash across the bar with a wink. The poor sod he'd grabbed stood there near perfectly still with his palms raised. Bruno suddenly dropped this guy and spun around, letting go a rant of insults at Dion for not opening his door when he stopped by weeks ago.

'You were in there! All of you were!' the nut spat, rotating his finger at everybody but Bobby and myself. He then plopped down on a stool. Not another word. A complete mystery.

Bobby soon smiled and Dion did too. And a few others nearby. The barman continued pulling pints and some old tough guys rolled their eyes at their women and resumed drinking. Those who stubbed out a cigarette produced another, springing all about like burning bushes.

A lofty Janner then whispered to Bruno, 'Bang Bang Boys are lookin for yah,' he said. The barlady swept about our feet. Her cleavage looked up at me. I footed together shards of glass, before telling Dion I was going to spend a penny, wandering off to the gents.

With my beer balanced atop the urinal, I stood there holding my Johnson, waiting for a maybe. I didn't need to go—just wanted to get away from the crowd, catch a break. Some unexpected piss sputtered out, enough to convince the big fella to my right that I wasn't a lavatory peeper.

I took my sweet time washing my hands. Slammed the dryer, which rattled several seconds of rank air. I stuck to it, humming a tune, before wandering back into the aftermath of a crazy ruckus.

All the front windows were smashed, chairs and tables turned over, and broken pool sticks clenched in the fists of five or so guys, blood running along their faces.

'What happened?' I asked Dion.

'Bang Bang Boys,' he said. 'Twenty of 'em rushed in, came for Bruno. Started a massive brawl before being run out by the oldsters.'

We both looked at his hand. It was bleeding.

'I landed on some glass tryna get out the way,' he said, pincing tiny pieces from his fingers.

'I didn't hear a thing,' I said. 'I just took a piss.'

He got up to leave. 'Well,' he said. 'I'm off. Be lucky, Judas.'

After sinking several more beers, I followed Bruno and Bobby out the door. The streets were busy. I walked alongside Bobby, looking where he looked, repeating what he said in my own words.

We stopped at a corner near a busy club on Union Street. Bobby said he was cold. I offered up my jacket. The jacket looked good on him. He zipped it closed and concealed the blood on his shirt.

Bruno tissued his bleeding head before bounding away to interrogate some toothless junkie on the street corner. Knots of drunken young yobs passed by, eyeing me and Bobby, sensing the tension.

Two police officers walked to us.

'Watch out, old bill,' Bobby said. 'Don't bother with 'em.'

'Why not?' I said, wanting to impress Bobby.

'It ain't worth it,' he said.

'Copper's don't scare me,' my drunkard brain clacked back.

One spoke into his radio while the other made a turn for Bruno.

Bobby whispered again, 'Don't say anything. I can't get nicked.'

I didn't answer. I was disappointed, insulted maybe.

'What you boys up to?' asked the copper.

Bobby shook his head and shrugged. The cop pointed to Bobby's collar. 'How'd you cut your neck, son?'

'It's a rash.'

The cop looked at me. I stared back coolly—that sixth beer had only reached my toes.

'Well okay,' the cop said. 'Just try and stay out of trouble.'

'What'd you mean, officer?' I finally said.

He turned back and gave me a tired look. 'I *mean* it gets rowdy round here, fella. So watch yourselves.'

I huffed mockingly. 'Well you too, officer.'

'And what's that supposed to mean?' he enquired.

I allowed the words to come slow. 'And . . . you . . . also . . . ' I said.

The cop bounced his chin, looked again at Bobby's collar. 'Is that fella over there with you boys?' he asked, pointing to Bruno.

'What of it?' Bobby said.

'Why's his head bleedin?'

'Ask him. He's right there,' I chipped in.

The boy in blue gave me a staredown, pinning me as the cocky kid. 'Know anything about a riot at the Tavern about a half-hour ago?'

Bobby shook his head. I gnashed my teeth.

Having had enough, the cop let off a weary sigh, turned and walked, tossing a few parting words over his shoulder. 'Just watch yourselves!'

'And you also!' I quickly yelled back.

Bobby shook his eyes at the floor. The copper sighed as he returned. 'You wanna take a ride to the station young man?'

'Not right now,' I said.

'Well, you're going the right way about it, lad.'

'What's the wrong way?' I asked him.

He stepped closer. 'Are you gettin lippy with me, son?'

I leaned to him and politely sneered, 'I ain't your son.'

He looked back at me for a moment, working me through. And then said, 'One more word and I'm booking you for public nuisance.'

I started coughing profusely, loud and speechlike: 'Aachpussie! Kassslickher! Pisshpertit!'

The copper shook his head and tutted, turned on his boot and walked to his partner.

Dropping the act I stuffed my fists in my pockets, imagining fighting all the yobs out for trouble. Like that drunken idiot jumping in and out of traffic, frightening the meek in their cars. And his laughing cronies, I think to myself, every last one of them. These pig-faced fucks. I was sick of it.

Resting my hand on a pack of Marlboro, I pinched one out and lit up. I was a curious case, I was sure. Curious because I kept an eye on whatever was arranging all this madness. Because there, as I saw it, right in the centre shitheap to all this clueless, fucking savagery, presiding over it all—the King of Kings, the Lord of holy fucking Lords—was this Yahweh fella, the omniscient, cutting those men down, the morons, the meatheads, *the brutes*, keeping tabs on my moves, which way I'd go, plotting to hack me too.

53

Sliding my feet back to Jacob's, two tough guys in identical Rockports, travelling alongside a skinny brunette came down the road. I saw it all from fifty feet. They swallowed the whole stinking pavement. But I kept my lane. Three of you, one of me, I thought.

One took a puff of his cigarette before retracting his arm without considering how little room he offered. I tensed every fibre in my shoulder, knocking him aside. He stopped. They all did.

'Problem?' he asked.

I stood my half-drunken eyes against his. 'In fact, yes, yes I do have a problem, seeming you asked. I have a big fucking problem with the *CUNT* your mother spawned you from.'

He stopped smirking. He looked confused. 'What did you say?'

The girl grabbed him. 'Leave it alone, Jerry,' she said.

I sneered. 'Yeah, listen to her, Jerry. Listen to the girl very closely. I'm doing my upmost to maintain a sense of serenity alongside pieces of shit like you. Like the monks do, Jerry. Like the monks do.'

'Let's just go!' she screamed out, pulling Jerry's arm. But Jerry stepped in. Both guys did. I was cool, tanked, stupid. We all formed a close-knitted triangle. His friend was short while Jerry towered above.

'Just leave it!' the girl clacked, getting visibly upset.

I noticed Jerry had a cheap tattoo of lucky dice behind the ear, while his small pudgy companion sweated profusely about the eyes, pincy little eyes with flashes of God save the Queen.

During our standoff, Jacob appeared, calmly stopping ahead of the little fat one. 'You alright there, mate?' Jacob asked the guy.

Jerry scoffed awkwardly, got hold the brunette by the arm and dragged the bony bitch down the road, followed by fatso. We watched the trio turn a corner before heading inside.

Jacob sat immediately at his desk flipping pages of his Bible.

'I'm pissed,' I informed him.

'Oh yeah?' he asked, eyes fixed on his book. 'Where you been?'

'Pub with Dion.'

'I had to sign on at the dole office.'

'Well, I gotta do that tomorrow.'

Jacob put his Bible down. 'I'll come with you if you like?'

'Sure. And for your information, your mum said I could stay.'

'Told you.'

'You didn't tell me shit. Anyway, all we need now is a job.'

'We can pick up a jobs paper tomorrow.'

'Decent idea. You got any money? I gotta pound . . .'

'I'll go ask my mum.' With that my friend vanished out the door.

Popping open a warm beer I discovered on his floor, I sat on the end of his bed contemplating the enigmas of life. Leaning over his desk I pushed open his Bible and read a few lines. Several pages stuck together. Peeling them apart I curiously read a few of those lines, took a swig of beer, placed the can on the desk and tried touching my toes. I see only one jar of piss beneath his bed. Not so bad, I think, straightening up and looking out the window.

The last of the sun spiked between the clouds, lighting up the street like a prison watchtower. Some gulls flew by, wailing between the light. I squint at the birds until all I see are tiny silhouettes, chasing the bin truck. Closing my eyes, the lowering sun warmed and soothed my mind, reds and golds, while hearing the faint desperation of Jacob running up the stairs.

'Judas!' I didn't answer. 'Judas!' he yelled again, throwing open the door out of breath. 'JUDAS!'

I opened my eyes and turned my face. 'What is it?'

'I got a tenner.' He kissed a ten-pound note. 'More beers!'

54

The next morning Jacob and me strolled to the dole office. We came down Greenbank and over Bretonside bus station.

We reached the Job Centre. 'Queue was worse yesterday,' he said.

Security at the door bridged his arm across my chest. 'Wait here, gents,' he said, flashing his name badge: *Ricky Miller, HOS.*

Ricky's trousers were immaculate, sitting perfectly upon tightly laced, military-style black rubbers. He folded his hands in front of his groin and cracked his neck to one side.

There was no light in the doorway, just grime and a bunch of cardboard scraps left by the homeless drunk lingering across the road.

Ricky Miller then nodded and said, 'Okay gents, in you go.'

He ushered us and several others through the door like a line of cattle. I scowled back at some guy clipping my heel. The asshole apologised with a grief-stricken face—behind him a row of similar faces all pulling the same miserable expression as Ricky Miller, Head of Security, moved us along on schedule.

Putting on the brakes I halted the procession before reaching the welcoming committee. A jelly-armed woman, clasping a blue clipboard and a half-sized government-branded pen, peered steely over her tiny green spectacles, fixing her gaze upon me. 'Name?'

'Judas Nobody,' I said. She looked me over suspiciously before running her pen up and down her clipboard, repeating my name to herself. And I think, a strange thing, hearing your name on repeat. Glancing around, the building performed as a doctor's surgery, yet instead of prescriptions, people collected wage slips for being sick, coughing and itching for mere pennies an hour. Above me, two out of four fans were keeping viruses airborne and well circulated. I let my head hang back, looking up at the fans, listening to my name on repeat and Ricky Miller arguing with some guy outside:

'You 'ave to wait lyke the rest of 'em. You're nuffin special.'

The guy replied in a pissy-headed slur, 'Neeeberrrre*youuuu.*'

'Judas Nobody, Judas Nobody...'

'I've no interest in bein special,' answered Ricky. 'Now, just stand 'ere and wait your turn.'

'Fuuuhhkdissss... Izafuckinjoke, datswhatdissizz.'

'Judas Nobody... Judas Nobody...'

'There's no comedians 'ere, fella. But if you keep this up, you're at the back of the queue, and you won't find that funny.'

'Ooooyeeeahhh?'

Silence.

And then, 'FuuuhkyouyouasscuntpotatofacePRICK!'

As I stared at the fans I hear a series of thuds, like pigs colliding with iron gates. 'Ahh yes, *Judas Nobody*, found you. Please take a ticket from the machine over there and wait for your number to be called.'

I looked down from the fans. 'Thanks,' I said.

She raised an eyebrow at Jacob. 'And you are?'

'He's my friend. He's with me,' I said.

Jacob pointed his thumb. 'Yeah, with him.'

The floppy-armed woman waved us on. 'Next!'

We stepped through the threshold over a small pile of crisps, dodging a toddler with salt and vinegar snot. When we reached the ticket machine a queue of ten or so had already formed.

Jacob shook his head at the toddler as she followed us.

'Go find your mum,' he whispered back. 'Where's your mummy?'

She looked up at us with a single bubble enlarging from her mucky nose. Stopping suddenly, her knees popped forward as she hit the deck, her piss-soaked nappy hovering an inch above the carpet as though she was doing poo poo.

But Chucky's bride wasn't doing poo poo. She instead scooped up a fist of dirty crisp and held it out to Jacob.

'Gaa-buba?' she said.

Jacob shook his head. 'No thank you little one,' he said.

She pointed to herself. 'Ga-bah?'

I elbowed Jacob. 'Just ignore her, she'll find her mum.'

'Gaa-buba?' she said again, pointing back to Jacob.

'You eat it,' he told her. 'Yum yum, all for you.'

'Seriously mate, just leave it,' I told him, before narrowing my eyes at the axis of evil. 'She's tricking you.'

The kid turned her grubby finger back to herself. 'Ga-bah?'

'Yes!' Jacob said. '*You* eat crisp . . . '

Her finger, again, turned back to Jacob. 'Gaa-buba?'

'Fucksakes,' I said.

Jacob shook his head like he'd just woken up from a twelfth-round knockout. His drunk-looking face-waggle must've hit home to the kid, for she then shoved the crisps and her fist and whatever else from the shitty carpet into her toothless gob before waddling off toward an open space where small pods of welfare clients sat with telephones to their ears, anxiously chewing their nails.

We kept an eye on the queue.

#78. 'That don't sound so bad,' I said.

We took a seat and watched the big monitor overhead. #51.

'Not too long now,' I added cheerily.

'Depends,' is all Jacob said and needed to say.

Three hours later . . .

'Please take a seat.'

'Thanks.'

'Judas Nobody?'

'That's me.'

'Any previous criminal records we should be aware of?'

'Nope,' I said with a stupid grin.

The man in the suit lifted his sleep-deprived eyes, noticing me for the first time. A face devoid of expression, he buried his pimpled nose back into his desk.

'Any disabilities that prohibit you from working?'

I sat up against the chair. 'No,' I said.

'Medication?'

'Medication?'

'Do you take any medication?'

'I do not.'

'Can you drive?'

'Yes.'

He lifted his eyes. 'Do you have a license to drive, Mr Nobody?'

'Negative.'

Eyes again to the desk. 'Age?'

'My age?'

'Yes. How old are you?'

'Eighteen.'

'Are you currently looking for work?'

'About to start.'

Eyes up. 'When, Mr Nobody?'

'Today?'

Eyes down. 'What was your most recent job?'

'Petrol Station Cleaner.'

'Are you happy to do a similar job?'

'Happy.'

'When did that employment cease?'

'About three months ago . . . '

'Why?'

'Why what?'

Eyes up. 'Why did that employment end, sir?'

'I walked out.'

Eyes down. 'How have you supported yourself since?'

'Odd jobs here 'n there.'

'Cash in hand?'

'Correct.'

'Did you declare this to H.M. Revenue?'

'H.M. *who?*'

Eyes up. 'Her Majesty's Revenue and Customs. It's how you're taxed and paid, Mr Nobody.'

'Negative.'

'Well in the future, please be sure to do so.'

'Agreed.'

Eyes down. 'Any other skills or work experience?'

'I tiled walls in a massage shop. I'm good with my hands.'

'Tiler, *riiight*. Do you know where your local post office is?'

'Yes. I'll find it.'

Eyes up. 'Mr Nobody, you'll receive seventy-five pounds and sixty pence fortnightly. You'll receive a giro cheque in the post. Please take this cheque to your local post office to receive your money. Please be sure to take along ID, otherwise your money cannot be released.'

'What ID?'

Eyes down. 'Passport, national insurance card, utility bill . . . '

'Okay.'

'You'll meet with me once a week to review your job search.'

'Decent idea.'

Eyes up. 'Good,' he said. 'All done. You're free to go.'

I noticed for the first time his nametag: Sidney O'Reilly.

I stood up and pushed my chair. 'Cheers, Sid,' I said.

55

We located a patch of green with no dogshit in the park, hiding our six-pack beneath Jacob's jumper keeping them cool from the sun.

'We're gonna get a job,' I said.

'Yeah,' Jacob said, popping open a cold can of Carlsberg. He then leaned to me with an expression he'd been festering all morning and said, 'You know I'm not a Christian, Judas?'

'I know.'

'You don't have to be to read the Bible. Jesus wasn't a Christian.'

'And I don't care,' I said, drinking my beer.

'Proverbs twenty-nine fifteen: a rod and a reprimand impart wisdom, but children left to themselves disgrace their mother.'

I sunk the rest of my can and wiped my chin. 'I don't know what you're saying, Jacob.'

My friend shrugged. 'I'm too dumb to know what it means.'

I popped open another can. 'Maybe you're too smart to care.'

He paused . . . and then asked, 'What's life about, Judas?'

'Pissing in the toilet.'

'Let's finish these and go to the pub.'

'Decent idea.'

'Hello boys!' cried Ruby, the landlady, cleaning glasses at the end of the bar. 'What can I get you two ansom fellas?'

'Couple pints of lager, please Rube,' Jacob told her, slapping both hands down to the bar.

'You make sure you tell people you're eighteen if they ask, got it?'

'We are eighteen,' Jacob said.

'Oh, okay. Two pints for the men, coming up!'

Ruby finished polishing the glasses before placing them on a rack, her grey hair wrapped up in a blue headscarf with one curly strand dangling at the eye. She had a tiny nose and large, protruding cheeks, like golf balls, and never smiled. Not even to her regulars.

Once she stacked the glasses she walked over, parting thin strips of cigar smoke with her pointy tits. Picking up a couple glasses she began filling them both at once with lager.

'How are you men today?'

'Good.'

'Good.'

'How's pops, Jakes? Haven't seen the old man for a while. He ain't joined the alkie anon, as he? Those Higher Power busybodies are stealin all me bleddy regulars.'

'He's working.'

'Well . . . be a darlin and say ello from me, will ya? Tell him Ruby's got some fine Scotch in the basement. His favourite tipple.'

'I will.'

She had a little sparkle in her eye, her cheeks flushing pink.

'He said he'd come by and give my boiler another service is all.'

'I'll remind him,' Jacob said.

'Thanks, hon. Ask him to drop by soon. Old Ruby needs the heat.'

'I'll tell him, don't you worry.'

She slid our drinks across the bar. 'On the house, chaps. Welcome to the cure.'

56

Jezebel cleared a shelf while I went and grabbed a cloth.

'I haven't told Dion that Moses is living downstairs,' she started. 'He'd be here all the fucking time. I'd never be rid of him!'

'All I hear is you swearing,' I said, walking back in the room.

'Shit, sorry.'

Moses was lofty and gangly, with an arching nose, overcrowded teeth and incredibly smart facial hair, with a full-time fondness for fraud. I think he was mixed Indian or Pakistani or something there. As fate would have it, I was to reacquaint with Moses later.

'I got a job at the video shop,' said Jezebel, twisting the cork off a red.

'Great,' I said.

She poured us a glass. 'I've got some pills too, stole 'em from Dion months ago. Let's do them!'

'Where are they?'

'Stashed inside one of my dolls. I know it's bad to steal, but he's put me through fucking hell.' Jezebel sipped her drink. 'Sorry, swore again.'

'Christ.'

She suddenly smiled. 'So you'll move in, Judas? Do we live together now?'

'Yes. But try to relax a little. Don't fly off the handle so easy.'

She hugged me and screeched, 'I promise!'

The graveyard across the street was black and empty. Almost midnight. We had each taken a pill. Jezebel refused to follow me to the graveyard. She believed in evil spirits. Instead we stripped off all our clothes and crawled onto the bed.

'It gets really hard,' she said, leaning my hardon side to side. 'And it's the darkest part of your body.' We both hang our heads curiously.

'D'you like being circumcised, Judas?' she asked me.

'Don't know any other way,' I answered while tugging her tiny brown nipples to form pyramids. She closed her fist tight around the head of my cock and commented, 'I think it looks smarter.'

'What's Bruno's like?' I asked.

'Really long! Like a snake. But his foreskin is *whiffy*.'

As I manouvered her buttocks near my face she had to swivel on her knees, keeping clutched my cock in one fist, a rollie between the fingers, with her elbows stabbing the mattress until her crotch was an inch from my nose.

'What was the sex like?' I asked.

'I don't think he liked sex,' she said.

Opening up her bumcheeks, I had a good stare at the hole. 'Everyone has their thing,' I replied a few seconds late, half-pretending not to care. I had seen and heard too many secrets. Finally, I stopped trusting the infancy of love and had started to embrace something real: they just wanted sex, good sex. Girls were hungry, deprived, in some sort of famine. That's what I told myself. I was reassured of it. If love was a shared economy, then what made sex so different? Perhaps I just couldn't satisfy her, wasn't big enough, rough enough, didn't last long enough. Perhaps I should stick a cucumber between her flaps, grab her by the throat and slap her wall to wall, tie her to the bed and whisper *my beautiful whore* while attacking the cunt.

'Are you looking at my asshole?'

'Yes,' I answered quietly.

She squirmed, '*Oh Judas,* is it clean? IS IT CLEAN?'

'Yes,' I said again, making my inspection. She passed the joint between her thighs. I took a slow, deliberate hit, blowing smoke onto the hole, watching it tighten like something alien. Then I noticed the pink of her flaps. Its pinkness. Its fertility. My finger made its way there. By now Jezebel was busy glossing my hardon with baby oil, humming a series of tra-la-la's . . .

'It's warm,' I told her, feeling about inside. But she was too preoccupied with whatever was amusing her, too absorbed in her own perverse world to hear me. So I slid another finger in. Pulled them out and smelled them. Sweet. Sticky. I rolled my fingers together until the goo dried up. Sniffed again.

'Ah ah, no no, *mister.*' With that I reversed my finger from her asshole. Gave it another sniff.

'*Judas,*' she whined.

'It's just poo,' I told her, my head rolling in chemical pleasure.

She reached for the drawer and cleaned up my finger with a wet wipe. 'These E's are strong as hell,' she said, turning sluggishly on the bed back to my erection. 'No more fingers up my bum, please. Only my fannyhole tonight. Just my fanny.'

Caught in some wild ecstasy rush, brought on by the pill and the wine, she bounced her fist hard and fast, oil lathering and spitting along my shaft. We both watched on eagerly like devoted spectators at the races, willing our horse coming down the final stretch. She beat the thing without pause, her eyes bright with excitement.

'Almost there!' I yelled.

She kept beating.

'Not far now!'

She beat it faster.

It suddenly shot up like glue paste.

'*Ahhhhhhhh!*' she shrieked.

57

My kit stood ready by the door. It was 7 AM. I left Jezebel asleep beneath the sheets. We'd been up all night. I had pissed inside her cunt. I thought I was coming, but I was pissing. And it felt good. Better than come—that long, drunken piss that empties both legs with a satisfying sigh. I realised in time, just before it could spill over, squeezed, and pulled out, made a run for the toilet and finished off.

Jezebel just lay back gazing at the ceiling, fondling her nipples, peaking off these pills. The sheets were fine, surprisingly. I had checked. Just more fluid. She didn't notice. We'd been fucking for too many hours to take note of something so trivial. So we drank more wine, then argued. We argued from 4 AM till we were too exhausted, nothing left in us but cheap booze and a cheaper comedown. She kicked all the furniture and screamed murder out the bathroom window with the door bolted. I punched a hole in the door. It was a horribly big hole. The police rang the bell at 6 AM—complaint from a neighbour. I somehow talked the coppers away while Jezebel sobbed with the cat on her lap. When the sun came up she rolled under the bedsheets with a doll, and stirred as I moved strands of hair from her teary eyes, kissed her forehead. She told me to have a good day football training. I told her to do well at the video store. And then I left.

It was a bright morning. My eyes tightened. The streets were busy. My knees cracked as I walked along Ford Park Road, then up across Central Park to the stadium. Stood outside, I breathed in that clean, sporting fresh air. My thigh muscle twitched. I watched the team arrive and laugh, they laughed well. I was down here and they were up there. Throwing my bag over my shoulder I popped open a can of Stella and guzzled it back. Lit a cigarette. It tasted good with the beer. Gave me a high, a warm, dirty fuzz in the brain.

I walked to a bench and sat down beside a homeless fella who was sat on the other side. He didn't ask for change. He just sat there, with his rusty bag on his back, drinking his morning beer too. A moment later I had opened another can and lit another cigarette, watching Sunday morning dogwalkers look at me with suspicion. But it only served to bring me back to reality: a street kid, working things out from the gutter. By now I needed the pills to end, but knew I had to let it pass through, ride the low as I did the high. That was the agreement. That's how it all balances and evens itself out, each our own judge, critic, and supporter, and in some cases, executioner. I felt stupid, worthless. And to make matters less humorous, the homeless stink had decided to reach his dirty little palm to me and mumble something with his tongue too swollen. I shook my head at him. And saw that now I was made to appear better off than he, having to act out a fictitious exchange of poor man and fortunate man, my morning beer somehow seeming more civilised.

I had read somewhere that no price was too high for the privilege of owning yourself. I think it was some *Neechee* fella. I couldn't recall. With this in mind, this intent on owning yourself, I would have gladly exchanged seats with the tramp on the other end of this bench. A nobody, a no one. There was light there. He had light. It was enduring. I could feel it. You could walk in any direction and keep going. Stop whenever you pleased. He had it good. I knew.

My knees cracked as I got up to leave. The foul-smelling scrounger had ruined our sitdown. I had eight hours to kill. In a few strides I made it to another bench and opened another beer and kept my eyes to the floor while I came down from my high. The gutter to slowly reappear and consume me like a bad dream.

The following day I strolled over to Jacob's. We started training hard. We went all out. Ten-hour days. Jacob was just shy of six feet. Stocky, a strong work-horse, the natural type that could lift big and finish a marathon, sink eight pints down the boozer and spring up at the crack of dawn.

I kicked the medicine ball to one side. Jacob slammed his thigh down like an empty glass, glaring from beneath those bushy eyebrows. He gave my arm a sly backhand. I told the idiot to let me know when he was ready. He gave me another. This time harder.

'There there, sweetlips,' I says. 'Play nice.' He jerked that dumb head of his down like a hot bull and lunged at me, coming fast and low. He took my ribs and drove me back to the wall, knocking the wind out of me. The sly dog then tried to hoist me up from the ground, hugging his biceps under my ass. We collided along the wall with a clunky thud. The lamp flew. The Bible followed.

I leaned into his ear. 'Whenever you're ready, cherrypie.'

'Take me seriously, Nobody!' he spat back, slamming me down against his desk. I coughed and snatched my arm around his waist, giving him the Yokozuna squeeze. He curled his buttocks down, trying to wiggle his way out. But I got the scoundrel, heaving him topsy-turvy with his toes walking the ceiling and his head tucked under my vicelike grip. I dropped the chucklehead on a pile of cushions, scooped up a twenty pound medicine ball and stood over him.

'*One!*'

'Have you told Jezebel you quit playing football?'

'*Two!*'

'Are you gonna tell her?'

'*Three!*'

'When you gonna tell her, Judas?'

'Soon. *Four!*'

'I don't think you need to.'

'*Five!*'

'She don't deserve it.'

'We live together now.'

Jacob held onto the ball. 'So what!' he said.

'I'm lying every day. It makes me gutless.'

He threw back the ball. 'She cheated on you! Just move out!'

I threw the ball back at him. 'I can't go back home.'

He tossed the ball aside. 'Move back here. My mum don't care.'

'I'll keep that in mind, buttercup. Now, fifty pressups.'

We later washed up and wandered along Greenbank toward The Albion. All around seemed bleak, the future was bleak, and everyone was gladly racing toward it. Was I the only one seeming distracted by it all, the only one wary of the sewer of success spewed out ahead by our highly regarded predecessors, or was I just another fool, stumbling blindly toward an inevitable fate like everyone else?

We finally made it to the pub and sidled up to the bar. Four dedicated musclebuilders with thick necks and ironlike confidence fed coins into a fruit machine. The place wreaked of piss and vinegar, the walls coughed, and the carpet raised up a stink that remained airborne, teetering just below the nose.

'Two pints of lager,' Jacob said, getting more convincing with pub talk. 'What about that guy?' he then whispered to me.

I followed his eye, catching sight a creature in his forties perhaps clutching his ribs and rocking back and forth. He looked mean, foul, cruelly kept alive, seeming as though he could take several metal poles to the skull, dust himself off and hop back to his feet. He yanked a bony yob to his right by the crook of his neck and gave the poor bastard a terrible shake, making this strange, inhuman sound, like a seabird. He then let go and put his straitjacket back on and was again silent, lifting his beer, smoking his fag.

'Harmless,' I said, turning my worry back to the meatheads.

We downed our drinks and ordered another, plus shots of whiskey. Another two whiskeys. Another couple beers and a shot of Smirnoff and perched at a table tipsy and lightheaded, wondering why the hell we were sat in this shithole. Then a very old fellow took the third chair and just looked at us. His name was Bill.

'I'm Bill.'

'Hello Bill.'

'Hello Bill.'

'Have I seen you boys round here? I think I recognise you.'

'Not likely.'

'Nope.'

'Oh . . . you look familiar . . . how'd I know you?'

We both shrugged.

Bill got excited. 'D'you boys box? Are ya boxers?'

'Nope.'

I shook my head.

'*Hmm*,' the old man sighed, clasping his brittle chin. His fingers were fat and yellow and beaten, his cheeks sunken as though he'd lost all his back teeth. Coughing, Bill slipped a pack of Marlboro Red from his top pocket and tapped the bottom with a nail. 'Fag?'

I leaned in. 'Sure, Bill,' I said.

'I've seen it all in this town,' began Bill. 'These youngsters don't know what respect is. They're too angry.'

'Right,' I said, taking a long, satisfying drag.

'When I was growing up, in the thirties, we never fought when we were angry, me and my pals. We drunk. Got drunk.'

'Amen,' said Jacob, raising his glass.

Bill's right hand shook a little. He rested it on the table. It stopped shaking. 'Kids today 'ave no reason to fight. It's all muscle and intimidation, a total lack of what it is to be a man.' Bill scratched some neck gravel. It was loud, like a scourer to a greasy pan. I glanced at Jacob then back at Bill, unsure where this was going.

He then said, 'If your house ain't in order, you don't *ever* fight.'

'What'd you mean, Bill?' I asked. The old guy stared at me, his reddened eyes tombs, tightening his brow, gleaming with new light.

'D'you boys believe in *God?*'

'Yes,' said Jacob without pause.

'I'm a Buddhist,' I declared. 'Like the monks who catch fire.'

The old man waved me off. 'Don't matter either way. What I mean to say, is that you must never fight when you're angry, you've nuthin to lose, blind, full of hot rage. There's no *life,* no *control.* The angry man's house ain't in order, it's *chaos!* Do you understand me, boys?'

Jacob and I nod together.

Bill leaned back in his chair. 'His lights are off. Just blind and angry, swingin at shadows, shadows he finks will do him harm. Still a frightened little *cockshit*. Are ye listening?'

We nod again. Bill's eyes rest a little. 'Too frightened to face up, to be a man, a good, fighting man, conquering *himself.*'

Bill sunk more beer. Took a long, reflective pull on his cigarette. 'No, no,' he said, blowing smoke under us. 'Never fight when you're angry. Your house is a bloody mess. Am I gettin through to you boys?'

The musclemen hit jackpot. The machine lit up like a theme park.

'I have to put up with this shit every day,' said Bill, tilting his head. The bolshie lads swung to the bar and slammed their winnings on the table. One finger-called menacingly at the barkeep while his steroid-tooting pals shoved nearby punters aside.

'You boys look like good lads. Good fighters. Not like these lot. These are not *men*. They're just angry boys with a bit of brawn, like to throw their weight about, protect dumb sluts, be heroes, all that stupid shit. No. Real men don't fight when they're angry. They suck it up and put themselves together. And it starts 'ere.' Bill thumbed his chest. 'This is your home,' he said. 'If you get hit, right 'ere, right to the chest, over some provocation or other dumb shit, and it drops you to your knees, metaphor-wise, makes you appear weak—the *worst* kind of insult. You just get yourself back on your feet and don't you *dare* swing back, you boys got that? You suffer it!' Bill kept his thumb. He stopped a tear. 'Where 'ave all my pals gone?' he asked himself, gazing around the four corners of the pub. His hand shook again. He put it on the table but it kept jumping. He looked at Jacob, then at me. The tear fell and stopped at his chin.

'You look like good lads is all I'm saying. Keep this clean and these for God.' Bill held up his fists while thumbing his chest, smoke smearing his eyes from the cigarette. 'Put yourselves together, and you'll fight for somefin worth a life, you 'ere me?' He swung a left hook. Stopped. Glared at us. 'And, if need be, if the heavens wanna show, only *then* should you let it swing—' he paused . . . 'And God'll swing right back atcha!' The crazy fuck plugged his fag in his gob and threw a couple neat uppercuts, cigarette ash exploding above the table. 'A Good man is just as monstrous as an Evil man,' he said, now taking a drag of his smoke. 'And that, my boys, is the fight.'

'The fight?' asked Jacob.

The madman swung his eyes left to right, scanning the bar. Looked again at me and Jacob. 'Yeah,' the loon whispered. '*The fight*. It's the only fight there is. You against Him. The toughest kind. Send you to the madhouse. Make you seem like a real *nutjob* among all these spoilt little cunts. Brutal. Lonely work. Becoming a man. All that inglorious, flawed, misunderstood shit, exposed to the world—a world overun by manchilds and ladybabies, too cockshit scared to face themselves!'

The old coot leaned across the table with another grin. 'Don't be *nice*, boys, be good monsters.' He put out another combo of fists, punching the air as if he were twenty-five all over again.

Jacob nodded. We both nod at Bill. Then Bill got up and walked away. He fixed his jacket, downed his beer, squashed his cigarette, and walked across the pub floor and out the door.

58

Double-checking if I had the right house, I fumbled the keys again. One was for my mother's place, the other, Jezebel's. Examining the keys, I flipped them over as though it were a trick. While doing so I noticed my shoelace undone. I didn't tie it. I was too drunk.

It was unnecessary to see over the wall of the graveyard to know how bare it was on the other side, grey stone as far as the eye could stretch, keeping death contained. The sudden privilege of being alive made me tie my lace. As I do, Moses's eyes peer from beside his curtains. He pushed the curtain and smiled when realising it was me. I stood back up and offered a tipsy nod, beginning to puzzle again these damn keys. They were both gold and made by Yale. I had mixed them again while tying my lace. I tried the one in my right hand, dropping that key in my right pocket and repeating *Mum* in my head before slotting the second one in and pushing open the door.

Moses's teeth stuck out from the wall like a broken fence. I wanted to be alone, wasn't available to humanise, shoving the other key in my left pocket along the hall repeating *Jezebel*.

'Judas Nobody!' my downstairs neighbour cheered.

I stopped walking. 'Hello, Moses,' I said.

He kept that false humour up and asked me in. I was weak, cornered, filled with remorse from all the alleged abuse screaming through the floorboards of 33A.

His flat was all white, everything: white walls, white carpet, white picture frames. I sat down on his white sofa.

'Tea?'

'Yeah.'

'Been out on the beer?'

'Yeah.'

'Where'd you go?'

'Albion.'

'Shithole.'

'Yeah.'

The coffeetable was littered with unopened letters, with several credit cards neatly piled to one side next to a pair of white latex gloves. I thought it odd but was too wasted to care.

Moses returned with two cups of milky tea.

'Thanks,' I said.

'No problem. So, how's it upstairs?' I knew what he meant. He banged on our door a few times. We never answered. Pills wouldn't let you answer a bang at the door at three in the morning. It instead made you crawl silently along the carpet away from the intruder and into the shadows, whispering back and forth until the headless horesman had galloped back to hell.

'Upstairs, yeah . . . it's okay,' I said.

He laughed. 'You two argue more than a married couple!'

'If that's what marriage is, then I guess we're committed.'

He stopped laughing. 'Could you please try keeping it down a little? Drives the missus nutty. She's falling asleep at work, Judas, thinks you'll hurt Jezebel bad someday.'

'We'll keep it down.'

'I don't mean to say you're knockin her about. We don't—'

'It's okay,' I interjected. 'I understand.'

'Anyway . . . listen, Judas,' he said, eager to get to the point. 'I wondered if you wanna earn a little extra cash?'

I sipped my tea. 'How'd you mean, Moses?'

'Well, I've got these 'ere credit cards.' He scooped up a box and fiddled out a latex glove, strapping the glove on before finger-picking a card from the dustless glass table. The card read: *Mr Alfonso Anderson.*

'He doesn't exist. He's completely made up. He earns more than a hundred grand a year, married, and lives at *this* address.' He fingered a letter with an address in another part of town.

'Alfonso?' I said, the only part of his spiel that amused me.

'You can be Alfonso. You could even be Abdu'llah. You're easy.'

'Your mum is easy.'

'My mum's dead, Judas.'

I took another sip of tea. 'I didn't know.'

'Listen, all these cards have a credit limit of twenty grand each.'

'Right,' I said, feeling the whiskey return to my oesophagus.

'You can use 'em anywhere. You just sign for whatever you buy.' He flipped over the card like he's pitched this a thousand times to a thousand other idiots. 'The signature just needs to match yours when you sign. And that's that! Easy-peasy.'

'What's your point, Moses?'

He shook his head. 'I'll give you one card if you test it out.'

'Worth twenty grand?'

'Yes. But you can't spend it all in one shot. Just a few hundred 'ere an there, test the waters.' He took a slow sip of his tea, the eyes of a cunning man hiding inside the cup.

'So what's in it for you?'

He took his time answering, setting his mug down steadily. 'It's a new batch. I just need to make sure they're squeaky clean.'

'Give it to me straight, Moses.'

'The card is yours to keep, twenty grand! If that card is *clean*, it means the rest are clean, comprende?'

'And if it's not clean?'

'Well, you know, *the risk* . . .'

I set my tea down and puzzled all that money. I grew up with cash: Gold. Silver. Copper. You held onto it, zipped it in your pocket, counted the correct change after buying a portion of chips and a bottle of cherryade, scooped up treasures from your mother's handbag. Though my brain, now, was doing something new. I was accepting cash as a metaphor, some sort of analogy. There were no limits, it seemed, no boundaries to this new arrangement. It was all a metaphor, a figment of the mind. Perhaps all along?

'No price is too high to owning yourself' But how far was I from myself? And how much will it cost me to get back? And is everything a fucking *metaphor*?

'Did you see that brand new silver Range Rover outside?' he said.

'Maybe.'

'I picked it up this morning, using this.' He pointed to a shiny amber card looking like Wonka's golden ticket. 'I've got some bloke coming to pick the car up for fifteen grand cash. Free money!'

'Fifteen grand, eh?' I say to myself. Moses nodded along, his latex thumb stuck to that shiny ticket.

'I'll do it,' I said.

'Great!' he said.

The room suddenly transformed into a crime scene, every sunlit floating particle a prime suspect, making sense to all the white goods.

The bandit hastily made his way to the curtain, making sure there were no interrogating beams of light, while I stared at that pile of credit cards, wondering, quietly to myself, where all that money *really* was.

59

Jezebel was at the video shop working overtime, helping the owner reorganise his display and advise on popular film. I was fortunate, I could meander at home while she ducked out the door, all because I had a better, more convincing lie.

I had spun a story that training had started later, a change of schedule at the club, some revised contractual agreement that I'd signed. Brewing myself another PG Tips, I returned to the window.

Jezebel bragged about the five-hundred quid she snagged for it, a bargain, she said. I watched the two burly delivery blokes haul that thing up the stairs, asked if they wanted help but they insisted they were fine. The hallway was narrow but they knew what they were doing. Just another day on the job.

The antique chair, carved as a human hand, sat oddly in the dark corner of the room, next to a new forty-inch colour TV. Sipping my brew, I sat back and wondered, 'How the hell did she afford this?'

Two mornings later, those same delivery men lugged a carved statue of a naked tribeswoman shaped as a side table up the same narrow staircase, a token gift from the boss for meeting target.

Lenny, her boss, was lean and crooked and pushing seventy. He stood crooked, his big spading hand clasped around his lower back, with a nose resembling a rotten, beaten down carrot. He was a bit of an enigma. I knew diddly-squat about the old coot, other than he owned a video shop and employed my girlfriend, and that his grey wig lapped over his forehead like a letterbox.

Popping open a bottle of beer with my back tooth, I stood examining Lenny talking with Jezebel. I was concealed across the road from the shop. Never had I seen her make those gestures. She smiled different, and her laugh wasn't real. He didn't smile, this Lenny fella—the aged had a license to be cold and ruthless in the company of spurious amusement of the young. It was commonly accepted—a privilege reserved for the almost dead.

Hmm, I think, taking a gulp of beer followed by a long, thoughtful puff of my cigarette. I needed to piss, but couldn't just abandon my post—not while they were closing up.

Lenny had bolted the door and flipped the sign to *'CLOSED'*. As he did, I was pissing against the wall with one eye on the shop, ready to lock my todger away if anyone surprised us. I rolled the cigarette to the corner of my mouth and propped my beer upon the wall. The stream of piss found all the cracks in the pavement, causing it to detour from out the shadows and across the street beneath the high sun, glistening like a golden spiderweb.

The wall held my chest upright, cigarette smoke wafting over my face. I had already put back six beers and a handful of party-sized Russian Standards, so I didn't feel much for the dark splash of piss about my feet. Us boys have watered against many something or other, felt the eastern breeze of an angel. My only shame was to take my eyes off my business for too long for it to swamp the soles of my shoes. But that ain't so bad. Wringing my cock, I quickly tucked him away. That little excess pee being absorbed by my pants was alright, it'll soon dry. *'Ahh, it'll dry,'* I muttered to myself, turning back to the video store.

Slipping another beer from my pocket, I watched Jezebel skip toward the back office door with Lenny. The old man carried her by the elbow while clasping that crooked back of his. The office door then closed.

She said he owned an enormous collection of videos in the back room, too much for one shop. He was thinking of opening a second shop and putting Jezebel in charge. I tried not to care much, air contently between the rent being secured and our new forty-inch television keeping me entertained.

Though that didn't stop me from kicking open the shop door, sending shards of glass all over the gaff, making my way toward that back room with a bottle wrapped up in my fist. Before I could toe-punt the second door, Lenny opened up and swung a cricket bat, but instead clutched his cheek from the bottle I'd served to the perverts face. Jezebel jumped behind with her hands covering her naked titties. 'Judas! Judas!'

'Are you gonna take that there beer bottle to the bin, sonny?' asked an old lady running a broom along her doorstep, glaring down at me swaying in a drunken daydream.

'Sure,' I muttered, fixing my zipper while looking once more at the video shop before retreating back to base, a hobbling series of dark-amber piss-prints following me down the street.

60

'Alright,' she said, taking a seat next to me. 'Lenny asked if I wanted to earn a little extra money.'

'Wait,' I said, feeling that jolt of nervous excitement and not wanting to rush into it. 'Okay,' I told her, 'nice and easy.'

'Handjob,' she said. 'Two hundred cash.'

'Knew it.'

'Two hundred, Judas!'

'Christ, Jezebel. Gimme a sec, will ya?'

'Sorry.'

I stood up, walked to the kitchen, uncorked a bottle and poured a long glass. Life's got a fetish for repeating itself. Was my mother a whore? No clue, a complete mystery. Necking the wine, feeling the cool liquid soak my brain, I walked back and sat down.

'Have you done it already?'

'........'

'Fucksake, Jezebel. How many times?'

'Twice. Two times.'

'At the store?'

'Yes.'

Punching the wall would be a nice act, a put-on show, so I refrained. Lit a smoke. Didn't care. Never was it the dirty rag of humanity that bothered me. That I could withstand, relate.

'He's got no one to spend his money on. He's loaded, Judas!'

'Loaded from a video rental shop?'

'He's got more,' she stressed, already way ahead of me.

'Jesus, Jezebel, juss gimme a second.'

All the new furniture was hers, she reminded me whenever we argued. That was fair. She was making things easier, I knew. We spoke some more. Some time passed. Without much thought I grabbed her by the crotch and stuffed three fingers straight in. She gasped and gripped my wrist, fought my zip open and wrestled me out, swung her leg over my lap and guided me inside.

Giving up our problems to the cunt was easy. Now we were both satisfied. Sex was often like that. We were both happy to just fuck, whatever it was, just like any other function in our relationship, like cleaning the loo or putting out the bins.

I knew she was a whore, that her and her cunt had discovered a way out. And yet, in some screwed-up, wonderful fashion, I was happy for her. More, I admired her.

She tensed her pelvis and out slipped my dribbling cock. She rushed to the bathroom, returning with some bogroll, immediately cleaning us both up while making sounds of light disgust. Looking onto the graveyard, it had started to rain, a light spit against the window. It seemed a decent moment to tell her that I wasn't a football star. That I had a hot credit card tucked away in my pocket with enough cash to wake up whenever we pleased, ease into the day, take our sweet time. But instead, I just sat there silently with my lap soaked in cum, admiring rainclouds drift across the sky. I was cornered but played along, knowing that I never objected when Lenny paid for the antiques, drove her shopping, funded our drugs and booze. I benefited, said yes to it all, encouraged it, took advantage of the old man.

'Do you hate me, Judas?'

'No,' I said, downing the rest of my wine. 'Of course not.'

'Do I need help? Am I fucked up?'

'We're both fucked up, Jezebel.'

61

A few days later I found myself wandering up and down the street. Tuesday. Raining again. I kicked a stone to the video shop and waited outside.

Lenny's green Range Rover was old, but it imbued wealth, that old, effortless, aristocratic farmhouse four-wheeled drive kinda money. You could kick a dent in the bonnet and smash out a head-lamp, wrench a wing-mirror from its face and snap the ariel and leave the thing sideways, yet it'll somehow continue to drive with charm, that old thing, parading the town like a traumatised veteran with his pistol sprung high.

The old man flipped the sign to '*CLOSED*'. He doesn't see me. But I could see myself reflected in his shop window, leaned back against the railing with a piping hot bag of chips.

Jezebel secretly signalled one more minute. I held up the bag of chips like a simpleton. She pouted '*sorry*' so clear and sweet with her lipstick-red mouth that all I could think was that juicy kisser wrapped around the old man's cock, which seemed to excite me.

We walked home.

'He knows about me?' I asked.

'Yes.'

'Okay,' I said. 'Well that's good. It's good that he knows.'

'He asked if I would stay over his house. Five hundred pounds.'

'And do what?'

'Company. He's lonely, Judas, and too old to keep it up.'

'Have sex you mean?'

'No! He asked if I had a girlfriend. He likes to watch.'

I went quiet for a second. 'It's a bit strange. I dunno, Jezebel.'

'Five hundred pounds for a few hours. I'd sneak out at midnight and leave him sleeping. He doesn't care, honest he doesn't.'

'What if he does something crazy?'

'He's just a lonely old man.'

'I should come and wait outside.'

'No, it's fine, I promise. He gets drunk on two glasses.'

'You've had a drink with him?'

'At the shop, yeah, some wine, just some wine.'

We reached home and I sat next to the window, again, that graveyard. Jezebel fetched her best plates from the cupboard, the ones with the abstract fruits painted by some artist I could never remember, no matter how many times she mentioned it. As she plated our chips, I brushed my finger over the soft lambswool throw on the sofa. And that television. The antique wardrobe. Persian rug.

I was proud of her. Watching her squeeze all she could from the little tomato sachet I said, 'I'm proud of you.'

'No you're not,' she shot back.

But I was.

'I've got something to tell you,' I said.

She scooped up her pager, unwilling to turn the thing off. Losing patience I snatched her by the hand and took us to the bedroom. She threw the pager to the sofa and ran her nail over the dent I put in the wall weeks earlier. It hurt good the third strike, that dent, feeling my knuckle swell an inch. No matter how hard I tried to reason with her screams, I did what all men were warned never to do: I made the dent look like her face, one impressionable oblong. Half an hour later, once my knuckle had stopped hurting, her old lady showed up in the hallway, stood behind one of her lovers, a hefty Russian with fists like hooves. Jezebel turned on the act, pacing about the flat with her eyes low, repeating, 'He's gonna kill me!'

I eyed the Russian, squared the fuck nicely in the eye. He was twice my size, thick-bodied, and was a nut. You could tell a nut. But I thought I could take the swine somehow, take his back and poke the bastards eyes while thumping his ear.

'I vill kum back eef you hoort her my friend,' he said to me, putting on the act to impress the women.

'You're here now, Rasputin,' I said.

Jezebel screamed, 'Stop it, Judas!'

'Judas, dear, please think,' motioned Frida.

'Your bodyguard here's making me nervous,' I said.

'I lose patience! Zis guy is mash fotatoes!'

'Mash what, cowtits?'

'Judas! Stop!'

The oaf stuck his finger under my nose. 'Votch it,' he snarled.

I stuck my forehead against his finger and locked eyes. 'Watch what, Babushka?'

His woman was quick on her toes, lunging in his way and stopping the brute from swinging. Sure, I was just some mouthy kid to him, water and bones. To ease the tension, the thick-headed dunce was ordered promptly out the door. And I watched the fuck leave, saw the angry cretin out, staring back at me with those small black holes that I was sure had seen and done some awful things.

The door finally closed. And I sat with her old lady and listened as she told me again how a frightened seven-year-old Jezebel had to watch her father put her mother's head through a door window, and then clean up all the pieces of glass.

She was right. I knew...

But it didn't count now. Was too late. She was already a whore.

62

The next day, while Jezebel was at the video shop with Lenny, I decided to take the credit card for a walk.

Stepping into a Buy n' Sell, I picked out a games computer, the one Jacob mentioned—The Sega Mega Drive—and wedged it under arm walking casually to the till.

I read the credit card while waiting in line:

Mr Alfonso Anderson: EXP END 10/00.

. . . and masterminded my escape if all went tits up, clocking the whereabouts of all the cameras in the shop.

The young kid behind the till looked as though he'd been working here long enough, on autopilot, racing through the queue. The gel had hardened his green-dyed hair to one side, pointing away from his head like one half of a Christmas tree. And his peepholes, swollen red beneath a pair of thick spectacles from all the overtime and punctuality, doing his very best to accommodate. I couldn't make out his nametag from where I stood, but knew he was my guy. Cleaning up his nose with his sleeve he coughed the next customer forward.

James '*The Hitman*' Ronaldson.

The shop tannoy screeched, but my friend James paid no attention, waving me forward like a pro. As I approached I slipped him a well-to-do smile, arching my mouth like some dapper Don.

'Good morning, sir,' he said sprightly.

I placed the computer on the counter. 'Morning, *Hitman*,' I said.

The kid grinned proudly, readying his scanner. 'Sega Mega Drive?'

'Oh yes,' I said. 'Can't wait to set this thing up for my kid.'

'Great choice,' he answered swiftly, more interested in blabbering about the games on offer. The Hitman flung six or seven cartridges onto the counter with a running commentary of each while boxing and bagging and tapping buttons. I stopped the green-haired emo on Streets of Rage II and told him those three would do just fine.

'That'll do just fine, Hitman,' I said, tossing him the plastic.

He swiped it up. My nerve-ends pricked. 'Just sign here, Mr Anderson,' he said. I stole a second glance at the exit before squiggling the mark of an impostor. My good friend and pal then handed me back the card without examining its authenticity.

'Good to go, Mr Anderson!' he said.

I pocketed the card and spun out of there. 'Thanks, Hitman!'

The next morning I marched straight back to the same Buy n' Sell with a shiny new Mega Drive that I had just procured up the street. Taking it directly to James, I informed my snot-nosed accomplice that I'd misplaced the receipt, that it was a birthday gift and that I had no way of returning the thing. My pal promised me a good price. Minutes later I whistled out the shop with a fistful of free cash.

Within a week, Alfonso Anderson had bought six brand new computers across town, then immediately sold each one in various flog-easys, pocketing four hundred notes of free money, ready for something more adventurous.

'I've got some speed,' I told Jacob.

'Oh yeah?' he said excitedly.

Lifting a snowball from my pocket, I said, 'I've got a shitload. Five grams, maybe. We're rich!'

We sniffed through the lot while playing chess for two straight days without sleep. By the third sunrise we went for a stroll along the coast, stopping by the cliffs and squinting at the hostile morning light. We plonked down and listened to the sea crash against the rocks as our teeth quaked uncontrollably.

'It's beautiful,' Jacob said.

'The sea?'

'All of it.'

I nodded. Knowing what he'd meant.

'Do you believe in God, Judas?'

'We have an agreement to ignore each other.'

'We should be firemen.'

'I used to start fires when we were young, big ones, remember?'

'Let's save people and put out fires.'

I tossed a stone. 'Fire's alright.'

'Not when people get burned alive, Judas.'

'Fire will always be alright, Jacob.'

My friend rubbed his cold hands together. 'It's freezing,' he said.

'Okay,' I said, climbing to my feet. 'Let's head back.'

We mooched back along the pier to Jacob's place. He crawled into bed with his clothes on while I rolled up in a sleeper on the floor. We said nothing but goodnight. We were cold and moody and out of shape—our first comedown together.

Jacob soon shot back up in a crazy fit, determined to fold a towel over the top of the curtain, attacking the coming light. He remained there for some time, in some sort of persistent quarrel. I listened to him struggle while staring at jars of piss beneath his bed, trying to ease my mind. I was flat-out exhausted, ignoring the cackle of pigeared shadows flitting by the corner of my eye.

Several moments later Jacob woke me up with the sound of pissing in the corner of the room.

'Did you sleep?' I asked him as he crawled back into bed.

'I don't know. I don't remember.'

'It was morning a second ago, now it's suddenly dark,' I said.

'I tried reading my Bible,' he said. 'It's terrifying, Judas.'

I rolled over. 'Well stop reading the bloody thing.'

'I can't stop thinking horrible thoughts, either,' he whispered in the dark. 'I think I'm going mad.'

I mumbled against my pillow. 'Take it easy. You're coming down off the speed.'

'I thought you were the Devil! I was convinced of it.'

'I said take it easy...'

He sighed. 'I thought you were putting me through some test.'

I sighed too. 'Yeah, these comedowns feel that way sometimes.'

'It was real, Judas!'

I rolled on my back. 'For Pete's sake, I believe you, now take it easy.'

He moved in his bed. 'Thought you were gonna kill me in my sleep. Christ, I believed it for hours. I was gettin ready to kill *you* first!'

'Your farts are killing me.'

He jumped up. 'I'm serious, Judas! I thought my whole family were demons, spying on me. *Inside my head.*'

'Oh yeah?'

'Yeeeah,' he whispered. 'They could hear my thoughts. I believed everyone could hear my thoughts. I almost lost it. I couldn't trust anyone, not even myself! That's why I tried reading the Bible.'

'It's a heavy book, Jacob. Try figuring things out yourself.'

He let go another long, quiet sigh, the back of his head sinking into his pillow. 'Man,' he said, 'I thought I'd lost it.'

I rolled over again. 'May not be such a bad thing,' I said.

He turned in his bed. 'You mean to go mad?'

'Well,' I said, 'what's the other option, continue with what we got?'

63

A few days of recuperating from the comedown I found myself back in town with the credit card, seated on a bench, staking out my next hit. While doing so, I noticed some sketchy-looking runt in a phonebox, cupping his hand over his mouth, rubbing his junkie eyes while sputtering into the receiver. I didn't know why I found this so amusing. The phonebox stood adjacent to the public loo where a homeless fella sat with his palm up and head low, ankles swollen blue over ragged boots, face brown in doorway soot.

After a while the homeless fella stood himself up, fixed his pants and straightened his head, stumbled over to the phonebox and politely tapped the window. The sketchy-looking guy ignored the stinky tramp, continuing to jabber into the receiver. A second later they took off together in a hurry, laughing, counting coins.

Lifting myself from the bench I made my way to a nearby clothes store. A young girl, no more than sixteen, loitering near the entrance with her hair neatly pinned back, smiled at me and said good morning. She quickly corrected herself. 'I mean good afternoon!' she said, triple-checking her oversized, glittery watch.

'Afternoon to you,' I repeated back in a dignified manner.

This particular retail store had only two security cameras, keeping an eye on all the stiff fabric and jewellery.

'Can I help?' the young girl asked behind me.

I turned and brushed a pair of trousers. 'Only browsing,' I said.

She grinned, bowed and retreated away like a lovely Geisha.

I reached high for a leather bag. Considered the price. A tall gent nodded my way. His nametag read "*Brian, Store Manager*".

Returning the nod, I slipped the bag back and stepped closer to Brian. I don't know why I hovered near him, but I did, for some time, pretending to be interested in leather jackets and trews. Something said get out of there, but instead I wandered over to the till and picked out the most expensive watch. Brian waved to the girl.

Five minutes later she'd gift-packed the watch into a small paper bag and took the plastic. 'I'm not sure why it's not working?' she said, swiping like a lunatic. 'It says to call a number.' Her eyebrows furrowed at the blue screen. And although my heart was racing, I couldn't help appreciate such mature tits on such a young girl.

The store manager took the card. 'Is it new?' he asked me.

'Everything okay?' I said, breaking out in a cold sweat.

'We just have to run a few security checks, Mr Anderson.'

The jobsworth took a corded phone from the wall and dialled the number on screen while examining the card suspiciously.

Several moments later he handed me the telephone.

'Just a few standard questions, Mr Anderson,' stated a woman.

I gave my best highbrow speak. 'Go right ahead,' I told her.

'What is your occupation?'

'Writer of fiction. Have you heard of *The Great Funfair*?'

'Are you married?'

'Many times. In fact, my current wife is also a writer.'

'Children?'

'Little Monty and Agatha. Twins.'

'Thank you. Please hand the phone back to the store manager.'

I cleared my throat and handed it over. Brian said yes three times before hanging up. I was surprised he passed me back the card.

'One moment,' he said, before disappearing through a back door.

Once the stickler was out of sight I slid my toes in reverse. The young girl flashed me a smile as I backslided between the aisle, pausing to try on a felt hat. Out the corner of my eye I see her fold a sweater. Seizing my chance, I flung the hat and bolted out the store.

'I told you!' Jacob cried out.

I fell on his bed, breathing heavy. Jacob locked his door and marched straight for his desk, producing a large pair of scissors from his drawer and handing them over.

Agreeing for once, I took the choppers and split the card in two. All that money and freedom, gone, twenty thousand big ones up in a figurative cloud of smoke—the words of that *Neechee* fella ringing in my head: 'No price is too high for the privilege of owning yourself.'

I started to laugh.

'What is it?' Jacob said.

I laughed a little harder.

'What is it, Judas?' he snorted more angrily.

Then it all came out of me, big howls from the gut.

'It's not funny, Judas!' he yelled. 'You could've gone to jail!'

I kept laughing. 'Twenty thousand pounds! *Ha Ha Ha.*'

He took back the scisssors. 'I don't care!' he blasted, bunging the blade across the room and snatching up his Bible.

I immediately stopped laughing and shook my finger at him. 'Put that thing away, Jacob. I'm warning you.'

Slamming the book shut he collapsed on his bed. 'Let's just forget it,' he said. 'I don't wanna think about that card or anything else.'

So we left it. I wasn't to be a criminal fraudster, as it happens, I had tried, but it was not to be. Ticking that off, I was now left with murderer, rapist, madman, or priest.

64

Jacob's mother yelled at us from the street below. 'Get down!'

'Not yet, Muh!' Jacob yelled back. 'I'm winning!'

'No you ain't,' I said, as we dangled side by side from the roof of his house, our fingertips wrapped over the drainpipe with our legs suspended forty feet above Joan.

'Down! Down! Down!' she yelled again, pacing the street below like a wild jungle cat. Unable to take much more, she shielded her eyes and vanished through the front door.

'Give up yet?'

'I could do this all day.'

'I could do your mum all day.'

'I'm sure she won't mind, Judas.'

'You really think?'

'Whyn't you go ask her?'

'I will. I will ask her.'

'Good, look forward to it.'

'I'll make love to her and get married and make you my son.'

'Stepson.'

'Right, stepson. No more pissing in jars. I won't allow it.'

'I'll piss in your mum's jar.'

'Jesus, Jacob.'

'Sorry.'

'Mother fucker, that was good.'

'We'll be here all day at this rate, Judas,' he said. 'One handed?'

We both released one hand on the count of three, just as Joan's hair and eyes appeared horizontally through a side window.

'Now, boys . . . this is the last time,' she said calmly. 'Please come back inside, you're scaring me, and I don't like it.'

'Judas got something to ask you, Muh.'

'It can wait, Jacob. Just come inside, now. You boys are crazy.'

We get another circuit going. Jacob had gotten big, his chest, his arms. I told him to go easy with those barbell lifts. He heaved the thing over his head with fire in his eyes, calling *more weight!* like Giles Corey.

After punching each other in the gut for as long as we could stay standing while repeating 'fine by me', we headed over to Ruby's.

'So, Jezebel's grandma told her she doesn't like me.'

'Jezebel's *grand*ma?' Jacob said, wiping froth from his lip.

'Yeah. Jezebel went to see a psychic and the psychic told her.'

'Wait. Her grandma's a psychic?'

'Her gran's dead. Jezebel spoke to a psychic.'

'Oh.'

'Yeah. So I've been talking with her dead grandma non-stop.'

'Why?'

'Cus I been lying to Jezebel, that's why—even *I'm* starting to believe I'm still some football star. I figured that's the reason her gran don't like me. Cus I'm lying to Jezebel.'

'I still talk to my nan and she died when I was eight.'

'I mean a full-blown conversation with the dead, not a prayer.'

Jacob turned to me. 'She don't deserve the truth. She's a bitch.'

I downed my beer. 'I'm telling her tonight. She has to know!'

After seven more beers and plenty shots of rum, we staggered out the pub. Jezebel was at Lenny's performing a double sex-act with her best mate, so we headed back to the flat.

I stuck the key in the door and we both tumbled inside. We decided to climb the stairs on our hands. Halfway up, Jacob crashed back down, jumping back to his feet like a man possessed.

While he was keeping from puking, I stumbled into the kitchen and stacked as many sausages as I could fix into the grill, tossed the cat a treat of tuna and set up the chessboard.

Jacob collided between the hallway before collapsing into the chair opposite me with vomit on his chin. I informed the God-lover that it's his move on the chessboard and that we've got twenty sausages under the grill. And that's the last I remember.

The fireman was a giant. 'C'mon, son, stay with me,' he kept saying. The thick smoke was suffocating. My arms swung like a sleeping toddler. Coughing, I whispered something to the fireman, something to the effect of, 'Listen to me . . . listen! I have to go back, *phut! phut!* my best friend . . . he's in there. Listen to me!'

In the midst of complete disorientation while choking up black smoke, I managed to tremble at the thought of being carried in the arms of a strapping man, the queer romance of it all. And then there was the cold night sky, darkness and a thousand twinkling stars as my hero in the red helmet lifted me to safety, gently setting me down against the wall before returning to the smoke.

Jacob turned his drunken eyes to me with the cat on his lap and shrugged. Moments later Jezebel came bounding down the street, scooping up her beloved kitty. We gave each other a look. Hers wasn't pleasant. She wasn't pleased. She walked away. Came back. Informed me the sausages caught fire. Walked away again.

'I love you, mate,' Jacob said.

'I love you too, pal.'

'No need to tell her a thing,' he said. 'God don't like her.'

65

Bob Gillingham's torch was more of a nightsearcher, lighting up the 2 AM sky at the foot of Levington's Ice-Cream factory.

Joan parked the car and kept the engine running. With a yawn, she told us to enjoy our first day of factory work and to please try and follow the rules.

'Thanks for the lift, Joan,' I said, slipping out the backseat.

'I'll drive you boys your first week. After that, you're on your own!'

Levington's was an hour's drive out of town, deep inside Devonshire moorland. Just as Joan pulled away, a large bus, one of those antique fifty-seater types, with oversized headlights and a flat face like a milk float, pulled up to the wide-gated entrance, pushing out twenty or so first-dayers all marvelling Bob Gillingham's tremendous light display. There was a chill in the night air as Jacob and I shuffled along to the entrance, leading the small brigade as they solemnly, with graven eyes, emptied the bus. We stuck our frozen hands into our pockets and stopped short of the gate.

Bob Gillingham hadn't budged an inch. There he stood, perfectly still, way back from the entrance on the other side of the gate, eyes big and shiny, with what looked to be a neatly waxed moustache upwardly twisted at the ends. We all eventually huddled together, some even walking blindly into the gate as it was so bloody dark, causing the gate to rattle like an organ of cold iron. And then silence. We all remained perfectly quiet as though we were sat in the gods of an empty coliseum, peering down far below at some villainous creature stood alone in the pit, a surreal shitfaced Salvador with a crazy eye.

It felt like the earth had spun by the time Gillingham called out: 'Welcome to Levington's Ice-Cream faaactoryyy!'

Three or four in the group mumbled back hello. Someone clapped twice—with one birdlike croon whispering somewhere close to me, the voice of a young angel repeating *'welcome'* while fiddling with her zip, seeming as though she would soon raise her hands to the moon and dance on her toes. I removed any thoughts of an easy fuck in the woods with this angel and instead focused again on Bob and his big shine of light that was now punching about the night sky before stopping suddenly at his rubber boots. We could no longer see the man's face, just green rubber treading toward us. And then the sound of a large bunch of keys, rattling like bones. Straining to see the mysterious figure as it stood at the gate, I drew from the darkness the whites of his eyes. From here I could pencil his face and pretty much piece the rest of him. I was happy to do this. It pleased me. I liked to see things. I did not like surprises.

His key locked in and turned. 'Everybody take one step back!' he said, in this raised, militant tone. We all shuffle-stepped backward. Jacob trod on someone's foot and apologised twice.

'It's okay,' said a little voice twice back.

'The Levington family built this factory in 1926,' Bob went on, swinging open the gate. I wondered why we had to step back when the gate swung inward, making me think twice about Bob.

'Procedure is important so you *must!* listen carefully. Do I make myself clear?' We had all managed to move as one membrane across the threshold and continued to turn as one and face our new boss who had locked the gate and had returned the lamp to his beady eyes.

'Yes,' most answered.

I kept shtum—a man who sends you backward when swinging a door inward didn't earn such a swift reply.

'Now come along!' he said.

We each follow behind Gillingham and his green boots across a hundred yards of gravel, stopping short at an unseeable door. He then switched off the lamp and swung open the door. The light on the other end shone so bright that I sharply looked about at our group and noticed the feeble fragile body of homosapiens with new surprise: the ears, the hair, clattering chins, quivering lips, all looking to each other like a walk to the gas chamber.

'Come along!'

As we filed one by one, I caught Jacob offer a modest smile to the young girl whose foot he'd trodden on. She smiled back. It was sweet. The ceiling to the factory was very tall, with strange-looking machinery, tendrils of repeating rhythms at compact stations with grey worker-people pushing mundane movements over and over, all functioning as one organism it seemed. I rubbed my bleary eyes awake, delirium settling in, with just a few hours' sleep—if any at all.

Once Gillingham ticked off names from his clipboard, he led us to the wash area with a running commentary upon hygiene and safety. We washed our hands—we washed our hands just as Gillingham dryly demonstrated.

We emerged unexpectedly from the next room wearing hairnets and plastic blue overshoes, sliding along an opening returning us to the main arena. A large freezer clanked open, thick steel releasing a rush of compressed air from its bounded rubber frame, suctioned to the wall, whining at our approaching parade. Dry ice poured forward from its doorway, curling at our feet in metallic plumes, followed by a very small man clad in an oversized rubber suit.

'Come along!' the boss yelled again.

Jacob caught me up. Her name was Sandy. He said she was nice and that she just got out of rehab and that she enjoyed table tennis.

'I approve,' I told him.

Bob Gillingham handed out small cards while escorting us to the clocking in machine. We simply insert the card and agree to the time shown by pressing the green button. On exit: red button.

'Do not lose your card! It will cost you an hour's labour to replace, one hour!' He then pointed his pen to me, Jacob, and two others, instructing the rest to stay put and await orders.

'The Levington family valued hard work, and above all . . . ' he prattled on as we toured the factory. I caught eyes with all the little workers as though they were warning us of something, each silenced by some unspoken decree. I saw people caged and ageing. There was no light or courage, no wild horses galloping into the sunset.

'Right, you two will be operating the ice dome,' he said, gesturing to Jacob and me. 'And then you shall advance promptly to the next machine every two hours once you hear the buzzer.' He pointed his pen up to a very large clock, just numbers and long, protruding hands, with a tick reverberating across the vast hall.

As soon as Jacob and I took a seat we were greeted by a short-armed fellow nicknamed Badger, wearing an extra hairnet over his streaky beard. He fixed a small cone-shaped wrapper onto each ice lolly as it rotated past our station. Badger won our gratitude while Gillingham loomed over us, his pen trained at that clock.

'On the strike of four, you follow Mr Badger. Are we clear?'

'Alright,' answered Jacob.

I kept shtum. It sounded rhetorical.

'Are we clear?' he said again, sensing a loose cord.

'Four, right,' I said.

Spinning on his boot, the henchman instructed the two other new starters stood blankly to turn twenty-eight degrees to the right.

Badger leaned in. 'He's been with the company for thirty years,' he told us as they marched away. 'We all know he's an asshole. Just get your head down and get it done and take your pay.'

'How long you been working here?' I asked.

He stood back up. 'Twenty three years,' he said proudly.

'Do we get free ice-cream?' Jacob asked.

Badger grinned. 'Yeah, but you'll be sick of the shit in no time.'

Our friend then slumped into a chair, the spine and shoulders folding with years of ache and sorrow, the posture of a dying, hollow man. He picked up an empty wrapper and slid it perfectly over an orange ice stick, fitting exact. He then took another wrapper from the neverending supply that kept appearing once one was taken and slid that one over the next ice stick, which was green.

'And that's that. Just two hours of putting 'em on the lollies. But if you miss one, just let it go—don't chase after it. They'll be put back on the conveyer belt by Agnes and come right back around so you'll get a second try. Alright then, gents. That's a wrap!'

Badger sniggered to himself as he stepped away from the chair, rolled up his spine, as far as it would stretch, and hobbled back along to his station, disappearing into the grey wall.

66

Fred Snr drove his old Astra G banger steady and slow. Fred was a handsome, powerful man of seventy. His jaw was square and his heart big. And he never muttered—never needed to repeat himself.

On the ride to the factory I sat on a tub of paint in the back of the van, watching the night sky through the rear window. On this particular 1 AM drive, Jacob and I agreed neither of us had had any sleep. We'd sniffed our way through two grams of whizz and had been up high as shit the whole night discussing the most painful types of death between bouts of arm wrestling. I moved my things out of Jezebel's, then phoned my old lady while at the extreme end of a speed rush, gnashing my teeth while assuring my mother that everything is fine. She was worried. Said Pastor Tom would like to see me at church. I told her I didn't care for her pastor. She said okay. That's alright. And that she would pray for me. I told her I didn't need her prayers, either. She hung up.

'You boys should never sniff! Always blow your nose!' commented Fred at the wheel. 'If the body wants it out, you let it bloody out!' He handed Jacob tissues. 'Here, Jakes,' he said. 'Blow!' We blew our nose to please Fred, nothing emerging but rancid air. Swallowing spit, I wondered how the hell I was going to survive a twelve-hour ice-cream shift with no sleep and black thoughts pecking my skull.

'You boys will have to find your own way tomorrow!'

'Thanks, Grandad.'

'Cheers, Fred.'

'You need a day job! It's inhumane working through the night, six days a week. INHUMANE! You'd think we're still at war!'

Our silence reassured Fred he was heard. I smiled a little crazily at my reflection in the car window. He smiled back. I then watched my finger draw a house with happy stick people against the condensation. Small droplets of water run down. Wetting my face with my finger I stretched open my eyes and let go a deep sigh.

Fred Snr was a man of character, like those gallant figures of old tales of valor and romance. Jacob admired him, perhaps more so than his old man. Scratching the tip of my nose, trying not to think too much upon it, I disregard the seemingly petty act as having any coincidence as Fred said, 'You boys *knows* what to do.'

We both clambered out the van. I slammed my door shut the second try and gave Fred a thumbs up.

The last of a no-nonsense generation stuck his head out the window. 'Work hard, boys! Even in a storm, you see it through to the end!'

'Yes, Grandad.'

'Sure, Fred.'

His old banger blew up the lane until all we saw were headlights zigzagging in the blackness, looking like something nonterrestrial.

'I feel bad, really bad, Judas,' Jacob muttered with a shiver.

'You'll be fine,' I said.

'I can't keep sniffing speed every day. I'm losing my mind.'

'Calm. Breathe. It's just the comedown.'

'I'm panicking. I think I'm having *panic attacks*, and seeing things too. I was one-hundred percent convinced I was talking with John the Baptist last night while lying in bed. John the fucking Baptist!'

A great big clock and suspect glances for twelve straight hours. Gillingham burning his eyes into our backs, asking all sorts of regulatory questions. And Badger, peering at us strange and indirect, making us paranoid. And our hands feeling unclean and carcasslike after we'd scrubbed them a zillion times. And our hearts beating right up to our throats, chests wheezing empty, hollow.

67

Jacob slid his Bible beneath his bed, pulled up his socks and tightened his lace. Switching off the desk lamp, he allowed the streetlight to seep in, stood motionless, gazing into nothing, his arms captured to his side, eyes adrift, the mind furling deeply over the brow, desperate to remember what he was doing stood at the door and for what.

'C'mon,' I said, snapping him out of it.

It was ten after midnight. We made our way along Prospect Street toward the bus station. No one was about but a guy stood with one palm against the brick wall, urinating.

'Can you gentlemen spare any change?' he asked us, twisting his neck as we came by, spraying a long trail of hot piss along the wall.

'Sorry mate,' I told him. Jacob reached into his pocket and produced a fifty pence piece, dropping the coin to the concrete.

'Thank you so much, kind sir!' the bum called out, speaking like a nineteenth-century bootboy. His dirty white buttocks appeared from beneath his filthy coat as he raised his arm, the heels of his bulging feet crushing the backs of broken shoes.

'Another fifty pence and I can get me shelter tonight!' he yelled.

'Haven't got it!' I said.

'What about your kind companion?'

'Nope!' Jacob answered.

The desperate man yanked up his trousers and scavenged the fifty, keeping one hand clenched to his pants.

'Thank you, kindly!' he said over, following us down dark alleyways.

'He's following us,' Jacob whispered.

'Your fault,' I said.

'Twenty pence?' the needlehead pleaded, closing in.

I turned and faced him. 'That's your lot, mate,' I said angrily.

'Fifty pence won't do *anything*!' he moaned.

'Listen,' I said, 'just leave us the fuck alone.'

Jacob tugged my shoulder. We continued walking to the bus station. The scrounger followed in his busy silence, the drag of shoes kicking cans, low senseless mumbling in the dark.

'I'm gonna give him my sandwiches,' said Jacob.

'He doesn't want food, he wants booze, and probably crack.'

'I know, Judas, but I feel guilty.'

'Even if he was hungry you shouldn't feed him.'

'Let him starve?'

'Correct.'

'It's just a sandwich, Judas. No big deal.'

I stopped. 'No big deal? It now means I'll have to give you half of *my* sandwich. You give to him, you take from me. This ain't the parable of the Good Samaritan, Jacob, some bloody holy conquest.'

But Jacob had already loosened his bag from his shoulder, unzipped and fingered out his sandwich. 'Here you go, mate, a sandwich.' With a kind turn, he placed the foil-wrapped ham-feast to the cobbled stone and took a step back.

'Thank you, kind sir!' the guy said. But the parasite ignored the sandwich, wasn't interested. And instead scooped up a can of beer from off the floor and emptied whatever was left into his up-facing gob. 'Thank you, sir! Thank you, kindly!' he kept spitting as we turned a corner and ran for our bus.

'Need I remind you both what happens when an employee is late!'

We watched as Gillingham unloaded his contempt for lateness, his moustache pricking the air with each high-nosed inflexion. And that clock ticking across the hall, coming alive. I had forgotten it. It almost had me like it did the rest.

Gillingham rotated his pen along work stations occupied by slow suicidal cases and sneered. 'When *you* are late, the factory is late!'

Noticing Jacob's bag was open, I zipped it closed.

'Thanks, Judas,' he tiredly said, turning back to our boss.

'Your first hour will be worked freely for the company,' he'd decided, pointing to the clock. 'Pay will begin at three-thirty AM!'

'We were just helping out some homeless guy,' Jacob pleaded.

'Your problem, young man,' the tight-lipped asshole replied while attacking his clipboard with his pen.

I nodded at Jane and Agnes, Billy and Marg. I gave old Ronnie the Bishop a chin, and his son, little Harry. A wink for Pat with the curls, sitting alongside tobacco Lin and Badger. Sandy waved to Jacob from the wash area. Jacob waved back. Tipping my head to the door, Jacob's eyes brightened, suddenly full of new sparkle.

'Now come along!' said Gillingham, beginning to walk off alone toward the clocking in machine.

I turned around and walked out.

Jacob followed.

68

We found another job. Royal Mail—Her Majesty's.

Reggie's handshake was firm, with fingers full of gold rings. 'It's a good ol' lot here,' he told me and Jacob, walking us through the warehouse. 'You lads live close?'

'Twenty minute bus ride.'

'I'm homeless,' I said.

Reggie tutted. 'Ain't we all been, mate.'

'I ain't,' Jacob put in.

'Plenty time!' Reggie laughed. 'You'll see!'

Our escort led us to the heart of the sorting space where hordes of workers buzzed about like bees. The place was a labyrinth of narrow partitions, each filled with rectangular holes where letters were being sorted and arranged, rows of people perched on stools, their faces flushed pink as they fingered through the endless stream of post. Amidst the racket, I glimpsed groups of workers gathered round large pits, their grubby hands filling large brown sacks with more letters.

Reggie flashed a set of gold teeth. 'I'll leave you lucky fellas with our lovely Jen,' he said before sauntering off into the noise.

Jen was about fifty and stood with a perfectly straight spine and no smile. Her shoulders were very wide and her legs extremely thin, like a paper aeroplane. She removed her tiny round spectacles from her nose and allowed the glasses to dangle from the rubber band around her neck, nestled between a pair of tremendous tits.

'You boys smoke?'

'We do,' I said, expecting a handout.

She started walking. We took the cue to follow.

'No smoking inside the warehouse,' she said.

'Right,' I said. 'Lots of flammables around here . . . '

She turned and locked eyes. *'No smoking inside the warehouse.'*

'Do Menthols count?' I returned smartly.

She stepped to me and fixed her copper eyes on mine and scoffed, 'So, you're the cocky kid, eh?'

There was no joy in her. It was attractive. I found Jen very attractive. As we stood there I couldn't help imagine meeting her outside around the corner someday. That she would whisper a time and place in my ear. And she'd be there, behind the bins, a minute past lunchtime, her skirt hiked up, her enormous briefs hung about her ankles, bent over, smoothing out the flaps with two fingers while ordering me to get a move on, that she needed to go grab a steak and kidney pie from the caff before it shut.

'I've seen one fire in twenty-five years. My two girls work here.'

'Got it,' I said.

She gritted her teeth. 'Don't be a smartass,' she said. I kept whatever misunderstandings we had to myself. She was boss.

We walked on. 'You'll both be in Pit 12.'

We passed by Pit 6 and 7, then 10.

'Lunch is one hour. We have a canteen where you came in. Food is standard: chips, beans, pies, sandwiches, usual grub. Reggie'll show you boys how to clock in tomorrow—if you decide to come back that is.'

We reached Pit 12. 'Right, I'll leave you gents with Big Greg.'

An almost seven-foot tall of a human, all limbs and feet, rose up and lunged at us with his monstrous arm outstretched.

Jen winked. 'Have a good first day, lads,' she said, collecting her glasses from between her almighty tits before strutting away.

'I like her,' Jacob said.

'Yeah, me too.'

Big Greg, a hefty-boned Cornishman, talked us through the operation. Letters came in. Letters went out. You were either sorting things *in* or sorting things *out*. There was no favoured side, and both were equally important, the giant reminded us. Just *in* or *out*.

'We sort into *postcodes*,' he continued, leading us about the pit. 'Marjorie, these 'ere boys will be with you till lunch, me sweet.'

'Tuck in, chaps!' said Marjorie, shuffling along a bench. Marjorie had worked here the longest, thirty-nine years, starting when she was just nineteen. Her nails were long, manicured, her wrinkled skin singed to a rusty orange. She had very small teeth and pushed her oversized specs back up her nose frequently.

'Squeeze your bums in, boys, I won't bite.'

'Not till she gets frisky!' joked Barney, a fat queer fella sweating buckets on a stool.

'Don't you listen to him,' she whispered to us. 'That walrus is too ugly to get any ass. His poofter pecker is covered in scabies.'

'Oi!' Barney popped. 'I heard that you cheeky cowcunt!'

Marjorie swung around. 'You were meant to you lazy pigshit!'

Barney laughed out loud. We squeezed up. Marjorie calmly turned back and fixed us a smile. 'I spend all me money on tans, you see, keeps me young-looking—especially in this shitheap.'

Me and Jacob got to work sorting letters from PL1 to PL3.

'You're up, Barn, me dear,' said Mildred. 'We're on "B", me love.'

Barney's head scrambled for one. 'Barcelona!' he said.

'Canada,' followed Mildred.

'That there's a country, Milly,' Big Greg remarked. 'We're naming cities from A to Z anywhere in the world, my sweet.'

'Alright then, Cairo! My Rodger took me there in 1970.'

'Dafur,' followed a young girl sat next to Mildred.

'Where'sat?' shrieked Barney.

'India, I fink,' the girl claimed.

'You just made that up!' Marjorie heckled.

'They probably have a Dafur somewhere there,' the girl argued.

Big Greg shook his big nose. 'Sorry, no point.'

'I don't care,' she huffed.

'Pass?' Big Greg said.

'I hate this bullshit game,' she said, picking out a fresh bundle of letters from a sack while angrily chewing gum.

'Right then—Durham,' said the big guy.

The young girl jumped up. 'That sounds like Dafur!'

Big Greg chuckled. 'Durham is up north, babe, near Newcastle.'

She plonked back down. 'Still a stupid game,' she said.

69

Following my shift I came up Victoria Park, hoping to catch my sister, Tabi. Heathcliff swung open the door with their youngest wrapped around his arm and a spliff pinched between his lips.

'Tabi's over at Gail's,' he mumbled, eyes drained and bloodshot.

So I left Heathcliff and walked to Gail's flat and held the buzzer, peering up at that sky. While waiting, I counted my money: five pounds sixty pence. My Casio told me it was one in the afternoon.

Gail lived over the road from my old primary school. Catching sight of the tractor tyres in the playground, that used to fill with rainwater during a storm, gave me pause for reflection: all the choices that I had made from there, bringing me to where I now stood here. And the sandpit, with the little buckets and spades. Childhood, I think, recalling the attack of a thundershower against the window, drenching everything and everyone—clapclapbaroom!

I crushed a Coke can beneath my foot and pressed the buzzer again. The last time, I thought. My stomach was rumbling, eager to get to Ivor Dewdney for a steak pasty before they'd run out.

Then I hear, 'Just a minute!' followed by Gail's heavy silhouette thudding down the stairway.

The door opens. 'Oh . . . alright, Judas.'

Gail always looked up the duff. Her hair was greasy thin and her face regularly exhausted. She took a long drag of her cigarette, twisted her lips to one side and blew. 'Tabi's gone home. You just missed her, me love,' she said, taking another drag.

A strong breeze hugged her nightgown as she stood there on her doorstep, blowing tobacco. I could see how she looked beneath and I liked what I saw. On her nightgown were soup stains and baby vomit and smeared jam. She clawed her neck and took another drag, looking me over.

'Wanna come in for a quick drink? I got Scrumpy.'

'Alright,' I said.

The instant offering of watching her fat buttocks rise and fall as she plodded up ahead had reminded me of being a little special in the eyes of the Lord.

She grabbed hold the bannister, panting.

'You okay?' I asked.

'I'm a fatty, Judas,' she said, taking another drag of the cigarette on the upstep. 'Haven't seen you in a while.'

'No,' I said.

'You could've raped me by the time I got to my door!' She laughed. We laughed together. Reaching the third floor she flicked the fag-butt through a side window and swung open her door, the stink of baby poop rushing up my nose.

'I'll go check on Abigail. Cider's in the front room. Help yourself.'

Locking the door, she vanished down the hall. I discovered the front room. It was a tip: crushed bottles of cider, bloated ashtrays, with dirty sheets tossed over the settee.

My eyes landed on a bottle of Scrumpy next to a child's dummy. Stooping down I picked it up, guzzled a quarter, and cleaned my mouth with my sleeve.

Gail appeared. 'Did you find it?' she asked.

I held the bottle up. ''Thanks, yeah.'

She flopped on the floor, scooping up a pack of cigarettes.

'Want one?'

I shrugged.

'Shitty Superkings. You don't mind shitty Superkings?'

'All the same to me,' I said, putting down the cider.

With an unlit fag in her mouth she picked her waist, adjusting her knickers. As she did a lock of greasy hair slapped her in the eye. Her breasts perched unusually. I liked how unusual her body was—short stocky arms sitting angular from her fat body, with small punchy tits fisting the air, like a circus freak. I realised then that my taste in the opposite sex was of the margins, all of us barely hanging on by the fingertips.

With all her struggles she finally picked out the wedgie and lit the cigarette and passed it over, lighting one for herself.

'Abigail's out cold,' she said. 'Won't be up for hours.'

'Where's her dad?'

She collapsed back against the settee. 'Went to the shop to buy nappies for Abigail and never came back. Took all his clothes an all.'

She picked up the bottle of Scrumpy and had a good pull. Drying her lips with the back of her hand, she stretched out both legs and came straight out with it: 'You wanna stick your dick inside me?'

I coughed and nodded. 'Yeah,' I said, still coughing, 'okay.'

She switched off the telly, spat on her cigarette, and turned one ear to the door, thinking she heard the kid. Flinging her nightgown up over her head she threw it to one side.

'C'mon,' she whispered. 'We'll have to do it quickly.'

The cigarette burnt my thumb as I hurried to stub the thing out. She laid out sheets along the floor, pausing every so often to listen for a squirm, a wince. Her stomach was big and round, nipples soft and pink and flat, no sign of a teat.

'We haven't got long,' she whispered again. 'Just a quickie.'

Kicking off my shoes, I rolled down my jeans and threw away my jacket and unbuttoned my shirt, tensing, for her, for them all, like a glorious bronze figurine. She pushed down her pants, fussing them to one side with her big toe. She was too fat and lazy to use her hand. She wanted very desperately to fling the pants off by her toe, getting more frustrated as they clung on. A shit stain sat in her pants. She didn't care that I saw. Neither did I. I liked that she didn't care. After a small war with the pants, she finally gave in and heaved forward and slung them away. As she did, lying sideways, with her legs tucked in like a giant lady-fetus, her muff emerged thick and gooey from behind, glistening pink flesh bulging like boils. She rolled over and opened her thighs. I whipped off my boxers, dropped to my knees and crawled between bowls of baby porridge and half-eaten wotsits.

She gasped, 'Condom!' Stretching to a small wooden chest she snatched from it a silver packet and looked at me. 'Medium?'

I shrugged. I think I'm more a smallish-medium, like a half shoesize. In any case, she ripped it open and helped the oversized rubber along my five and three-quarter inch erection, with plenty roll at the bottom.

We began fucking.

'Can't feel a thing,' I said. 'Can't even feel my own dick.'

She reached down and tugged me out, snapped off the condom and flung it aside. 'You make sure you pull out, mister,' she said.

We get going again, bareback. I noticed tiny hairs along her chin. Her eyes were small, green, pretty, blinking at the ceiling, keeping a fraction of her thoughts with the kid. She didn't mind that I watched her so closely. Her lips fell apart, her tongue appeared dry and dull from all the booze and fags, the waft of cheesy crisps lifting from her mouth and spreading across my face.

By now I was going for glory. She grabbed her knees and heaved them back, taking me deeper, my dick discovering new ground. I nibbled her nipple. Sweat rolled along the nipple into my mouth, rolling from her neck, or maybe worse, the pit! With disgust I spat it back out, watching the slime run back to where it sprung.

'I'm gonna come,' I said.

'You pull out!'

I kept fucking. 'Any moment now.'

'Don't you bloody come inside me, Judas!'

'I can feel it!'

'Do it on my belly! Come on my belly!'

'Here it comes!'

'On my belly! Do it on my belly!'

I jumped out in the nick of time and made two squirts. The first shot up and hit her left nipple, the second slithered into her belly button. My dick was still gagging, like it needed to throw up.

She stretched her neck forward. 'Is that all?' she asked, inspecting the small spatter, rolling her cheek side to side with a teasing grin. 'You shouldn't jerk off so much, Judas.'

Gathering my clothes together, I quickly dressed. She turned over and re-lit her cigarette. 'You can really fuck,' she said in a good mood. 'Not much cock, but you can fuck!'

Then, like the cue for the next low-budget act, the kid woke up.

She pushed me out the door. 'Seeya, Judas,' she said, slamming it shut. I stood at her doorstep and smelled my fingers. I didn't like smelling of her but I couldn't stop smelling them. I smelled them all the way down the stairway, thinking what it smelled like. It was a rotten stink but I was obsessed. I wondered if she was pleased but quickly suspected it didn't matter. She didn't care. And neither did I.

Once outside I inhaled and looked upward. The sky was less grey. There were no people on the street—only the little school kids screaming and running about the playground.

I reached into my pocket and recounted my coins, then legged it all the way to town before they sold out of steak pasties.

70

Jacob threw aside his Bible and told me again, 'I love her, Judas.'

'I know,' I said. 'But it's your birthday, and we need to get drunk.'

Bonnie had decided to travel, her first stop, Australia. She had no plans to return. She wanted adventure, needed to see the world.

'Three years we've been together, Judas, since we were fifteen. We were going to make babies. And they were all going to look like her.'

'Okay,' I said, 'a bit much . . . but alright.'

He called her family home every day, left long, desperate voicemails, and went and knocked on her door unannounced. Her mother had enough sense to turn the sore sop away, saying Bonnie needed space, time to think. I told him to quit turning up at her doorstep. The sentimental fool paced the room, chewed his nails.

'Christ almighty,' I said, 'we just got paid. Let's go for a drink!'

The sky was clear. There was good sun. A bunch of gypsy kids ran amok throwing water balloons at regular people. They stopped and asked us to sponsor their boxing competition, one kid producing a battered handmade flyer with drawings of stickmen.

Jacob and I laughed together. It was very funny.

'Whey feckin not?' the older kid asked, folding away the flyer.

'Because it's a scam,' I said, a part of me admiring their little hustle. The kid gave me a menacing stare and raised up his water balloon, ready to bust it on my shoe and leg it. His caravan buddy was much smaller than he was, slower, less willing. Jacob was still in small hysterics over the drawing while I simply shook my head at the kid, transmitting a stern 'dontchu fucking dare'.

The pikeys ran off. We walked on, crossing Freedom Fields.

'Judas, am I too nice?'

I shrugged.

'Is Bonnie leaving me cus I'm too nice?'

I shrugged some more.

We picked up a couple Cobra, some new Indian beer making headlines, and drank them on our way to the pub.

Following many shots of whiskey and a gallon of Scrumpy, we swung our football boots over our shoulders and made it to Saint Budeaux Fields, the spot I played my first ever game as a kid.

'I'm pissed.'

'We've got a game to win. It's your birthday.'

'I'm still pissed.'

I pointed down the street. 'Chinky!'

We stumble-run to the Red Dragon and ate noodles with our fingers. 'I'm gonna be sick,' he said, turning and puking chunks of vegetables washed in brown liquid across the pavement.

I placed a hand on his back. 'We've got a game to win, sweet-cakes. Get it together.'

Chase Matthews strolled by. 'Fellas!' he said. 'You boys okay?'

Jacob wiped his face. 'We're pissed.'

'We're fine,' I said, swaying while stuffing my gob with noodles.

'You sure you boys can play? You look wasted.'

I stared longly at Chase with a greasy chin of chow, finishing my mouthful before telling him again, *'We're fine.'*

Chase's old man, Homer Matthews, was waiting for the squad. He gave a good team talk. Gallant. Kirk Douglas saddling his horse in Spartacus, addressing a thousand men.

'Gentlemen!' Homer started as we gathered round. The sun melted overhead. I inspected my hands, witnessing two of everything.

My blurry eyes found Jacob. 'I can't see,' his lips mouthed, pointing to his eyes. I liked Homer. He was a good man. I didn't want to let him down.

Taking my usual central position, with Jacob on the wing, I made sure to keep him busy. The downward wind favoured sudden attacks, continuing to square him the ball, the ball rolling past his feet each time. He looked amazed.

I staggered to him. 'You okay?' I asked.

'I'm too pissed, Judas. I'm seeing two balls, two of everything.'

'Try crossing your eyes,' I told him. 'It makes things one again.'

It worked for me, I'd been playing cross-eyed the entire time.

Homer clapped his big hands next to his wife, Betty—a sixty-something former pin-up with a purple dye shaped like a beehive. 'C'mon, chaps!' she called. My lungs croaked heavy with tobacco. I got outplayed all over the field, inebriated beneath the hot sun. Giving one final push, I switched the ball to Jacob near goal. He swung his leg like a skipping rope, crashing to the mud, fetching his ankle in both hands.

I got to him first and dropped to my knees. 'You okay?'

'I think so,' he groaned. 'Did I look ridiculous, Judas?'

'Yes. Yes you did.'

He buried his face in the mud.

But I grabbed the idiot. 'You scored a goal!' I said.

His eyes lit up like a jackpot machine. 'I scored a goal?'

The final whistle blew. I turned back to Jacob. 'You just scored the winning goal, you jammy git!'

Homer saw to his ankle. 'You'll be just fine,' he told Jacob. 'Lucky for you, it's just a simple sprain.' Homer patted our shoulders and climbed back to his feet. 'Now, you boys get yourselves home and sobered up. I appreciate you fellas making the effort. It's not easy playin after a few bevvies, especially under this heat.'

We arrived back to Jacob's half sober. His old lady was busy hoovering the stairway, fully clothed. In his room, I bandaged his swollen ankle, with quiet thoughts of Homer's tolerance.

'I'm serious, Judas!' Jacob went on. 'I'd do it for you!'

'Christ,' I said, taking a pen and paper and sitting at his desk.

During a twelve-hour shift of sorting letters at the Mailhouse I had promised to help the lovesick pudding-head write a letter to Bonnie, putting the idea to him. 'Just write her a letter,' I urged, after whipping Barny's ten-year record for postcode sorting speed.

Jacob hobbled about pouring forward his heart, some sadness, much laughter, and a long, brooding spell of quiet, sober reflection.

'Am I too nice?' he asked again. 'Am I just too nice, Judas?'

For some reason I started quietly singing a tune my old man often sung: 'Don't you love farce? My fault, I fear. I thought that you'd want what I want. *Sorry, my dear!* Send in the clowns . . .'

He hobbled to me on his sore foot. 'Don't patronise me, Judas!'

I turned from the desk. 'What makes you think you're too nice?'

'Her! *Bonnie!* Are you even listening to me?'

I gave him my back again. 'Let's just finish this letter,' I said.

We finished the letter. It was a damn good letter. Honest. Tender. With just the right amount of withdraw. I was fond of it. But the heartsick sop screwed the thing up and flung it out the window.

'Too soft!'

Leaving his house, I winked at Joan as she opened and closed both fists three times. 'Thirty minutes,' she said. 'Don't be late, Judas.'

The pub was overcrowded. Feeling uneasy, I told him to drink up.

'Let's just go for a walk,' I said. 'This place is a dive.'

'One more pint,' he said, readying some change.

I downed my drink and stood up. 'Let's get outta here!'

'Okay, okay,' he said, downing his beer too.

As we stumbled along, I informed my friend all about Gail and her porridge-smelling lady-parts. He laughed and said I could do better.

'Sometimes better looks worse,' I tutored him. 'It wasn't fancy or anything, it was straightforward, none of this romance faff.'

I sniffed my fingers again, couldn't believe she was still there.

'And she had shit-stains in her pants!' I remembered out loud.

Jacob hobbled along on crutches. 'You're a perv, Judas,' he said. 'No more information, please. It'll make me puke again.'

We came up Nelson Street, then Clifton Street to Clifton Place.

'Okay,' I said, stopping short of a big red door. 'We're here.'

'Here?' he asked, swaying on his sticks.

'Ain't my idea,' I said drunkenly, pushing the door open.

Perhaps fifty people yelled at once, 'SURPRISE!!'

Jacob clipped my arm. 'You knew all along!'

We stumbled through the huge crowds and onto the stage, surrounded by balloons and party blowers and colourful decorations.

'Thank you all for coming!' his mum announced on a microphone.

Just then, like the third act of a cheap budget flick, the big entrance door swung open and in walked Bonnie. She tiptoed to the back of the hall, a birthday card clasped in one hand, suitcase in the other, all set to leave this old town and Jacob for good.

I turned back to the birthday boy. He'd seen her too.

Joan took a large knife to the cake while his old man juggled a tall deck of paper plates. Bonnie quietly raised her hand to Jacob in a show of truce, smiling funnily.

Suddenly the front row went silent. And half the room stopped cheering. Following the eyes of the crowd I glanced to my right and saw Jacob unbuttoning his trousers. For a moment there, as my tipsy peepholes assembled the picture ahead of me, I figured birthday boy might be buttoning them up, that they had somehow come loose. But he wasn't. The shit wasn't buttoning them up. Pushing his pants down he threw his arms up to the ceiling, eyes glued to Bonnie at the back of the hall with a big dumb smile on his face.

The whole room gasped at his dick. I looked at his dick. His uncle Gary and Aunt Jennifer both looked at his dick. Stephanie and Larry, his godparents, they looked at his dick too. And all the little children sat close to the stage, they all pointed at his dick.

His mum was first to act. Leaping toward her boy with a paper plate, she tripped to her knees, fumbled along some floor, one desperate arm outstretched, finally securing the plate over his dangling pecker.

Bonnie, in her amazement, had dropped the birthday card and her suitcase, bringing both hands to her mouth in horror.

Seeing this all play out, I grabbed him by the collar. 'You did it,' I cheered quietly. 'Blooming hell, mate, you did it! You bloody did it!'

His mum was yanking up his pants, yelling at me with her nose an inch from his weeny. 'Don't you encourage him, Judas!'

Jacob blew a kiss to his girl. 'Remember us!' he cried out.

Bonnie snatched up her suitcase and ran out the door.

71

The midmorning sun spiked over the curtain. I was looking up at the light from the floor, hadn't slept or eaten in two days. Ignoring the cold set in my toes and the bloodied tissues scattered about my pillow, I think only of the arguments inside my head, bitter from all the cheap cornershop wine and speed.

Jacob moved pages of his Bible. 'Did you say something, Judas?'

'No.'

'What you thinkin?'

'Nuthin.'

'Oh. I thought you said something.'

I stuffed tissue up my nose. 'I heard the library's closing down.'

'Not as bad as the junkie next door found dead with a needle up his arm. His body decayed into the carpet—can you imagine? Three months he's been dead. I told you I could smell somefin.'

'The library closing down is worse,' I said.

A pigeon landed on the window. I stared at the pigeon.

'Judas?'

'What?'

'A lot of young kids saw my dick.'

'Yes they did, Jacob.'

'The Bible don't help with that.' His laugh was short and pointless. I kept my eye on the pigeon. The pigeon flew. As though some beckoning cue from its takeoff, I decided to sniff the last of the powder.

'Funny thing,' Jacob mused. 'The sun's dying. Burning and dying.'

'We're all burning and dying,' I said, snorting back the last of it.

'We can't escape it,' he added. 'We can't escape death, Judas.'

I grunted aggressively. 'May as well burn as we live then, eh pal?'

'Suppose so,' he said, closing his book. The rusty springs of his mattress squeak as he sits up in bed. 'Suppose so,' he muttered again.

'Suppose so, what?' I asked, replacing another bloodied tissue.

But he didn't answer.

Thinking only what it took to delay the comedown, steer away the madness, I came up with more speed as the solution. 'I'm gonna get more. One more gram will do. Sleep tomorrow.'

Jacob panicked. 'No, Judas! I can't! We can't do any more!'

'Alright,' I said, resting my head back to the pillow, 'take it easy.'

My friend sighed, staring into his book. He then slid out of bed, walked to his desk and pulled open the top drawer. With his Bible clutched in his hand, he rummaged through the drawer, muttering this and that while shoving aside sweet wrapers until he found what he was looking for—a box of matchsticks. 'Found 'em!'

I heard the sound of a plate touch his desk and looked over at him. Smoke wafting above his head, he scrambled toward the window with his arms outstretched and something burning on the plate. I didn't react. I was too empty to react. I just watched, hypnotised by the smog billowing over his face, his eyes squinting between the smoke as the flame flickered from high yellows to low reds.

'That's it,' he choked, placing the plate on the ledge and swinging open the window. The cool outside air rushed in, swallowing the smoke and taking with it little burning pieces of paper.

Jacob put out pieces on the carpet with his bare foot. The plate smouldered. Smoke thinned away. And I waited, waited for the point to all this. But the fool just brushed char from his foot and clapped smut from his hands.

'That's it,' the lunatic said again.

I sat up. 'That's what?' I asked.

He looked pleased. 'No more Bible.'

72

The ceiling low and the room dark, sat in the corner of Disco 2000, the last nightclub to close, stocked with muggers and dealers and prostitutes, I watched the crowd with an uneasy grin, warm waves of ecstasy creeping along my arms. A bunch of ravers danced ahead of me, their jaws grinding round like a laundrette. The big hardmen remained in the darker corners, their cold, lifeless eyes examining the turf, forming all possible punchups. And the music, bouncing off the walls and inside beer glasses, abandoned glasses that rattled from the repetitive bass thumping from the speakers. Scenes of hollow-cheeked needleheads with bulging scheming eyes moved along the outer reaches in some endless fidget, one junkie scrambling across the dancefloor.

Almost four in the morning. My back ached against the wall. I got up and took a seat on a sofa. Folded in among loose tobacco was half a pill, stuffed in my right pocket. I had given some guy three coins for it in the pisser, some scrawny, shifty-looking rat with black greasy hair and a sly smirk. We stood mostly in silence on pools of pee with the cubicle door locked. It didn't matter, everyone knew what went on in there. I wasn't worried about being seen as a lover of men.

Using his sleeve to clean down the toilet seat, my bathroom companion pulled out a pocketknife to finely chop the gear. As he did a loose cigarette slipped from his shirt pocket. He bent over the seat, his rear-end thrashing about the air as he searched for his lost fag, inspiring images of fucking him up the ass, primal impulses that jumped into my mind merely for our close proximity.

Did it make me some sort of queer or was I just a reckless pervert, powerless over my compulsions?

Locating his cigarette, the louse jumped back up, pursed his lips and tried blow-drying the piss that it had collected from off the floor.

'Fuckit,' he finally hissed, slipping the fag back into his pocket.

That last pill was yet to kick in, beginning to twist more paranoia. I'd somehow planned on killing him before he killed me—take his throat with his knife and call it a moral duty.

We each sniffed a line from off the toilet seat. Unlocking the door, I walked slowly to the sink and washed my hands. My face in the mirror noticed me first, or I it, I wasn't sure. With my fingers rested on the tap I listened to the water run down the plughole, inspecting the dark circles under my eyes.

The shitter had been empty, just that greasy scum now taking a jimmy. As he flushed I stuck my fist in the mirror. 'What the fuck was that?' he asked. I didn't bother explaining. I was busy searching for that demon lurking behind the glass. I foresaw jail-time—10 to 15—cracked jaw, teeth scattered like confetti. The thought of prison gripped me in terror, yet my willingness to die overcame the threat, reduced the enemy as it were, all that dark, otherworldly think-stuff pleading to be outed, displayed, spat out.

Closing the tap, I blinked my eyes back to the present hour and wiped my hands along my jeans, cleared broken glass from off the sink and turned around. The soulless weasel stepped out from the loo with a wet cigarette dangling from his smirky lips. He lit the cigarette and took a drag, examining my mood. And I think he is the worst kind, nothing to lose, full of schemes and tricks—a petty con with a blade in his back pocket, ready to stick the next guy for being short-changed, mistreated, downtrodden.

Pushing his greasy hair from his slippery eyes, he looked at the crack in the mirror and noticed the cut on my knuckle, shook an abandoned bottle of beer left on the sink before helping himself and walking out the door and back into the club.

The bar was closed. It was after five in the morning. Managing to haggle a can of Special Brew from some fella in exchange for three Marlboros, I rested beneath the crowd, watching the same old story unfold.

'What the fuck are you doing here?' I heard myself say.

And then, 'Judas!' over and over. 'Judas! Hey Judas!'

From out the darkness Sibie appeared. The first thing I noticed were her eyes, two black holes, her face spoiled with much mascara. She wiped her mouth dry before falling beside me on the sofa, handing me a peck on the cheek. I barely knew Sibie from our school days—had written her several sicknotes without charge. She was an outcast, always bunking off to go pinch from Dingles.

Considered now adults as we were, I was afforded the time to notice more of her, her hair, which was bleached yellow, shoulder-length, with thick brown eyebrows and a distinct mole on her chin. She kept licking her lips, complaining of the dryness. She wasn't attractive to the general populous, but to me she had something, a one of a kind free flyer.

She stretched out her bottle of water. 'Want some?' she asked. Pushing her hand away I said *'I'm good, Sibs,'* more bothered she had the nerve to shove that thing in my face ahead of the crowd.

I glanced around at the hardmen.

'Gerald is here,' she tells me, fingering somewhere to the corner of the club. I didn't know Gerald all that well either. He went to a different school: Buckland. The toughest kid of Buckland once offered me to a scuffle. I never claimed to be tough, but it was expected, my ancestry, the kin. And so I occasionally, throughout school, had some idiot wanting to go at it. It seemed I was in his way, prompting unfamiliar voices inside my head, making comments. And I only made them worse, the voices, the threats, forming monsters, depraved, murderous ones, conjuring a plan to club me with a bat, hack me to pieces.

Therefore it seemed only rational to go find the threat before it found me, shining a bright light upon the danger inside my head. In other words, I'd go straight to where the threat was, such as being stood outside Buckland School. Afraid and not afraid. Alone. I walked there alone. To then be greeted by some lanky kid with a skinhead running across the street, informing me the kid who wanted to scrap couldn't scrap that day as he'd gotten himself detention. The errand boy introduced himself as Gerald.

Gerald fell to the sofa. 'Judas!' he cheered.

'Hello, Gerald,' I said.

More followed, more fledgling speedheads. I was now coming up on the pill. And that little bump of powder was feeling good. Sibie introduced an Italian girl named Andrea. Seeing that she was pretty I jumped up and gave her a squeeze. She was petite and bubbly and chewed gum while smoking. Everyone was flying high. I felt good, damn good.

Finishing my beer, I looked through the crowds. Surprised, I see Frida, Jezebel's mother, sitting alone at a table.

'Just a sec,' I told Sibie and Gerald and the others before criss-crossing the dancefloor, falling beside her.

'Judas!' Frida said, slurring but not yet all the way drunk.

That pill came on strong, producing a fuzzy charm along my face. The skin-tickling euphoria convinced me that I had been in love with Frida all along. She looked tired, her hands fiddling with a pack of Camel's. 'I need a drink, Judas. This place is dry.'

Slowly, she pushed herself to her feet, arched forward and put her lips on mine. We kissed. Or she kissed me. I wasn't sure. All I knew is that a kiss could be better than sex.

'That girl of mine,' she said against my mouth, stroking my

face. A second later Sibie and the gang leapt on me and snatched me by the arm. 'Let's go, Judas!'

Reaching someone's house on lower Lipson I found myself looking up at the morning sky, that tender, reasonable part of the brain pleading to stop, to sleep, the other half to keep going, outrun the comedown. Perhaps six or more bodies crammed through a door. And in that pause, like an infant child, I had forgotten how we arrived there, if we walked or rode a taxi. I hacked up a bitter clog of speed from my throat and choked it down. The street is alive. A slight breeze wrapped around my wrist, my neck, heavying my eyelids. Closing my eyes, I sway and suddenly there's no ground beneath my feet. No traffic. No human noise—only the birds and the wind and their freedom.

'Judas!' Sibie waved from the door. 'C'mon!'

I stumbled through the hallway, passing a room with several bodies sprawled out on the floor and slumped down on a large beaten-up sofa. The place was dingy, moist, had no life, no colour, no pictures on the wall, no television, no plants, no furniture—just one flea-ridden sofa dragged in from off the street. I fell opposite Sibie in what seemed to be the livingroom. My old school pal made some wild gestures sitting cross-legged, her eyes struggling to remain open. She unfolded a block of dope from her pocket and began making preparations. I figured it was heroin by the delicacy in which she cut through a sheet of tinfoil, followed by the thick puff of brown smut circling above her eyes. She soon slipped into a dope-haze and went someplace else.

'Chass'er de drrrahgon,' she said, Andrea, the Italian chick. She sung it again while looking my way. *'Judas . . . Chasss'er de drrrahgon.'*

I liked hearing it. I liked how she said it with the soft inflexions of her accent, dancing upon her pretty pink tongue. I hadn't spoke a word since we all greeted. Sibie was now sucking plumes of smoke through a cheap plastic pen, charring the dope beneath the foil. She rolled her gaze up to the ceiling, allowing the smoke to tip from her mouth. Dropping her head to one side, she looked me over, her pretty emerald eyes at peace.

'Judas,' she muttered, holding out the dope, 'take a hit.'

I took a hit.

And held it in.

Then blew it out.

Closed my eyes and fell into a dreamhole.

It was still daylight when I woke. Being the only one with open eyes made me feel less like them. Gerald was rolled up against the wall, the cute Italian tucked in beside me—the rest scattered about the floor shivering like dying flies.

Lifting myself from the sofa, I made my way toward the front door, stepping between legs and torsos. Before reaching the door I had passed the same room where Sibie was now tangled up with another girl half-naked. They'd tried to undress to lady-fuck but had both passed out. Sibs had bigger tits than I imagined. Her arm hooked awkwardly in her sleeve, protruding upward like a broken wing, one pink nipple on show.

My first thought was what a beautiful image, like the dark-end of some Michelangelo masterpiece. Next was to slip my cock inside her while she was out cold, playing out its sordid scenario inside my head. She'd never know—or maybe she'd come alive and get into it, want it harder, rougher. 'Yes, Judas, yes!'

All the buttons of her jeans were unpicked, a tuft of brown pubic hair spread across her tummy. I paused, looked her over some more, before opening the door and stumbling outside.

The wind moved the branches on trees. My mother's home was nearby so I aimed my feet that way.

When I reached I merely said, 'Hello Mum.'

'Oh,' she replied, switching off the hoover with her foot.

I hadn't seen her in over a year. 'I'm tired. I'm going to bed.'

'Okay,' she says. 'I made casserole.'

'Mm,' my mouth sputtered back, already halfway up the stairs.

Stepping into my room for the first time in a long time, I stared into the mirror with a carefree slant, looking like death come alive. I shadow-boxed like a hopeless has-been, pushed off my jeans and noticed a Mars bar melted to my back pocket, the same one I saw on that sofa in the squat when I had taken a seat.

I laughed shortly. It seemed funny—that I had walked the busy streets in broad daylight with a melted chocolate bar stuck to my ass, my energy reserved simply upon putting one foot in front of the other. I laughed some more, empty, useless laughter.

Slept.

73

I woke up the next morning having been out cold for fourteen straight hours. Making my way downstairs I finished two bowls of potato casserole, and then, bloated, decided on a bath.

Trying to toss off in the tub, I gave in and instead watched my dick slip below the water, held my breath and slipped down too.

While buttoning my shirt a car came blasting down the street. I glanced out the window to see Chase, parking his new Nova SRi. The car looked like a deathtrap, with a half-done spray job. He got it off his uncle. His uncle ran a cut-price dealership in Pennycross.

'Let's go, Judas!' he yelled out.

'Christ,' I said, stepping out the house. 'Go easy, motherfucker.'

'Ahh, you know me, Judas!'

He slipped it to first and revved, yet the car didn't budge, and his eyes growing more crazy.

'I said take it easy.'

My mother waved from the kitchen window. Chase leaned out and gave her a thumbs up.

'Cars coming behind us, titrag.'

'Shit!'

'How the hell did you even get here?'

Laughing madly while cursing he shoved the gear stick in and out like we were in some video arcade. Defeated, finally he cut the engine, lowered his head to the wheel and spoke in a whisper:

'Don't give up on me now, cupcake. C'mon, there's my girl. Today's gonna be a good day, you and me and Judas at the beach.'

With that little promise he twisted the key, his eyes charged with superstition. The engine rumbled back to life, and he grabbed the stick, eased her to first and away we rolled . . .

'You goddamn beaudeee!'

'Luck.'

'Nawh, Judas, she juss needed attention, that's all.'

'How about giving the road your attention.'

He laughed and wound down his window. But I knew Chase. He was unpredictable and did nothing to please the crowd. He was like a yappy terrier dog that never tired playing fetchy, racing back each time with madder eyes.

He fiddled with the stereo.

'I'll find the music,' I said. 'Just keep your nose in the lane.'

Chase had only been behind the wheel for just one week before passing his test first try. Somewhere between gushes of wind rushing through the window I heard him say that his uncle knew the test examiner and that the examiner told him that his uncle did a blooming marvellous repair on his exhaust not too recently.

The car felt like a tin can, it was quick, but it was tin, loose screws rattling all over the place.

'How much you pay for this thing?'

'Two hundred.'

'That's cheap.'

'Uncle.'

'You sure it can get us to Fistral?'

'Mate . . . *friend* . . . relax . . . *we're going to the beach!*'

Tuning the radio I stumbled upon Stone Roses, *Wanna Be Adored*, and braved to admire the view from my window. Neither of us said it but we were excited, four wheels and a bit of pocket change, racing forward as free men.

We hit 70 . . . 90 . . . 95 . . .

I grabbed my seat. 'Feels like the doors gonna fly off this thing.'

'Everything's intact, my good friend, don't you worry.'

'Remind me again what kind of garage your uncle runs?'

He answered that question by laughing. A high pitched, crowlike cackle. In my sleepy daze and lack of vitality, Chase to me morphed into a crow. His long, crowlike snoot yakking back in his own private hysterics. He was a handsome kid, with his old man's beach bum looks. And he enjoyed life, thoroughly enjoyed being alive.

'We got wheels! We finally got wheels!' he yelled, howling and punching the steering wheel like we just pulled off a robbery.

'Hands on the wheel, Chase. Keep both hands on the wheel!'

'Ha Ha Ha.'

We barreled straight over the A38, zipping by Saltash and Bodmin. We were making good time so decided to stretch our legs about a Welcome Break, picking up snacks while embodying our entry into manhood.

'My dad'll be there already with Mum,' he said. 'They took a cooler with enough food for a refugee camp! And my old man already waxed our boards, Judas, at five this morning.'

'Shit, he didn't have to.'

'He's up at dawn every day. He even made us jam sandwiches! Pissed my mother off. She was planning on making tuna.'

When we reached back to the car, I got behind the wheel and rolled us about the carpark, showing Chase how to slip gears, treat her easy.

'Who taught you to drive?'

'A pimp.'

He jumped back to the driver's seat.

'I've got a joint, Judas, wanna get stoned?'

'No.'

'How about some acid?'

'Just fucking drive, moron.'

Fiddling with levers and knobs, I said, 'It ain't too shabby.'

'Thanks,' he said. 'But I know it's shit, Judas.'

'It's your first car. A to B banger. They're meant to be shit.'

We hit the bypass and raced along the A30, then up over the A392 to Newquay, passing Mountjoy. The Cornish air fresh.

Reaching Fistral Bay we spot Homer and Betty perched on yellow deck chairs sucking ice-cream. By midday we were out in the ocean. I'm not an open sea person. I find it terrifying. Fortunately waves were few and short-lasting. By five the sun had lost its prime, with shore fishermen and metal detectors outnumbering beachgoers.

Coming to a roundabout as we sped back to Plymouth, Chase, in one of his manic headspins, bounced his nose at the windscreen.

'And the heavens said, let there be flight . . .'

'What?' I said. 'You mean light, let there be *light* . . .'

'Over the roundabout,' he says with that crazy look. 'We're going over the roundabout, Judas.'

Before I could disagree the lunatic kicked it to third, then fourth, by fifth gear all four wheels briefly took flight as we collided into and over the kerb. Bits of car took off past my eyes as we whipped through hundreds of flowers.

'Sheeeeet!' Chase rattled through his teeth, both hands gripped to the wheel. The car slid sideways, mud and dust shooting up all around, eventually terminating in the middle of the road on the other end of the roundabout where the bonnet smoked and the engine shut off.

The general public moved from shock to outrage. I grabbed Chase by the collar. 'What the fuck!'

'C'mon baby,' he whispered to the car, cranking the ignition.

'Get us out of here, Chase!'

'C'mon baby. . . Judas needs us to go, we need to go.'

Crowds were forming all around us. 'Get this thing started!'

Cars swerved by, punching their horns. 'I'm trying! I'm trying!'

Just as I was assessing the time we had before the cops arrived, before we had to run, and down which street, the engine roared back to life. 'Yes!' Chase cried, throwing it to first.

Back at Chase's place, and while Betty shouldered dough for an apple pie, Homer pulled out a tin of Carnation milk and simmered it upon the stove. Topping two large bowls with cornflakes, he poured the white goo straight over without being precious, drawing Betty's attention to each fleck of milk missing its target. Sliding our bowls across the table, Chase's old man then spaded over a jar of crystal white sugar.

'There you go, me boys, fill ya boots!'

Betty sung a little tune while sweeping Homer's mess. 'Don't go overboard with the sugar, chaps,' she says—which meant no more than a couple tablespoons.

Homer crossed his arms over his giant belly, his chest broad, thick with golden hair—like some Mexican wrestler named El Gato. He then hunched over with the cornflakes box. 'More?' he asked.

Chase munched his last spoonful and looked at me.

'Thanks, Homer,' I said. 'But I'm stuffed.'

The big guy turned and winked at his woman. Betty giggled.

'Fancy gettin on the beer?' Chase whispered across the table.

'Can a black man boogie-woogie?' I said, fully committed before realising all I had was salty shorts and a damp shirt.

Chase shot out his chair with an idea. 'Follow me!'

I was almost two of Chase, and Homer was twice my size. I needn't try anything belonging to either men. So we walked up the stairs to his brother's old room and swung open the wardrobe.

'Brace yourself,' he said.

I quietly gasped. 'Holy what in the fuck?'

His older brother had recently declared that he was gay and had been gay since forever. He first spilled the beans to his girlfriend, then his family. Betty was delighted. Homer was quiet and supportive.

I looked at all the colourful clothing. 'It's . . . . GAY.'

I told Chase to quit agreeing with everything I mentioned. He took a step back. I had never seen anything like it: a satin blue shirt with gold sequins, a rainbow-striped waistcoat, skinny black flares, a pair of feathered stockings, and an undershirt with two little holes missing to show off the nipples, presumably.

'This is all he left,' said Chase. 'You shoulda seen the rest!'

Then I said it. I don't know why or where it came from, but I said it. 'It's fine. No problem. I can pull it off. Who gives a shit.'

'Who gizsa shit!'

'That blue satin shirt will do, minus the sequins. And those flares look normal enough.' I turned to Chase, holding up the bell-bottom trousers. 'You got any shoes?'

He flew across the room opening boxes before jumping up, clutching a pair of black shoes. 'He's your size!'

The heels were extremely tall, and thick. We necked some of Homer's whiskey. I smoked a cigarette walking in circles, looking at the outfit in the corner of my eye.

I got dressed. Chase stood back.

'I look like a fucking Bee Gee.'

'You look good!'

I faced the mirror. 'You can't go round wearing this stuff in a fishing town. This ain't Mardi Gras.'

'What's Mardi Gras?'

I didn't answer. I instead poured another shot of Jim then started picking away the gold sequins from the shirt.

'You look good. You can make anything look good!'

'Stop talking.'

'Okay.'

'Right,' I said, stretching the ass of the trousers doing squats. 'This ain't too bad.' I slipped on the shoes. 'You sure these is all we got?'

'You look good.'

'Stop saying that.'

'Okay.'

I gave the funny shoes another inspection in the mirror. They were ridiculous, beyond anything I'd ever wear. But I didn't mind. All I wanted was to go out and get shit-faced, and forget about the next day, and all the other days to follow.

'Alright, alright. Let's just get the hell out of here.'

Chase made a run for the door.

I stopped walking. 'Wait,' I said . . . 'do I look like a homo?'

He spun around. 'No,' he said.

'Don't fucking lie to me, Chase.'

He took a moment, a second too long.

74

'Look at that queer!'

Some guy ran off as I flew after him, these damn trousers clapping in the wind. Chase was right on my heel and stopped when I stopped. Too sober to be dressed up in dolphin-blue satin and bellbottoms on Union Street, I scored a bag and sniffed a heavy line down a side alley, stepping back beneath the lights a new man.

Mobs of partygoers swarmed all about us, louts chanting from one side of the street to the other, jeering patrolling police—with miniskirts falling from taxis, knocking back Babycham, cackling like zoo monkies. The mood was erratic. I hated it. I was a clown in a goddamn circus.

Almost sunrise. Disco 2000. Stood in front of the same broken mirror, I rested both hands on the sink and looked closer at the stranger looking back. The dark circles under my eyes had gotten heavier, gums sore and swollen red. Blood tipped from my nose, running along my lip and gathering at my chin. I watched the blood as it slowly dripped to the sink, with a tiredness no amount of sleep could cure.

'You're bleeding, Judas,' Chase said over my shoulder.

I kept my eyes to the mirror. 'I know,' I said.

'Just use the shirt. My brother don't care about that shirt.'

'Let's score another bag.'

'It's gone four in the morning,' Chase pleaded.

I didn't answer.

'Let's just go, Judas,' he sighed. 'I'm getting the shakes.'

We stumbled from the bathroom back into the club. I wiped my nose with my sleeve though the blood continued to drip across the dancefloor. We passed between the same old bunch raving and chewing their tongues. I gave attention to some fella I thought I knew, some scrawny, shifty-looking sort with black greasy hair, lurking in the corner trying to catch my eye. I smiled stiffly at him like a happy drunk. He returned a demure ladies charm, a flirtatious glint of self-conscious intrigue—the bathroom guy with the pocketknife, I recalled. Man or woman, I didn't care, I felt glorious, a fucking first-rate fantasy.

Fishing out my last pill, I dropped it on my tongue and ripped open the last of the powder and sniffed it up on the dancefloor, raw chunks of speed shooting up both nostrils. A cloud of white chalk consumed my face, stopping my nosebleed long enough to be taken by the music. I closed my eyes and let the sounds wash over me, a deranged shimmer of satin-blue swaying in the centre-cluster of early morning junkheads. I licked the cellophane bag and raised my arms and fell in among the crowd, a gathering of bliss and euphoria, admiration, admiring their admiration over me.

Chase stood around waiting, trying to catch my attention. It had gone six in the morning before we finally made it through the crowds, ignoring the rare point and snigger, my bloodied shirt and sweatsoaked flares fading off into another hellish sunrise.

75

One week later it was me and Jacob who found ourselves back in Disco 2000. Jacob fell on the sofa holding his crutches away from all the idiots trying to borrow them to race across the club high on whizz. He'd been waiting a good hour—said he was ready to go an hour ago. It was dawn. I stretched open my eyes. And there, beneath red strobes of disco lights, appeared Jezebel.

'Judas?' she said. 'Judas, can you hear me?'

I tried focusing, my pupils swimming in chemical bliss.

'Are you alright?' she asked. 'You look trashed.'

I made a nod.

'You wanna pill? I can get Doves. You wanna Dove?'

I nod again. She walked away. Came back. Placed a pill on my tongue and vanished with her new drug-vending loverboy.

Disco 2000 was now all but empty. Fed up of waiting, my good pal hopped toward the exit on his crutches, persuading me out of this shithole. The street outside held a ghostlike silence as the morning sun crept over the horizon.

'Let's go back to mine,' Jacob said.

Three guys lingered at the foot of the road with hands in pockets. I helped Jacob down some steps. His ankle had ballooned up again.

'Wait here,' I tell him, heading toward those guys. They looked suspicious to me stood there huddled together. My loaded brain assumed we were under fire, that we were gonna get lynched.

The street is deserted. One guy I recognised, I wasn't sure—the scruff from the toilet? The other two appeared shy while the one I assumed to know smiled my way.

I gritted my teeth, delirious, ready to start swinging.

Jacob hobbled alongside. 'What's wrong?' he asked.

'Just go,' I said. 'I'll catch you up.'

He didn't move.

'Go,' I pushed again. 'You're on crutches. I'll deal with this.'

Like a downbeat dog he limped away, leaving me to suss the situation. From the corner of the street my friend swung his crutch, beckoning me to abandon this madness. I shook my head at him. Lowering his eyes, he slowly turned the corner and was gone.

Two I could easily take, I think, but the third was more pronounced. I stepped closer, choosing a commanding angle.

Take him first, I thought wearily, balling my fists, and just take blows from those scrawny two until you put down the big guy.

The one I recognised then said, 'Back to mine for a smoke?'

Relieved, my arms dropped to my side. The other two simply walked away. We jumped in a cab. I wound down the window and put my face against the wind. I couldn't speak, those last few pills had crept on me at once, along with all the boozing and speed-runs the whole week, my mood a twisted hell of fever.

'North Prospect,' I heard him say to the cabbie.

Moments later we're on his bed. He drew the curtain. It got dark. In a clouded daze I watched him burn a block of dope, body-rushes of otherworldy evils heavying my mind, slipping in and out of here, out of consciousness and back again, wondering where the hell I was, who the fuck he was.

He passed the joint. And I smoked. And kept smoking.

'Slow down,' he stressed worryingly. 'That's a lot of dope, man.'

But I didn't care.

I just needed to keep numbing, keep the hounds at bay.

Then in a flash, I blacked out.

76

I stumbled through my mother's door straight into another Bible gathering. Curled up on the floor as though that would keep out the world, I needed them all to go, but my jaw was locked shut, the room shifting this way and that way.

'Hahlayleuyah!' the congregation cried.

'Thank yeuuu, Jeeesus!'

'Praizze heeem! *Yesss* Lord!'

Desperate, I noticed all the shoes encircling me, all with their palms faced up from the waist, spouting holiness.

'O Lord! Take this demon!'

'Grace us, dear Jesus. Show us you live!'

My mother's feet moved hesitantly from beyond the circle. Words collapsed inside my head to nothing. From the corner of my eye I glimpsed someone inside the television with copper coins over his eyes, lips moving. But the television was off.

'Be strong, Judas,' I heard my mother say.

Peering up, the midday sun peaked through the curtain, casting light into my eyes.

'Praizze God Almighty One!'

'We serve *you* O Lord! Work your grace!'

As I shielded my eyes from the light there came a loud knock to the front door, followed by another, the next one lowering the congregation to a faint whisper.

The sides of my head throbbed in my hands, small electrical currents stabbing my temple.

The knock on the door persisted.

My mother's feet shuffled from the room, leaving the congregation. 'Lord, take this demon from this boy,' Pastor Tom declared, stooping lower with a crucifix in his fist. 'Seize this Devil!'

My mother's feet shuffled back to the room. In a hush, she told them all something. I couldn't make it out, but whatever she said caused the gathering to break from the circle and collect their coats.

They blessed my mother. They blessed her one by one.

'Bless you, Mila. God is here. God is with you.'

'Thank you.'

'Bless you my love.'

'Thank you so much for coming.'

'He will be saved. The demon never wins.'

Seeing Pastor Tom's polished shoes pause before my mother's flat-footed jungle feet, a sudden cry of laughter erupted inside my head, entertained by the absurdity of it all. A smile crept over my face, a wicked, intoxicated smile. I even laughed a little as their feet pranced left to right. It was ludicrous. And then they were gone.

Finally left alone I stared at patterns in the carpet, wiping snot from my nose, thinking, 'This is extreme—an extreme turn.'

And yet between those thoughts, a part of me curiously looked upon the hysteria with a casual eye, where there was no madness, no left or right turns, no ups, downs, good or bad.

Things then began to shift that supposedly shouldn't, common words becoming hundreds of repeating utterances—as if the world about me was breaking apart, revealing a strange new reality.

'It was a traffic warden,' whispered my mother as she returned. 'They had to move their cars. Pastor Tom will be back tomorrow.'

I could hear her fine but I didn't pay her attention. I didn't want to force a false grin and for her to be frightened into thinking I was the serpent in the garden. So I instead concentrated upon something different once the previous thing twisted out the ordinary.

'Be strong, son,' she said. And I almost bust out laughing. She

shuffled from the room, and I see something long and red protrude from her backside, like a tail. It was there and it wasn't there. Her feet soon returned. This time placing a Bible on the settee.

'You muss fight this,' she proclaimed. 'You muss win!'

Laid out on the floor, I peered up at her Bible, its pages gold and shiny. I somehow believed the congregation had gathered quietly in the next room, fucking my other body. That I had a second body in some lower existence yet that body couldn't die, but appeared lifeless.

That must be Hell, I think to myself.

'Try to read,' she begged, placing the holy book on the rug.

Once she disappeared from the room I slowly reached across and moved a page . . .

And there was a war in heaven, Michael and his angels waging war with the dragon. The dragon and his angels waged war, and they were not strong enough, and there was no longer a place found for them in heaven. And the great dragon was thrown down, the serpent of old who is called the Devil and Satan, who deceives the whole world. He was thrown down to the earth, and these angels were thrown down with him. Then I heard a loud voice in heaven, saying, 'Now the salvation, and the power, and the Kingdom of our God and the authority of His Christ have come, for the accuser of our brethren has been thrown down, he who accuses them before our God day and night!'

And they overcame him because of the blood of the lamb and because of the Word of their testimony, and they did not love their life even when faced with death. 'For this reason, rejoice, O heavens, and you who dwell in them Woe to the earth and the sea, because the Devil has come down to you, having great wrath, knowing that he has only a short time.'

77

It was the last time I saw all those church shoes surround me. Alone in the house, my mother had left for work. Looking out the window, nothing made sense, and the walls changing shape, and dead faces speaking from the television and some other body of mine, a lifeless one in Hell, being fucked and beaten. I had started to get used to it, thinking that I had died, that this was some lower place which clung to where I was before.

I forced away all the soft-feeling, figuring this was it, I wasn't going to last. Some pious part of me even dropped in fisted prayer. I watched him kneel. And this other side of me continuing to look upon my attempts at salvation, waiting for me to get up off my knees and think matters straight.

So I went and sat on a chair and just thought about this Hell, this unending comedown I was in. Hours passed by, and I watched who was watching. And continued this way, watching who was watching, back and back into myself until there was nothing left but to watch who was watching, no emotion, no human drama, no Judas Nobody. And I stayed this way for many more hours, noticing the light in the room grow thin, watching the watcher in a state of calm quietude until my mother returned home past midnight.

'Please, Judas, you're scaring me,' she said, turning up the light.

I took myself to my bedroom and stood in front of the mirror, my cheeks full of bruises that weren't there, broken teeth beside my bloodied mouth that isn't real, and yellow pus pushing from my eyes like veins of cloud paste. Stirring some crazy, I looked about this Hell. Something birdlike loomed somewhere near. I couldn't get to it, when I tried, that body was chained back to the wall in the next room like a dog, chained and buggered by impish things, with lots of small, puncturing stab wounds pulling out with them entrails of blood rivers. Vomit spewed from my mouth and out the holes of my throat. I was terrified.

'Judas, are you okay?' whispered my mother outside my door.

I told her I'm fine without speaking, knowing she can hear perfectly my thoughts, the cunning trickster.

Days later my eyes wandered up to the roof of the church, noticing the light pouring through the stained glass window, thinking how she got me there.

Everyone stood and sang hymns. Choosing to remain seated, hunched to my lap, I listened to my mother sing all the wrong words, turning pages and singing louder when she knew a line or two.

Following the service I stood up and faced a broad, hefty Mexican. His eyebrows a permanent frown, jaw wide, rough copper skin. The guy wore a typical gold medallion outside his shirt, and had spent half his life in and out of prison.

'Tro your televeeesion awayyy, me ameego,' he told me, his eyes small and sincere. 'God told me to do this. I tro it from my weendow.'

I had a hunch the Mexican was thinking himself as some self-help liberator, a one-man mariachi Samaritan. I laughed nervously, still half-crazy in my own way, still figuring who the hell blindfolded me and smuggled me into a damn church.

78

Two seasons had passed, I was sure, watching many shades of light move to an eerie dusk each day. Often, I'd spend my days sat at the window like a home cat, studying the light from morning till evening, listening to sounds that were no longer ordinary. And at times I'd listen to who listened. And this obsession went on, listening to the listener. Turning from the window, I nodded at the old lady. At odds with what else to do, she'd booked a consultation.

I watched myself pick out a belt and strap it on. I watched my fingers button a shirt, and my hands move a toothbrush. I saw how I looked at my reflection in the mirror, catching hollow assurances compliment how handsome I stood, familiar comments that previously paved a favourable path on the outside.

'Ready?' she asked.

I nod again and follow this strange woman down the stairs and into a taxi. Strap on a seatbelt.

'Where to me love?' asked the driver.

'Central psychotherapy ward, please.'

'Right you are,' he said.

The woman read out the address from a headed piece of paper from inside a white envelope while I watched the sky and listened to the driver wheeze. And then silence. We drove for half an hour without a word. I then found myself in a white reception room alongside others, some seeming like real certified headcases, with several half-loaded on meds.

'He hasn't spoken in months,' she told the shrink. She also informed the stiff-faced man that I had taken drugs, that they had made me someone else, and that I had not returned to my former self.

The shrink faced me. 'Nod if you understand me, young man.'

I gave the guy a nod.

He scribbled something down. Looked back up.

'Do you know where you are?'

I nod again.

'Good,' he said. 'Now, where are you?'

I had perhaps ten or so answers multiplying by the second, they were all convoluted and likely correct but different. There was, Human Sacrifice Mind-Surgery, Soul-Stealers, Evil Entity Lab, Alien Body-Snatcher Facility—and maybe, just maybe, a regular Psych Ward.

As he scribbled, I took note of his penmanship, moving about his pad with a calligraphy just like my dead old man. What did it mean? Was it some uncanny message from the other end?

'You seem to be enduring a prolonged psychotic breakdown, son,' the doctor suggests. 'Quite remarkable, really, how long it's lasted.'

Me and the woman then walked out the door and out of the centre. We walked up a long road, nothing being spoken. Passing by a shop window, I froze, seeing myself with no clothes on.

'Judas?' my mother said. 'Please, Judas . . . what is it?'

I said nothing, trying not to disturb what I saw in the reflection, quietly considering the metaphor. What the hell does it mean? I thought to myself curiously. Peering down, I saw shoes, trousers, a shirt. I was fully clothed . . . but I think people are seeing me naked?

My mother not a clue as to why I've stopped ahead of a shop window, turning my eyes between my reflection and my shoes, hurried quickly to the High Street and threw herself in front of a bus. She dragged the bus driver from his seat and all the passengers aboard looked upon from the window.

'Please help my son!' she cried. 'Please help him!'

Seeing this guy dragged my way, I turned and ran.

79

With time I started to form coherant sentences, new, more exact ones, speaking out loud the order of events while pacing my room.

My mother listened outside. 'I can't take anymore!' she yelled out.

I flung open my door. 'Now you behave yourself,' I said.

She cried in her hands. 'A man had sex with you?'

'Christ, it was me that . . . this has nothing to do with . . .'

She swung up her hands and screamed, 'JEEEESOOOSSS!'

'Take it easy, woman,' I said. 'It ain't how you think it is.'

The maniac ran down the stairs, yelling, 'We need to flush the Devil out!' I went after her. She fell to the floor and wept. 'I'm a bad mother! Oh, God help me!'

I snatched up my bag.

'I should kill myself!' she yelled. "That's what you want!'

Slinging my bag over my shoulder and lowering my cap, I looked back at this figure as she lay at the front door, wailing like a child. Reluctantly I turned back and waited patiently for her tears to stop. It took a long minute for her to wipe her eyes, climb to her knees. Once she stopped her crying and stood firmly on her feet, I took off.

Climbing a fifteen foot wall, I bulldozed through ten yards of brambles, landing on the edge of the train track. Swinging a glance, I jumped over the tracks toward Esther's place.

'Mum's been calling,' said Esther. 'Says she's gonna kill herself.'

I walked in. 'She wouldn't know how,' I said.

'You should be lucky. She's been telling me that since I was a kid.'

Big Henry was in the kitchen reading a newspaper. He offered me a beer. Since I shook my head he went on reading whatever it was:

'A County Judge praised an eight-hundred thousand pound illicit sex operation as being *well run* . . .'

'Eight-hundred thousand?' laughed Esther. 'And the rest!'

Henry read on: 'Judge Jeffrey Rucker said that Paradise had treated its prostitutes so well that many had remained for years.'

'Of course!' Esther piped in.

Henry continued: 'If you're going to run a brothel, you could do it a lot worse than Paradise . . . Mr Cooper,' he said, 'was ably and at times energetically assisted by Miss Nobody. And you can't ask for more than that in a partner.'

Esther got excited. 'He's worded that well, eh babe?'

Henry shook his head and finished the article: 'None of the prostitutes had been bullied or coerced and no children were involved.'

'Of course no children are involved, cheeky so-and-sos!'

Henry sighed. 'They mean underage girls, honey, calm down.'

Esther looked at me. 'Wanna cuppa tea, Judas?'

'No.'

'Take off your coat and hat? You look like a burglar.'

I took off my coat.

'Hat?'

'No.'

'Mum doing your head in?'

'Do you mind if I just go sit down?'

'Sure love,' she said, peering over Henry's shoulder at the article.

Dumping my bag, I went and sat down in the front room. It took only a minute for the walls to twist out of shape, revealing a black ship floating along the ocean, its sails tattered and its hull creaking in the wind, with groans of the dead singing up through the deck. An old sea shanty came quietly. Two jolly pirates then appeared from inside the wall, drinking, singing. The walls of the house drooped and the smell of sea brushed under my nose like a fond memory.

From there on, many imagined agonies passed through as fully as I could take before exhausting myself to pass out, usually from a make-believe limb being sawn away in some bygone age, or my skull forced open by a wild gang of headsmen. The scenes in my mind would continue in my dreams, and immediately as I woke, as much as I could endure minute by minute.

'You alright, Judas?' my sister asked, her eyes pushed beside the livingroom door. Rotating my head slow as to keep all that I had seen in focus, I said, 'Fine.' I said, 'Fine' but how you would say 'fine' to someone who had doped you and tied you to a chair with thick rope and had set the chair down to the concrete floor of a windowless basement, and had asked if you were comfortable while they sharpened knives. To then find this other to be a version of you, hunched over the chair, running a blade along his own fucking scalp.

Another sunrise. The third without a shower.

'Judas, I think you should really shower now,' said Esther.

This time her tone was a little more bold. When she suggested if I would like a shower two days prior, I shrugged and instead spent day and night thinking of physical movement and how it gave you purpose to do so, just sat thinking my finger to life for two or more hours until it jumped, moving on to the next finger and arm, toe, foot, spending hours on end willing body parts to move with only my mind. Until now the third day, and Esther asking me again to shower. I had no reason to shower. I didn't feel unclean. But I stood up anyhow and took the towel and walked to the bathroom. The last thing I needed was to be seen as a cruel smelling lunatic sat unwashed without sleep for three days staring at walls.

And so each day I relearned to speak from this lower, more terror-filled place, forming coherence through the chaos. Preferring fresh, uncooked foods, such as tomatoes and lettuce, cucumber, I chewed the stuff to a mushy pulp.

'Tortoise food,' Esther put in.

And so I tried eating fried egg and bacon on toast with plenty of butter. Sat there with the hot plate on my lap, I looked at it suspiciouslike, picking up the meat with my fingertips and sniffing the grease and discovering its veins and lifeless fat, poking the thick, white bread as though it was not food, as though the fiends were fooling me to eat something that would make me docile and compliant.

80

Clutching the waistband of the pyjama bottoms handed to me after another afternoon shower, I clutched them as they were three times my size with no string to fasten the thing tight. So I yanked them up with one hand, a damp towel in the other, wearing only this, stark naked beneath.

'Thanks,' I said, handing Esther the towel.

'Just drop it in the washing basket, Judas,' she said.

I walked past Henry, tossed the towel in the basket, and walked back to the kitchen, sitting on a stool at the breakfast table with those oversized pyjama bottoms bunched up in my hand. The trousers often slipped from my hand and I'd catch the bleeders below my ass like some retard. Henry chuckled. Esther coughed nervously.

Taking a fork in one hand while clinging to the bottoms in the other, I tried to choke down some of that tasteless slop. Now and then I'd pick up the knife to hack a sausage, in which I had to let the back of the trousers droop, and my buttocks air.

While they frolicked excitedly over a new whorehouse, I sat chewing the fatty tissue of a pig, lost in my own thoughts, with scenes of some long-forgotten life flashing before my eyes . . .

I see Henry and his siblings, screeching like a pack of wild animals around their drunken father. The old man was slumped in a wide chair, his bloated body sloppily sagging over the sides. The kids beat the shit out of each other, tears streaming down their faces as they scratched and clawed while the father just sat there grinning. His hands were swollen blue, teeth yellow with rot, and his breath stinking like a pile of shit under the sun. And nothing good came from this fuck, other than the once overenthused delight of a newborn that he himself once was, gushing helplessly from some poor woman's cunt. Then there was the little girl, the only daughter, gone, vanished into thin air, no one ever allowed to speak of her again.

That's when Henry turned to me chewing a mouthful of slop while pointing his knife and said, 'They were my old man's trousers.'

More weeks had passed, perhaps a month or two.

'We need to air this room,' Esther would rant.

I had known my slow-going refusal to participate was a burden as she walked from the livingroom, dumping her kid to play at my feet with a bowl of cheese puffs and a wooden train track.

I kept the kid company, noticing my second body in Hell trying to stand up. I don't know why he was trying to stand up. I'd wished he'd just lie still and keep the fuck quiet.

'Choo choo!' cheered Henry Jnr, tapping my knee. 'Uncle Judas!' he went on, pointing a cheese puff to the window. 'Look, seagulls!'

'Yes,' I said.

He kept pointing to the birds and cheering, 'Choo choo!'

Then almost suddenly I'd find myself laid on my back on the sofa looking up at the ceiling while the house slept, wondering how the hell I got there and where the kid had gone and who rolled a duvet over me. Another blink of the eye and I woke again in the middle of the night, finding Henry stood beneath a dim light with his pants around his ankles and a new prostitute on the books knelt at his feet with her mouth full and her fist busy.

Days later Henry received news that his younger brother had been arrested for murder, 42 times with a hammer. The deceased was a young woman, a neighbour. Esther was alone in the house with Henry's brother the morning of the murder, the news had her chain-smoking. And then the police called for me.

The address was a beige house. Throwing up my collar was the best crack I had at any sort of distraction from the output of intensity that was now my normal. Two knocks to the door was soon answered by a supposed policeman in jeans and an off-duty shirt. And then I was sat on a plastic chair with thin steel legs, looking between three plain-dressed coppers. I of course do not believe that they are coppers. My nerve-endings put together some sort of shorthand, outlining the current situation of which my brain summed conclusively that it was kill or be killed, that this was a setup by the underlord himself.

I gripped the chair leg ready to swing. A quiet voice in my head reminded me they knew more, these mindreading tyrants. Everyone's an imposter, everyone's reading the damn mind pretending to be clueless with all these decoying pleasantries. Am I the only one left in this hellheap? Are there more out there??

'So, Judas,' one cop said, doing his best to keep a straight face, 'were you or were you not, um . . . *raped?*' His plain-dressed friend couldn't hold it together, hiding a smirk behind his fist.

I knew how I looked. I was a nut.

'Right,' I said, realising my mother made the call.

'Your mother informed us. We're following it up, is all.'

'My mother is not well,' I said.

They spoke cop-speak among each other, putting away their notepads. 'Well, I guess that's it,' one said.

'I guess so,' I replied, releasing my grip on the chair leg.

81

I moved on a second time, back to walking the streets like a bum. Henry Jnr had barricaded himself by the front door, staring down at his slippers, clutching his little wooden trainset by his side.

I scooped him up. 'Hear those seagulls?' I said.

He shook his head. Once back on his feet, he just ran away.

'You wanna ride to Rudy's house?' asked Esther.

'No.'

'Alright, well, you come back if you need to.'

'No thanks.'

'Alright . . . okay . . . well be safe, watch how you go.'

'You watch how you go.'

'What's that supposed to mean, Judas?'

I picked up my bag and walked off down the road.

My other sister Rudy answered her door holding a spatula covered in pink icing. 'Hi Judas!,' she started. 'I make cake!'

'Great, Rudy.'

A tiny face appeared beside her with golden hair and big blue eyes. Little Evie gave a shy smile and licked another pink spatula.

'We're baking cake,' said the kid.

'I can see,' I said.

It was late afternoon. The sun had fallen behind a thick blanket of clouds. Burt, this sister's husband, said hello. Burt wasn't much of a talker, which suited me fine. He and Rudy had been attached at the hip ever since graduating from 'special school'.

'We made up a bed in Evie's room,' said Burt.

'Thanks, Burt. Sofa's fine.'

Burt picked his nose. 'Rudy's making cake,' he said cheerily.

'I know... I know that, Burt.'

The crafty human hunkered down to watch the telly while I paid attention to some soldier-figure dragging his severed body from beneath the glass cabinet across the carpet. I knew he wasn't real, but I still wasn't sure how he had squeezed himself from beneath such a small crevice, or why there was no blood from his entrails? Burt clicked the remote and chuckled at Tom and Jerry while I quietly puzzled the vision.

Night had fallen.

'You okay, Judas?' whispered Burt, his voice slow-coming.

'Fine, Burt.'

'I'm eating Frosties at midnight?' he said cheerily.

'Why not?' I said.

The happy lump plodded back to the kitchen. The clock on the wall struck three in the morning. The kid was first to arrive, playing with her doll on the rug, wiping endless snot from her nose.

'Did you sleep?' asked Rudy coming behind her.

'I don't know,' I said.

'You can nap in Evie's bed if you want?' she said.

The kid's pillow was soaked in mucus. I rolled to the other end, taking another moment to consider how completely crazy this all was, how the ordinaries of life had taken a turn. The thought carried with it some strange deluded peace, welcoming madness as something to admire. With that I knew no end, a voice in my head calling for more. 'Too easy!' it mocked, goading the Devil.

Turning in the pillow trying to shut the voice up, I came face to face with a skeleton, its skully eyes looking back at me with a permanent grin. Real or not, it didn't matter anymore. Up or down, it was all the same. You only live twice, I thought, succumbing to the sweet release of exhaustion.

82

The taxi guy said belt up please young man and the weather keeps changing its blinking mind, before driving.

'You're my last customer,' he barrelled on. 'I've been at it all night—kids these days, lemme tell ya. Today's youth just turn into animals—if you know whadda mean? They just don't give a monkeys. I see it all from start to end . . . start to bleedin end.'

Tabi, my last sister and final chance at a roof, lived across town. The cab rolled up. Several moments later I'm sat on her foul-smelling sofa while Heathcliff cradles chubby Timmy while smoking a joint. An awful pop song looped from the stereo where little Tabitha tapped her shoes, dancing in a pink tutu screaming Disney ballads into a toy microphone. And as they congregated, familiarised with one another, that strange, unquestioning, relatable fix to your breed, I remained a useless hollow shell, unable or willing to participate in any such sickening charade.

After Heathcliff took off, abandoning the whole *family* business, Tabi wasted little time luring some other halfwit to her bed, smoking endless dope with her new man. While the two of them frolicked under the sheets, young Tabitha danced alone and little Timmy taught himself new tricks. I didn't take to this new guy, always half-stoned, bringing along with him one strong-armed black kid, who'd supposedly just got released from a two-year stretch at Belmarsh.

Speaking only a few words a day, only ever in response to some meaningless matter, I'd spend much of my time eavesdropping trivial conversation. The point was irrelevant, just seeing it laid out like a cheap stage play was enough to keep my interest.

The ex-con grew uneasy around me, skulking in the corner. He was dangerous, maybe, but it was clear—while I stared seemingly between the air, screwing over this whole business of what is real—that he no longer knew what constituted fear. As did I.

Having suggested an honest song to Tabitha, I left her twirling and made my way past the strong-armed goon up to Tabi's bedroom, where she lay with her new friend and his endless supply of grass.

Stepping into her room, I stood over the two of them and knew I looked a crackpot but stood there anyhow, trying to catch a word.

Tabi asked if I was alright. Her friend turned his face away, cough-laughing into the pillow. In a few strides I was at the sidetable, taking the hefty bag of weed and heading to the crapper.

Loverboy leapt from the bed and followed behind, spewing all sorts of threats, but instead kept well back while I opened the bag and dumped all his stash down the loo, flushed it away. The bathroom spun as I rose up, white spots clouding my vision.

'You're fucking crazy!' he spat, clenching his fist. 'You dunno where I'm from, mate.'

Waiting for my vision to clear, I replied, 'No . . . no I don't.'

'Saaf London mandem, yah get me? Me and Beast dannstairs.'

'Sure,' I said, now seeing fewer flecks of light.

He started tapping his temple repeatedly with his finger. 'Iz dare somefink wrong wiv you big man?' he asked curiously.

I looked at him, really looked. 'It's been a rough year,' I said.

Beast came running up the stairs, pushed his friend aside and stepped forward. I looked at him. He looked at me. His little buddy then said, 'Dis wasteman flushed all our weed dann the loo.'

Beast kept nodding, perhaps waiting for more information from his friend, but nothing further came. So he turned back to me.

'Iz our grass, man,' he said. 'Datsa lotta cash dann the shitter.'

I brushed the remaining weed from my hands, straightened the words in my head and spoke back, 'Well I guess we all have to endure this little matter together. I did what I did.'

'D'you know where we're from?' he said.

His friend tapped his arm. 'I said to him, innit—'e don't know.'

'Listen,' I cut in, 'I appreciate you both wanna share yourselves fully. But right now, right this moment, we're all here. So if something happens, it happens now. Let's not waste our energies with improbable threats.'

I had stopped feeling dizzy. I wasn't going to pass out. Beast clapped his little friend on the shoulder and told him, 'Allow it, man—dis geeza ain't right in the head.'

Unable to keep up conversation, I stepped between the two. Enraged, the smaller one jumped in my path, continuing to inform me how Beast could hurt me bad.

As I approached my sister she was lying half-naked beneath the duvet looking bleary-eyed. I went to sit in a chair to try and form the correct set of words for my actions. But I missed the chair, and fell to the floor. Tabi let off a nervous giggle, while loverboy hunched over me with his fists clenched.

Collecting myself up off the floor, my eyes stood against the window. Outside, a thick haze of smog hung in the air—a dirty blue horizon above tall, bleak tower blocks, looking like tombstones for giant men. A tear rolled along my cheek. Tabi's playmate quickly began packing up his stuff while calling me a madman, slamming the door behind him as he and his pal, Beast, made their hasty exit.

83

'Have you thought about studying psychotherapy?' the shrink asked, sipping coffee while observing me from across the room.

I looked about the place, surrounded by the stench of desperation, taking in the cheaply framed diplomas on the wall.

The shrink hesitated before speaking again: 'All I'm saying, Judas, is that I don't think you need my help.'

It was our third sitdown and I craved to screw her, showing up just to sit in her company. She had an elbow rested on her pleated skirt, coffee mug in one hand and spectacles in the other, tapping her penny loafers—the perfect image of prim and proper. While meanwhile, I just sat there, trying to appear more or less ordinary.

Though the more the clock ticked over the more hopeless I became, all because she wasn't dressed for the pleasure of a man yet her clever open mind struck me something good. I couldn't care less what she wore, how she fixed her hair, or even the shape of her behind—that cleverness, of getting straight to the thing without sugarcoating around, confronting what's true, was the most attractive thing I had come to know.

That was the last time I would see her again. Stepping back to the streets, I walked for an hour until I found myself once again sitting in the dim livingroom of Tabi's place, watching the lowering sun through the net curtain. The usual shadows stretched across the walls like black whales, and the phone rang, her little red phone with its rattling handset ringing like a fucking brigade.

The flat was empty, and so I just sat there on the sofa, watching the light and listening to rustling from behind the drapes. Was it another figment of my curious brain, or could there really be a shadowy figure lurking on the porch, honing a butcher knife like some phantom blacksmith? I believed anyhow this was the end, the final act, a deep psychic cut to the place that spawned all this absurdity. My heart bounced, thoughts go numb, succumbing to the ghostlike terror before passing out.

When I came to, my trousers were soaked in piss. Overstating the case I jumped up and pulled a knife from the kitchen drawer and held it against my throat.

But I wasn't the type—I was no suicide stunt. The humour, the twisted irony of it all was compelling enough puzzlework for a heretic like me. 'Christ, you *are* a nutcase,' I muttered with an amused sigh, sliding the knife back and taking a wash.

Then came a knock to the door.

In strolled Tabi's babysitter—K'sandra, she called herself.

'Where's your sister?' she asked, making herself at home.

'Out,' I said, zipping up a clean pair of trousers.

She plonked down on the settee and adjusted her bra, told me she had just turned sixteen. 'Happy birthday,' I said, lighting a cig.

You could easily tell this town had dulled her mind already so young. Her skin was a sickly white and she could only breathe through her mouth. Gormless looking. Craving sugar. Teeth a little crooked, but a nice body, young and new, like soap. She reached into a blue plastic bag.

'What's in the bag?' I asked.

She pulled out a pinkish bottle. '20/20,' she said.

'You drink that stuff?' I asked surprised.

She unscrewed the cap. 'I'm sixteen, ain't I?,' she said again.

I took a drag of my smoke and sat down. 'Why not?'

She necked some, made a sour face and held up the bottle. We passed the wine back and forth. She complained her bra's too tight.

'Why don't you take it off?'

As the weeks flew by I found solace in The Red Book, immersing myself in Jung's brilliantly mad and clever mind—all that he'd lost and found and penned so accurately and with such shameless detail that I ate up his words with a hunger bordering upon obsession, to the point of considering eating the book itself. On a whim, I decided to try my luck at becoming a shrink, perhaps for the criminally insane? But I'd need to leave this shitheap, I pondered to myself, pacing up and down with newfound belief.

I first began journeying across the busy town centre, getting over misunderstandings of being mistaken queer if word got out, or worse, a fucking rape case. Though truth be told, it was that self-pity which had taken root in my mother's literal-minded ways that really troubled me—the child of an unsympathetic God. Yet the worse part, the holy rotten grace, was somewhere deeply detached from all this fuss and noise, in some shape or matter, I was grateful.

Following a keen search I found a study in London: *The Regent's School of Psychology*—sounding too impressive for a kid like me. Problem was, I was a mere twenty year old—five years too young to apply. Yet once I'd put forward my proposal to override their prerequisite, resolute on getting a spot and getting out of this town, I had discovered they accepted younger students on the merit of meaningful life experience, which was to be handwritten and submitted before the approaching deadline.

So I got to work putting it down, three or four pages of half-decent stuff. Yet returning to my sister's place after posting the letter, I found her chucking all my things outside her door, slamming the door shut and twisting the lock.

Gathering up my stuff, I flipped open the letterbox and thanked her for the stopover. Her silence was enough to tell me I was too much of a madman to stay another minute. So I got moving, down the corridor and back into the streets, a bin liner slung over my shoulder, back to the old lady till I received my reply from London.

84

Second-rate news travels fast. My mother had blabbed to her friends and the church all about what had happened to her. The man I thought I would become was stripped away, cornered like a thief. I had to start anew, figure what else, a different sort of take on things.

Deciding on another aimless stroll to clear my head, I picked up a four-pack and drank them all in a hurry. After pissing against a wall, I headed to the house where I stumbled out of that taxi almost a year from now, lurking in the shadows half-boozed. And then I see the scrawny fuck. The little cockshit was unmistakable.

Darting across the street I got the runt by the neck, pinning the dirty queer against the wall. His bony throat swelled in my hand, fists flying either side of my vision. The filthy rat scratched my cheek, but I was half-tanked, continuing to choke the bastard blue.

He tried speaking, spit falling from his chin. 'You wanted me!' he sputtered, his eyeballs turning red. 'You wanted me!'

I had a couple of choices that I could see—a few inevitabilities.

Why can't I do it? I heard myself ask.

And a part of me answered: it's just the way it is.

Pressing my eyes down, pressing away the cheap corollary, I let the faggot go. Coughing and wheezing, his trembling fingers fumbled for a key, checking over his shoulder before disappearing through a door.

He was somehow a perfectly greased little labouring cog in this sanctifying turn of events. I had some sort of illness, I was sure, like a monk gets ill and goes very far away to be alone. I could have wept, but the truth refused to let me. Everywhere my eyes turned I see people possessed. Slipping my hand in my pocket I pulled out a cigarette, lit the cigarette, and made it down the street, taking long, heavy drags, dizzying as I walked.

Stumbling upon a corner shop, I pinched a brew and walked to a bench in a small park crammed with pigeons and sat down. An elderly bloke across the way saw to the birds. He seemed content, busied in afternoon routine, tossing bread. The old timer spotted me and soon began packing up his things, gathering his walking stick and his hat, gradually finding his feet. Just as he was leaving the park, he turned my way and tipped his hat.

Lifting my beer to the old man's departure, a brown mutt charged past my eyes, sending columns of pigeons into the air. Being the sole human in the park, the dog trotted over and sniffed my shoes, his wet nose seeking my drink.

I took another swig. And we watched together all the birds flutter back. The sky had become grey. In the distance, a solitary balloon tied to a string climbed the sky. I briefly admired the balloon, wondering where it'll end up. My doggy friend suddenly sucked in his tongue and pricked up his ears, detecting a whistle somewhere to our right, jolting the mutt back on all fours and sending him on *his* way.

Alone again, I tossed the empty can in the bin and made a move to Madam Yula and her crystal ball on the Barbican.

'Your name won't be up in flashing lights,' the gyspy woman told me as I stared at my shoes, fiddled with my lighter. 'But you'll be known well enough,' she said, '. . . well enough.'

85

Things had gotten familiar again, the walls stopped moving, and the phantom beatings were manageable, letting it all pass through. There's just no sense in fighting the ghost.

I walked into the house to the smell of roasted chicken. My mother and I ate alone, saying nothing—other than a mention of new Bible classes, and that my letter had been accepted for the shrink study in London.

I said good luck.

She said well done.

Dinner over, I retreated to my room and tuned my radio to the shipping forecast, and packed a small bag, enough to travel light. Snatching my mattress overhead, I gathered loose change. That done, I relaced my shoes, and without much thought made two final spits against the wall. God and the Devil slithered down, meeting together at the bottom, equally absorbed by the abyss of the carpet.

I walked downstairs. 'I'm leaving for London,' I said.

'But it's almost midnight,' my mother replied.

'There's a late coach. I'm leaving now.'

'You're leaving?' she said. 'Where will you sleep?'

'I'll figure that out when I get there.'

She scooped up her purse. 'Take it,' she said.

And I did. I didn't like it, but I took it.

'I'll pay you back,' I said.

'Okay, son. Have a safe journey. I love you.'

I kissed her forehead and turned for the door. 'I love you, too.'

The coach station was filled with homeless drunks, staggering, with others curled up quietly inside sleeping bags. Crippled pigeons with swollen feet and greasy wings pecked aimlessly at anything beneath the streetlamp.

And then the coach pulled in: LONDON

Seated with a cheese sandwich and a pack of salt n' vinegar crisps in my lap, I rode the bus through the black country, leading onto the long motorway. In theory if not in practice I already knew how to get by in the world. I reread my acceptance letter for the course, counted my cash—and spared a thought for my old pal, Jacob.

After six hours of back stiffness, I was soon watching the sleepless fidget of London arrive.

Stepping off the coach at Victoria Station, it's gone five in the morning, with London city beggars occupying the exit with limp wrists and palms upfacing. I wandered about, taking in the hustle and chase. Once I read all the accommodation notices I considered sitting somewhere until the help desk opened at nine, but instead kept wandering along Buckingham Palace Road.

'Hey mayte!' yelled a guy in a rusted yellow Volks in what sounded like an Australian drawl. 'Need a place to crash the noight, eh?'

Tossing my bag in the van, I hopped in, and we chatted along the way to the hostel—the big city and the long open road. Leaving the van, I walked into what appeared to be a hedonistic choir singing campfire circle songs, crammed in the reception, sitting on boxes and suitcases and whatever else. A short guy took a fiver from my hand and waited while I scribbled madeup details on an irrelevant piece of paper like all those screwed up pieces in a small mesh bin before walking me to a room stacked with thirty or so bunk beds stinking of ballsacks and feet.

'I'll take this bunk,' I told the guy.

Climbing a ladder and over those metal poles that keep you from rolling, I told myself to get a few hours kip before looking for work. But I couldn't sleep. Restless, I clambered back down and zigzagged my way between tens of noisy backpackers to the bathroom for a quiet smoke.

Looking at my reflection in the mirror, I lifted my chin and thinned my eyes, lowered my gaze, tensed my brow and flared open my nostrils, raised my cigarette to my lips and took a mean-fuck puff, letting the smoke slowly fall from my nose.

Shaking off the act, I turned and noticed a book sat on top of the toilet. I picked it up. The cover had been ripped away. I flicked it open, and the waft of a musty library filled my senses with nostalgia, the smell of old wood and typewriter lifting from its pages. I noticed the title section was also missing. Taking another pull on my cigarette, I settled down on the toilet seat and read the first few lines of the prologue . . .

I cannot tell my story without going a long way back. If it were possible I would go back much farther still to the very earliest years of my childhood and beyond them to my family origins.

I searched quickly behind the loo for its cover. There came a knock on the door. 'One minute!' I called out.

Straightening up, I took one last drag on my smoke and dropped the butt into the bowl. Placing the book back, I flushed the crapper, brushing cigarette ash from my trouser leg while walking to the door, opened the door, the brightness of a new day come rushing in.